P9-DCC-534

PRAISE FOR *THE LAST DRAGONLORD*

"*The Last Dragonlord* by Joanne Bertin features villains who have not lost their humanity, and heroes who are still capable of making mistakes. Court intrigues are entangled with unabashed romance in this fast-paced and satisfying story. The reader gets a sense of the world's rich history and unique magic."

—Robin Hobb

"Joanne Bertin's *The Last Dragonlord* is fresh and different, a story nobody's ever told before. The writing is clear and powerful, and the characters appealing. Altogether, I had a wonderful time!"

—Joan D. Vinge

"Action brews constantly at several interstices within the web of characters in this honest and engaging first novel. The flow of action and many layers of intrigue will float readers toward her novel's hard-fought conclusion."

—*Publishers Weekly*

"A convincingly colorful welter of plots and stratagems set forth with confidence and finesse."

—*Kirkus Reviews*

"Newcomer Bertin launches a winning fantasy epic. What with political intrigue, romance, bloody menace, and sweeping adventure as well as well-realized characterizations and intricate, believable world building, this is full-bodied fantasy, sure to be a hit with fans of Dickson's *Dragon Knight* and McCaffrey's *Pern*."

—*Booklist*

Tor Books by Joanne Bertin

The Last Dragonlord
Dragon and Phoenix (FORTHCOMING)

The *Last*
Dragonlord

Joanne Bertin

TOR®
fantasy

A TOM DOHERTY ASSOCIATES BOOK
NEW YORK

THE LAST DRAGONLORD

Copyright © 1998 by Joanne Bertin

Edited by James Frenkel

A Tor Book
Published by Tom Doherty Associates, LLC
175 Fifth Avenue
New York, NY 10010

www.tor.com

Tor® is a registered trademark of Tom Doherty Associates, LLC.

ISBN: 0-812-54541-9
Library of Congress Catalog Card Number: 98-21186

First edition: December 1998
First mass market edition: September 1999

Printed in the United States of America

0 9 8 7 6 5 4 3 2 1

To Sam, because he didn't laugh

With thanks to

eluki bes shahar, Shawna McCarthy, and Jim Frenkel for all they've done.

Judith Tarr's novel-writing workshops at Wesleyan for advice, energy, and enthusiasm.

Judy herself, for lots more advice, unstinting help and horse neep, a virtual baseball bat when I needed it, and especially for her friendship.

And the biggest thanks of all to Walter "Sam" Gailey for loving support, advice, computer expertise, and patience above and beyond the call of duty. Sam, you are hereby nominated for sainthood.

Prologue

The storm was close now. The mage heard the rumble of thunder, heard the rising wind soughing through the tops of the pine trees. Chanting softly, he knelt before the stone altar and all that it held, then took up a silver scrying bowl and watched the scene revealed in the black ink.

He saw the barge rock as the first little waves slapped against it. The pennants at bow and stern came alive as the wind caught them. Although the colors were muted, he knew them to be the royal scarlet. The waves rose as the waters of the Uildodd River grew darker, reflecting the leaden sky above them.

More . . . Just a little more . . .

Now!

Moving swiftly, he set the silver bowl down and caught up a knife in one hand. With the other he seized the hair of the youth who lay bound and gagged on the altar. He ignored the boy's terror-filled eyes, and, with a practiced motion, yanked the head back and slashed the blade across the exposed throat. All the while, he chanted.

He caught the hot blood in a bowl carved from the same stone as the altar, impassive as the blood spilled over his fingers, staining them red. When the deadly flow ceased, he nodded curtly. His servant pulled the body from the altar.

The incantation changed, became harsher, more urgent. He opened a small box that rested beside the bowl. First he removed a bit of wood, carved in the rough likeness of a barge, wrapped in a thread of scarlet silk. Both wood and silk had been taken from the same barge whose progress he had watched in the scrying bowl. He set them to float in the blood.

Next he took out a small bottle. From it he let three drops

of water from the Uildodd River fall into the bowl. The blood stirred as if a tiny wind raced across it.

Overhead the sky grew darker as the storm closed in and thunder walked the land. In the bowl, the waves rose higher. The crudely carved bit of wood slewed around as if turned by an unseen hand. The man watched in satisfaction as first one, then another of the tiny, crimson waves splashed against the "barge's" stern.

He raised his voice, weaving the blood magic in a net of death. Slowly he stretched out a finger. Slowly, and with infinite satisfaction, he pressed down on the wood, forcing the back end under. Blood splashed up and over, wave after miniature wave, as he continued to push the little boat down.

It disappeared. Nor did it surface again. The chant ended on a note of triumph.

He stepped back from the altar, aware now of a sudden drop in temperature. "Clean it up," he ordered the servant as he wiped his bloody hands on the wet cloth the man offered him. Then he walked down the slope to where he'd left his tunic.

As he picked it up, a necklace of silver chain fell out. He caught it in midair and let the heavy links slide through his fingers a moment before putting it on.

He smiled, fingering the necklace. Soon he would be able to cast it aside forever.

The first drops of rain began to fall.

One

The dragon gleamed in the light of the setting sun, his scales glittering as he soared toward the castle that crowned the mountaintop. His gaze shifted to a wide, flat area ending in a cliff, wreathed in shadows cast by the dying light. A slight tilt of the powerful wings and the red dragon turned, silent, beautiful, deadly, intent on his goal.

He landed, claws scraping against stone, the sound harsh in the crystalline air. A red mist surrounded him and the great dragon became a wraith; the mist contracted, then disappeared, leaving behind the figure of a tall man.

Linden brushed a strand of hair from his eyes, his blood singing from his long flight and the magic of Changing. He crossed the shadow-dappled landing area. As he reached the first step of the long stairway that led to the castle of Dragonskeep, a voice, old but still clear and strong, rang out.

"Dragonlord."

Linden paused and looked up. On the stairs high above him stood an elderly *kir,* his silvered fur catching the last of the sunlight, no expression on his short-muzzled face.

Sirl, personal servant to the Lady who ruled Dragonskeep and the Dragonlords, regarded him in return. "The Lady has need of you," the *kir* said.

Why? Linden wondered as he raised a hand in acknowledgment and bounded up the stairs, his long legs taking the steps three at a time. It had been long since he'd had such a summons.

When Linden reached the step where Sirl waited, the *kir* bowed to him. "If you will follow me, Dragonlord," he said. Then he turned and led the wondering Linden to the Keep.

No words were exchanged as they walked through the

white marble halls of Dragonskeep. Globes of coldfire, set to hovering in the air by various Dragonlords, lit the way. At last they came to the tower rooms set aside for the ruler of the Keep. Sirl opened the door and bowed Linden inside. Linden entered the chamber; Sirl followed close behind, shutting the door once more.

Globes of white coldfire lit this room as well, setting aflame the gold threads running through the tapestries that covered the five walls. Dragons soaring against blue skies, sunsets, a river of stars, or among mountain crags covered four of them. The fifth, incongruously, was of a hunting scene: a stag, a pack of baying hounds, three huntsmen, all forever frozen as they raced through the forest. A reminder, perhaps, of the Lady's life before she Changed? Linden doubted he would ever know. They were the only decoration in the room, which was sparsely furnished. What few items of furniture there were looked lost in the emptiness.

The Lady sat in a high-backed wooden chair. Her long fingers cradled a cup of tea as though seeking its warmth. She looked unreal in the cold light. Even the pale albino's eyes that watched him seemed colorless. She beckoned.

As he crossed the room, he studied her. She had been very young, he knew—only fifteen—when she'd Changed for the first time. Their kind aged slowly; how many centuries had the Lady seen to give her face that delicate tracery of wrinkles? After more than six centuries, he himself still looked only twenty-eight.

Without thinking, Linden touched the wine-colored birthmark that spread across his right temple and eyelid. It was his Marking, as the Lady's icy paleness was hers. He'd hated it until he'd discovered what it meant: that he was one of the great weredragons, the lords and servants of humankind. A Dragonlord.

Linden knelt before the Lady. Setting his hands on his thighs, he bowed till his forehead almost touched the floor— the salute of a Yerrin clansman to his lord. "Lady?" he said.

The Lady studied him for a long moment. Then she said, "Yes, I was right. You will be the third."

Linden frowned slightly as he accepted a cup of tea from Sirl. *And what does she mean by—*

Memory returned and with it came understanding. Lleld, smallest of the Dragonlords, had been late to breakfast that morning, bubbling over with news and speculation—more of the latter than the former. Linden thanked the gods he hadn't taken her up on the wager she'd demanded when he'd laughed at her notions. Sometimes Lleld's wild predictions had a way of becoming real, and he'd no wish to lose that particular cloak brooch.

The Lady's long, pale fingers tapped against the cup. "You have never sat in judgment, have you, Linden? Then perhaps it is time, little one—" She stopped at his chuckle. "Impudent scamp, you know very well what I mean!" she scolded with an affectionate smile.

Linden hid a grin as he drank. Over six and a half feet tall in his stocking feet, he towered over everyone else at Dragonskeep. The Lady herself barely came up to his chest. But with only a little more than six centuries behind him he was the youngest Dragonlord, the "little one."

And, to his great grief, likely the last.

"You've heard by now that a messenger from Cassori arrived early this morning, yes?" she said.

Linden nodded. "Lleld said something about it at breakfast; she'd heard it from the servants. Is it about the regency? I'd thought that was already settled some time ago and the queen's drowning proven to be an accident. Wasn't there an investigation?"

"There was; it found no cause for suspicion. And now that the period of mourning is over, we had all thought Duke Beren was to be confirmed as regent. But then came this challenge, the messenger said. The Cassorin council is divided; they cannot settle the matter and many of the barons are becoming restless. Luckily the messenger came before the *Saethe* and I left to confer with the truedragons."

Of course; on the morrow, the Lady and the Dragonlords' own council—the *Saethe*—were to consult with the true-dragons on a matter of grave and growing concern to the

Dragonlords. For there had been no new Dragonlords, not even a hint of one, since his own First Change. It explained the Lady's haste, then, in choosing judges—if Lleld had guessed right once again.

Aloud he said, "Most of the Cassorin royal family are dead now, aren't they?" Bad luck attended this reign, it seemed; he'd seen its like before.

"Yes; all save for a little boy, Prince Rann, and two uncles: the challenger, Peridaen, a prince of the blood, and Duke Beren, who has a strong lateral claim to the throne."

Linden considered as he sipped his tea. Another of Lleld's guesses confirmed. He went on, "So the Cassorin messenger came to ask for Dragonlord judgment." At the Lady's nod, he smiled. "That was Lleld's guess. She also predicted Kief and Tarlna would be sent as arbitrators, since they're Cassorin and have done this before."

"Lleld," the Lady said, sounding exasperated, "is entirely too clever by half. Someday she'll guess wrong. But not this time. Kief and Tarlna are indeed going to Cassori. And so, I have decided, are you, as the third judge required." The Lady set her empty cup on the low table to one side of her chair. Sirl appeared and took it.

Linden carefully schooled his expression to stay blank. A mission with Tarlna, who chided him at every chance for his lack—by her prim standards—of dignity as befitted a Dragonlord? Oh, joy. He wondered what he'd done to deserve this.

Yet to sit in judgment was his duty as a Dragonlord. But why him, Yerrin by birth, and the youngest, least experienced Dragonlord to boot? True, he spoke Cassorin—a talent for languages seemed to go with being a Dragonlord. But there were others far more experienced in such things. Surely one of them was to be preferred.

He held his tongue.

"The three of you will leave in the morning. Since there is no time to be lost, you will all Change and fly to Cassori. The court has not left the city for the summer yet; the claimants shall await you in the great palace in Casna." The Lady smiled. "I know you'd rather ride Shan, but I fear Cassori cannot afford the time it would take." She beckoned Linden to rise.

He offered her his arm as she rose from her chair, and escorted her from the room.

They paused in the doorway of the hall, watching the dancing that began every night after the evening meal. The Lady leaned easily on his arm, nodding her head slightly in time to the music.

Linden said, "Lady, if I may ask . . . Why did you choose me? Kief and Tarlna, yes, they are Cassorin. I'm not. So?" He waited as she considered her answer.

Finally she said, "For the sake of a feeling that I have, little one." Her soultwin Kelder emerged from the dancers and came toward them. She held out her hand to him.

As Kelder led her into the dance, the Lady looked back. "But whether this matter needs you," she said, "or you need this matter, I don't know."

On his way to his chambers Linden met Lleld coming the other way down the hall.

"Hello, little one," Lleld said with a grin as he stopped to talk to her.

"You love being able to say that to me, don't you?" Linden replied, unable to keep an answering smile from his face as he towered over her. Lleld's Marking was her height; the little Dragonlord was no taller than a child of perhaps ten years. "You weren't at the dancing tonight," he said.

"Ah, no—I had something else to do," she said. "So tell me—was I right?"

He nodded. "About everything."

She heaved a sigh of regret. "Blast, but I wish you'd taken that wager."

"I've learned," he said dryly.

"You're to be the third judge, aren't you?" She cocked her head at him.

Laughing, he said, "Right again, you redheaded imp. I just hope it won't take too long."

"Or be too boring; regency debates usually are, you know," Lleld said helpfully, "as well as taking years to settle, sometimes. A pity this isn't one of your friend Otter's tales, isn't it? It would be much more interesting then."

One of Otter's—That would be all he'd need on top of Tarlna's company. Linden asked in some exasperation, "And what did I do that you should wish that on me, Lady Mayhem?"

Lleld just grinned. "Ah, well; I'd best be off. It's getting late." And with that she sauntered off down the hall.

Linden continued on to his rooms, shaking his head. The things Lleld thought up . . . And she had looked entirely too innocent as she'd walked away.

When he entered his chambers, he found Varn, his servant, almost finished packing for him. Sirl must have sent word on.

Varn looked up. "The boys are already asleep. They stayed up as long as they could to say good-bye, but . . ." He smiled and shook his head.

"Tell them I'm sorry," Linden said. And he was; he was fond of his servant's twin sons.

The golden-furred *kir* straightened up from closing the last buckle on a leather pack. "They'll miss their pillow fights," Varn said with a grin. "Though I should warn you that they've bribed Lleld to join them for the next great battle. Something about honey cakes, I think it was."

Linden shook his head, laughing. "Have they now, the little hellions? And that explains where Lleld was. Thanks for the warning. Ah, well; I shouldn't be gone long."

"You hope," Varn said as he eased Linden's small harp into its traveling case.

Linden sat on the wide stone rail of the balcony. Behind him was the open door to his rooms, some ten of his long strides across the balcony floor. He looked out into the night, savoring the coolness, the spicy scent of the night-blooming *callitha* rising from the gardens below.

Varn had gone home to wife and sons long ago. Now there was only one thing left to arrange before sleeping; Lleld's earlier comment had given him an idea. Closing his eyes, Linden made ready to "cast his call on the wind" as the Dragonlords said.

He let his thoughts drift, seeking a particular mind. There came a faint stirring, an impression of the sea, the whisper of wind in canvas, a ship gently rocking. To his surprise he had to strain to keep the link; Otter was much farther away than Linden had thought he'd be.

Then the link wavered on the edge of dissolving; the distance was just too great. Linden was about to abandon the attempt when he felt a sudden surge of power.

What on—? Then he realized: his quarry was on board a ship. That burst of magical power must mean some merlings, the half-fish, half-human people of the seas, were nearby. They often followed ships for days at a time. Somehow their magic must be augmenting his own.

He was not slow to take advantage of this bit of luck. *Otter?* he said.

A wordless rush of delight, then, *Linden? Linden, is that really you?*

Linden smiled. *It is indeed, old friend. I'm leaving Dragonskeep in the morning.* Quickly he told the bard all he knew. *I'm flying there in dragon form. I thought we might journey together afterward. I could come back for Shan and meet you wherever you are—or rather, are going to.*

Otter said, *You're not taking Shan? Have you told him yet that you're leaving him behind? I wish I could see it when you do.*

Linden grimaced at the thought of how his Llysanyin stallion would take the news. *I thought I'd wait until the morning. He'll probably bite me. Where are you bound for?*

Otter replied, *Believe it or not, we're on our way to the great city of Casna, as well.*

There was a sly feel to Otter's mindvoice that Linden knew well. Someone was in for a teasing. Wondering who was the intended victim, he said, *What are you doing at sea?*

For the past few months I've been visiting a kinsman who lives now in Thalnia. You might remember him—Redhawk, a wool trader. His son Raven's best friend is a trader-captain, one of the Erdon merchant family of Thalnia. I asked to go with her; I've an itch to travel again. She agreed to let me sail with her.

Redhawk? Raven? Linden thought a moment. *Ah! I remember them now, especially the little boy; red hair and a passion for horses.*

Otter's chuckle tickled in his mind.

Little? The lad's now nearly as tall as you are! And still horse-mad, much to his father's despair. A pity he's not along; the two of you would get on well together.

Linden nodded, forgetting as he always did that Otter couldn't see it; it felt as though the bard stood next to him. *And why are you going to Casna?*

It happened to be the first northern port the Sea Mist is bound for. I'd planned to journey to Dragonskeep to drag you out of there and go traveling with me. Poor Maurynna; when she heard that, she was wild to come with me. Tried to talk her uncle, the head of their family, into letting her take a trading trip overland, but he was having none of that.

Linden wondered who Maurynna was, then decided she must be the captain. And from the feel of Otter's mindvoice, he now knew who the intended victim was to be. *Otter— what bit of mischief are you planning?*

Never you mind, boyo. Then, wistfully, *Gods, but it's been a long time.*

Linden sighed. He'd forgotten how long the years were to truehumans. It was part of the magic of Dragonlords; to be caught out of time until the dragon half of their souls woke, years passing with the swiftness of days—both blessing and curse.

He rubbed his temples; even with the aid of the merlings' magic, his head was beginning to ache. He said, *Kief and Tarlna are coming, as well.* A brief wave of sadness washed over him. He hoped Otter didn't feel it.

Tarlna, eh? Aren't you the lucky one, Otter said. *But Mau-*

rynna will be delighted—three Dragonlords in Casna!

Linden raised an eyebrow at that. *Oh?* was all he said, but he put a world of meaning into it. *When will you make port?*

I'd guess in a few tendays or so, but I'm not certain. Perhaps sooner; we're making good time or so I'm told. We left Assantik two days ago, looking for something Maurynna calls the Great Current. Ah, Linden—may I ask you a favor?

Here, then, was his answer. *Of course. What?*

Would you mind if I introduced her to you? She'd be thrilled.

Oh, gods. Another one looking for a Dragonlord as a lover's trophy, no doubt. He hoped she wasn't the sort to gush. Still, she was a friend of Otter's; he couldn't refuse. *No—I don't mind.*

I should warn you right now that you're one of her heroes. She's always loved any story about Dragonlords—and about Bram and Rani and the Kelnethi War. This will be a dream come true for her. You're not only a Dragonlord, boyo— you're Bram's kinsman who fought alongside him and Rani.

Linden cringed. This was going to be worse than usual.

Kief and Tarlna. A moment's hesitation, then Otter said, *I'm sorry, Linden; it will be hard for you, won't it?*

Linden bowed his head. Somehow, at Dragonskeep, although there were soultwinned couples all around him, he could ignore it. Whenever it became too much, he had friends he could escape to in the outlying villages or he could go riding in the mountains. But in Casna, the only people he would know would be Kief and Tarlna. And theirs was one of the closest bonds in the Keep. Being with them would be like having salt water constantly poured into a wound. Perhaps there would be someone in Casna to help him forget for a little while.

He should have known the bard would catch that quick betrayal of loneliness before—and not have forgotten. He made light of it. *Ah, well; at least* I'm *not the one tied to Tarlna.*

To lighten the mood again, he told Otter what Lleld had said earlier.

The bard laughed. *She said that, did she? Imp. You've enough to worry about with Tarlna; you don't need a wicked mage.*

The mage, Linden said, *might even be preferable.*

The power that had been aiding his effort wavered; the group of merlings must be splitting up. *Otter, I can't hold this link much longer.*

I understand. Shall I look for you at the palace when we make port? I'm known there; I played many times for Queen Desia.

Yes, Linden replied. *Good-bye.* He let the contact fade, groaning a little at the ache that had settled behind his eyes. The scent of *callitha* blossoms returned, spicy and soothing. Afterward he sat watching the night sky for a long time.

Nethuryn never knew who slipped the note under his door. Perhaps it was Joreda, who sometimes saw the truth in her fortune-telling sticks. But anonymous as it was, it had the ring of truth.

The cold-eyed one sends his wolf for you.

Nethuryn's hands shook as if with a palsy as he read it over and over. "Gods help me," the old mage pleaded in a whisper. He looked wildly about his comfortable lodgings.

He knew who hunted him. And what they wanted. He even knew who the "wolf" would be.

"Mmmrow!" A black-and-white cat twined about his ankles, demanding attention. Annoyed when the customary pat didn't follow, the cat batted at the hem of the old man's robes.

The tug brought Nethuryn back to himself. "Oh, Merro-lad, I'm sorry. We've been happy here for so long, but now . . ." He swayed and caught himself on the back of a chair. "Now we have to run."

But was there anywhere he could hide and not be found? Pelnar wasn't big enough to hide him; not from—

Despairing, he sank to the floor. Perhaps he should just give up; he was old, useless, his magics nearly gone . . .

Merro jumped into his arms and purred in delight. *What*

will happen to Merro if you die? Nethuryn demanded of himself as the black-and-white head butted his shoulder.

The old mage took a deep breath. "We shan't make it easy for him, eh, boy? No, he'll have to hunt for us, he will. Hunt us and . . . and *it.*"

Setting the cat down, Nethuryn clambered stiffly to his feet and set to work.

Two

Linden gritted his teeth. Resolving not to lose his temper, he ignored Tarlna and went to the window of the small meeting room.

Outside, Varn and the other servants were moving the departing Dragonlords' packs to the distant cliff. He stared at their small figures retreating along the track. And counted to ten once more, trying not to wish they'd drop Tarlna's packs into the green valley below.

Then he said, "For the last time, Tarlna, I am *not* wearing the ceremonial regalia now. Once we reach Cassori, yes—but not today."

Her voice tight with exasperation, she said, "One would think you're ashamed—"

Linden rounded on her. "I'm not ashamed of them. Far from it. But blast it all, they are uncomfortable!" He folded his arms across his chest and glared at her.

Tarlna returned the glare. She stood with her arms akimbo, blue eyes flashing, blond curls tossed back. Her lips parted as a gleam filled her eyes.

Linden knew Tarlna had thought of an especially scathing retort—even for her. He gambled everything on a final toss of the dice. With his most innocent look, he said, "What if it's raining there? That'll ruin the silk."

The blue eyes narrowed.

Linden wondered if he should start running now. If Tarlna guessed he was jesting, and at her expense . . .

Kief's voice came from the doorway. "He's right, love. Let's get there first. We'll be formal later." He sauntered into the room, grinning. "Won't we, Linden?"

Linden grumbled but agreed. While small, slender Kief

looked younger than he, Linden, did, in reality Kief was much older. And as eldest, Kief would head the delegation to Cassori.

Tarlna turned her glare on her soultwin. Kief smiled and shrugged. She advanced on him.

Linden worked his way to the door. Just as Tarlna, her voice ominously soft, said, "Why do you encourage him—?" he slipped out of the room. He hurried to put as much distance as possible between himself and the inevitable explosion. Once outside, he heaved a sigh of relief.

Then he remembered he still hadn't told Shan he was leaving. He looked back at the Keep with longing. He'd rather face Tarlna than his stallion.

The stone stables were cool and dim, sweet with the smell of freshly cut hay. Linden paused a moment to breathe deeply. He closed his eyes; that scent brought back so many memories of Bram and Rani. He smiled a little, then opened his eyes and continued on. He stopped by Shan's stall. It was empty.

"Shan!" he called.

A big black head appeared in the doorway to the paddock outside. The stallion whinnied a greeting as he entered. His ears were cocked forward and there was a bright, inquiring look in his dark eyes. He dropped his head over the stall door to be scratched.

Linden obliged. *Oh, gods,* he thought. *He thinks we're going for a ride.* He cleared his throat.

"Ah, Shan? There's a problem in Cassori. . . ."

Shan tilted his head. The ears flicked back and forth. He rumbled deep in his chest and nodded.

"There's a question there about the regency, and I'm one of the judges."

Shan whickered. He clearly relished the idea of a long journey.

Linden inched backward. "I have to fly to Casna—and that means—"

He threw himself back as the big head snaked out. The stallion's teeth snapped together, just missing his shoulder.

"I'm sorry, but it's the Lady's orders. You know I'd rather ride you—"

Shan turned and raised his tail, flicking it insultingly.

"Don't you da—!" Linden looked down at the fresh pile of manure as Shan stamped out the paddock door.

"What did you expect?" a voice said. "If you Dragonlords must insist on riding Llysanyins . . ."

Linden turned and found Chailen, the head groom, watching him. The *kir*'s expression was sour.

"You know he'll be impossible until you come back," Chailen said. "The stable boys consider it a punishment to clean his stall whenever you leave him behind." The *kir* sighed. "Ah, hell; dodging Shan'll keep 'em lively.

"I came to tell you Varn was looking for you. Everything's ready."

As Linden strode down the well-worn path, he saw a familiar figure waiting for him at the head of the stone stairs leading to the landing cliff.

"Come to see us off?"

"Come to see how much Shan left of you," Lleld said, looking him over. "You've gotten good at dodging him, haven't you?"

Linden winced, remembering times he hadn't been so quick. Then he said, "I've news for *you* this time. Remember Otter? I'll be bringing him back with me."

Lleld clapped her hands in delight. "Oh, good! He always has the best tales about evil mages."

"And this isn't one of them," Linden said.

"How boring," Lleld retorted. "It makes a much better story my way."

Before Linden could say anything, a voice from the landing cliff hailed him. "I must go," he said and continued down the broad stone stairs.

She called after him, "Tell you what, little one—I'll wager

my dagger with the crystal hilt against your cloak brooch that
it is—"

"No!" he yelled back. "With my luck you'd be right!"

Lleld crowed with laughter.

Linden shook his head as he continued on. Lleld and her
ideas! He reached the landing place in time to see Kief move
to the very edge of the cliff.

The updraft from the valley blew the fine brown hair back
from the smaller Dragonlord's face. Kief bent, adjusting the
carrying straps holding his baggage, then said something Linden couldn't hear to the *kir* servant beside him. The servant
ran back.

Kief raised his six-fingered hands and closed his eyes. A
rapt expression came over his lean face. The air shimmered
around him. A red mist formed; the outline of his body quiv-
ered, melted. The mist spread, darkened, became a ghostly
dragon.

A heartbeat later a brown dragon crouched on the cliff's
edge. One six-clawed forefoot stretched out, closed talons
around the stout leather straps of the packs. Kief dragged the
bundle closer, arranged it between his forelegs, and launched
himself from the cliff. Spreading his wings to catch the wind,
he spiraled upward.

Servants ran up with Tarlna's belongings. When they were
gone, she limped to take Kief's place. She paused to watch
her soultwin high above.

Linden looked up as well. The brown dragon hung in the
sky now, his wings motionless, gliding in lazy circles as he
waited for the others.

"Luck to you, Linden."

The Lady's voice came from behind him. A deeper voice
echoed her. Linden looked over his shoulder.

The Lady and Kelder stood together. She leaned on her
soultwin's arm, her head cocked to one side. "I've a feeling
that there's something you must do in this matter, Linden, but
I don't know what. I wish—"

A ringing cry cut her off. They watched Tarlna, now a pale

yellow dragon, spring from the cliff. Varn and some of the other *kir* brought up Linden's bundles.

The Lady spoke again. "Go, little one. Once again—luck to you. And keep your eyes open."

Linden ran to take his place at the cliff's edge. Varn helped him arrange the bundles. A quick clasp of hands, a whispered, "Good luck," and Varn ran back. To Linden's amusement, everyone moved much farther back than before.

For pity's sake, I'm not that *large!* he thought.

He let his mind empty, freeing his thoughts to savor Change. He felt his mind and body melt and flow. For a moment he was weightless, nothing more than a breath of air, a wisp ready to drift apart on a breeze. If something should distract him now, or cold iron pierce the mist he'd become, he'd be lost.

A thrill of terror stole through him, an old, familiar friend, spice added to the wonder that was Change.

Then, as always so quickly he could never put his finger on the moment it happened, the tenuous feeling evaporated and he was solid once more.

He craned his long neck around. Maybe he was that large after all; he covered nearly twice the area the others had. His scaled hide, the wine-red of his Marking, glistened in the sun. He seized his packs in his claws and opened his mouth, tasting the air. The wind called; he leaped to meet it.

The silken, sensuous feel of the air filling his wings delighted him. A few powerful strokes caught the same current Kief and Tarlna rode. He soared up toward the summer sun. The air was warm and to his dragon senses tasted of honey and wine. He threw back his head and trumpeted.

Kief and Tarlna wove their voices around his. Their harmony filled the air, echoing from the mountain peaks as one by one they wheeled in the sky and flew south.

Three

Maurynna shook her head to clear it as she left her cabin. She'd had the oddest dream last night; a pity it had faded upon waking, leaving behind only vague hints that vanished even as she snatched at them.

She inhaled deeply; the early morning air was fresh with the tang of salt. This time of day had always been her favorite. And now that she was captain of her own ship it had a new savor.

She looked down at the wide gold bracelets of rank that covered both wrists. She still had trouble believing it. From first mate to captain in little more than two years; she'd never thought it would happen so fast.

Three trips on her own were not enough to dim the excitement of her new status. Sometimes she woke in the night, thinking Uncle Kesselandt's gift of the *Sea Mist* and a small partnership in the family business but a dream she'd had. Then she'd remember and drop off again, glowing with a warm happiness.

The wind blew Maurynna's long black hair across her face. She shook it clear, greeting the sailors on deck, waving to those working in the rigging. From the mainmast high above the deck the Erdon pennant fluttered in the wind: a silver dolphin leaping on a sea of green silk.

She called up to the first mate on the quarterdeck, "All well, Master Remon?"

Remon looked over the rail, one hand still on the ship's wheel. "Aye, Captain. Kara reported a quiet night with a brisk wind. Keeps on like this, we'll make Cassori a few days early."

"Thank you, Master Remon. I hope it continues as well."

Maurynna walked along the deck, squinting into the sun off the starboard bow, pleased with the world. This trading run had gone well so far. And if the first half was an augury for the rest, she'd do very well indeed. So much for the protests from the senior partners that at nineteen—almost twenty, she amended—she was too young for so much responsibility.

She nearly jigged a few steps for joy, then remembered it was beneath the dignity of a captain to do so. Instead she leaned on the polished rail and hummed.

The door to Otter's cabin opened. The Yerrin bard stepped out, yawning. A smile crept across his face when he saw her.

"You're a sleepy one this morning," she said as he joined her. "Didn't you rest well last night? You turned in earlier than I."

"I was talking to a friend late last night," Otter said, "and had trouble sleeping again afterward." His smile widened.

"Who?" she asked, idly curious. "Remon?" She knew that wasn't right even as she said it. For one thing, the first mate rarely stayed up late; he rose at dawn to take the helm. And Otter's grin said it was someone very different.

He looked around. "Lovely morning, isn't it? Think I'll stroll the deck for a bit."

Maurynna pushed off the rail to stand squarely in his way. "Not until you explain." She tugged the bard's grizzled beard. "You're teasing me—I can tell. You always get that look in your eye. Out with it!"

He looked hurt. "You wound me, Rynna. You've known me since you were a child and—"

"Exactly; I know you. Ot-*ter*!"

He leaned on the rail, looked out over the waves, and laughed. Maurynna turned her back to the following wind. She knew she could outwait Otter.

Behind her the crew hoisted another sail, singing a bawdy chorus to keep the time. The creaking lines and the flapping of the canvas formed part of the melody.

At the final "Ho!" from the crew, Maurynna looked over her shoulder to see the woad-blue sail belly out as it caught the freshening wind. The *Sea Mist* leaped forward on the waves. Otter grabbed the rail. Maurynna swayed with the motion of the ship and pretended not to notice.

She said, "Now—who was this mysterious friend?"

Slowly relaxing his white-knuckled grip, Otter said, "When we were in Assantik, do you remember that captain telling us that the Cassorin queen had died?"

"Ah—you mean Gajji. It's old news; Gajji was in Cassori a long while back. It's tragic about that pleasure barge foundering in a storm, but what has that to do with your friend?"

"A great deal, actually." Otter smiled, clearly waiting for her to beg him to go on. When she didn't give in, the bard gave her a fatherly nod, his eyes alight with mischief. "You'll find out when we reach Casna."

At her yelp of protest, Otter raised a cautionary hand. "And each time you threaten to keelhaul me, I'll put off telling you even longer. Mm—perhaps I should wait for your birthday anyway."

Maurynna's frustrated curiosity nearly choked her. *Blast Otter!* He knew she wouldn't snoop around the crew to find out to whom he'd been talking; it would lessen her standing as captain. She was still new enough to be touchy about her dignity.

"You—you . . . Pah! Why I ever agreed to give passage to an intolerable, troublemaking, annoying, and outright obnoxious Yerrin bard . . ." Her fingers itched to pull out Otter's beard hair by hair.

And the bard knew every thought crossing her mind as if he could read it. She saw it in the laughing eyes. She snarled something rude in Assantikkan and stalked off, feeling a little better.

Otter leaned on the rail again and laughed.

No, she wouldn't snoop. But she could keep her ears open in case she overheard one of the sailors talking about the conversation.

Yet it still puzzled her. Which one of the crew had Otter been talking to? What had they heard in port that she hadn't? And why should that sailor care about what was happening in Cassori? She climbed to the quarterdeck and let the clean salt air blow her annoyance away.

Ah, well, she consoled herself. *Whatever Otter's surprise is this time, it will be well worth the waiting. They always are. But must he be such a tease about it?*

Four

The field outside of Casna was jammed with people awaiting the Dragonlords' arrival. They crowded behind the line of scarlet-clad palace guards who kept the larger section of the grassy sward free. The guards' tabards shone like splashes of blood against the green of the grass. Banners stuck up here and there above the throng, gold and scarlet and blue, hanging limp in the still, hot air. Folk of all classes jostled and called to one another. Wine-sellers shouldered through the crowd doing a brisk business. It looked as though the entire city had come to see the fabled Dragonlords.

Kas Althume stood beneath Prince Peridaen's canopy, enjoying the shade. Thank the gods his role as Lord Steward of the prince's lands and possessions entitled him to such comforts; he had no wish to join the sweltering masses in the sun. Still, it irked him he could not sit in public with the prince. Standing like this made the old wound in his thigh ache. He rubbed it lightly.

"That leg bothering you again?" the prince asked.

Althume shrugged. "My leg is not important. This is. Look at the fools," he said, his voice scornful. He leaned closer to Peridaen. "This might as well be a fair. Look how ready they are to welcome what's been holding them back for centuries—and glad of it."

Peridaen shrugged. "They don't matter. And if the Fraternity has its way, the end will begin here and Dragonlords will cease their interference in truehuman affairs once and for all. Do you think your man has reached Pelnar yet?"

"Pol? He left the day we knew for certain that the Dragonlords would be appealed to. Barring unforeseen accidents, he should arrive there soon. It may take time for him to find what we need," Althume said. "It's been years since I've had word of Nethuryn."

Seated to Peridaen's right, Anstella, Baroness of Colrane, asked, "Kas—when he returns, do you really think you can loosen the—"

"Quiet, Anstella," Peridaen said.

She tossed her head. "Don't hush me, Peridaen—I'm not a child. The servants are well out of earshot. Not that they could hear me above this jabber."

"Not a truehuman, certainly," Althume said. "But can the Dragonlords read minds, sense intent? And from how far away? Remember, that's one of the many things we don't know about them. Keep all this from your mind if possible."

Anstella inclined her head, conceding the point.

Althume looked beyond her to the nearby canopy that sheltered many of the younger nobles. One young woman caught his eye. She had the same delicacy of feature and form, the same glorious auburn hair as the baroness. But unlike the baroness, who wore the intricately twined braids of a widow, the girl's hair spilled unbound down her back. She looked bored. Her lip curled disdainfully at the other young women as they chattered, their voices high with excitement.

Yet her hands belied that seeming aloofness as her fingers toyed incessantly with the rings adorning them. Althume guessed she was as excited as any of them.

"I see Sherrine is not succumbing to the excitement," he said, sipping spiced wine from a chased silver goblet.

"She knows what is right, not like those empty-headed chits," Anstella said with a toss of her head. "I've taught her well. No doubt they hope to snare a Dragonlord as a lover."

So she hadn't heard the sarcasm; he hadn't expected her to. All too often Anstella heard—and saw—only what she wanted. Despite her dedication, that narrow-mindedness limited Anstella's usefulness to the Fraternity. A pity Peridaen had taken up with her.

"And if the judges are all women?" Peridaen asked. "Such tears of disappointment!" He sighed and pressed a hand to his heart with a flourish. The movement disturbed the large amethyst pendant he always wore. It flashed purple fire in the sunlight.

Althume smiled thinly. "Even so, there will be male Dragonlords. It is my understanding that Dragonlords prefer not to be separated from their soultwins; the judges will no doubt bring theirs. We may have as many as six Dragonlords descending upon us."

"Oh, gods," the baroness said, her voice heavy with disgust. "That many?" Her lip curled much like her daughter's.

"Calm yourself, my lady. It's more likely there will be only four. My guess is that two of the judges will be a soultwinned couple; the fourth will simply be accompanying the third judge," Althume explained.

"So the little fools will still have their chance," Peridaen said, stroking his beard.

"Not likely. It is said that a soultwinned Dragonlord is immune to seduction." Althume drank again.

"Pity; it might have sown some dissension in their ranks." Peridaen shifted in his chair. He beckoned to a page who bore a tray of sweetmeats. The boy hastened to obey. The prince chose one. The page offered the tray to the other two, then fell back out of earshot.

"Well trained," Althume said.

"I insist upon it," Peridaen said as he surveyed the field once again. "Hmm—a pity even your magery couldn't manage a love philter to ensnare a Dragonlord. Blast; I forgot. Because we don't know if they can sense magic, you've had to cease—Damn! Rann is running about. Too much of that and no one will believe he's sickly. Kas?"

Stung by Peridaen's slight, Althume angrily craned his neck to see across the field into the pavilion of Duchess Alinya, the interim regent of Cassori. He saw the young prince capering with his wolfhound. He snarled, "I'll see he gets more of the potion. He must not have received this morning's dose. It won't happen again."

Peridaen grunted, then said irritably, "I still can't believe Desia signed that warrant. If I'd known . . ."

"You really had no idea she'd named Beren as regent if the contingency arose?" Althume said.

"None whatsoever. Damned nastiest surprise I've had in a long while," Peridaen said. He scowled.

Althume shrugged. It had been a setback, true, but he'd seized the opportunity to set an even more ambitious plan into action. One always had to be ready.

A scream from the crowd made him look up. People milled about, some shrieking with excitement, all pointing to the sky in the north. He shaded his eyes. After a moment he made out three dots against the blue sky. He searched for, but couldn't find, any more.

"I thought you said there would be at least four," Anstella said. Althume couldn't tell whether she was disappointed or pleased.

He didn't reply. Instead he watched the dragons approach. And wondered.

Two dragons, one brown, one yellow, flew side by side. Large as they seemed to his truehuman eyes, they were dwarfed by the dark red dragon behind them. Scales glittered in the sunlight. The three wheeled above the crowd, graceful as swallows, momentarily blotting out the sun.

Althume could feel the wind from the powerful wings as their shadows slid over him. All across the field the banners snapped in the sudden breeze, then fell limp again as the dragons passed. People screamed and ducked even though the dragons were far above them. The dragons settled on the grass well away from the crowd.

They dropped the bundles they carried between their fore-legs and folded their wings. Then they moved to stand well away from each other, almost clumsy upon the earth. Their claws scored the turf. The yellow dragon limped; its right hind leg was smaller than the left.

And still no other dragon winged down from the north to join its fellows.

"I don't understand," Althume said. He was aware of an unreasoning annoyance deep inside. The Dragonlords had proved him wrong. And he had rushed to the edge of the canopied area to watch them as though he were one of the common herd of fools. That Peridaen and Anstella had done the same was small consolation. "Where is the other one? There should be at least one more."

On the field, a red mist surrounded each dragon, drawing more shrieks from the crowd. Moments later three human figures stood in their places. One stood head and shoulders above the other two. Althume could see the long clan braid of a Yerrin hanging down the man's back as he joined the others.

A glimmer of an answer came to Althume. He tensed. "Peridaen—I must see who the Dragonlords are. If the third one is who I think—"

Looking surprised, Peridaen nodded. "Since I'm a claimant for the regency, I suppose I must greet our . . . honored guests—" he spat the words "—and be civil. No one will think it odd if you come with me. But what—?"

"If I'm right, the fools have played right into our hands." The memory of Peridaen's doubt stung Althume again. *We'll see if even a Dragonlord is a match for my magic!* "And do be cordial," Althume continued. "But don't worry; it won't be for long." He shook his head in mock regret. "Not long at all."

Five

Sherrine swept into her bedchamber, surprised at the dim light within. Her gown clung damply to her. She was sticky with the heat, had a headache, and wanted a bath.

"Tandavi," she called.

No answer.

Sherrine frowned, a tiny, becoming frown that she'd practiced many times before her mirror. Where was that fool maid? Nothing had been straightened since she'd left. Even the brocade curtains still hung across the many-paned windows.

She forgot herself and scowled at the unmade bed with its linen sheets tossed about, the gowns she'd tried on and discarded still scattered over the embroidered cushions of the chairs. The dark green silk, one of her favorites, lay crumpled on the tiled floor. Sherrine picked it up and flung it onto a chair.

Stupid cow. How dare she leave without—oh, bother. I did tell her she could go to the field, the silly chit was so excited about seeing Dragonlords.

Sherrine sniffed, glad that she was above such idiocy. Since the arrival of the messenger yesterday with the news that the Dragonlords had broken their journey just north of Casna, all she'd heard from anyone was Dragonlords, Dragonlords, and yet more Dragonlords. Tandavi was as bad as any of the fools at court.

Grumbling, Sherrine yanked her pale blue linen gown over her head, allowing it to fall to the floor. Let Tandavi pick it up. Dressed only in her fine lawn undergown, she sat on the featherbed and kicked off her satin slippers.

The fuss when those empty-headed ninnies had caught

sight of the man the red dragon had Changed into! No doubt Tandavi would come back singing the praises of Linden Rathan as well.

A small voice at the back of her mind said, *Ah, but he was handsome, wasn't he?*

She considered that as she threw back the lid of the carved box on the table by her bed. Catching up the small lavender-filled headache bag within, she held it to her nose. She closed her eyes and breathed deeply, the scent soothing her.

A pity he was a Dragonlord. Not that that put her off—rather the contrary; Sherrine did not share her mother's fanatical devotion to the Fraternity of Blood. To her, the Fraternity was merely a road to power.

She recalled her first glimpse of Linden Rathan: tall, with bright blond hair to his shoulders. It was only when he'd turned that she'd seen the clan braid, the long, braided lock of hair at the nape of the neck that a Yerrin man never cut.

Sherrine imagined running her fingers through the unbound length of it. She smiled; she'd always had a weakness for handsome, fair-haired men. And Linden Rathan was handsome despite the birthmark. A dalliance with him might be amusing. And to score such a coup on the other women at court! The idea appealed to her.

How unfortunate that she couldn't act upon it. Her mother would have a fit. And that would be tiresome.

A timid knock broke her reverie. The door edged open; Tandavi peered around it.

"My lady," the maid began. "I'm sorry; I thought I could get back before—"

Sherrine was in no mood to be understanding. "How dare you leave my chamber in this con—" She broke off at unaccustomed sounds from below. Frowning, she strained to hear.

The house steward's voice, surprised but respectful; the click of bootheels on the tiles—more than one man, she thought—and the soft hiss of satin slippers; a low rumble of voices crossing the common room. She recognized the woman's voice.

*And what is Mother doing here, in the city house? She's
staying with Prince Peridaen. Why didn't she go back there?
Ah, gods; don't tell me they've quarreled and she's come
back.*

Annoyance flared. Since her mother had taken to staying
with the prince at his estate across the river, Sherrine had
been mistress of the Colranes' city house. She'd come to
think of it as her own. She didn't relish yielding control now
to her mother. And her mother would accept nothing less.

The other voices. She thought she could guess who they
were. A meeting, then, before going on to the palace.

And with Dragonlords in Casna, there was only one reason
for her mother, Prince Peridaen, and Peridaen's ever-present
steward to be conferring.

This was Fraternity business.

And they hadn't thought to include her—in her own house!

Sherrine dug her fingernails into her palms, seething at the
slight. Then she smiled, the merest stretching of tight-pressed
lips. Since she was the lady of this house, she should play
the charming hostess, shouldn't she?

Sherrine beckoned to Tandavi. "Fetch me a basin of cool
water and a fresh gown. I must greet my guests."

As he was escorted to the city house one of the nobles had
put at his disposal, Linden thought over what they'd learned
so far.

Prince Peridaen, the brother of the late queen, had been
away for some time traveling in Pelnar, and had returned to
Cassori only a few days after his sister's death.

Good timing, Linden thought wryly. It had certainly incon-
venienced his rival, Beren, Duke of Silvermarch, the young
Prince Rann's other uncle.

The uncle who, although invited, had not been on the barge
that day. More good timing.

In the normal course of things, Peridaen would have assumed the regency without question. But it was Beren who
had the warrant naming him regent to Desia's children should
ill befall her and her consort.

But not one of the Cassorin Council had known of the warrant's existence until after Queen Desia's death. Yet from what little Linden had overheard so far, most agreed that the document was indeed in the late queen's hand.

Caution on Desia's part? Or trickery on someone else's?

Sherrine approached the study. A servant bearing a tray laden with a flask of wine and four goblets followed. Voices murmured beyond the door. Without a pause, she opened it and entered.

Her head held high, she crossed the patterned tiles to the table that dominated the center of the narrow room. Surprised—and angry—faces turned to her. She had guessed rightly who would be here: her mother the baroness, Prince Peridaen, and Lord Steward Kas Althume. Before any of them could speak, she swept the prince her deepest, most graceful courtesy. Another for her mother, a lesser one for Althume.

At her gesture the servant entered. He set the tray upon the cherrywood table. Sherrine dismissed him and poured the wine herself. "I am sorry, my lords, my lady, that you were not served before this. The servants were derelict in informing me that I had such honored guests.

"And I apologize for coming late to this meeting; I would not have you think me lacking in dedication to the Fraternity." She took a seat at the end of the table opposite Prince Peridaen, fluttering her lashes at him, enjoying her mother's obvious annoyance. Peridaen nodded benignly at her.

Now admit—if you dare—that you had meant to keep me out of this.

Anstella snapped, "And what makes you so certain this is Fraternity business, girl?"

Sherrine said nothing, letting her look speak for her: *Don't be stupid, Mother.*

Prince Peridaen raised one elegant eyebrow. His hand covered his mouth. Sherrine was certain he hid a smile.

She looked down, feigning modesty. "May I ask what you were discussing? I wish to learn more of the ways and wisdom of those greater than I in the Fraternity." She gazed at the prince, letting her face fill with awe, before looking down again. She watched the others through the curtain of her lashes.

Vain as always, Peridaen took her bait. "We discussed the feasibility of trapping one of the Dragonlords by magic." His glance strayed to Althume.

From the corner of her eye, Sherrine caught the flash of Kas Althume's hand cutting Peridaen off. The prince fell silent.

The sight nearly startled a gasp from her. To see the Prince of Cassori, who demanded every courtesy and mark of respect due his rank, meekly accept an order from his steward was unfathomable.

Therefore, things were not what they seemed. She wasn't stupid, whatever her mother said to the contrary. Anstella of Colrane simply refused to acknowledge that her daughter— and chief rival as court beauty—might in any way equal her. Sherrine was content to let her mother keep her illusions— for now. She considered what she knew of the man sitting to the prince's left.

Ever since the prince had returned from his travels, the mysterious Althume had accompanied him everywhere. The tale at court was that he was a Pelnaran noble, a friend of Peridaen's, down on his luck and given a stewardship.

If so, I'm a scullery maid. Aloud she asked, "Magic? To what end?"

Anstella made an impatient gesture. "What do you think? The Fraternity wishes to know more about them. We need to discover their weaknesses—they must have some."

Sherrine stifled a sigh. The Fraternity always wanted to know more about Dragonlords. The time never seemed ripe, however, for the Fraternity to act on their knowledge. She doubted they ever would; like bards and Healers, Dragonlords were the chosen of the gods. To harm any of them was to be cursed for eternity, even if one escaped punishment from one's fellow men—which very few did.

It was all so dull. But thoughts of the Fraternity could be dismissed. She wanted to know what these three were plotting. If she could turn that plotting to her own ends . . .

Peridaen said, "Linden Rathan is the only Dragonlord without a soultwin. I had joked earlier about a love philter—"

This was a gift from the gods. "There is no need of a love philter," Sherrine said. "If, as you say, the tall Dragonlord has no soultwin, surely he is lonely.

"Am I not my mother's daughter, my lords? Her very image I am told. And you would not deny her loveliness, would you? Bards have sung of it." She favored her mother with a smile that had no mirth, knowing how it galled Anstella— who was without blemish—that her daughter should be held her equal in beauty.

Abandoning all pretense of modesty, Sherrine continued, "Think you this lonely Dragonlord will refuse a dalliance with the most beautiful young woman at court? I will ensnare him, learn all that I may from him, find out how we may strike at them."

She folded her hands and waited. She had no doubt of her ability to do as she'd said.

"Of all the stupid . . . ," Anstella began.

Expected though they were, the words cut her. She wished that for once her mother would bestow her ungrudging approval. But as much as she desired it, this time it was not her mother's approval that was of vital importance.

It was the prince's approval that she needed—and still more, she suspected, Althume's. While her mother and Prince Peridaen argued, Sherrine studied the supposed steward's profile as he traced a pattern with one long finger on the table.

He was thin to the point of gauntness; his heavy-lidded eyes looked bored, even sleepy. Light brown hair winged back from his temples, falling straight to his shoulders. His nose was straight with flaring nostrils.

His clothes, as always, were somber—dark gray and green—and conservative in cut. Not for him the more fantastical parti-colored tunics of the court dandies. He dressed, Sherrine decided, to remain unobtrusive; there was nothing about him to catch one's eye, to imprint him in one's memory.

He had made only one mistake in his chosen role: the quality of the cloth from which his garments were cut. It was far too expensive for a man supposedly living on the prince's charity; Sherrine knew Peridaen was not *that* generous.

She found it an interesting error. Unconscious vanity? An unwillingness to sacrifice those luxuries he considered his due? She would find out in time; for now she knew the man was more than he seemed.

As if to confirm her speculations, Althume shifted in his chair. Immediately her mother and the prince ceased their debate and turned to him.

He murmured, "We've nothing to lose if she doesn't succeed." He rested his chin on his steepled fingers, looking thoughtful.

The baroness opened her mouth as if to argue. Althume glanced at her, however, and she shut it with a snap.

That impressed Sherrine more than anything she had yet seen of the man.

Peridaen said mildly, "Hmm. True, Kas, but . . . We appreciate your unselfish sacrifice, my lady, but if upon thinking further about it you find it repellent and wish to withdraw—"

The memory of Linden Rathan's face came back to her. She almost laughed aloud. Sacrifice? Now she could have what she desired while advancing her status in the Fraternity. She congratulated herself on her cleverness.

"For the sake of the Fraternity, my prince, anything may be endured," she murmured.

The prince looked again to the other man. Althume shrugged and nodded. The fire in her mother's eye boded ill for someone, but Sherrine knew the older woman dared not forbid her now. She'd won.

Woe to the first servant to cross my lady mother, she thought with mock sympathy.

Prince Peridaen stood up. Sherrine hastened to rise. So did Anstella. Althume did not.

For the second time in less than a candlemark, Peridaen ignored a breach of royal etiquette. Sherrine's curiosity nearly choked her.

Stroking his beard, Peridaen said, "The Dragonlords will be feasted tomorrow night. I will see that you're introduced to Linden Rathan. You will see to it that he becomes interested in you.

"We shall talk to you again tomorrow." He held out his hand to Anstella. "Come, my dear; we must go on to the palace."

Head bowed, Sherrine dropped a low courtesy as the prince and her lady mother passed. They left the room without a backward glance. She rose.

Althume stood before her.

As her gaze met his directly for the first time, Sherrine's skin crawled. She had never seen such cold eyes. Her breath caught in her chest. It was as if she'd fallen through ice and was drowning in the frigid water below.

In a whisper like dead leaves blowing across slate, he said, "Remember—this is for the *Fraternity*." Then he was gone.

She stumbled back to her seat and drank the rest of her wine in a single gulp. She knew now; gods help her, she knew what the man was. Despite the summer heat she shivered. And wondered if she hadn't been too clever.

Six

"So, you got your way."

Sherrine rose and turned from her mirror to find her mother standing in the doorway. Tandavi quietly laid the hairbrush down and slunk off to a corner. "Indeed I did, Mother."

Gods, how that must rankle, Sherrine gloated inside.

"See that you don't fail."

"Why should I? Am I so ugly, then?" Sherrine asked, all innocence. If there was one insult her mother never offered her, it was that.

Her mother studied her for a moment. "Oh, you might catch his fancy for a time. Just until he sees past your face."

There was a note in the older woman's voice that alerted Sherrine. "Why, Mother—I do believe you're jealous."

Anstella stormed into the chamber, hand raised. But even as she drew it back, she checked herself.

"No, it wouldn't do to mark me, would it?" Sherrine said. "Not this night." Victory rushed to her head like strong wine as she watched her mother seethe with impotent fury.

At last her mother managed to say, "Time will see me right." Without another word Anstella turned and swept gracefully from the room.

"Not this time," said Sherrine as she sat before the mirror again. "Not this time." She clapped her hands. "Tandavi! Finish my hair."

As Tandavi ran the brush through her hair once more, Sherrine laid her plans.

Her hands trembled as she fitted the key to the lock of the chest. If Beren found her here, all was lost. Yet all those who could were at the feast, hoping for a glimpse of the Dragonlords. It was now or never.

There! The lock clicked open. Lady Beryl threw open the chest. To her dismay, it was filled with parchment scrolls. Oh, dear gods—was she going to have to examine each one?

A sound from the hall outside made her jump. She pressed a hand to her breast; beneath it, her heart hammered and thumped wildly. But the noise wasn't repeated, and no one came in. At last she remembered to breathe again.

This was much harder than she'd thought it would be. But she couldn't trust anyone else with it. It was too important. Her lord had to have the time.

She only hoped she wasn't hurting his cause; she'd not discussed her plan with him. She looked in the chest once more. This time she made herself think rationally.

The scrolls, she saw, were tied with different colored ribbons. But only one bore a ribbon of the royal scarlet. This was it, then.

Beryl lifted it gently, shielding her fingers with a strip of silk she'd brought for just this purpose; who knew what magics the Dragonlords had? Could they sense her if she actually touched the parchment itself?

She slid it up one of her long sleeves, between gown and shift, and cradled it against her body.

Now to hide it in the place she had marked days ago, a place where no one would ever find it.

Linden heaved a sigh of relief. The interminable feast was finally over and the last Cassorin noble had been presented to them. Now Kief, Tarlna, and he stood on a balcony overlooking the great hall below, talking quietly.

"What do you think?" Tarlna asked.

"It all seems straightforward enough," Kief said. "This may be just what it seems: a question of who shall be regent, nothing more." He paused to sip his wine. "Still . . ."

"Still we keep our eyes and ears open," said Linden. "I've naught to say against that; it's only good sense."

"And mingle as much as possible," Tarlna added. "It's

amazing what someone will let slip in a conversation at dinner or a hunt, especially when they don't realize just how sharp your hearing is.''

"That won't be hard," Linden grumbled, thinking of how many invitations had been pressed upon him already.

"You, too, hm?" Kief said sympathetically.

"Mm. I'm going to get more wine." Linden set off, looking about in curiosity.

He'd never seen anything quite like this. Galleries for minstrels, yes; even his father's small mountain hold had had one. But never before had he heard of a balcony for the guests of honor to survey the room. Here and there were small tables with comfortable chairs set around them. Larger tables held refreshments so that the favored occupants need not brave the crowd below to seek food and drink. At either end of the balcony wide stone staircases spiraled down to the dancing floor.

It was all very elegant, with the carved stonework of the railing, the bright tapestries covering the granite walls, the torches blazing in their sconces of gold.

And it was extremely public.

Every time he or one of the other Dragonlords went to the rail, Linden's sympathy for the denizens of a wild beast show grew. Half the people in the place seemed to be standing just below, waiting for a Dragonlord to look down. Even from this distance—and despite the music—he could hear the rising buzz of conversation every time one of them approached the rail. He noted glumly that the squeals and giggles seemed reserved for his appearances. As Linden waited for the servant to fill his goblet with spiced wine, he tried to decide whether he felt more like the trained wolf or the dancing bear.

Stop looking so sour, Kief's mindvoice said.

Linden growled back, *And why shouldn't I? You wouldn't be so smug if they were hunting you as well. But no; they see that you're with Tarlna and shy off. It wouldn't be so bad if there were someone else to distract them.*

I went through it as well before Tarlna Changed. You'll

live, little one. It's nothing; stop making such a fuss. Kief's laughter rang in Linden's mind.

Linden grumbled. He knew Kief thought him silly. But it bothered him that so many women saw only the rank and not the man. He had accepted many long years ago that all too often he was pursued as a lover's trophy, a conquest to flaunt before rivals.

He accepted it, but he didn't have to like it.

From the corner of his eye Linden saw Prince Peridaen come up the stairs. Since the elderly Duchess Alinya had retired early, the prince, as the ranking member of the family, was now their host. Linden had noticed that Peridaen and Duke Beren of Silvermarch had been carefully avoiding each other all evening.

Peridaen was flanked by two women, Baroness Anstella of the council on one side, a young woman on the other. The girl's eyes looked down modestly as she walked. Another man, dressed in sober grey and green, followed them; he looked vaguely familiar.

Linden thought a moment before he recognized the man: Peridaen's steward. The fellow certainly looked the part; he had a lean face that revealed nothing; his master's secrets were well hidden behind it. The torchlight glittered on his heavy silver chain of office.

Peridaen and Anstella led the girl to Kief and Tarlna and introduced her to the older Dragonlords. The five of them chatted. The steward stood to one side, awaiting his lord's bidding.

Linden knew he was next to be introduced to the girl. He groaned, wondering if this one was a giggler. That was better than those who stood before him terrified, as if he might Change and gobble them up. At least he thought it was better.

He waited politely as Peridaen bore down on him, the girl following. He inclined his head, saying, "Your Highness."

Peridaen made him a small bow. "Your Grace, may I present my lady Anstella's daughter, Sherrine of Colrane?"

As the girl held out her hand, Peridaen excused himself.

Mentally cursing Peridaen for trapping him like this,

Linden turned his attention to the girl and took the proffered hand, bracing himself for whatever might follow. As she made him a courtesy, he absently noted that she had beautiful auburn hair. The heady scent of wood lilies came to him.

The girl raised her head. Long lashes hid her downcast eyes.

Linden started in surprise. Gods, the girl was breathtaking. He'd seldom seen such beauty. "My lady Sherrine, it is a pleasure to meet you." He hoped for once the words were more than polite emptiness; it would be a pity if she proved a fool.

Her gaze met his. To his surprise, she neither giggled nor gasped. Instead her slanted hazel eyes held cool amusement. Their look intrigued him. Without realizing it he bent closer.

"You honor me, Dragonlord. I thank you." Her voice was low, pleasing to the ears.

Was that a laugh he heard behind her words? She took her hand back a moment before he wanted to release it.

"I would welcome you to Cassori, Your Grace—" she tilted her head "—but I'm certain you've heard it too many times already this evening." She smiled then, a mischievous smile that both conspired and commiserated.

He grinned. This girl had spirit. "Perhaps; then again, perhaps not, my lady. If you—"

But someone else, with daughter, niece, or sister in tow, was fast approaching. Linden cursed under his breath.

Sherrine laughed, a sound as delightful as a rippling brook, and made him another courtesy. "*Perhaps,* Your Grace," she said, her tone gently mocking him, "we shall meet again."

Sherrine spun away before he could stop her, looking back over her shoulder to arch an eyebrow at him. She disappeared down the other stairs as the Duchess of Blackwood shoved her terrified daughter into his arms.

When he had disentangled himself from the girl and freed himself from her mother's tenacious grasp, Linden went to look over the rail. For once he was oblivious to the commotion below. His eyes searched the crowd for a mane of auburn hair.

Sherrine was nowhere to be found.

He drank, taking his time to empty the goblet. There had been a challenge in Sherrine's look as she'd left him, as plain as if she'd spoken it aloud: *You will see me again when I wish it.*

Her boldness amused him. So did her challenge; he rather thought he'd enjoy playing her game—and letting her win. Perhaps—just perhaps—it would help to ease the loneliness. He put his goblet down and set off down the stairs.

Maurynna cradled the brass astrolabe in her arms. She'd taken her reading long before but couldn't bring herself to return to her cabin. For the past two nights it had felt like a cage. On the deck, with the familiar emptiness of starry sky and black ocean, her conflicting desires didn't crowd so close.

By sunset tomorrow they should be far enough to catch the Great Current that would carry them first north, then east along the shores of the northern kingdoms. Next port of call was Casna and whatever decision she would come to there. The thought scared the daylights out of her.

Ever since Otter had told her of his intent to journey north to Dragonskeep, she'd been tormented by a hunger to go with him. To everyone's surprise—especially her own—she'd proposed leading a trading expedition overland to the north.

You've worked so hard to get your own ship, she scolded herself, *and at the first chance to see a Dragonlord you're ready to abandon it. And for what? Otter's friend might not even be there—Otter admitted as much himself. And even if that friend is Linden Rathan, what's to say that you'd even like him? Maybe, just maybe, it's sometimes better to let a dream stay just that.*

But . . . Dragonlords! Especially the Dragonlord from all the tales she liked the best—even if he hadn't yet Changed in the stories with Rani eo'Tsan and Bram Wolfson.

Maybe this was the time to chase a dream.

She heard booted feet on the deck behind her. Not one of the sailors, then; they were all barefooted. There was only one person it could be.

"Why are you still up, Rynna?" a musical voice asked from the darkness and then Otter stood beside her. His eyes met hers in the faint light of the deck lamp, his head cocked in inquiry. He said gently, "What are you worried about?"

She shrugged to hide her surprise. "Why do you think I'm worried? I—um, I was just thinking how good it will be to see cousin Maylin again. And Kella. She must be a big girl now."

He made a rude noise. "I've known you since you were a child playing with my imp of a great-nephew by the fireside— remember? Believe me; I know when you're worried. You don't eat and you stare off into nothing, chewing your lip all the while. Hah! You're doing it again. Now what is bothering you?"

Memories of childhood came back to her: she and Raven sitting at Otter's feet as he spun his tales for them before the winter hearth, and so many of them about the Last Dragonlord.

. . . Raven's fifth birthday, a time of both great solemnity and great rejoicing. For on this day his hair, allowed to grow unchecked till now, was cut off at his shoulders, all save the lock at the nape of his neck that was braided for the first time. As of this day Raven was truly a part of his clan. Maurynna was happy for him, of course, but most of her joy was for the man who had traveled far for this day and now sat before them, for Otter told her stories of her hero.

Raven rocked back and forth in excitement, the firelight glowing in his red-blond curls. "Did you really see the hag before Linden Rathan did, great-uncle?" he asked breathlessly.

Otter nodded. "I did, boyo, and barely had time to warn him. It was pure luck that he heard me yelling in that storm; the wind was howling louder than all the souls in Gifnu's nine hells."

"Why didn't you mindspeak him?" Maurynna demanded. "You can do that, can't you?"

"Ah, but I didn't know him well then, remember; it was only the second time I'd met him. And I can't really mind-

*speak Linden, even now. It's just that if I think hard enough
about him—*

*Here now; haven't you ever known—just known—that
someone was thinking about you?"*

*Maurynna turned to Raven, knowing he'd be doing the
same. "Oh, yes," they chorused. "We know."*

*"Well, then, that's how Linden knows when I want to talk
to him, Rynna. I can't be too far from him, either, or it won't
work. But to get back to—"*

*"Linden Rathan killed the evil hag, didn't he?" Maurynna
bounced in anticipation. "He can do anything!"*

Otter laughed and went on with the tale. . . .

Linden Rathan had indeed killed the evil hag. Gods; he'd
been her hero for so long. . . . She blurted out, "Otter—hang
the *Sea Mist!* And hang what my family will say! I want to
go with you to Dragonskeep."

There. She'd said it. She waited for the bard to pin her ears
back for an idiot. And Otter could do that very well indeed.

But beyond a gasp of surprise, the bard said nothing for a
long time. When he did speak, his voice was quiet, concerned.
"Rynna, you wouldn't, not really—would you?"

She gripped the astrolabe so hard it was a wonder the brass
didn't buckle. "Yes. No. I don't know. It's just—It's just that
ever since you first talked about it, there's been a yearning in
me to see Dragonskeep, to meet a Dragonlord, to meet *him.*
It's tearing me in two. I want my ship; it'll kill me to lose
her. But even more I want, I want—oh, gods; I don't know
what I want."

But she did. She wanted to follow the fool's dream that
burned in her soul.

"Have you spoken of this to any of your crew?"

Maurynna snorted in disgust. "Of course not. I may be
mad, but I'm not stupid."

He laughed at that. "Don't, then. Because I promise you
this, Rynna: I will bring Linden to meet you. However I have
to do it, I will."

Her breath caught in her throat. "Otter, is this a joke?"

"No, dear heart, it isn't. My word as a bard on it."

He smiled gently at her. She couldn't speak. Otter loved to

tease, but this he meant body and soul. Tears choked her; she swallowed them.

"Thank you. I'll be patient, then." Her voice was husky. She turned to look out over the midnight sea before he could catch a glimpse of the betraying wetness on her cheeks.

When she could, she said, "Do you think I'm wrong? Would I be better off not meeting him? He's been my hero for so long.. Linden Rathan—he's not, I mean, he's not an ass or anything like that, is he?"

Once again Otter made a rude noise. "Of course Linden's not an ass. Dragonlord or no, I wouldn't inflict him upon you if he was. Gifnu's hells, girl, I wouldn't have inflicted his company upon myself these past forty years!"

Other fears rose to torment her. What if he thought *she* was an ass? What would she have to talk about with a magical being more than six centuries old?

She buried the first and asked the second.

Otter shook his head. "You'll find he's not that different from you, Rynna."

Puzzled, she asked, "What do you mean?" How could Linden Rathan not be different? He was a Dragonlord, magical, nearly immortal.

Otter paused, as if considering his next words carefully. He said, "Linden told me once that something happens to Dragonlords when they go through First Change. He didn't know how to explain it beyond 'we fall out of time.' My guess is that once they Change, they mature the way a truedragon would—incredibly slowly. To a truedragon, Linden would be considered a babe, even though he's over six hundred years old.

"He wasn't that much older than you when he first Changed—only twenty-eight—and many times over the years I've forgotten that he was older. True, sometimes I've seen something more ancient than I can ever imagine in his eyes, but the next moment it's gone."

Flinging a hand up to take in the *Sea Mist* and the ocean all around them, Otter said, "As for what to talk about . . . Tell him about your ship, Maurynna; tell him about sailing and what the sea is like in calm and storm. Tell him about making a port for the first time, the patterns of the waves and what they mean, what the gulls sound like at dawn. He's rarely sailed and he likes learning new things. Don't be surprised if he asks if he can sail with you someday.''

Maurynna's head reeled. She couldn't speak; there were too many things to say at once. Linden Rathan? On board the *Sea Mist*? That would be a dream come true indeed.

Sherrine hid behind a pillar. She peered around it, taking care not to be seen and laughed quietly as she ducked back into hiding.

Linden Rathan was descending the stairs. From the way his head turned this way and that, she knew he searched the crowd.

And she had little doubt for whom he searched. She was well pleased with herself. She'd struck just the right note with him: unafraid, bold yet not overbearing, challenging. She'd seen the look in his eyes change from boredom to interest as she'd dared to tease him.

She peeked out once more. He'd paused on the steps. Her gaze roved over him with appreciation. The ceremonial regalia of a Dragonlord suited his tall, powerful frame well. None of the young men she knew would be able to carry off the antique cut of the black tunic, the wide sleeves with their imdagged ends and scarlet silk lining. They'd be laughable even at a masquerade.

But not the tall Dragonlord. He wore it with an unconscious dignity that made him look . . . She pondered a moment. Dashing. That was it: dashing, like the hero in an old tale.

He was at the foot of the stairs now, ready to plunge into the crowd.

Keeping to the shadows, Sherrine made her way out of the hall. It was not part of her plan that he should find her again this night.

She would find *him*—and at a time and place of her own choosing. She thought she would enjoy that next meeting.

There was something in his face that she instinctively liked, a kindness in the dark grey eyes.

She shook her head. Bah! She sounded as bad as Tandavi. This dalliance was business. War even, her mother would say; truehuman against weredragon.

Still, she hoped she need not wait long.

Seven

Maylin was just taking the last loaf of bread from the oven in the fireplace when her little sister Kella came running into the kitchen.

"Maylin! Guess what? Guess, guess, guess!" Kella squealed, hopping with excitement.

Untying the apron from her plump middle, Maylin asked, "I can't even begin to guess, gigglepuss. Tell me."

"Mama said that since we couldn't go to watch them arrive the other day, we could go watch the Dragonlords ride up the Processional before we have to help her in the shop! Today's the first Council meeting."

The apron sailed across the kitchen, missed its hook on the wall, and slid to the flagstones unnoticed. Maylin whooped and seized Kella's hand. "Don't just stand there! We'll have to run if we want a good spot."

They yelled their good-byes as they dashed out the door. Laughing in the early morning chill, they ran through the streets of Casna, stopping now and again to rest—but not for long. Their excitement urged them on each time before they'd completely caught their breath.

"I know a good place to wait," said Maylin, gasping between each word, at one such stop. "Under that big elm, the one where that little street behind the temples meets the Processional. It will be a bit of time yet before they go to the palace, and we can wait in the shade."

"Yes!" Kella agreed, and was off like an arrow.

Maylin groaned and ran after her. At least it was still cool enough to run; the day had not yet begun its descent into the sultry heat that had plagued the city for the past two tendays. Still, Maylin was puffing by the time she caught up with

Kella. Taking her sister's hand once more, Maylin kept her to a slow jog.

Although they made good time, when they reached their goal they found a great many other people had had the same idea. The Processional—the great avenue leading to the palace—was thronged with people as far as Maylin could see.

"Oh, bother," she grumbled as she eyed the crowd. "Kella, grab on to the hem of my tunic and hold on for all you're worth."

Kella seized a double handful of cloth; Maylin plunged into the crowd. She twisted and turned, Kella clinging like a burr, worming a way between the tightly packed spectators. One ill-mannered yokel in farmer's garb wouldn't let her pass, although he could easily have seen over her head even if she stood right in front of him. When he turned to leer at her, she thrust her face up at him, eyes wide, making certain that he got a good look at them. He stumbled back from her, making the sign against the evil eye. Maylin seized the moment to slip past him, grinning wickedly.

That's right, fool—they're two different colors. And a pox on your ignorance, thinking they mean evil. They simply run in my family.

At last she fetched up against a back clad in scarlet livery; someone pushed her and she jostled the palace guard. The guard turned, frowning. Maylin stared up at him, frightened, Kella hugging her. But frown turned to smile, and the guard said kindly, "Hoy, lasses—little bits like you won't see nothing over us. Come stand 'twixt Tully here and m'self. Hurry; here they come."

"Th-thank you," Maylin stuttered as the guards shifted to make room for them. She gathered Kella up in her arms so that the little girl could see better and craned her neck to look down the Processional.

The scarlet of palace guards and the blue-and-red of the City Watch lined the great avenue. They held back a crowd that suddenly erupted into happy shouting. Now Maylin could see a scarlet line of palace guards marching abreast down the avenue. The heads of their upright spears glittered in the sun. Behind them were three figures on horseback.

"Kella! There they are—do you see them?"

Kella nodded vigorously; Maylin hoisted her a little higher. She held her breath as she watched the riders.

Two were men—a smaller one on the right, the taller closest to their side of the street—with a woman riding between them. They looked wonderful in their ceremonial garb.

The small man had brown hair and a thin, mild face. He was slender and altogether most unextraordinary in appearance. *He's a Dragonlord? He looks like one of Father's journeymen,* Maylin thought.

The woman had pale blonde hair hanging in a tumble of curls down her back. She was pretty, but with a sharp set to her full red lips that made Maylin think she'd be chancy to cross.

Now what had she heard their names were? *Oh, yes—Kief Shaeldar and Tarlna Aurianne, the soultwinned pair. The other one is Linden Rathan. Won't Rynna be jealous when I tell her! I do hope she makes port here before this is over.*

She shifted her gaze to the one known as the Last Dragonlord as they neared her. Her overwhelming impression was of size: Linden Rathan, like almost every Yerrin she'd ever seen, was tall and broad of shoulder and chest. He was also blond like Tarlna Aurianne, but his hair was the bright gold shared by so many of his countrymen. It was thick and shaggy and hung down to his shoulders.

As the Dragonlords drew abreast of where they stood, Kella began frantically waving, well-nigh tearing herself from Maylin's grasp, caroling a greeting in her high, sweet voice.

The sudden movement seemed to catch Linden Rathan's eye, for he looked straight at them. Kella waved harder. To Maylin's everlasting astonishment, Linden Rathan smiled and waved back, calling, "Hello, kitten!"

Kella screamed in delight and dissolved into giggles, burying her face against Maylin's hair and drawing laughter from the crowd. Linden Rathan's smile grew wider; he winked as he and the other Dragonlords passed.

Soon all they could see of the Dragonlords were their backs. The magical moment was past. Maylin suddenly realized her arms ached. She set Kella down with a groan and tried to shake the pins and needles from them.

Kella jumped up and down. "Did you see, Maylin? Did you see?"

"I certainly did. We'll have to tell Mother all about how Linden Rathan waved at you," Maylin said. "And if you grin any harder your face is going to split, gigglepuss."

"*He* called me 'kitten,' " said Kella.

"So he did." Maylin took her sister's hand and led her through the dissipating crowd. "Don't forget to tell Rynna about this when she gets here."

"Will she get here soon?" Kella asked as they wound their way through the streets of Casna. "And I wish Papa hadn't had to go trading. He would have liked this, too."

"He'll be so disappointed he missed the Dragonlords. And I hope Rynna docks here soon; she'd like to see them. But the captain of the other Erdon ship that was here a few tendays ago could only tell us 'sometime around the solstice,' so I don't know."

Kella asked, "Will we take her to wave at Linden Rathan?"

"We certainly will, small stuff, if he's still here. And there's the shop—won't Mother be surprised!"

"I'm afraid," Kief said as he peeked into the council room through the barely open door, "that this omen does not bode well. My Lord Chancellor of the Council—"

"Wassilor," Tarlna provided. "Chancellor Wassilor. How unfortunate a combination."

"Is very long-winded," Kief finished. "The esteemed council members' eyes are glazing over."

"Oh, damn," said Tarlna. "This is *not* what I'd hoped for." She scowled at the walls of the anteroom as though wondering how long she'd have to look at them before escaping.

Linden rocked from foot to foot. Oh, bloody damn indeed.

First they had to stand about in this stuffy little room while some pompous ass brayed, then the herald would announce them, giving their human and dragon names, one by one. Then he would present the council—one by one.

What idiocy. They'd met these same nobles last night. But *now* it had to be done with proper ceremony and formality.

Bother the ceremony. He wanted to get started.

He pushed back his sleeves. Wretched things, always in the way. He wished they didn't have to wear the regalia for these meetings. He'd had enough of it last night at the welcoming festivities. He'd spent the entire feast waiting for the wide sleeves to fall into the gravy. They usually did; sometimes he thought they had a mind of their own.

And these blasted tight breeches pinched.

He wanted the soft, loose, Yerrin breeches and well-worn boots waiting in his quarters. And a tunic with sensible sleeves.

Yet the black, scarlet, and silver formal clothes were impressive—and necessary. They would remind the council that these were Dragonlords, the ancient Givers of Law, sitting in judgement. Without that reminder, some members would forget that the three before them were not the mere two decades or so old that they appeared.

He shifted his heavy torc of rank, fingering the dragonheads with their ruby eyes. His clan-braid snagged on the links of his belt. He pulled it free.

Damn these clothes.

Tarlna hissed, "I hope you're more dignified when you're out there. You're fidgeting like a child!"

She stalked him, drawing breath to continue. Linden retreated into memories of the night before, allowing Tarlna's scolding to wash over him unheeded. He'd grown expert at it over the centuries. Instead, he wondered when he'd see Sherrine again. Not one moment before she wanted him to, he'd wager. The memory of her perfume and laughing eyes came back to tease him. Tarlna continued venting her annoyance with the delay on him.

The herald's voice rang out from the other room. "My

lords and ladies—His Grace, Dragonlord Kief Shaeldar!''

Kief opened the door and made his entrance.

The herald's cry of ''Her Grace, Tarlna Aurianne!'' cut Tarlna's lecture short. She limped off.

Linden heaved a sigh of relief. Then the herald called ''His Grace, Linden Rathan!'' and it was his turn to face the Cas-. sorin Council. He stepped through the door.

This was his first look at the room where he would likely spend much of his time in the next few tendays; they had entered the anteroom from the hallway. It was longer than it was wide, with windows from floor to ceiling along the lowall to his left. The sunlight shone through, making rectangles of light at intervals along the floor.

At the far end was a massive fireplace of black marble. He wondered if they'd ever roasted an ox there; the. thing was large enough. The remaining walls were covered with the dark carved paneling that was in every Cassorin room he'd seen so far.

A thought drifted across his mind: *Perhaps there's a law requiring it.*

The heels of his tall, stiff boots clicked on the patterned tiles of the floor. He counted as he passed through the sunlit patches: one, two, three, four, five. The warm sun felt good on his face.

The table was closer to the fireplace than to the door to the anteroom, leaving him a long walk to reach it. Once again he felt on display.

The dancing bear; I definitely feel like the dancing bear.

Kief and Tarlna stood with their backs to him. Curious faces looked past them, watching him. He was able to put names to most of them. He avoided the Duchess of Blackwood's accusing stare.

To his surprise, young Prince Rann came forward to greet him. It was the first time he'd seen the child since the afternoon of their arrival. He was shocked at the change in only two days. Granted, the child hadn't looked robust before— but now!

The little boy's face was wan, with dark circles under the

eyes. For all that he was barely six, Rann moved like a tired old man.

Linden suppressed a frown lest Rann think it meant for him. Instead, he mindspoke the others. *Why is the boy here? He looks ill. A council is no place for even a healthy child!*

He has the right to be here, Kief said. *After all, it is his fate we are deciding.*

If we keep him here, we will be deciding his fate indeed. We'll send him to join his parents! Blast it, Kief, the boy looks ready to collapse.

Kief made no answer. Linden leashed his anger as the young prince bowed to him. He bowed in return. Then he held out a hand. Murmurs of surprise went around the table at this departure from protocol. Tarlna glowered. He ignored her. Instead he looked down at the young prince, waiting.

Rann studied him in return, his dark brown eyes too serious in his thin face. Then the boy nestled his hand into Linden's grasp. His eyes now were trusting, unafraid even when his small hand disappeared in Linden's large one. Linden walked with him to the empty chair by Duchess Alinya's side at the end of the table by the fireplace. It was far too tall for a child; Linden lifted him into it.

Linden winked as the boy curled up in the cushions. His reward was an impish, gap-toothed grin.

Linden circled the table to take his own seat beside Kief, ignoring the murmurs that followed his passage. He hoped his face betrayed none of his anger.

The herald introduced the men and women seated around the table. Each one bowed as he or she was presented, the claimants for the regency last of all.

Prince Peridaen had the slender elegance of a greyhound. A short beard neatly outlined his jaw. His dark hair, curled in the latest fashion, hung to his shoulders. By his expression, Peridaen looked to be a reasonable man.

The late consort's twin, on the other hand, sat tight-lipped and scowling. Beren had the Cassorin face one saw everywhere in the country: round, broad of cheek, snub-nosed. It was now nearly the same shade of brick red as his hair. He looked ready to explode. Yet the nervous way he licked his lips said that there was more than simple fury at work.

Linden frowned as his glance met Beren's and the man glared before looking quickly away. Gods knew, Cassori didn't need a hothead on its throne. And how much patience would he have with a child? Was his claim to the regency only a ploy to get power over Rann? If the warrant of regency was upheld and Rann died, the Cassorin throne would fall to this man.

I wonder if it's at his instigation that Rann is here. The boy looks sickly. How convenient if he should die of natural causes—aided by exhaustion.

Duchess Alinya, the great-aunt of the older prince, faced the Dragonlords from the other end of the long table. Until the regency was settled, she was the ruler of Cassori.

She was shrunken with age. But her pale blue eyes were fierce and proud and there was no weakness in her bearing.

Alinya greeted them. "Dragonlords, I thank you once again for coming to our aid. We have all agreed to accept your judgment—" She stared hard at the two claimants to either side of her. Beren scowled again. Peridaen nodded, smiling benignly.

The duchess continued, "Of who shall be regent until Rann is old enough to rule." She rested a wrinkled hand on the boy's head, then stroked his hair gently. Rann leaned into it like a puppy.

"Since we are ready and all are agreed to accept our judgment, shall we begin?" Kief said.

Linden leaned back in his chair and rubbed the back of his neck. The way things were plodding along, he looked to be in Cassori for the rest of his long life. Right now someone was praising her late Majesty's dedication to the country. He stifled a yawn.

The man droned on, "And there is no doubt our beloved queen would have chosen her consort's—"

Lord Duriac stood up. "Had Her Majesty not been so negligent, we wouldn't be wasting our time here! A proper selection of a regent, with witnesses—that's what she should have done. Then we wouldn't have to deal with this nonsense of a so-called warrant of regency only now coming to light.''

Beren—three chairs down from Duriac—slammed his big fists on the table. ''Are you calling me a liar, Duriac?'' he shouted.

Linden tensed, ready to break up a fight.

But instead a tiny whimper, barely more than a breath, claimed his attention. Rann was huddled in his chair, biting his lip. His eyes shone with tears.

Duriac smiled primly and said, ''Those of Silvermarch have always shown an overweening ambition for the throne of Cassori. Did you think to do what your brother had not succeeded in, my lord—to make yourself king in Cassori?''

Beren leaped up, yelling. Duriac shouted something back at him. A countess jumped to stand between the two men. Everyone began talking at once. Kief called for order, but his light voice was drowned out. Rann dropped his head to his knees, crying.

Linden stood up. His deep-voiced growl cut through the noise. ''Gentlemen, this is most unseemly. And if you will excuse me, I wish a conference with Prince Rann.''

Before anyone could react, he strode to Rann's chair. Rann stared up at him, tears flowing down his cheeks. Linden resisted the urge to scoop the boy up and comfort him. Though a child, Rann was a prince and entitled to the courtesies due royalty.

''Your Highness, would you care to step aside with me? I wish to speak with you privately,'' he said.

Rann nodded and stood up in his chair. Linden picked him up, meaning to set him down to walk, but the thin arms slid around his neck. Very well, then; if the boy wanted to be carried, Linden was more than willing. He settled Rann on one hip and carried him to the end of the room where the door to the anteroom still stood ajar. For a moment he considered taking Rann there. Instead he stopped by a window well away from the council.

Kief said, *Linden, just what do you—*

Tarlna sent a wordless blast of anger.

Linden ignored the older Dragonlords' barely suppressed fury. *Doing what should have been done in the first place. The child doesn't need to hear harsh words about his parents. Kief, please—do* not *interfere.* He felt Kief's struggle with his own temper, then his resigned agreement, and Tarlna's vexation at his high-handedness.

He sat on the edge of the deep sill, his back deliberately turned to the council, one leg braced to hold himself in place. Let them think him rude; he wasn't sure he could control his expression and he would not betray his feelings to them. He unlatched the window and pushed it open.

The window overlooked the gardens. Linden gazed outside, waiting while Rann finished crying, the child's face buried in his shoulder. Linden stroked the boy's hair, absently rocking him.

The heavy, sweet smell of roses drifted in. He saw that the beds of roses and their borders of lavender were arranged to form a maze of red, pink, white, and purple. Bees that only a Dragonlord's sharp eyes could see from this distance droned among the blossoms. Linden wondered idly where their skeps were kept; the kitchen herb garden, no doubt.

A breeze sprang up, bringing in the sharper scent of the lavender. With it, and the weight of the sobbing child in his arms, came a memory Linden had thought he'd forgotten.

. . . Closing the door of the small holder's cottage behind him, exclaiming, "Gods, it's cold out there!" And then Ash, running to greet him, stumbled, knocking his head against the trestle table.

He scooped the crying child up and kissed the bump already forming. "There, there, boyo, don't cry. It'll stop hurting soon." He tossed Ash into the air until the little boy laughed.

"Stop that, Linden," Bryony scolded, but smiling all the while. "You mustn't get him excited now or he'll never get to sleep!"

He laughed, hugging the boy, reveling in the tightening of the slender arms around his neck. "Did you get the blankets out? I saw a ring around the moon as I came back from watering the horses. We'll have a heavy frost by morning if nothing worse."

"Yes," Bryony answered. *"Fresh from the chest and still sweet with the lavender I packed them in. Here—smell."*

He breathed deeply as he tucked the blankets around the boy lying in the small bed. The scent clinging to the wool was sweet, clean.

"Goodnight, boyo," he said, and kissed Ash's forehead, turning his cheek for the child's kiss before stepping aside.

He watched Bryony kneel by the side of the bed. As much as he'd grown to love his stepson, he wanted little ones of his own. He imagined making more little beds, just like the one he'd made for Ash.

But so far he and Bryony had had no luck. Maybe tonight . . .

Instead the marriage had ended after festering like a tainted wound. Linden closed his mind to the remembered pain of Bryony's mocking words, chosen to hurt as much as possible. *Mule. Linden-half-a-man.* If only he'd known then . . .

Rann lifted his head and Linden came back to the present. He waited while Rann hiccuped once or twice, collecting himself.

"Do you really want to be here, lad?" Linden asked.

Rann hesitated. Linden watched him struggle with his answer. Finally he said, "No, Dragonlord. Some of them are saying bad things about my—my mama and papa." Rann swallowed a sob. "Uncle Peridaen doesn't think I should be here either."

"So why are you here?"

Rann shifted. "Because Uncle Beren said I should be, that it's my future to be decided."

Linden started at hearing Kief's reasoning echoed. He struggled to put aside his earlier suspicions. *Commendable perhaps,* he thought, *but hard on the child.*

Then Rann leaned in to whisper, "I'd really rather be outside with my wolfhound Bramble—and Gevianna, my nurse."

Linden grinned, wondering what Gevianna would think of coming after a wolfhound in Rann's listing. He asked, "What about your playmates?"

Rann shook his head. "There are only servants' children in the palace now. And Uncle Peridaen says it's beneath me to play with them."

Linden's eyebrow went up. *Oh, really?* he thought. *The hell it is; if it's not beneath a Dragonlord, it's not beneath a prince.* "I know two little boys I think you'd like to play with—"

Rann's tired face lit up.

Linden cursed himself for an idiot, getting the boy excited like that. He finished, "But they're too far away."

The boy nodded and drooped in Linden's arms, the happy light gone from his eyes.

This princeling needed some playmates. Linden vowed that somehow or another he'd find them for Rann. But for now, he wanted the boy well away from this squabbling.

He mindspoke the others. *I want Rann out. This is no place for a child.*

Tarlna said, *His uncle has asked that he be here—*

And the other one doesn't want him here! Kief, you are the eldest, our leader. For pity's sake, spare the boy this, will you? Linden pleaded.

Heavy regret tinted Kief's mindvoice even as he said, *If the majority of the council wants him here, Linden, he must—*

Linden roared, *The council be damned! I will not have it! If you won't back me up in this, I shall return to Dragonskeep. I will not be a party to this child's suffering. Even when I was a mercenary I never harmed a child. I certainly won't start now.*

You take a great deal upon yourself, Tarlna said. Her mindvoice was cold. *The Lady will not be pleased.*

The Lady may discipline me as she sees fit. Now—will you stand with me in this?

He felt the other two withdraw. He bit his lip, waiting, forcing himself not to argue further.

At last Kief said, *Knowing what a stubborn wretch you*

are, I don't suppose we've much choice, have we? Very well, Linden. Tarlna and I will stand with you. I must admit the child doesn't look well. Perhaps it's for the best he's out of this.

Linden strode back to the table as Kief announced, ''We feel that Prince Rann is better left out of these discussions, my lords and ladies. He has been ill. This will take too great a toll on him.''

He knew he'd made the right decision when Rann sagged against him with a soft cry of relief. But for a moment Linden thought Beren would challenge him to a duel. The duke's face was purple with rage.

Peridaen looked surprised but pleased. His voice grave and gentle, he said, ''Thank you, Dragonlords. I have already said my nephew is not strong enough for this. He needs his rest. Shall I—'' He stood up.

So did Beren. ''Sit down, Peridaen. If anyone goes with Rann—''

But Linden was already striding to the door. He opened it and leaned into the hall. The two soldiers guarding the room swung around to face him, hands on sword hilts, eyeing their prince sitting in his arms. Linden closed the door behind himself as he stepped into the hall.

''Hello Captain Tev, Cammine,'' Rann said, his head once again resting on Linden's shoulder. He yawned.

The soldiers saluted, murmuring, ''My lords,'' and relaxed.

''Would one of you send for His Highness's nurse—'' Linden looked down at Rann.

''Gevianna,'' Rann supplied, sounding a trifle petulant that Linden hadn't remembered.

''Thank you, Your Highness,'' Linden said gravely.

The younger soldier set off down the hall at a nod from her superior. Linden waited in the hall with Rann, grateful for the respite. The captain took up his post again, too professional to be distracted by anything less than an invasion of the palace.

''I hate these things,'' Linden muttered under his breath. He hoped Gevianna would take her time coming for Rann.

Rann lifted his head. "My mama and papa did, too. When I am king, I shan't go to councils. I shall be a soldier. Were you really a soldier, Dragonlord, with Bram and Rani—just like in the stories? There was a Yerrin bard who sang for my mama; he told me some of them."

Linden chuckled. "That sounds like my friend Otter. He's on his way to Cassori now, and if you want I'll ask him to tell you more tales." He returned Rann's grin of delight. "And yes, I was in Bram and Rani's mercenary company. It was the dead of winter when I ran away to join them. I was hardly sixteen at the time and hadn't enough brains to bait a fishhook with, as the saying goes, else I'd have stayed at my father's keep—at least until the spring."

Rann laughed aloud. Even Captain Tev allowed himself a small grin.

The boy leaned in and whispered confidentially, "There were some scary parts—all that about Harper Satha. It gave me nightmares. Otter didn't say much about him, but . . . Satha wasn't really dead—was he?"

Linden felt the blood drain from his face at the mention of the undead Harper-Healer's name. He cursed himself in his mind: *Damn it! You're not sixteen anymore to be frightened by him. Stop being a fool!*

Yet even as he railed against the old terror, cold sweat trickled between his shoulder blades as for the second time that day memories returned unbidden.

. . . The stench of Satha's rotting flesh and the croaking horror of his voice as it whistled and bubbled past the slit throat . . .

Worst of all, the memory of Satha kneeling over him as he lay mortally wounded . . . *Fingers of burning cold, slick with his blood, groping along the edges of the gaping wound, and a smell of rotting meat following him as he fell into the welcome darkness, away from the agony of the Healing . . .*

Linden looked into Rann's eyes. "No," he lied. It was not something he did lightly, but if a small falsehood would ease the child's mind, he'd lie gladly. Someday he'd come back when Rann was older and tell him the truth. "Satha wasn't dead." He smiled; it felt tight and false.

He thanked the gods that the younger guard returned then, sparing him any further questions. Cammine resumed her post by the door. Her eyes slid to look back the way she'd come.

A slender young woman turned the corner into the hall. The woman had a pinched face, with a tight-lipped mouth that had certainly never smiled. She looked as though she smelled a dead rat three days after the cat had hidden it.

Linden blinked in surprise. This Gevianna didn't look the sort to romp with a little boy and a wolfhound.

She wasn't. And she wasn't Gevianna, as he found when Rann sighed and said, "Good day, Lady Beryl." Then, to Linden, "Dragonlord, this is my governess."

"My lady," Linden began. "Prince Rann—"

Lady Beryl cut him off. "Come with me, Your Highness. It's time for your lessons."

A quick pressure of the thin arms around his neck and then Rann twitched, asking to be set down. Linden obliged. The governess snatched Rann's hand and turned away—but not before Linden saw her expression change. Now she looked like a cat that had a baby bird fall from a tree straight into its paws.

She walked so fast Rann had to trot to keep up, hopping at every third step. His shoulders slumped as he pattered along, head down.

Linden called after her, "Lady Beryl, it would seem best if Prince Rann—"

She kept walking. "I believe I know what's best for the child, Dragonlord." She made the title sound like an obscenity. "Good day."

He stared as Rann and his governess disappeared around the corner, then glanced sideways at the guards. They stared intently at nothing.

"Ah," he said under his breath. He looked thoughtfully at Captain Tev, one eyebrow raised. After a long moment Tev met his eyes. The captain gave a tiny nod and a wry smile and opened the door for him.

It seemed Dragonlords were not in favor with Lady Beryl. As he entered the council chamber once again, Linden wondered how many others in Casna shared her feelings.

Eight

The door to the gardens was open. He could smell the roses from the maze on the breeze. Somewhere in the nearby darkness the brass chimes hanging from one of the peach trees rang softly. Linden sat with his back to the dining table, looking out into the warm night, rolling the stem of a silver goblet between his fingers.

He'd never known of such chimes before coming to Casna. The first night he'd heard them, the sweet sound had lured him into the garden until he'd found the source. Entranced, he'd called Aran, the house steward, and questioned him.

"They're from Assantik, Your Grace," the steward had told him. "A trader brought the first about two years ago; they immediately became all the rage among the high-born. A pleasant sound, isn't it, my lord? Very soothing."

Soothing indeed. Linden yawned. He must remember to get some and bring them to the Lady; she would enjoy them. So would Lleld. He drank, savoring the wine and the melodious chiming.

Memories of Rann's haggard face sprang up to shatter the tranquil moment. The muscles of Linden's neck and shoulders knotted with the remembered tensions of the council chamber. He shook his head angrily.

What is wrong with the boy that he could take such a turn for the worse? Isn't there a Healer at the palace to attend him?

Linden slouched down in the chair, his long legs straight out before him. He studied his boot toes and came to a decision.

There must be a Healer, blast it—and I'm going to talk to him or her. Tonight.

"Aran," he called aloud. When the house steward appeared, Linden said, "Tell Captain Jerrell that I wish to return to the palace, but not to rouse the full escort. He and one other soldier will do."

The young woman pulled her hooded cloak tighter as she hurried through the starlit gardens, clinging to the pools of deeper darkness by the walls. Gods, how she hated these meetings! It always felt as though eyes watched her, eyes that belonged to creatures best unnamed. Tales that her grandmother had told long ago came back to haunt her and the flesh at the back of her neck prickled.

At last she reached the part of the gardens known as the ladies' bower. A huge sigh of relief escaped her as she made out a figure already there. At least this night she wouldn't have to wait while her imagination peopled the heavy darkness with bogles and demons.

"You're late." The dulcet voice was cold and imperious.

"My apologies, my lady Baroness. I could not get away before now." She made a courtesy.

The Baroness of Colrane sniffed. "Try harder next time." From beneath her cloak she drew out a small flask. "Here. This is the new tonic for the boy. Be certain he gets it; you have been careless a time or two lately."

The young woman dropped another courtesy and took the flask. "I will try, my lady. But sometimes the Healer or the apprentice Quirel is there when it's time to dose the child and I cannot." Then, gathering up her courage, she said, "My lady Baroness . . . These potions—they're not . . . poisonous, are they?" She looked at the earthen bottle in her hand as if it might turn into a snake.

"Second thoughts, girl? You're in too deep to back out now. Besides, what would happen to your worthless brother?" A pause, then, "If the money to pay his gambling debts stopped, of course." The baroness smiled coldly. "You really should let him lie in the bed he makes for himself, you know."

All the gods as her witnesses, she didn't trust that smile.

She didn't trust any of this lot; she had her suspicions about the queen's death.

But what could she do? The woman was right; she was in too deep to back out now. And the money . . . She had no choice; if Kerrivel couldn't pay his debts to the young lordlings, he'd be imprisoned. And that would kill Father, he was so proud.

The baroness went on, "Still, if it is any consolation to you: no, none of the tonics you have given Rann are poisonous. None will be. They are merely meant to keep him quiet and biddable. Do not ask why this is necessary; it is the business of your betters and not yours."

Once again the noblewoman's hand disappeared beneath her cloak; this time, when it reappeared, it held a pouch that clinked. She tossed it to the young woman. "From this day forth you will go to Prince Peridaen's steward when you need more. I have other things to do. Now go." The baroness turned her back, signaling the end of the interview.

The young woman dropped another courtesy to that uncaring back and hurried off, the flask clenched in one hand, the pouch of coins in the other.

The whole way back the eyes watched her, digging into her very soul.

Her "cave," her apprentices called it. Not fitting for the dignity of the castle's Healer. But Tasha felt comfortable in the odd little room she used for a study. No one alive now knew why it had been built the way it was. But Tasha had fallen in love with it when she'd first come to the castle. Filled with shelf after shelf of books, jars of medicinal herbs, and soothing oils, the beehive-shaped room had been her refuge.

These days it felt like her prison.

The oil lamp guttered, threatening to go out. Chin resting in the palm of one hand, Healer Tasha sighed and lit a sliver of wood from the sputtering flame. Moving slowly, she held the tiny fire to the wick of another, full oil lamp and went back to her books. There were three of them spread out on the desk before her—and none of them were any cursed help in figuring out what was wrong with Rann. Certain of his symptoms matched those of some of the illnesses described—yet others didn't. The treatments prescribed for those illnesses did nothing—or else made Rann sicker.

She pressed the heels of her hands into her eyes, stifling a yawn. As much as she hated to give up and admit tonight's search was as fruitless as all the others, she knew she was getting stupid with exhaustion. She'd have to sleep soon; a fine thing it would be if she missed the cure because she was too tired to recognize it.

If only the scribe who'd copied these books hadn't had such a crabbed hand. Perhaps he'd been trying to skimp on parchment and ink, the stingy wretch. She hadn't the energy to curse him. Not tonight.

She'd close her eyes briefly, then read until the wick burned down a little. Just a little while . . .

A soft knock at the open door made her jump. Her head snapped up. Hang it all! She'd fallen asleep. Tasha shook her head, trying to clear her wits.

"Yes?" she said, peering shortsightedly at the door. *Please—not an emergency. Not tonight. I haven't the strength.*

Someone loomed in the darkness just beyond the doorway—someone large. Tasha racked her memory to remember who in the castle was that tall. Then the man detached himself from the shadows; for a moment she didn't recognize him without the ceremonial garb. When she did, she stared at him, speechless.

Her wits returned. She scrambled to rise. "Your—Your Grace!" she stammered. Apprehension seized her. "Oh, gods—you're not ill, are you?"

Linden Rathan waved her back to her seat. He made the warding gesture with his other hand. "I'm quite well, thank you. Healer—" He looked an inquiry at her.

Her tongue tried to trip over itself, but she got her name out. "Tasha."

He nodded. "Healer Tasha, this visit is an informal one,

so please sit again. You look—if you don't mind my saying it—exhausted."

Tasha sank down gratefully on her chair. She passed a hand over her face; her gaze dropped automatically to the books before her.

The Dragonlord asked gently, "Seeking answers for Rann?"

She nodded.

He pulled the only other chair from its place against the wall and set it backwards before her desk. He straddled it, arms crossed along the top, his long legs stuck out to either side. "What's wrong with the child?"

Tasha bit her tongue to keep from snapping. Rann's uncles and half the damned castle asked her that same question ten times a day. And she had no more of an answer for this Dragonlord than she did for them.

But at least there was no angry accusation in his voice, just honest curiosity—and a hint of sadness. She remembered Rann telling her how kind the big Dragonlord had been to him.

He cares. The revelation surprised her. She'd always thought of Dragonlords as remote, unfeeling. To find that they were prey to the same emotions as any truehuman moved her. In token of that, she spared him the flood of her frustration, saying only, "I don't know," tensely, bitterly.

Linden Rathan seemed to ponder her words. He looked down at his hands, one thumb rubbing along the knuckles of the other hand. The lamplight glinted in his fair hair. At last he asked, "Have you ever seen anything like it before?"

Tasha shrugged. "Yes—and no. His symptoms are puzzling; sometimes they seem to indicate one thing, then another. I'm told one of his grandmothers was sickly all her life. Perhaps Rann just takes after her. For no matter what I try—whether it's medicines and tonics, or a Healing—it doesn't help. Sometimes a Healing even makes him worse."

She shook back her sleeves. Bared to the oil lamp's feeble glow, the tattoos of ivy vines encircling her forearms looked black. She raised her arms for his inspection.

"Not even a Master Healer can cure everything," said Tasha. "And as you can see, I'm only of the Fifth Rank. Not good enough for poor Rann, I'm afraid." The admission burned like bile in her mouth.

Shaking his head, Linden Rathan said, "Don't blame yourself, Healer. For that matter, there are illnesses that Dragonlords—or even truedragons—can't cure with their Healing fire. Only the gods can cure everything."

Tasha's despair lifted from her like mist before the rising sun. How could she have forgotten? "Dragonlord, would you be willing—Ah, sweet gods, Your Grace, you must try!" she cried.

"Changing and then using my Healing fire? It might not help him, you know—it might even be dangerous for him."

She wanted to scream. It was a chance—he had to try! He had to, damn it! She would—his last words filtered into her mind. She reined in her emotions. "What do you mean it might be dangerous?"

His dark grey eyes met hers. "Didn't you just tell me that sometimes a Healing made him worse? How much worse? And if the power of the Healing increased, would it make him that much sicker? I could even kill him."

Gods help her, the man was right. And Rann's condition was not desperate enough to warrant that kind of risk-taking. Not yet, anyway. "You're right, my lord."

For a moment he looked as if his thoughts were far away; then the corner of Linden Rathan's mouth crooked up in a wry half-smile. "Your pardon. I was remembering something a friend of mine said just before I left Dragonskeep. This is silly, I know, but . . . Could Rann's illness be magical in nature?"

Whatever Tasha had been expecting, it wasn't this. For a moment she just stared, openmouthed, at the Dragonlord. "You—you're not jesting, are you?"

"Jesting? No. Nor do I take the idea seriously. But it popped into my mind, so . . ." He shrugged.

Tasha smiled. It was a poor excuse for one—she knew that—but it was the best she could do. "Was there magic involved, Your Grace, I think I would have felt it during the few Healings I've dared. No, I don't think we can blame this on sorcery—no matter how much ill-luck has dogged Rann's family.''

At his questioning look Tasha said, ''Rann's father died two years ago while hunting deer. The gods only know where the boar had been hiding in the woods; the villagers in that area had had no idea there was even one about, let alone one that size. Thank the gods no one else has fallen victim to it since. Prince Vanos's—Rann's elder brother's—horse went lame. He dismounted to look for a stone in its hoof; his father, the prince consort, stayed with him, letting the rest of the hunt go by.

''Vanos told me later that he never saw the boar until it knocked him down and gored him. His father flung himself upon the beast, armed with only his dagger. The boar escaped; the prince consort bled to death. I don't think Vanos ever forgave himself that his father died in his stead. He never fully recovered from his wounds. When the winter sickness came that year—and it was bad here in Cassori—he fell an easy victim to it.''

Tasha stared into the air beyond the Dragonlord's shoulder. She'd failed Vanos, just as she was now failing his young brother. A memory of Vanos's grey, haggard face danced before her mind's eye, taunting her with her inadequacy. She shook her head to banish it and made to close the book in front of her.

Gods—when had she clenched her hands like that? Her nails had dug deep half-moons into her palms. She eased her fingers open, wincing at the cramped muscles, and closed the book.

''Did the storm come up suddenly the day the pleasure barge sank?''

The question came out of nowhere. Tasha jumped. Lost in her memories, she'd forgotten she wasn't alone.

Puzzled at the turn the conversation had taken, Tasha blinked stupidly at Linden Rathan for a moment before answering. ''What? Oh—no, it had been threatening all day.

Still, it wasn't a bad one, Your Grace. That's why it was such a shock, you see; the barge had weathered worse.'' At the memory an icy chill settled in Tasha's stomach like a stone. Damn him for making her remember that time as well. She stared at the Dragonlord, willing him to say more.

He didn't. Not for a long while. Then he said, half to himself, ''I should have taken that blasted wager after all.''

When she said, ''Pardon?'' he laughed a little and said, ''Just thinking aloud, Healer.''

He stood up and returned the chair to its proper place. ''Thank you for taking the time to explain all this to me. I hope you'll find the answer soon, for Rann's sake and your own peace of mind. Now I'll leave you to get some rest.'' He turned and walked to the door.

Tasha heard the hint of command in the deep voice, subtle though it was. She nodded. He raised a hand in farewell. A moment later he was gone, lost in the shadows once more.

Tasha started. Gods, how could such a big man move so quietly and disappear so easily? It was like something out of a bard's tale—a cloak of invisibility or some such thing.

The thought made her remember what he'd said about magic. A shiver danced down her spine. Drat him; she'd likely have nightmares now over *that* bit of moonshine.

But thank the gods that's all it was: pure moonshine. She yawned. The Dragonlord was right; it was time for some sleep. Wearily she blew out the lamp.

As he retraced his route through the halls of the palace, Linden turned a corner and nearly ran into Duke Beren hurrying the other way. The duke had the look of a man on some secret errand.

Beren swore in surprise and jumped back. Linden saw him realize who the other late-night wanderer was and the glare that seemed reserved for Dragonlords was back in Beren's eyes. *Why does he hate us so?* Linden wondered.

''What are *you* doing here at this hour?'' the duke demanded.

Linden raised his eyebrows at Beren's rudeness, though all

he said was, "I wanted to talk with your Healer."

"Tasha? Why?" The questions snapped out like the cracking of a whip.

Linden reined in his temper. "I asked her about Rann." Then, prompted by some perverse impulse, he said, "I asked her if Rann's illness might be magical in nature."

A strange look passed over Beren's face. Fear?

"What did she say?"

"That it isn't."

Relief at that—but relief mixed with something else. As if—

Beren pushed past. "I must leave now. I'm . . . I'm tired."

Linden let him go, wondering.

Nine

She waited in the solar, rubbing her temples with her fingers in slow, even circles, trying to will away the tension that was her constant companion these days. It was late, the room was stuffy with heat the tiles had soaked up during the day, her head ached, and she wanted nothing more than to go to bed. She hoped he would get here soon. At least she'd managed to get here before him; she'd worried about that. He would have fretted, otherwise.

Thank the gods the solar was deserted. Where once she had enjoyed the crowds of ladies that filled the solar during the day, chattering like sparrows over their embroidery, she'd avoided as many people as she could since Queen Desia died.

The door opened. "Beryl?" a soft voice called.

"In here, my lord," she replied.

She could make out a figure moving through the shadows. Slowly it made its way through the gloom and into the yellow pool of light cast by the oil lamp next to her.

Duke Beren sat on the bench next to her. "Gods help me— I just ran into Linden Rathan. I'll tell you about it when I stop shaking. How was Rann when you left him?"

Linden Rathan? She could understand Beren's reaction; she'd been terrified during her own encounter with the big Dragonlord. But what was Linden Rathan doing in the palace at this hour?

Beryl swallowed her questions; Beren would tell her as soon as he was ready and not one moment before. "Well enough, though he still looked tired and pale from this morning. I left when Alinya came to bid him good night. I think he was still upset by some of the things said at the council meeting."

"I know, but it couldn't be helped." Beren smacked one big, meaty fist into the palm of the other hand. "Damn that Dragonlord! I want Rann under your eyes or mine as much as possible."

She patted Beren's hand. His fingers curled around hers for a moment. "At least I managed to get there before Gevianna. And Beren, for whatever comfort it might give you, I do think the Dragonlord only did it out of concern for Rann. The boy was clinging to him like a drowning man to a rope."

He pulled his hand free and hunched over, elbows on knees, face buried in his hands, fingers wrenching at his red hair. "No doubt you're right, sweetheart, but still! If only that old idiot Corvy hadn't insisted on having Dragonlords mediate this and gotten the majority of the council to agree. I'm certain I could have swayed enough of them to my side. Damn the Dragonlords!"

Beren turned his head enough to look at her. Worry lines that hadn't been there a few months before creased the skin around his eyes and of his forehead and threads of grey shone at his temples.

Her heart went out to him. He was a country lord, happiest in the saddle after a deer or looking over his own fields. Beren was not meant for this kind of intrigue. She wished for the words that would comfort the fear she saw in his eyes. If she could only talk some sense into him. If only she dared tell him . . .

"Dearest," she began, "you've no proof against Peridaen. Nothing at all."

Beren looked stubborn. "The queen saw fit to . . . suggest . . . he travel."

"At your brother's instigation. You know very well she could never say no to Dax. Even so, she didn't exile Peridaen as he asked her to. She was even considering calling Peridaen back. Have you ever considered that all this was no more than your brother's jealousy of the influence *her* brother had?"

Beren snorted. "My brother was neither jealous nor a fool. He knew something about Peridaen. What, I don't know. But that's why he did what he did. I need to find out what Dax knew.'' He drew a long breath. ''You say I have no proof against Peridaen. And that's true. I just wonder what proof he has against me—and how did he get it? And tomorrow the council will call for—oh, gods.

''Beryl,'' he said, his voice shaking, ''what if the Dragon-lords find out?''

As the council made ready to enter the chamber the next day, Kief said to Duke Beren, ''My lord, I understand that you have the warrant of regency in your possession. Would you please send for it?''

Beren's face paled, but he said steadily enough, ''Very well, Dragonlord.'' He beckoned to a castle servant. Yet when the man answered his gesture, Beren said nothing for a long moment.

What's wrong with Beren? Linden said to the others.

I don't know, Kief replied. *Surely he expected this once we were past the first round of discussions.*

Linden was about to ask the man if all was well when Beren said, ''Go to my chambers and tell my steward to bring the warrant to the Council Chamber.''

''At once, my lord Duke.''

Beren watched the man set off on his errand; for a moment Linden thought Beren would call him back. Then, grimacing like one about to face the hangman, Beren turned and stalked into the Council Chamber.

What ails the man? Linden wondered, remembering Beren's odd behavior and furtive air last night. He glanced at the others.

Kief shrugged and raised his eyebrows as if to say ''We'll soon find out,'' and followed Beren.

They found out all too soon. The council had just begun debating various points when the door burst open. A man Linden didn't recognize stood framed in the doorway for a moment. He wore the heavy silver chain of a steward, though, so Linden could guess. The man's face was deathly pale. He held out empty hands to the duke.

Beren stood. "Vatrinn—what is the meaning of this? Where's the warrant?"

The steward's mouth worked, but at first no sound came out. Then, "My lord Duke—it's gone!"

Had the kitchen cat settled itself upon the council's table and lectured them on the differences between the nine hells of Yerrin belief and the three that Cassorin priests held to, the council members could not have looked more surprised. A stunned silence fell over the room.

Duke Beren was the first to find his voice. He confronted Peridaen. "You!" he bellowed. "What did you do with the warrant?"

Peridaen shook his head, sending his carefully arranged curls flying, all elegance forgotten. His jaw hung open like a country yokel seeing a two-headed calf at a fair. "Beren—I swear to you, I've no idea where it is!"

Chaos erupted in the chamber.

Either he's telling the truth, Tarlna said, *or he's the most convincing liar I've ever seen!*

The same with Beren, Kief added. *That was honest surprise; I'm certain of it.*

Their uneasiness came through the mindlink. Linden regretted adding to it, but it had to be done. *None of them did; I'd take oath on it. Gifnu's hells, I'd even make a wager with Lleld, I'm that certain.*

The three Dragonlords exchanged puzzled glances.

Could it be some sort of honest mistake? Linden said. Not that he believed it for a moment. But if none here were responsible, then who?

You mean a servant misplaced it? said Tarlna with a touch of derision.

Linden shrugged. *It might be the safest course.*

You're right. I fear whoever did this, did it with the intent of fomenting civil war. Very well, then—we won't play their game. We'll treat this as some sort of mistake. The servant gambit will be useful; no one will believe it, of course. But we'll force them to accept it or openly rebel against us, then continue as if nothing's amiss, Kief said. With a mental sigh, he added, *This will make our task much harder—and longer.*

The slender Dragonlord stood up and called the excited nobles to order. While Kief did so, Linden continued to watch for clues in the faces around them, and saw none.

So who did this? And why? And what was next?

Ten

Linden guided his horse through the gates, acknowledging the salutes of the startled guards. Luckily there seemed to be few others who recognized him without the ceremonial regalia. He was just another of the many Yerrins who had business in Casna at any given time.

A moment later he was outside of the city. He thanked the gods that no council had been set for this day. Casna stifled him; he needed to break free.

This early in the morning carts and wagons still crowded the dusty road as they made their deliveries to the marketplace. He wove a way between them, dodging a cart loaded with early beets on one side, the next moment skittering out of the way of a wain laden with tanned hides. All around him the carters cursed one another and anyone else unfortunate enough to be caught in the crush. As he cut in front of one lumbering wagon he heard a flood of invective cut off in midtirade. By the strangled yelp that ended the impressive display, Linden guessed the driver had just realized who the "Yerrin son-of-a-bitch!" was.

He looked back, grinned, and saluted. That driver could have held her own amongst Bram and Rani's mercenaries without trouble.

The heavy wheels and plodding hooves churned up the pale dust of the road. Because the air was so still and heavy, the dust hung in it like a fog. It tickled his nose, gritted in his eyes and clung to his clothes, hair, and skin. The gelding snorted, tossing its head in displeasure.

After two or three miles the press eased. Linden rode aimlessly along the road. The people he passed seemed to take him for one of their own. He had no particular destination in mind; he just wanted to ride and think. Maybe then he could make sense of everything.

There were undercurrents in the council meetings that he couldn't put a finger on. So vague was the feeling, he was ready to dismiss his premonitions as moonshine, but something wouldn't let him do it. But neither would that "something" tell him what was wrong. It merely chafed at him.

He was not happy. And this idiot horse wasn't helping. Every time his attention wandered, so did it—straight for the nearest patch of grass. Cursing, he pulled its head up. Ill-mannered beast. He couldn't ignore it for a moment the way he could with Shan.

Hardly fair to compare the poor beast to a Llysanyin like Shan. It's one of the few mounts in the city capable of carrying someone your size, he scolded himself. *You shouldn't complain.*

But he still missed Shan. If the stallion were here, he'd be telling Shan his problems. Shan couldn't answer, of course, but he nodded in all the right places. And somehow, talking to Shan helped Linden get things sorted out. Linden wondered just how much the stallion did understand. Ah, well. He'd just have to make do.

A half mile or so ahead a smaller track met the main road. It went east, which meant he'd be riding with the sun in his eyes, but there was no one on it for the distance that he could see.

Moved by a sudden urge to explore, Linden turned his horse onto the new road when he reached it. That it was deserted appealed to him; he wanted to get away from any reminders of the overwhelming press of humanity that was Casna. Kief would likely blister his ears for him, going off without bodyguards or even his greatsword, Tsan Rhilin. But the company of even one or two silent guards would have been unbearable that morning and the greatsword was too noticeable.

Still, the thought of Kief's—and Tarlna's, too, no doubt—fussing was enough to blacken Linden's mood. He urged the gelding into a canter.

To his surprise, the rangy, pied gelding's canter was a pleasure to ride. The long, easy stride flowed along the road. It certainly made up for the stiffness of the gelding's trot and its slouching walk. A pity he couldn't canter through the city streets.

The sun rose higher in the sky. After a time, Linden slowed the reluctant gelding as the road veered south. He smelled the tang of salt air and guessed he was nearing the coast.

He held the gelding to a ground-eating trot. While the sun no longer shone into his eyes, it was now high enough to be uncomfortably warm. The road turned due east again. Linden debated whether to follow it or strike off to the north and cross the wide swath of fields and meadows to the woods he'd seen from the air the day they'd arrived in Casna.

He was certain the road would run along the sea cliffs at some point farther on; perhaps there was a beach he could climb down to. The idea of swimming decided him.

He rode on. And soon wished he'd thought to bring food and wine with him. Or even a flask of water. The sun and salt air made him thirsty.

The road passed within a quarter mile of a circle of standing stones on a headland that jutted out into the water like the prow of a ship. He turned off the road to investigate them. They sat peacefully in the sun, one trilithon with nine single stones in attendance, their shadows tucked around their feet with the nooning. Beyond them sparkled the sea.

Linden wondered who had raised them, and why. There was such an aura of eternity about the stones that he felt young in comparison. He tied the gelding's reins to a scrubby, wind-dwarfed pine, loosened the saddle girth, and went among them.

The stones were easily twice his height. He paused by the trilithon in the center and rested a hand on one of the uprights. The stone was cool to his touch. But from deep inside it came a faint pulsation that spoke to him of magic. It was like the hum of the lowest string of a harp—yet no harp could resonate so deep. He felt it, faint and clear, in his bones, a magic born of the earth as his own was.

This magic slept deeply inside the grey stone. Even so it comforted him somehow. He leaned his forehead against the cool, lichened roughness, letting all his frustrations at the council and his worries for Rann come to the surface of his mind. He imagined they drained away into the stone.

For a moment he thought the pulse within the upright changed. He pressed both hands to the stone, seeking with the magic that bound his soul and concentrated. No; no, there was no difference—he thought.

He pushed away from the stone, continued through the circle to the cliff. There he saw that while there was a rough path to the beach below, it was hellishly steep; line it with sword blades and it could be the path Gifnu, lord of the nine hells, sentenced kinslayers to climb, bearing their victims on their backs.

No, climbing back up that would undo whatever good a swim did him. Nor could he Change here; there wasn't enough room. Besides, there was no water or shade for the horse. He'd have to wait.

"Bah," he said as he went back to fetch the gelding.

It was the glint of reflected sunlight among the trees that alerted him. A truehuman would have never seen it. Linden recognized it at once: sunlight sparkling on the rushing waters of a stream. He turned the gelding toward the promise of shade and water.

As he rode, Linden studied the land before him. The forest came close to the road here; before he'd seen it only as a dark line far in the distance. His unnaturally sharp vision confirmed that there was grass aplenty growing amid the trees at the edge of the forest. He could hobble the gelding and leave it here with a clear conscience.

Then he'd be off to find the perfect spot to swim.

He launched himself from the sea cliff, his wings sweeping down and out in short, powerful strokes.

This was freedom! He spiraled up into the sun, exulting in the feel of the sun on his scales, the wind sliding over his wings, the sheer power of his dragon body. When he had enough height, Linden tucked his wings close to his body and rolled just for the fun of it.

He came out of the roll and set off along the coastline, humming one of Otter's tunes in his head.

He'd gone a fair distance when a beach below caught his eye. He hovered a moment, struck by the look of it.

It was a wonderful place for a child to play, with odd-shaped rocks to climb over and hide among. Rann, he thought, would like it. He'd have to remember this place, though what good it would do the boy, Linden didn't know. He couldn't carry the prince here in dragon-form and it was too far for the child to ride.

Still, it wouldn't hurt to look at it a bit closer, just in case. . . .

He rumbled happily deep in his chest. There, right below him, the rocks formed a pool perfect for soaking. He landed and Changed. A moment later he was stripping off his clothes.

He sighed happily as he slid into the water.

Time to ride back to Casna. Not, he reflected as he dressed once more, that he needed to take the direct route back. No sense in wasting the benefits of the swim by riding along a hot, dusty road in the sun. He'd go back by way of the woods. He had no fear of losing his way. By long habit, he'd scanned much of the countryside surrounding Casna as they'd flown in and had a fair idea of the way he planned to take.

Gods, what a scout he would have been if he could have done that when he was with Bram and Rani. Of course, if he could have, he wouldn't have been fighting alongside them. He would have been duty-bound to find a peaceful settlement, he mused as he let himself flow into Change. Somehow he didn't regret not Changing earlier in life.

With a powerful spring, he leaped into the air once more and flew back along the coast.

After a time he recognized the cliff that he'd jumped from earlier. His holiday was nearly over. He landed on the edge of the cliff and walked back to the woods.

The gelding, dozing in the shade of the trees, was annoyed at being asked to work again. It snapped halfheartedly at Linden as he laid the saddle on its back once more.

"Give over, gooserump," Linden grunted as he tugged on the girth, "and give me one more notch. Now for your bridle." He stowed the hobbles in the saddlebags once more, then swung into the saddle and set off through the trees.

Linden continued west through the woods. He'd been riding for three candlemarks or so now, enjoying himself; the forest here was oak and maple, ash and beech and birch. It had a friendly feel to it. As he entered a large clearing, he heard laughing voices close by. He kept silent and rode on.

He wished he didn't have to return to the city. Still, he'd have to go back sometime—and explain to Kief why he'd ridden off alone.

Not that I truly need a bodyguard—

On the very heels of the thought, the branches behind him crackled as someone rode out of the forest into the clearing. And he, gods curse it, had left Tsan Rhilin behind.

Linden pulled his horse around in a tight, rearing turn. One hand reached for the greatsword that he knew wasn't there. He dropped the hand, feeling supremely foolish when he saw his attacker.

Sherrine tossed her hair. "Did I startle you, Dragonlord? My apologies!" Her voice was husky, enticing even as her eyes laughed at him. The woods lily scent of her perfume filled the air.

He smiled, wishing everyone who'd sneaked up behind him in his long life was so welcome a sight. "Good day, my lady. I'm sorry—I didn't notice you."

She frowned, but there was a smile hiding behind it, like sunlight behind a cloud. She asked, "May I join you, Dragonlord—or do you prefer to ride alone?" Her eyes said she hoped he didn't.

Her gaze warmed him. Oh yes, this girl wanted a dalliance. Her boldness enchanted him—as did her beauty. It had been too long since he'd had a lover. Perhaps his stay in Cassori would be more interesting than he'd thought.

"I would be delighted," he said. Then, because he couldn't change old habits, he asked, "To what good fortune do I owe this meeting, lady? Surely you don't ride these woods alone."

"Sometimes I do, Dragonlord; the woods this close to Casna are safe. But today I was riding with some friends."

He remembered the voices he'd heard.

"We'd thought to have a picnic, but they returned to the city instead, leaving me to go on alone. And by sheer luck I found you instead."

He hid a smile. Her laughing eyes made Linden certain she had spotted him and sent her friends off. Nor, he thought, did she much care if he guessed it. They both knew what game she played.

She smiled as she rode up alongside him. The scent of her was warm, dizzying. *My luck or hers—and do I care?* he thought.

"Are you enjoying your stay in Casna, Dragonlord?" she asked, and urged her horse on. "Aside from the council meetings, of course." She looked back over her shoulder at him, a glance of mingled amusement and sympathy.

Linden urged the gelding to catch up. "I'd enjoy it far more if there were more moments like this and less of the council," he said.

She laughed. "Mother says the council *is* terribly boring. Especially when old Lord Corvy starts rambling."

Linden grimaced. With his huge, bristling mustache, Corvy looked like a dyspeptic walrus—and sounded like one. "Too true. Though when Baron Chardel threatened to shorten Corvy's tongue for him if he didn't get to the point, it almost became interesting. Almost."

Sherrine smothered a laugh. "Be thankful you weren't there when Corvy and Chardel were fighting over the swamps that lie between their lands. Chardel wanted to drain them to make more farmland. Corvy refused."

"Why? It seems laudable."

Now her shoulders shook. "Because it would drive away the bullfrogs, you see."

Linden wasn't sure he'd heard that correctly. "Bullfrogs?"

Sherrine nodded. "Corvy is inordinately fond of frogs' legs and was livid at the thought of losing his favorite dinner. They sniped at each other for months. I thought Mother would resign her seat on the council. She still won't have frogs' legs served at home."

He could see the two feisty old men going at it in his mind's eye. Laughing, he said, "Thank you. Have you any idea how tempted I shall be to whisper 'ribbit, ribbit' the next time Corvy starts?"

Sherrine laughed in turn and told him more about the nobles of the Cassorin court: Lord and Lady Trewin, who had a joint passion for collecting Assantikkan ceramics; the racing rivalry between Lord Duriac and Lord Sevrynel, the Earl of Rockfall, the latter also being well known for the impromptu feasts he gave for whimsy's sake—"And somehow nobody minds; most people think they're great fun and go just to see what he's celebrating this time"; Lord Altian who was "rather light-fingered, keep an eye to your things should he visit you," and his unfortunate sister, Lady Dovria, who spent much of her time rushing about and returning the things her brother had "absentmindedly picked up" from various residences; the efforts of the Duchess of Blackwood to marry off her six daughters; and many other foibles and oddities of the Cassorin nobility.

Linden listened with amusement; Sherrine's descriptions were droll and witty, and showed him the very human side of these people he dealt with every day. He also made a mental note to warn Kief and Tarlna about Lord Altian.

The horse took advantage of his inattention to snatch at another bush. Sighing, Linden hauled its head up once again. "Bloody idiot," he said. "I wish Shan were here."

"Shan?" Sherrine asked.

"My Llysanyin stallion. I had to leave him behind."

Sherrine chewed her lip. Then, as if she'd made up her mind on something, she said in a rush, "Dragonlord, the stories about your kind . . . ah, make it sound as if your horses are, well, more than horses.''

Linden had an odd feeling that that wasn't what she'd started to say. He pondered what he should answer. The Dragonlords deliberately kept truehumans as ignorant as possible of their strengths and weaknesses. And even those few truehumans whom they did trust—such as Otter—didn't know everything. But Linden thought he could tell this girl about the Llysanyins. Just not everything about them.

''They're more intelligent, for one thing. Oh, they can't think, not as we do,'' he said lightly, apologizing to Shan in his mind, ''but they're much smarter than a horse like this.'' He nodded at the gelding. ''But then, with this one, that isn't very hard, though I'll grant he has a fine canter.

''And Llysanyins are very long-lived. Shan and I have been together for over a century now. We're used to each other.''

''A century?'' Sherrine said. ''Are they magic, then?''

Linden smiled and shrugged, pretending he didn't know. He'd already told her as much as he meant to.

They were deep in the woods now. The white trunks of birch trees rose around them. Linden picked a way at random. The coolness and the earthy scent of humus and leaf mold revived him.

''This is what I needed,'' he said. ''I've been walled up in that stone city for much too long.''

''Dragonlord,'' she said, ''would you like to see my favorite spot in these woods?''

He raised an eyebrow. Ah; now her game began in earnest. And he was quite content to play. ''I'd love to, my lady,'' he said. ''Please—lead on.''

She urged her dappled grey mare ahead. About a half a candlemark later, Linden guessed, she turned onto another path. It twisted and turned around boulders and fallen trees. More than once Linden had to duck or be swept out of the saddle by a low-hanging branch.

They came out by a stream. Its high narrow banks dipped down where the trail crossed, then rose up on either side.

Sherrine rode her horse into the water and turned it to walk upstream. Linden followed her.

The banks rose higher as the horses moved slowly along the bed. The water rushed and bubbled around their hooves as they splashed along. Linden heard a vireo in the distance, the bird's liquid song echoing the rushing water.

The stream twisted and turned, the steep banks cutting off any view ahead. Sherrine looked back once or twice as if to make certain he still followed. He heard falling water somewhere.

When the banks had risen to as high as he could stretch his hand, the sound of falling water became louder. He rode around a last bend in the stream and stopped his horse in surprise.

The banks opened sharply, curving around a small dale. The hollow was shaped like a rough triangle, its walls running nearly straight up and down. Beech and alder, hawthorn and basswood ringed the top, looking down into the hollow. Grey rocks jutted out from the ferns and shrubby growth that covered two of the walls.

They had entered at one "corner" of the triangle. The wall opposite him was a stone cliff. Its harsh lines were softened by the bright green of the ferns that grew in every available niche.

Water spilled from a breach in the rock to bubble merrily over the stones below. It trilled and sang as it splashed from ledge to ledge until it formed the stream.

The stream divided the floor of the dale into unequal halves. To his right was barely enough room to walk. On his left, though, the earth was covered with patches of ferns and long hummocks of grass. Ground ivy wove its way through the grass, its tiny purple flowers vivid against the green. He could smell where Sherrine's horse had crushed it.

"Does this suit you, my lord?" Sherrine said as she dismounted.

Linden followed. "Indeed, yes. It smells wonderful here—so cool and fresh. I wish we had that picnic with us. This is—"

With a sly wink, Sherrine reached into her saddlebags. He watched, curious, as she pulled out a stone flask and set it in the cold rushing water.

"You do prefer your wine chilled, Dragonlord, yes?" she said. She reached into the bags again.

"Yes," he answered, and bit back a laugh. For Sherrine had pulled out two goblets, a fresh loaf, and a cheese. And a blanket. He couldn't help smiling at how neatly he'd been trapped.

Yet he wondered what she would expect of him afterward when it came time for him to return to Dragonskeep.

She looked at him over her shoulder. Her smile was sweet and slow.

Warmth spread through him. Still, he hesitated. Best to get this out in the open. "My lady," he began.

She laughed at him. "Oh, Dragonlord—don't look so worried! Are you afraid that I'll read more into this than a dalliance?"

"Yes," he said, relieved to be honest.

She smiled. "Don't be. I'm not fool enough to think that you'll fall in love with a truehuman." She unfolded the blanket. "And," she said, slanting a look at him from under her eyelids, "what makes you so certain you would be the only one I dally with?"

Linden laughed. The girl had spirit. "I deserved that. As long as you understand the same of me. And I will warn you now that a friend of mine is coming to Casna. When he arrives I will likely see a great deal of him. He's my oldest truehuman friend."

Sherrine smoothed the blanket upon the grass. "Thank you for that warning, my lord. I think we shall get on very well together, Dragonlord, now that we understand each other."

He nodded. "I'll hobble the horses," he said. "And Sherrine—I am Linden to you."

This time her smile was pure pleasure.

He settled the horses, slipping their bits and loosening their girths. After making sure they were hobbled securely, he bent to retrieve the flask from the stream.

"For pity's sake," he murmured. "I haven't hunted those since I was a boy!" He sat down and pulled his boots and linen stockings off and rolled up his breeches. Then he waded out into the stream, staring into the water.

"What are you doing, my—Linden? What is there to hunt?" Sherrine asked. She stood on the bank and watched him.

Linden's hand darted underwater. "These," he said, laughing as he held up his prize. The crayfish wriggled its claws furiously at him. Linden poked at it. "Ow!" he cried and dropped it. He held up a finger and examined it ruefully. "Out of practice, I guess."

Sherrine said, "Dragonlords feel pain, then, as truehumans do?"

Linden showed her the red mark left by the angry crayfish's claw. "Yes, save the pain of burning; fire can't hurt us." *And it is none of your business, my curious lady, that too much smoke will kill us as surely as a truehuman.*

"I'm fairly conquered," he said and retrieved the wine flask. "I'll leave the stream to that crayfish. This looks much more interesting." He nodded to where Sherrine had spread the blanket and arranged the goblets, bread, and cheese upon it. Linden knelt and filled the goblets.

He raised his. "To you, my lady—and an unexpectedly delightful day." He stretched out on the blanket, resting on one elbow.

"You honor me, my lord," she said. She fed him a sliver of cheese.

He closed his eyes. Oh, very interesting. . . . Her fingers trailed gently along his jaw. He opened his eyes and fed her in return. They traded back and forth, laughing at each other.

He was teasing her, holding a piece of bread just out of her reach when she bit him. He flung the bread away and pinned her down. "Vixen!"

She tilted her head back, her lips parted. He kissed her. Her mouth was soft, welcoming. She pulled him close, her hands twining in his hair, running down his back.

He kissed her thoroughly. "That will teach you better man-

ners, little tease!'' he said, then lay back on the blanket. He
watched her from under half-closed eyelids. The sun-dappled
shade played over her hair.

She bent over him, nipping lightly at his lips. ''I am well
schooled, Dragonlord,'' she said formally. But her mouth slid
along his neck, trailing light kisses, a teasing counterpoint to
her words. ''You taste of salt. Were you swimming in the
sea?''

Linden nodded. He twisted his head so that their lips met
again. He gently pulled her to him, ready to let go if she
hesitated. He wanted her, but he wouldn't force her.

But she was as eager for him as he was for her. He slid
his hands under her tunic. Her skin was soft and smooth.

''Yes?'' he whispered against her mouth.

''Yes,'' she answered.

Linden lay on his back. One arm pillowed his head; the other
held Sherrine against him. She lay along the length of him,
one leg thrown over his, her head resting on his shoulder. Her
fingers traced the length of the scar running across his chest
and down one hip. Linden grunted when she reached the end
of it at the top of his right thigh. Sated as he was, her touch
threatened to arouse him again.

''Stop that or you'll make me late to meet with Kief and
Tarlna.''

She laughed. ''Ready again so soon? I'd heard that Dragonlords were strong beyond the lot of mortal men, but I had
no idea—''

He silenced her with a quick kiss. Laughing, he said, ''Ah,
Sherrine, what shall I do with you? You're a bold one, you
are.''

She snuggled against him. ''Is it true? That Dragonlords
are much stronger than truehumans?''

Linden said, ''Haven't you ever listened to the bards' tales
of us? The answer is 'yes'—just as in the songs.''

''And faster?''

''Yes.''

Now she turned onto her belly, propping herself up on her

elbows. Her tilted eyes were wide and innocent. "And can you truly read minds?"

Linden sat up and smiled. "Why? Have you something to hide fr—is something wrong?" he said, for she twitched violently.

"No, just a chill. It's getting cooler, don't you think? And do you really have to leave soon?"

"Do you want your tunic? No? And yes, I really do have to leave soon—but not just yet." He ran his hand down her spine, stopping just above her buttocks. With one finger he circled the wine-red birthmark there. It was as large as the palm of his hand.

"Don't," she said, quickly turning and pulling away. "It's ugly."

Linden raised an eyebrow. "Is it?" he said. "I don't think so."

He saw her gaze go to his Marking. She blushed a fierce, dark red at the realization of what she'd said. Linden saw with interest that the blush extended as far as her breasts. He regretted that he didn't have more time to investigate the phenomenon.

"I'm not insulted," he said, kissing her. "Before I Changed, I thought my birthmark ugly. I don't anymore. But yours—where it is—is no hindrance to your beauty. And you are beautiful, Sherrine."

Indeed she was. Linden could think of few women he'd met over the centuries who could match her.

"My mother says it's ugly."

Linden bit his tongue. It was not his place to call her mother a fool. "Let's get dressed," he said gently. "I shouldn't keep the others waiting."

They dressed in silence. As he helped her onto her horse, Linden said, "Would you bring me here again?"

Her smile lit her eyes. "Yes," she said. "I will. I'd like that. I'd like that very much."

He'd aimed his "arrow" well.

Althume looked up from the scrying bowl. "It worked," he said.

"Sherrine found him where you told her she would?" said Peridaen. "Oh, well done, Kas, working out which way he'd go once he got to the woods!"

Anstella leaned forward. "And?"

Althume pushed the bowl away. "As I said earlier, it was hard to see very much," he said. He stood up, hands pressed against the small of his back, stretching. He continued thoughtfully, "It would appear there's a magic about Dragonlords that prevents their being spied upon. The images become fragmented, blurry. But," he said in triumph, "it seems Sherrine has the dalliance she—and we—wanted."

Eleven

The chill of a mountain dawn hung over Dragonskeep as Varn and Chailen walked together up to the Keep. To the east the first apricot streaks of sunrise lit the sky. In the distance they could see farmers already working in the fields.

Mist drifted around the patchwork of the small fields of *urzha* tubers and the canals that separated them. The mist rose at night from the sun-warmed waterways and protected the delicate plants from the cold. As always, Varn thought how eerie it looked, seeing his neighbors moving through the fog, disappearing and appearing like wraiths as they jumped from island to island. It was more comfortable to watch the workers in the fields of wheat, oats, and barley, the plants soft gold and green in the growing light.

"It must be quiet for you now that Linden's gone," Chailen said.

"Very. And the twins miss their pillow fights." Varn grinned and said, "I daresay it's not the same for you."

Chailen made a wry face. "Very funny. No, it's not at all quiet in the stables. Shan's been in a foul temper ever since Linden left. And a stallion that size who's determined to make life miserable for everyone . . . Why can't Dragonlords ride ordinary horses?" he lamented. "Why do they have to ride Llysanyins? The wretched beasts are far too smart."

Varn laughed as they reached the courtyard. "I'll help you open the doors."

"Thanks; they sometimes stick."

Walking in companionable silence, they crossed the cobbled courtyard of the stables, the only sound the clicking of their boot heels against the stones. When they came to the stable, Varn waited as Chailen pulled back the bolt on the doors. He could hear the muffled stamps and nickering of the horses and Llysanyins inside. Yawning, he grabbed the iron ring set into the left-hand door. Chailen caught hold of the right.

"Ready?" Chailen said. "Pull!"

The heavy doors stuck on their hinges, then swung ponderously open. Puffing, Chailen said, "I keep forgetting to ask the smith to look at—"

A neigh drowned him out as a heavy weight threw itself on the doors from the other side. The *kir* went flying.

Varn raised himself in time to see a large black form bolt past and disappear from the courtyard. The thunder of hoofbeats faded away down the road.

A bitter voice from beyond the other door said, "Llysanyins. Why, by all the gods, do they have to ride thrice-damned Llysanyins?"

Not trusting his legs quite yet, Varn crawled to where the head groom lay on the ground. Chailen sat up, dusting himself off.

"Are you hurt?" Varn asked.

"Only my dignity," said Chailen. "I ought to be broken back to stableboy. He was too docile last night—I should have guessed then he was planning something."

"That was Shan, wasn't it?"

"None other." Then, with a wicked gleam in his eye that ill matched his innocent expression, Chailen said, "My—won't Linden be surprised?"

Both *kir* fell back on the cobblestones, laughing.

The three Dragonlords and their escorts rode down the wide avenue leading to the palace. The air hung hot and heavy even this early in the morning. Linden sighed and tugged at the heavy silk of his tunic. This was promising to be a miserable day for wearing the ceremonial garb.

Perhaps he could arrange to lose the second set somehow; then he could wear ordinary clothes every other day while this tunic and breeches were washed and airing. It was a lovely dream and the Lady would have his head if he did it.

Neiranal mountain silk was hideously expensive.

I've been thinking, Kief's mindvoice said, *about those standing stones you found yesterday. Both Tarlna and I are from the north of Cassori; I for one have never seen them. It would be interesting to visit them once this is over. What do you think, love?* He glanced at his soultwin.

I would like to see them myself, she said, *properly escorted, of course.*

She cast Linden a withering glance. He shrugged. Her nostrils flaring in annoyance, she went on, *I wonder who built it and why, and if there are any more.*

Linden said, *Let's ask.* "Captain Jerrell," he said aloud. "Yesterday when I rode by myself I came across a circle of standing stones overlooking the sea. Do you know anything about them?"

Though Jerrell looked surprised—Linden sympathized with him; the question must have seemed to come out of nowhere—the guard said, "Very little, Your Grace. No one knows who built it or why; it's not unlucky or anything like that. There are even some who say it's a lucky place."

Linden nodded; that fell in with what he'd felt among the stones. "Go on—any more? I've, ah, an interest in such things."

The captain looked wary. It was plain he considered any sort of magery as something best avoided. "That's as much as I know about it, Your Grace. It's lucky—not like the other spot in the woods. Leastways, the spot that the stories say is in the woods. No one I've ever heard tell of has found it; may not even be real.

"That place is said to be cursed; the old folk say it's bad luck even to speak of it. Good thing you didn't stumble upon that one, my lord, if it really does exist. Straight inland from the stone circle as the crow flies, it's supposed to be, like it was deliberate. And whether it's real or just moonshine, no one goes near that part of the forest if they can help it. People just don't feel welcome there."

Linden asked, "How do you know of it, Jerrell?"

The soldier grinned. "My granther used to scare me with

stories about it, my lord. All about the horrible bogles and such that are supposed to haunt it. When we were sprats my mates and I used to dare each other to go there at night; good thing it was too far away—or we'd've had to find it! Now and again more stories about it crop up.''

The three Dragonlords looked at each other in speculation. *Did you feel anything like that?* Kief asked.

Indeed, no. In fact, the part of the woods I found myself in felt most welcoming.

He must have sounded smug, for both Kief and Tarlna raised eyebrows at him, murmuring ''Oh?'' and then catching each other's eyes.

Linden tried not to smile. *I met Lady Sherrine of Colrane while riding. We had a picnic at her favorite spot in the woods.*

A picnic, Tarlna echoed blandly. *Of course.*

Kief hid a smile behind his hand. Linden swore he heard a snicker.

Then Tarlna said aloud, ''You'll make your other lady jealous, Linden.'' She nodded toward the side of the avenue.

Linden blinked in confusion. ''My other—? Ah—are we here already?''

He looked over to where a huge elm tree stood alone at the intersection of the main avenue and one of the side streets. Two girls waited beneath it; he'd seen them most mornings on his way to meet with the council. From their dress he guessed they were from a well-to-do merchant or artisan family. He missed them the mornings they weren't there; they were the only faces he recognized in the masses that lined the street every day to see the Dragonlords pass. They stood out from the crowd somehow.

As usual, the elder—a plump girl of fifteen or sixteen, he guessed—held up the younger so that she could see more easily. With their matching brown curls and snub noses, they were obviously sisters.

The little girl caught sight of him and waved. He waved back, returning her grin. And as she had every morning, the child dissolved into giggles; her sister set her down and waved. Though he turned in his saddle, Linden lost sight of them in the crowd as the procession continued along the avenue.

"I wonder who they are," Linden said to no one in particular.

Kief shrugged. "I doubt you'll ever find out; they're not likely to ever be at the palace, are they?"

"No," Linden agreed, thinking, *And a good thing, too; I wouldn't wish that cesspit of backstabbing on anyone, let alone two sweet-faced children.*

He'd just have to settle for waving at them each morning—and envying them the simplicity of their lives.

Twelve

Nethuryn looked up from his scrying bowl and groaned. Pol had found his trail once more; he would have to run.

But where? It seemed no matter where he fled, Pol tracked him down, barely one step behind. And he was so tired; even so small a use of what was left of his magic left him weak. He looked around his current refuge in despair, running his fingers through his long white beard.

The room was as shabby as the inn it was part of. Nethuryn was glad of Merro; the mice now gave this room a wide berth. It was the only bright spot he could see in a sea of troubles.

Where could he go next? Kers Port? Canlyston? Where?

Where could he hide himself and the last bit of real magic left to him?

Merro pounced on something in the filthy rushes. It squeaked. Poor little mouse. Probably it was just in from the country and hadn't heard—

Gods, what a fool he'd been! Of course Pol found it easy to track him; Kas knew him too well, knew all his habits. Habits that an old man would find hard to change.

"I'm a city mouse, Merro," he told the cat excitedly. "I always have been."

Merro looked up from the paw that pinned his supper to the floor. He cocked his head at his master. "Mrrow?"

"A city mouse and Kas knows it! So we'll do just what he won't expect—we'll become country mice!"

Althume let himself into the study where Peridaen and Anstella sat at a game of chess. Seeing that they were intent on their game, he went to the window overlooking the grounds of Peridaen's river estate. For a moment he stared out into the darkness. Then he pulled the window hangings shut.

Peridaen looked up. "Afraid of spies?"

Althume shrugged. "It's possible. After all, we have one in the older Dragonlords' household. Why shouldn't Beren or someone else have one here?"

Anstella moved a piece. "Checkmate," she said. As Peridaen studied the board, she continued, "A pity that Linden Rathan decided to stay in town. We had such a nice estate picked out for him here."

Grumbling, Peridaen laid his king on its side. "Where we could have wormed in a spy, just as we did in Duriac's household. But no, dear Lady Gallianna—and Beren's supporter— had to offer him her city house." He paused. "Stupid cow."

Anstella laughed. "Another game, Peridaen? No? But gentlemen—we do have a spy in Linden Rathan's household."

"Who?" they asked together.

She smiled. "Sherrine. Even as we speak, she's with him. He invited her to dine with him this evening. And I shall be most surprised—and disappointed—if we see her before morning."

Sherrine sat up, her hair falling over her breasts. She leaned over Linden, who lay on his back on the bed. "Surely, Linden, you can answer this one! Again—you say you like to dance, yet you won't. Or not very often. Why?"

He chuckled and caught her nipple between thumb and forefinger. She gasped as he rolled it between his fingers. "Stop that," she said, her voice husky. "You're trying to distract me." She slapped his hand—gently.

He rested his hand on her hip. "Because I'm afraid you might be offended at the answer. And yes, I'm trying to distract you. It's fun." He grinned at her.

"Beast," she said. "Do you mean I'm a bad dancer?"

"No, not at all. It's just that, well, you're too short for me, little vixen. Not that it matters in many things," he slid his hand back up to her breast, "the important things, but it is uncomfortable for dancing. All the women here are too short."

"We are not. *You* are too tall." She kissed him and straightened. The next words stuck in her throat.

Yet she had to ask them. Her mother would be furious if she didn't. Every time she returned from spending time with Linden, her mother badgered her for whatever information she'd gleaned. And every time her mother called her a fool for not learning more. It galled her beyond belief to meekly accept her mother's mockery.

As if she could do any better!

But the Dragonlord had chosen the daughter, not the mother. During every tirade Sherrine smugly congratulated herself for that as she kept her silence.

Still, she had to have some information to pass on. So she put on her most innocent look and asked, "Is it true that Dragonlords are immune to magic?"

"Sherrine!" he said, laughing. But there was also a note of annoyance she'd never heard before. It quelled her. "You're more curious than any cat, ferret, or even bard could ever be!" He rose from the bed, stretching. "I want more wine; do you?" A ball of coldfire blazed up in his hand. He tossed it into the air.

She gasped and jumped. This was something she couldn't get used to; each time it startled her anew. "Yes," she said, though she didn't. She watched him cross the room to the table. The coldfire cast rippling shadows over his body, glinting on the narrow clan braid that fell to below his buttocks. She watched the big muscles of his legs bunch and slide under his skin.

She bit her lip; she'd annoyed him. Well and truly she'd annoyed him. She saw it in his walk, the set of the wide shoulders.

A pang of unaccustomed remorse took her. It suddenly felt low, this pumping him for information. Maybe it would be best to let some other woman of the Fraternity betray him.

Then he turned, offering her a goblet, and smiled at her. Her breath caught in her throat. And she knew she'd never give him up to another woman.

Thirteen

Almost four tendays we've been here and this heat hasn't broken yet.

Linden sprawled across his bed, unable to sleep any longer in the sticky heat. He longed for the chill of a mountain dawn at Dragonskeep.

It didn't help that everyone assured him over and over that this was most unusual weather, that Casna was usually kept cool by breezes off the sea. Since he couldn't have it, he didn't want to hear about it.

He turned his head to look at the empty half of the bed. It was as much as he had the energy to do. *Just as well Sherrine has been with her other lover for the past two nights.* While he enjoyed her company and found the habit endearing, her trick of wrapping herself around him in her sleep was likely to stifle him in this weather. He'd lost count of how many times since they'd begun their dalliance he'd gently disengaged himself only to wake up a short time later and find her once again pressed against him. *Too hot for that.*

Yawning, he debated whether to get up or stay abed until the servants came to wake him. The linen sheets sticking to his back as he rolled onto his side decided him. *Perhaps it'll be cooler in the garden.*

He got up, found a pair of breeches to wear and decided against tunic, stockings, and boots for the time being. Pouring tepid water from the pitcher into the washbasin, he splashed his face and chest in a vain effort to cool off. He studied his dripping reflection in the mirror, rubbing the reddish stubble on his chin; time enough later to shave, he decided. Linden walked light-footed through the dim house. The clatter of dishes from the kitchen could be heard but otherwise the house was silent. He let himself out of the doors to the gardens.

It was little better outside. Even the dew seemed warm to his bare feet. But at least the air was fresher; that was something. He wandered among the topiary animals that populated this part of the gardens. As always he silently cheered on the fox running away from the goose.

A darkness in the western sky caught his attention. *Rain clouds? Pray the gods they are! We could use the relief.*

"Dragonlord?" a voice called softly.

Linden looked over his shoulder. One of the servants stood in the doorway. When she saw that she had his attention, she continued, "Your bath is ready, Your Grace."

"Thank you, Vesia; I'll be right in." Once more he looked at the sky, hoping for a storm.

Something's wrong. The thought jolted Otter out of his sleep. Only half awake, he groped for his clothes, trying to decide what was amiss. It wasn't until he stood up, automatically balanced against the roll of the *Sea Mist*, and nearly fell over that he realized the ship was still in the water.

"Oh, gods; what's going on?" he muttered as he pulled on his clothing as fast as he could. He stumbled out to the deck, still rubbing the sleep from his eyes, and went to the rail. The sea was glassy, with an oily look that he didn't like. "Rynna?" he called, apprehensive.

"Up here on the quarterdeck, Otter. Come have a look!"

When he reached the quarterdeck he found Maurynna, Master Remon, and Kara the second mate apparently just ending a discussion.

"So, it's decided, then? It doesn't look to be a bad blow; it might well push us out to sea a bit more than we want, but better that than onto the shore. We run before it," Maurynna said. "And I want as much canvas as is safe up; we may as well take advantage of this. Master Remon, the helm is yours."

Otter was appalled. "A 'blow'? You mean there's a storm coming and you're keeping the sails up? You're not going to anchor and ride it out? Heave-ho or whatever you call it?"

Master Remon and Kara laughed outright. Maurynna grinned and said, "That's 'heave to,' Otter, and no, we're not going to throw out the sea anchors. Why? The crew's fresh.

"And believe it or not, we're safer running before it. Besides, it's coming out of the west which means it will blow us east—and perhaps a bit south, but that's no matter—and east is the direction we want to go. We'll get to Casna that much sooner. Haven't you ever been on board a ship in a storm before?"

Otter licked dry lips. "No."

Maurynna jerked her head aft. "You'll be getting off easy, then. This doesn't look like a bad one."

He stared past her at the lowering sky. Black clouds were piling up with—to his eyes—ominous speed on the horizon. Not a bad one? It looked like the wrath of the gods to him. He swallowed hard. "I'm going to my cabin."

She caught his sleeve. "Otter, if you do, be warned: I can't spare anyone to clean it while the storm's on and likely not afterward, either."

"What?" Then, as her meaning became clear, "Oh. Gifnu's bloody hells."

Maurynna nodded at the starboard rail. "That will be the best place for you, my friend, while this is going on. Kara, fetch one of the oilskin cloaks from the stores for Bard Otter and get a safety line on him."

Maurynna went off to prepare the rest of the crew. Otter waited glumly by the rail for the second mate to return. While he knew a bard should always be open to new experiences, this was one he suspected he could well do without.

Since he was already awake, Linden decided to go to the palace early that morning. If Rann was up, he'd spend some time visiting with the boy before the meeting began.

Rann was, indeed, awake, and playing in the garden with his wolfhound and a slender young woman with a round, pleasant face. This must be Gevianna; Linden could imagine this girl romping with Rann and his dog.

"Dragonlord!" Rann cried with pleasure and trotted to him. Bramble the wolfhound pranced along behind.

Linden scooped Rann up and tossed the laughing child in the air. Damn! but the boy was little more than skin and bone. "Have you eaten yet, lad?" he asked.

"Yes. But if you're hungry, Dragonlord, Gevianna can bring you something," Rann said, mistaking his meaning.

"Only if you join me, Your Highness," Linden said, catching the nurse's eye. She smiled her thanks.

"I'll fetch some bread and cheese right away," she said as she rose from the grass. She made them both a courtesy and set off.

Rann watched her for a moment and then turned back to Linden. "Dragonlord," he said shyly, "could we play a game while we wait?"

"Of course, lad," Linden said, and set Rann down again. "What would you like?"

"Hide-and-seek. You hide and Bramble and I shall find you."

"Well enough; but wouldn't you like to hide, instead?" Linden asked, remembering his own childhood. He'd always hated being the Seeker.

Rann heaved a martyred sigh. "Bramble always gives me away," he said in disgust. "He bounces."

Linden hid a smile. "I see. Very well; you cover your eyes and count, and I'll hide."

"Good!" Rann clapped his hands over his eyes and began chanting aloud. "One. Two. Three . . ."

Linden turned and ran as quietly as he could through the garden. He ducked beneath the thickly hanging branches of a weeping willow. This shouldn't be too hard for Rann, and as long as he kept still, the keen-eyed wolfhound shouldn't spot him. Linden parted the branches slightly; if he craned his neck he could just see the prince between the bushes between them.

Rann dropped his hands and sang out gleefully, "Ready or not!" But the boy had taken only three steps when Lady Beryl came around a hedge and caught him up. She bore him away, protesting every step. Bramble followed with head and tail hanging.

It happened so fast that Linden had no time to protest. By the time he reached the spot where he'd left Rann, neither prince nor governess were to be seen.

Gevianna appeared, bearing a tray. She looked at him and sighed. "Lady Beryl, Your Grace?"

Nodding, Linden asked, "How did you—"

"She does this all the time, Dragonlord. The moment I leave Rann alone, she pounces on him even when it's not time for his lessons. Sometimes it's even Duke Beren. I swear they spy on us."

"Indeed?" Linden said softly. "Thank you, no, Gevianna; I'm not hungry." He waved the nurse away.

She left him. Linden stood alone beneath the lowering sky and brooded.

Otter tried to tell his stomach that there was nothing left, but his stomach refused to listen. Once more the bard leaned over the rail while that same troublemaking stomach tried to vomit up everything he'd ever eaten. When it gave up in exhaustion, Otter slid weakly to the deck, an arm wrapped around one of the posts of the rail, his eyes closed as he curled up like a miserable hedgehog.

It was some time before he paid attention to his surroundings. At first he thought the water sloshing around him was from the pelting rain. But when some splashed onto his lips and his befogged mind said *Salt!*, he came to himself enough to look around.

And wished he hadn't. A wall of green water was about to crash down on the stern of the *Sea Mist*. Maurynna and the first mate had their backs to it, blind to the danger. He pointed frantically.

The wall reared higher, its top curling down to engulf the little ship—and disappeared. Moments later it reappeared.

"What the—?" said Otter in bewilderment.

Maurynna finally noticed his pointing finger. She looked back at the wave towering over her and merely nodded. Cupping her hands to her mouth, she yelled, "Don't worry. It won't get us! It only looks like that because we're at the bottom of the swell right now. Each wave will slide under us—watch!"

He preferred not to, thank you very much. But he couldn't tear his fascinated gaze from each wave that threatened to devour the *Sea Mist*—and didn't.

Maurynna worked her way to him hand-over-hand along the safety lines strung across the quarterdeck. Keeping one hand on the line, she gripped his shoulder with the other. "How are you faring?"

"I feel as though I'm going to die and afraid I won't," Otter joked weakly.

"Quite frankly you look awful. I don't think the storm will go on much longer, and the moment it's over you're going to your cabin." A fresh burst of wind blew a loose strand of long black hair across her face. She pushed it back. Her odd-colored eyes sparkled.

"You're enjoying this!" he said in astonishment.

She looked surprised. "Of course I am. The whole crew is. This really isn't a bad storm, Otter; look how much canvas we have up. And we're making wonderful time. With luck we'll make port tomorrow."

"Gods help me," Otter moaned. "The girl and all her crew are mad. Just let me get to dry land and I'll never set foot on board a ship again." *Thank the gods I never told her what's waiting for her in Casna. She'd have* all *the bloody sails up in this bloody storm and the bloody crew paddling with whatever they could find.* "I ought to make you wait until your birthday for your surprise. It would only be just."

But Maurynna only laughed at him and made her way back to the ship's wheel, calling out, "Remember, Otter—I want that surprise when we reach Casna!"

Fourteen

Linden, sitting to one side of Kief, leaned forward, studying the document on the table before them. On Kief's other side Tarlna did the same.

So this is the warrant granting the regency to Beren, Linden thought to himself.

It had reappeared just this morning; a bewildered archivist brought it to the council chambers and delivered it directly into Kief's hands.

"I don't understand how it got in that drawer, Dragonlord," the baffled Ferrin had said as Kief slid the scarlet ribbon from the rolled parchment and smoothed it out. "And it's pure luck we found it at all; if the palace reeve hadn't needed to examine some older tax rolls . . ." The man shrugged.

Had it been, Linden wondered, some kind of honest mistake after all? That his convenient excuse of a servant's error was the truth? Surely if this had been done deliberately, the thief would have destroyed the document rather than take the chance it might be found again.

Likely they would never know.

He read through it a second time. It purported to be in Queen Desia's own hand, and from what he could see of the other documents from the late queen scattered across the table, it certainly looked to be.

The A's aren't quite right in this section, Tarlna said, tracing a circle with her finger around one paragraph. *Do you see the difference?*

Kief picked through the other sheets of parchment. Finally selecting two, he said, *But they match the A's in these. Perhaps Desia didn't write this in one sitting. Perhaps she wrote one part at her desk and another on—I don't know—a tray on her lap or something. That could account for that slight wavering.*

Linden nodded in agreement, then looked up at a muffled cough from one of the council. Until then, the room had been still, its quiet broken only by the breathing of the council members and the furtive shuffling of feet and shifting in chairs. Forty pairs of eyes met his. Forty accusing stares said, "What's taking you so long? Get on with it!"

Only one pair of eyes refused to meet his: Beren's. The duke stared at the table before him.

On a whim, Linden asked, "Duke Beren, the prince's supporters claim that you forged this. Is that true?"

Beren met his eyes then. Although the blood surged to his face in an angry tide, the man said quietly and firmly, "Your Grace, I have never forged anything in my life. Anyone who says I did that lies."

He's telling the truth, Linden thought. *Yet—something's not quite right.*

Maurynna stood in her favorite place in the bow, the polished rail warm under her hands, and watched the shore off to port. She could smell sun-baked earth and the green scent of fields and trees now.

Familiar landmarks counted off the miles. First the ruined tower on a cliff, then the beach that seemed so inviting and whose waters hid rocks like shark's teeth.

Then came the old fortress—still watching for sea reivers centuries gone—that told them the mouth of the Uildodd River was perhaps a candlemark's sail. Above her the great woad-blue sails cracked and snapped as the *Sea Mist* came hard about to sail closer to the shore. The Erdon banner stood out from the mainmast, its silver dolphin dancing in the wind.

She studied the position of the sun when they finally turned into the Uildodd itself. They would make Casna well before it set.

It will be good to see Aunt Elenna and Uncle Owin again. And very good to see Maylin. Why does the only female cousin close to my age have to live in Cassori instead of Thalnia? she wondered idly. *And Kella! I wonder if she'll remember me.* Maurynna balanced against the roll and pitch of the ship, staring across the brown expanse of the river. The wistful thought came: *I wish I could have grown up here instead of Thalnia. The Vanadins have always felt more like my family than any of the others since Mother and Father died. Ah, well; what's done is done.*

Behind her the bosun bellowed orders. "Furl all sails save the mizzen," he cried in a voice hoarse from years of out-shouting gales.

She listened to the sailors' bare feet thudding across the deck behind her. Soon the *Sea Mist* would dock. Then she herself would supervise the unloading of the Assantikkan palm wine. She'd trust no one else with that. And—finally— off to her aunt and uncle's house and a bath.

She ran a lock of hair through her fingers. It was stiff with salt. That bath would feel good. She'd not have long to wait for it now. The docks were just off the starboard bow.

She just hoped Otter wouldn't wait to reveal his surprise until the Solstice. While she was certain whatever it was would make a wonderful birthday present, she didn't think she could wait that long. Not with all the mysterious hints he'd been throwing out. *If he waits that long I will keelhaul him.*

"Good silver for those thoughts, Rynna," Otter said from behind her.

She turned. He stood, legs braced against the pitch and roll of the deck. One hand toyed with the broad leather strap of his harp's carrying case running diagonally across his chest.

Maurynna smiled sweetly. "You wouldn't like them," she said.

He laughed. "Still planning to keelhaul me, then? But if you do how will I ever introduce you to Linden Rathan?"

"Very well, I won't—but just because you've promised to introduce me someday. Gods—to meet the Dragonlord who knew Bram and Rani! But until then . . . Perhaps a week in the crow's nest instead."

"Don't even think it, my fierce little seahawk. I'd sing off key the entire time just to annoy you." Otter turned serious. He said, "Rynna, in case I forget to warn you when the time comes, I know how much you'd love to ask Linden about his time with Bram and Rani, but whatever you do, don't ask him about Satha. He still—Ah, just don't. If he volunteers information, that's one thing. But don't ask."

Astonished at the sudden change in subject, Maurynna asked, "Why? Can you tell me?"

"I don't know if I should." The bard ran a hand through his iron-grey hair. "Oh, hang it all—you might as well know what has been dropped from the tales over the centuries.

"Rani woke Satha from a magically induced 'sleep' that had gone on for a century or two. Yet Satha had had enemies in his own time; Bram and Rani guessed that someone got to him before the protection spell that was part of the magery was complete and cut his throat. But the spell was so powerful that Satha's soul was bound to his body—which began rotting over the ensuing years. He terrified hardened mercenaries. Imagine what he did to a boy of sixteen who'd never been away from his father's keep until he ran away to join Bram and Rani.

"Then one day Linden took a blow that was meant for Rani. It would have killed him but for Satha, who, when he had been truly alive, was Healer as well as Harper. You know how much a Healing can hurt, don't you, even with a skilled Healer? Satha," Otter finished grimly, "was not gentle."

Maurynna shivered in the hot sun. "I always thought that the part about Satha being undead was, was—"

"A bardic embellishment? Unfortunately no. It was quite real."

Otter stared out across the water. Maurynna studied him, thinking that he still looked drawn and pale from the storm, and waited for more.

He continued, "At one time Linden frequently accompanied me on my bardic journeys. More than once I had to throw something at him to wake him up from a nightmare when we were camping. I learned," he turned to her once again and now there was a twinkle in his eye, "after the first time not to shake a Dragonlord out of a bad dream." He made a motion suggesting someone flying through the air. "Linden is damnably strong."

Maurynna winced at the image in her mind's eye.

The *Sea Mist* came across the swift current of the Uildodd. Otter lurched for the rail as the ship tossed. Muttering a curse under his breath, he clung to the rail.

Maurynna swayed with the cog's motion. "Yerrins," she said with smug superiority. "No sea legs at all. Lucky for you there were no bad storms this trip." She went to oversee the docking.

"No bad storms?" he yelled after her. "What in Gifnu's nine hells hit us yesterday, then?"

The last of the sails came down and the ship bumped against the pilings. The sailors tossed lines to waiting dock-hands. There were far fewer workers than usual. Maurynna wondered if there was some trouble with the Dock Guild. She frowned. The Assantikkan wine had to go to the warehouse as quickly as possible; if left sitting on the dock it would soon sour in the hot sun.

Breaking into her gloomy thoughts, Otter said, "I've never seen a dock so quiet." He squinted into the afternoon sun. "Shall we go on to your aunt's now?"

Maurynna half laughed, half groaned. "Otter, don't tempt me that way. I have to stay while the wine's unloaded." To Otter's halfhearted offer to stay with her, Maurynna said firmly, "No. But I'd appreciate it if you'd go on ahead and warn them that I've docked."

And that will make certain that you get some rest. Aunt Elenna will take one look at you, my troublemaking friend, and pop you right into a bed. Good luck arguing with her!

Otter tried not to look relieved, and failed.

Maurynna slipped the bracelet from her right wrist. "Here; take this as a token since you've never met them before. Hire a wagon for our baggage and tell the carter to take you to Owin and Elenna Vanadin's house. It's on the little lane behind Chandlers Row. Tell them I'll want supper and a bath, please.''

''I'll do that,'' Otter said. He slipped the bracelet into his belt pouch. ''And don't worry; I'll take good care of this.''

''Thank you,'' Maurynna said. ''Then I'll meet you at the house later.''

Otter set off down the gangplank. Maurynna found one of the regular dockhands. ''Jebby—where is everybody? Why are there so few workers?''

Though tall for a Cassorin, the stocky woman who led this crew of dockhands came only to Maurynna's shoulder. Jebby shook her head, her lined face sweaty, and ran the back of her hand across her forehead. ''All the docks is shorthanded, Captain. Every merchant and his cousin is here. Daresay they're reckoning that between the Solstice and what's happening in the council, everyone'll be flocking to Casna. They're right. Can't find room in a tavern to lift your elbow.''

Jebby fumbled in her belt pouch and pulled out a strip of grimy cloth. She tied it around her forehead. ''Best get to work now.'' She ambled off, yelling, ''Go on, you lazy wharf rats! Move your asses!''

Maurynna looked down at herself ruefully. Her second-best tunic and a good pair of breeches—no, it wouldn't do to ruin them. And best take off the other bracelet; she might catch it on something. She pulled her hair sticks from her belt pouch. Twisting her long hair into a bun, she stabbed the sticks through it and called, ''Give me a few minutes to change my clothing, Jebby, and I'll be back to help.''

She went up the gangplank to her cabin.

The council was just breaking up for the day when Linden felt a tickle at the back of his mind. For a moment he wondered what it might be, then recognized it: the feel of a true-human mind seeking contact with his. And there was only one such mind he knew well enough for that. He waved Tarlna, who was speaking to him, to silence, tapping his forehead with his two middle fingers in the Dragonlords' signal for mindspeech. Tarlna nodded and herded a few council members away from him.

Otter! You're in Casna already?

Yes, by the mercy of the gods, came the tired reply.

The exhaustion he felt through the contact alarmed Linden. *What's wrong? Are you ill?*

Not since that damned storm ended. I'm too old for this gallivanting about, boyo.

Linden remembered the dark sky he'd seen yesterday morning. *You got the storm while at sea? My sympathies. It never made it here, more's the pity.*

The next words came with more of Otter's old spirit. *Then I bloody well wish you'd gotten it and not us. That madwoman Maurynna and her crew enjoyed it! They claimed it wasn't a bad one at all.*

Linden nearly laughed aloud at the outraged disbelief in Otter's tone. *Where are you now?*

I'll be on my way to Maurynna's family's house as soon as the carter finishes loading the wagon. They're also merchants, though this branch is landbound—the Vanadins behind Chandler's Row. Once I've dropped off our luggage, do you want me to meet you somewhere?

No, Linden said firmly. *You're exhausted. Don't argue with me, Otter. You forget that I can feel more through the mindlink than you can. And I don't like what I am feeling. You're ready to drop. When you get to the—Vanadins, did you say?—you are to eat a light meal and then go to sleep. Is that clear? And just in case you get any notions to the contrary, that's Dragonlord's orders.*

Yes, Your Grace, came the meek—and relieved—reply.

Tell me when you're settled; I want to make certain you reach the house in one piece. Until tomorrow, then.

Until tomorrow.

Linden cut off the contact, leaving a part of his mind to "listen" for the bard's next call. No sense making this any harder on Otter than it had to be.

He was alone in the council room now, undecided about his next move. Sherrine had other plans again this evening.

He shouldn't complain; he saw far more of her than her other lover did, and her absences only made their meetings sweeter. Still, he was excited by Otter's arrival and frustrated that he couldn't visit with his oldest truehuman friend that moment. He wanted to be about doing *something*.

Inspiration struck. *What was the name of those Thalnian merchants? Erdon! That was it.*

He went to the small side table that held parchment, ink, quills, and sealing wax for the use of the council members. Gathering what he needed, he sat down and scribbled a hasty note:

Sherrine,
The friend I told you about on our first afternoon together has arrived in Casna. As I warned you then, I
plan to spend most of my free time for a while visiting
with him, as we haven't seen each other for a few years.
You'll like him when you meet him, I think. Until
then—

Linden

He folded the parchment and heat-spelled a stick of sealing wax, dribbling it onto the note and pressing his thumb into the cooling puddle.

Well enough; he'd find a servant to deliver this to Sherrine and then go home to change into some old and comfortable clothes. Since he couldn't go visit Otter, why, he'd go look at the ship Otter came in on. A moment later he was on his way.

Fifteen

The oxcart lurched along the ruts of the country lane. Nethuryn, sitting beside the driver, braced against the jolting.
From the throne of his master's lap, Merro surveyed the country around and purred.

"Think 'ee likes it here," the driver said, nodding amiably
at the cat.

"Yes," Nethuryn answered. "And so do I," he continued
with some surprise.

It was true. Though the journey was hard on old bones, the
air here was sweet and the colors bright and new, from tiny
wildflowers nodding by the road to the towering pines. Birds
sang and everyone they passed called a greeting whether they
knew them or not.

The old mage looked over his shoulder at the two small
bundles that held his few remaining possessions. They looked
pathetically small tucked among the sacks of wheat. He'd
never been so poor; he'd never felt so free.

He was certain that somewhere ahead would be a refuge
for them and the thing he could not leave behind.

The cart rumbled on. Nethuryn stroked Merro's head and
was content.

There were far too few workers. Maurynna swore as the barrels piled up on the dock faster than the dockhands could get
them onto the carts. Much longer in this sun and she'd be
selling palm wine vinegar.

Bloody damn. She needed more workers.

She said to Jebby, "After we unload this barrel, I want you
to scour every dock for extra hands. Don't worry; you'll get

your usual wages. You're still working as far as I'm concerned.''

The Cassorin woman nodded her grizzled head. "As you wish, Captain. But I don't think I'll have much luck. The docks have been busier than I've ever seen 'em lately.''

"Do what you can.'' Maurynna wiped her forehead. "Ready?'' she called out.

"Ready!'' came the answer from the hold.

She, Jebby, and the two sailors working the line with them lowered the great barrel tongs into the hold. At the call of "Set!'' they hauled in the line foot by foot, Maurynna flaking it out upon the deck behind them. A barrel appeared, secure in the grip of the tongs. It swung gently in the air.

They paced the deck, walking the yardarm until the barrel hung above the dock. Then they paid out the line until another dockhand could snag it with the boat hook and guide the barrel down. Others freed the tongs and rolled the barrel beside the others sitting on the dock.

Jebby trotted down the gangplank and set off. Maurynna peered into the hatchway. Three faces looked up at her.

"I want to stop unloading for a bit. It's cooler down there than out here; the wine will be better off in the hold. We need more help to load barrels onto the carts.''

One by one the men climbed out of the hold. They followed her down the gangplank. She stared at the barrels in dismay. If she lost this shipment, there would be someone back in Thalnia screaming for her captain's bracelets.

"Let's get to work!'' She bent to a barrel. Three men jumped to help her.

Before long, she was soaked with sweat. Her patched linen tunic and breeches clung to her, chafing with every motion. To add to her misery the westering sun shone in her eyes, making her squint and giving her a headache.

She groaned as once more she and her team of workers gently laid a barrel on its side, rolled it to the waiting cart, and bullied it up the ramp to the bed of the cart. She urged the work crew mercilessly, sparing neither herself nor them.

"Look out! Look out!''

Maurynna looked up. The boards of one of the ramps had slipped and a barrel teetered on the edge of the cart. Two men struggled to hold it steady.

"Help them!" she cried, and sprang to help. She caught the end of the barrel and pushed.

It was no good. Bit by bit, the barrel pushed her down and back. The wood dug into her cheek. She could hardly breathe. If she didn't jump out of the way now, she'd be crushed when it went.

A deep voice said, "I've got it. Let go," and the weight miraculously disappeared.

Maurynna staggered and fell. She sat on the dock, watching open-mouthed as a tall blond man steadied the barrel on the tailgate of the waiting cart, then rolled it to rest against its mates.

By himself.

The others muttered their astonishment. Maurynna blinked. Where had Jebby found *this* one? Gods—she didn't care! He was easily worth any three men. She scrambled to her feet.

He was one of the biggest Yerrins she'd ever seen. His clothes were of good quality, though not new. But why was a Yerrin horseman working the docks?

No matter. The man was as strong as a bull. She hoped he was smarter than one, though. In her sad experience, that kind of strength and brains rarely went together.

The new man's head turned as if he'd been called, but Maurynna heard nothing. He smiled at her, saying, "Were you hurt? No? Good. If you'll excuse me, then." He walked away.

"You!" she yelled. "Where do you think you're going? Get back here. We're not finished."

He stared at her, looking puzzled. He looked around, then pointed to himself.

Oh, gods. Big and stupid as the day is long. "Yes, you! Get your ass over here and earn your pay!"

An odd smile played across his mouth. Then he stripped his tunic off, tossed it to one side and trotted back.

"What do I do?" he asked.

"What do you think?" Maurynna said, exasperated. "Load barrels. And hurry!"

"Then let's get to it," he said, grinning.

She wasn't sure how it happened—or even when—but she soon realized that the new man had claimed her as his partner. They worked together rolling the barrels and pushing them up the ramps.

She carried very little of the weight—and had a sneaking suspicion that the man didn't need even that token bit of help. His strength was frightening. Still . . .

She admitted to herself that she enjoyed working with him. It felt *right* somehow, as if they'd worked as a team for years. She studied him from the corner of her eye.

His clan braid was done in a noble's pattern; Raven had shown her the different plaitings once. She wasn't sure, but she thought the white, blue, and green cords tying it off were Snow Cat clan's colors. She wondered if she could get him to tell her his story. She smiled as she came up with one absurd plan after another to get him alone.

He saw her smile and answered it with one of his own—and a wink. She looked away, embarrassed.

He's nothing but a common dockhand, she scolded herself. *Maybe even an outcast.*

No matter. Her eyes slid back to him.

He had a thick, ugly scar running from his left shoulder diagonally down across his chest. It disappeared under the breeches at his right hip. She was curious to know how he'd gotten it. She wanted to know everything about him.

She thought, *Gods, but he's handsome. I even like the birthmark,* and wondered at the intense attraction she felt.

From the look in his eyes he felt it as well. She wondered if there was some way she could see him after this without her family finding out. They'd be furious if she took up with a dockhand.

At long last they finished unloading the wine. Maurynna thought they'd gotten it to the warehouse in time—thanks to the new man. She called for a break. She sent one of the men to the warehouse with a message for Danaet, the Erdon's factor in Casna. He soon returned, followed by clerks bearing pitchers of ale, mugs, and bread.

The workers hurried to collect their food. A clerk brought her her share. She carried it onto the ship, intending to examine what was left in the hold.

The gangplank shook behind her. She turned, somehow not surprised to see the big Yerrin behind her. After a moment, she realized that she still didn't know his name; she asked him.

He seemed not to hear her. His gaze roaming the ship, he said, "Where are you going?"

"The hold. I want to see just what's left, decide what must be unloaded before full dark." She bit into her bread.

He did the same with his, washing it down with some of his ale. "Can't you use torches?"

She smiled. "Too expensive. And the moon's far from full tonight, so there's no help there. You're new working the docks, aren't you?"

He came close to choking at that. "Yes," he said, an odd note in his voice. "I—I was a mercenary at one time. I've only sailed two or three times—short journeys."

She could see he was struggling not to laugh. She wondered what was so funny. But since he didn't seem to be laughing at her, she said, "Would you like to see the hold?"

He nodded. She set her mug and bread down and crossed the deck to the hatchway leading to the hold. She was down the ladder in a moment. He followed close behind.

Maurynna rubbed her eyes, grateful for the dim light. "Ahhhh," she breathed. "It feels good not to squint anymore," she said as she turned.

And stepped right into his arms.

Part of her was surprised; another part had known that this would happen. One of his arms encircled her waist. The other hand brushed her cheek.

I fit just under his chin, her mind said. Then, *I shouldn't let this happen. He thinks I'm just another dockhand. I don't even know his name!*

She was surprised that she had no fear of what he might do. She trusted him—and somehow this felt right.

His lips brushed hers, at first tentatively, then firmly. She sensed a hunger that should have alarmed her. Instead it awakened an answering need deep within her.

He ended the kiss before she wanted; she stared up at him, speechless, her eyes wide. Somehow her hands had come up to meet at the back of his neck.

Sounding a little breathless—and surprised—he began, "I hope I didn't fright—"

He broke off with a startled gasp. All at once he turned her face so that the light from the hatchway fell full on her. He stared into her eyes and began trembling.

"Gods help me," he whispered, his voice tight. "My lady—your eyes . . . This is the first time I've really seen them—they're . . . they're two different colors."

Confused, Maurynna tried to pull free, but he held her against him with absentminded strength. She saw that he'd paled.

That made her angry. He'd be making the sign against the evil eye in a moment. She said, "It runs in my family. My mother had them and one cousin here in Cassori does as well. If you think they're ugly, you needn't—" She pushed against him.

"Ugly! The gods as my witness, you've the most beautiful eyes I've ever seen!"

He was shaking now, not just trembling, and had the look of someone who'd been given a gift by the gods themselves.

"I don't understand. . . ." she said, uneasy. "What—?"

He placed a finger across her lips. He smiled, saying, "If I'm right, I'll explain soon, my lady, and then—"

Footsteps booming across the deck above their heads interrupted him. Maurynna instinctively sprang back; if that was Danaet, the factor would lecture her about dallying with a dockhand until the waves ran backward. And the gods only knew what would happen if Danaet told her aunt.

The Yerrin let her go.

One hand on the ladder, Maurynna, fumbling for words, said, "We'd best . . . I mean—"

He nodded. "You're right." His voice said he wished the opposite. "Up you go," he said, and boosted her to the top of the ladder.

She popped out of the hold like a cork from a bottle. Mustering her dignity, she strode across the deck, ignoring the speculative looks some of the sailors slid her way. Without looking she knew the Yerrin was right behind her.

She had to clear her throat twice before she was sure her voice wouldn't tremble when she spoke. "Back to work!"

Once again the Yerrin was by her side as often as the work permitted. She didn't dare look at him; she was afraid of what the others might read in her eyes.

Maurynna never knew when he left, only that it was sometime around sunset. She quartered the dock looking for him and even went back to the hold in case he'd hoped to meet her there alone again.

But her Yerrin had disappeared.

Bewildered, she kept the workers on long after she would have normally dismissed them for the day. Hang the expense of torches; maybe he would return. . . .

But now the empty ship rode high in the water and there was no sign of the man. And no reason to stay at the dock any longer. The work was done. She was tired and heartsore, and wanted the comfort of her family around her.

Maurynna found her cousin waiting in the street before the warehouse. The younger woman was mounted on one of the family's horses and held the reins of another in her hand.

"Thought you might be too tired to walk, beanpole," her cousin called cheerfully. "Your friend the bard told us that you had to help with the unloading."

"Bless you, Maylin," Maurynna said as she swung into the saddle. She was weary, far beyond what her aching body could account for. "You've no idea. How is Otter?"

"He told us about the storm you went through. He looked so exhausted that Mother sent him straight to bed—and he was so tired he went."

"With no argument? Otter? Gods, that storm must have taken more out of him than I'd thought. I'm glad he's resting." Maurynna rolled her neck trying to ease her shoulder muscles.

She listened with only half her mind as Maylin told her about how pleased the family was that she'd made port safely and the cold supper she'd find waiting for her. Instead she wondered how many docks in Casna she'd have to search before she found her Yerrin again.

Sixteen

"Linden? Linden?"

Linden looked up. "What? I'm sorry; I didn't hear what you said."

"So I've noticed," Kief said dryly, "all evening. You've been miles away tonight." He sat back to allow the servant to clear the plates from the table before him.

"Daydreaming about Sherrine?" Tarlna said. Her grin was pure wickedness.

Linden shook his head, smiling. "No; I met someone today." He felt a bit disloyal saying that, but if his surmise was correct . . .

"Oh, my," she mocked. "Sherrine has a rival? I don't believe it."

Linden pushed away from the table. "Shall we have our wine in the gazebo? It's a beautiful night."

He continued in their minds, *And away from the servants. There's something I need to talk about with both of you.* He let a brief touch of his elation flow through the contact.

The others exchanged brief glances. Kief said, "Of course we could."

Tarlna rose from her chair, goblet in hand. "A lovely idea, Linden." She took the hand that Kief offered her.

They didn't speak as they passed through the halls of the riverside estate given over to Kief and Tarlna's use. As they approached the many-paned doors leading to the gardens, Linden shook his head.

He said, "I don't think I'll ever get used to this. When I was with Bram and Rani, glass was rare. Now people have pane after pane of it set in doors or windows from floor to ceiling."

"I know what you mean," Kief said. "I didn't see glass—other than some small beads—until well after I'd Changed."

They passed through the doors to the warm darkness outside. One of the servants followed, carrying a flask of wine.

"No need, Harn; we'll serve ourselves. Just give me the wine," Kief said.

The man stood on the threshold, clutching the flask. A smile crossed his square, blocky countenance. "Your indulgence, Dragonlords; it would be my—"

Linden took the wine from him. "We don't wish to interfere with your regular duties, Harn. Don't worry about us." To himself he thought, *Lazy wretch. I daresay serving wine in the garden is indeed easier than what he usually does.*

Harn licked his lips. "But—"

"No," Kief said. His voice was gentle but brooked no argument.

Harn retreated.

They started down the brick path to the gazebo. Linden stooped and snapped off a branch from the lavender hedges bordering the walk. He sniffed the grey-green leaves, wishing for the scents of salt, tar, and sweat.

Kief chuckled, shaking his head. "While I admire dedication in a servant, there are times . . ."

"Dedication, my ass. He didn't want to polish silver or whatever he's supposed to do," Linden retorted, laughing.

"No," Tarlna said. "You're both wrong. Did either of you see the look on his face when he went inside?"

"No," Kief said.

"Nor I. What was it?" Linden asked.

"Frustration. Frustration and—," Tarlna paused. She continued in a thoughtful voice, "Hate."

Kief whistled. "I wish I had seen that. Do you think he's one of those who would have Dragonlords stay out of true-human affairs?"

Tarlna considered. "Perhaps."

Linden raised an eyebrow. "I wonder if there are many of that ilk in Cassori?"

"I wouldn't worry, Linden. That sort are a nuisance, but

have hardly been a serious threat for centuries," Kief said. "Not since Ankarlyn's death and the destruction of the Fraternity of Blood." He snorted. "*Our* blood, that is. But aside from a few ineffective, half-mad misfits calling themselves by that name now and again, no one has ever resurrected it."

"They'd need another mage the equal of Ankarlyn to make it work," Tarlna observed. "And I've not heard of any such."

"Nor have I," said Kief. "Besides, if there was some plot against us here in Cassori, surely something would have happened. We've been here for so long, with all of us going out and about so much, from this revel to that dinner and everywhere in between, that if someone were going to strike at us, they would have done it by now."

"True. I think this wrangle is nothing more than it seems," said Tarlna.

They passed through an archway covered with honeysuckle. Ahead was the gazebo; beyond it flowed the river. Moonlight made a path across the water.

Linden's gaze followed it to the docks. He thought he recognized the *Sea Mist*. His heart jumped. Silly, that; the dockhands would have all gone home by now. He hoped she wasn't too angry at the way he'd left without a word. He hadn't wanted to get caught in a tangle of half-truths. Still, the sight of the cog brought back the feel of his lady's shoulder touching his as they worked.

His lady. He savored the memory of holding her.

Tarlna's crisp voice cut through the night. "Linden—you're the one who wanted to come here. So why are you standing staring across the river? There's nothing there. And that's a remarkably silly smile, I'll have you know."

Linden jumped and felt his face grow hot. He mumbled, "Sorry," as he climbed the steps. A tiny ball of scarlet coldfire lit the interior. "Ah—more wine, anyone?"

The others held out their goblets. Linden poured wine for them, then for himself. They sat down.

He wondered how to begin. He hadn't felt this unsure in

centuries, like a stripling boy in love for the first time. He also felt very foolish.

"Out with it, Linden. What's so important that we had to come out here? Why not use mindspeech if you didn't want any servants overhearing?" Kief said.

"I . . . ah, I—"

Blast it all; the others were going to think him an ass. Why hadn't he used mindspeech?

For no other reason than he didn't want to share these feelings. And share them he would, with mindspeech, whether he wanted to or not. They were too strong to keep back.

Tarlna leaned forward, her eyes intent, studying him for many heartbeats. When she spoke, her voice was the gentlest he'd ever heard it.

"It's something very important, isn't it, Linden? Something not for sharing with everybody. I felt your excitement earlier. Tell us when you're ready."

He nodded. Looking out at the river again, he said, "What did it feel like when you two met?"

"Ahh," Kief said. There was a wealth of happiness in that exhalation.

Linden turned back to see Kief and Tarlna smiling at each other, lost in the past. He felt the all-too-familiar pang of jealousy and sadness at being with a soultwinned couple.

Kief said, "We . . . *fitted* together somehow. I can't explain it any better than that. Just that it was right, our being together."

Linden forgot his pain. His voice tight with excitement, he said, "I think I met my soultwin today."

There; he'd finally said it, admitted it even to himself. His heart jumped again. His soultwin; to never be alone anymore—gods, it was hard to believe.

He continued, "I'm certain of it. It felt like that: right, somehow. The sense of fitting together." He closed his eyes, shaking. An aching hunger filled him.

A hand gripped his shoulder. He opened his eyes to find Kief kneeling on one knee before him; the older Dragonlord's face was full of concern.

"Linden—listen to me. I'm sorry. I'm sorry, but whoever she is, she can't be. The truedragons have said nothing of a new Dragonlord. And they're always the first to feel the souls merge. Unless—oh, gods; please no." Kief's voice shook. "Unless it's like—"

Linden knew what Kief was thinking; the other Dragonlord's stricken face betrayed him. A sudden chill took Linden and his stomach twisted. He hadn't even thought about that. "You mean like Sahleen, don't you—twinned to a truehuman?"

He remembered the tale—and its tragic ending—heard by many a winter's fire in Dragonskeep. His mind's eye saw the unfortunate Sahleen dangling from a tree in the gardens.

Not realizing he spoke aloud, he whispered, "What use living when your soul is gone from you? Such a short time truehumans live." He felt cold despite the heat.

"Has she a Marking?" Tarlna's voice, hard and practical, shattered his fears.

He grasped at her words like a drowning man at a rope. "Yes! Her eyes. They're two different colors: one's blue, the other green. Even though she said others in her family have them, that doesn't mean they can't be a Marking for her. I'm not the only person—truehuman or Dragonlord—with a birthmark like this." He touched his eyelid. "Even Sherrine has one like it on her back. And didn't you once tell me that six-fingered hands ran in your family, Kief?"

"Um, yes," Kief said, still kneeling on the floor. "But the truedragons—"

Tarlna exploded, "Oh, Kief! Forget the truedragons! Somehow they didn't sense her birth."

She jumped up and bent over her soultwin. "Don't you see what's happened? For the first time, soultwins have met *before* they've both Changed!"

Kief fell back, landing with a thump. He stared up at Tarlna. "Gods help us, love—you may be right."

"Of course I'm right," Tarlna said. "And close your mouth; you look like a fish. The thing we need to think about is: what do we do about this?"

Puzzled, Linden said, "What do you mean? She's my soul-twin. I'll tell her, court her, and—"

"No!" Kief said. "That's exactly what you mustn't do—not until we know more about her." He scrambled up, dusting himself off.

Black rage filled Linden, a rage so powerful it frightened him. Before he knew what he did, he sprang at Kief, hands reaching for the smaller Dragonlord's throat. At the last moment he realized what was happening to him.

He was in the grip of Rathan's draconic rage. Shaking, he took control of himself once more. He forced his hands to his sides.

Kief met his eyes unflinching. "Force him back, Linden," he said softly. "Rathan is dangerous to you right now. To you—and your lady."

"Why?" Linden said. His voice was harsh with pain. "Why should I wait any longer? I've waited more than six centuries to be complete, to find the person with the other halves of my souls—far longer than any other Dragonlord has had to wait without hope. And you dare tell me I have to wait longer? Why?"

"Think, you fool! *She hasn't Changed yet!* Think what that could mean—you know what's happened from time to time to *full* Dragonlords."

As Kief's meaning became clear, Linden fell back a step. Despite the warmth, his skin was suddenly clammy and cold. "Oh, gods. I—I understand. I've heard the stories, but I'd forgotten."

"I remember," Kief said grimly, "because it happened during my first century as a Dragonlord. It's not something I ever want to see happen again. You may be a pigheaded pain in the ass sometimes, Linden, but I'd hate to lose you. Especially that way."

"Go sit down," Tarlna ordered. "You look as if you're going to faint or vomit. I'd rather you did neither. So sit down and have some more wine."

Linden obeyed. Tarlna might well be right; he felt shaky enough for either one. She steadied his hands as he drank.

"Thank you," he said. He closed his eyes for a few minutes, concentrating on the shape of the goblet in his hands. Rustling sounds told him the others had also sat down once more. When he could breathe evenly again, he looked at them.

"Thank you both. While I realize there's a danger to us, I can't not see her. Can you understand that?" he pleaded. If Kief invoked the Lady's name and forbade him to find his dockhand . . .

Kief sighed. "Yes, we understand. It would be cruel, having her so near and not being able to even talk to her. But hold Rathan in check, Linden; until your lady goes through First Change he's more of a danger to you than a dozen dark mages. And what's your lady's name, anyway?"

Linden looked down at the floor, feeling foolish. "I don't know. I never had a chance to ask her. We were working too hard."

"Drink some more wine; you're still pale," Tarlna said. She added suspiciously, "Working?"

He decided it might be best not to elaborate.

Kief said, "This will be painful for you, Linden—very painful. Every instinct you have, every fiber of your body, will drive you. It's an imperative for us to join with our soul-twins. I don't envy you one bit. Gods—I wish we could help somehow."

"You have," Linden said, "by telling me this. Just as Lleld did when she told me about—" He cleared his throat. Even after so long it was difficult to talk about. "About Bryony, after I had gone through First Change."

"Ah," Tarlna said, pouring more wine into his goblet. "This Bryony—I think I heard you mention her once. Was she the wife who left you?"

Linden drank off the rest of the wine in one gulp. "Yes."

Tarlna shook her head. "She must have been livid when she found out later you were a Dragonlord." Wicked laughter bubbled under the words.

"Oh, gods—yes. It was three years later and she had married someone else, so she had no claim on me." He leaned forward, resting his elbows on his knees, lost in the past.

"So how did you meet your unnamed lady today?" Tarlna said briskly.

Linden couldn't help laughing. Trust Tarlna not to give up. And if she disapproved of playing with the servants' children, what would she say to this?

"I went down to see the ship Otter came in on. She thought I was a dockhand—she heads a crew of them, you see. She told me to get my ass over there and earn my pay." Linden chuckled. "So I helped unload the ship as long as I could."

Tarlna shut her eyes. She looked pained. "Linden—there is no hope for you."

Kief laughed. "So that's why you were late." Then he sobered and said, "Don't tell her, Linden, until you know her better. If she's headstrong, she may try to force an early Change. That would be disastrous. On the other hand, it may make it easier for both of you if she understands what's happening and is patient enough to let things unfold as they should. She'll want you as much as you want her, I suspect."

"I'll ask Otter if he'll help me find her. I know, I know," Linden said, forestalling the other's objections, "he's not a Dragonlord and this is Dragonlord business. But I need him to search for me. A Dragonlord looking for a dockhand would set too many tongues wagging. And remember—he's a bard. He knows how to keep his mouth shut when needed."

He fell silent. *Gods; I hope I can hold back. No, not "hope;" I must hold back. I wish I could talk to Otter right now.*

He refused to think of what he'd truly rather be doing. This was going to be hard enough without torturing himself.

But when he reached out with his mind, he found that Otter was deep in sleep. This time he'd not wake the bard up; time enough to talk in the morning.

He sighed. Six centuries. Six long, lonely centuries—and now this. A memory drifted into his mind. Once more he heard Rani say, "Nothing worth having comes easy, you know."

He never noticed when Kief and Tarlna left him alone with his thoughts, the river, and the warm night.

The whitewashed walls of the bedroom glowed a warm ivory in the circle of light cast by the single rushlight. Shadows filled the corners that the tiny flame couldn't penetrate.

Maylin sat with her legs hanging off the side of the bed as she leaned against a bedpost at the foot of it. Kella, asleep long before Maurynna had arrived, lay curled up in the other bed.

Now Maurynna sat on a pallet made up on the floor between the beds. The tall girl sat with her legs folded to one side, nightgown rucked up to midthigh, displaying long, slender legs. She had pulled her long black hair over one shoulder to pool in her lap. The red-gold of her captain's bracelets winked in the rushlight as she brushed her damp hair.

Stroke, stroke, stroke. Maylin blinked, almost hypnotized by the slow, rhythmic motion. The ropes supporting the mattress creaked as she shifted to better study her cousin.

Half-lowered eyelids concealed the odd-colored eyes so vivid in the tanned, heart-shaped face. Maylin envied her cousin her long aristocratic nose—so different from Maylin's own snubby one—even if it wasn't quite straight, a legacy of being knocked to the deck by a loose boom.

As Maurynna switched hands, her nightgown of fine lawn slipped from her shoulder. The sharp line between the sun-darkened neck and the lighter, honey-toned skin of her shoulders was startling. Maurynna's lips curled in a dreamy smile.

It was the smile that worried Maylin. Just as it had worried her all during Maurynna's bare-bones recital of the docking and unloading of her ship as the taller girl ate the cold supper hastily prepared for her.

Something's not right here, Maylin thought. *That dockhand did an honest day's work—why should he run off before he could be paid? Perhaps he's not a dockhand—but then, why unload Maurynna's ship? And I don't like what she didn't say about him. That's not like Rynna. No funny descriptions. Not a bit about what he looked like—just that he was a big*

man and strong—or anything else about him save that they
worked side by side all day. Just that same dreamy smile.

Her mother had been too distracted to notice. Like every
other merchant Maylin knew of, her mother was worried sick
over what a prolonged regency debate—or, gods forbid, civil
war—would do to trade.

Maylin wondered what the bard would make of Rynna's
dreaminess; he seemed a clever fellow. She'd ask him tomorrow. Now it was time for a distraction—and she knew
just the thing.

"We've seen Linden Rathan," she said a touch smugly,
nodding at the sleeping Kella.

The distant look vanished from Maurynna's face. "What!
How?"

Maylin grinned. "Haven't you heard? There are three Dragonlords in Casna because of the debate over the regency. The
other two are Kief Shaeldar and Tarlna Aurianne."

Maurynna stared open-mouthed. "But, but—Oh! That
wretch! Now I understand! I'll keelhaul him," she fumed,
smacking her thigh with the brush. "He knew all along."

"Who?" Maylin asked, confused. "Linden Rathan?"

"Otter. Never mind, I'll explain later. Go on about the
Dragonlords. Please."

Maurynna rearranged her long legs. To Maylin it looked a
dreadfully uncomfortable position. But Rynna seemed happy
with it, so Maylin plunged into her story.

"We've seen him nearly every morning when Mother can
spare us."

When she saw the naked longing in her cousin's eyes,
Maylin was sorry she had announced it so baldly. Good thing
Mother had already told her she could bring Rynna to the
Processional tomorrow.

"Where—and how?" Maurynna begged.

Maylin warmed to her tale. "The council meetings almost
always start about three candlemarks or so before noon. The
morning of the first meeting Mother let us go to the Processional. We got there barely in time. They were earlier than I
thought they'd be."

Now she bounced with remembered excitement. The ropes of the bed complained. "Two kind guards let us stand right in front so that we had a perfect view."

Maurynna's eyes went wide. A soft "Ohhhhh!" escaped from her.

Maylin knelt on the edge of the bed, looking down on Maurynna on the pallet. "But this is the best part! I held Kella up so that she could see better and of course she waved. Linden Rathan waved back and called out 'Hello, kitten' to her! *And* he's waved every morning that we've been there— we always stand near the same spot if we can—whether he's alone or with the other Dragonlords. I really think he looks for us. He smiles whenever he sees us."

The brush fell to lie in Maurynna's lap. Her fingers caressed the handle carved in the shape of a dragon as her eyes closed. "Oh, gods."

To Maylin, the barely heard words sounded like a plea. "Although Mother needs us tomorrow, she said we could bring you to the Processional. I should have let Kella tell you this—it's really her story—but I couldn't wait. Just act surprised when she tells you."

Maurynna nodded. Then the odd-colored eyes opened again; they sparkled. Maylin wondered why her cousin suddenly looked smug.

She had her answer when Maurynna said with false diffidence, "Did I tell you that Otter's offered to introduce me to Linden Rathan? They're friends, you know."

"What!" Maylin's squeal brought a sleepy grumble from Kella. Contrite, Maylin clapped a hand over her mouth.

Maurynna nodded again. "But I don't know when he will, and I'd like to have a chance to see Linden Rathan before that. Do you think we'll see him?"

"It's likely. There should be another meeting tomorrow; they seem to meet for four or five days, then break for two or three, sometimes more—to let tempers cool, Mother thinks. The talk is that it would take very little for an open break in the council. And that would mean war. Only the Dragonlords have kept it from that." Maylin shivered at the thought. Her gaze met her cousin's, odd-colored like her own.

Maurynna made the sign to ward against evil. "Avert," she said. "Let's hope the Dragonlords can keep it from that."

The next few moments passed in troubled silence. Here, in the little bedroom with its age-darkened beams, the possibility of civil war should have seemed remote. But for the first time Maylin believed it could truly happen. Something hovered in the room like a shadow. Even the colorful tiles around the hearth seemed dimmed.

Then Maurynna shattered the darkling mood. She began brushing her hair again and asked cheerfully, "But what does he look like?"

Since there could only be one "he," Maylin began, "He's big—"

Maurynna was now staring at nothing, smiling again. The brush hung suspended in midstroke.

Maylin wanted to knock a head—her own or her cousin's, she wasn't sure which—against the wall. Belatedly she remembered that description fit the dockhand. Oh, gods; Maurynna wouldn't—Not with a common dockhand, would she?

How to ask without offending her? Maylin considered the problem and could see no way around it. A frontal attack it was, then.

"You look like a lovesick calf," Maylin said. "You're thinking about that dockhand again, aren't you? Oh, don't try to deny it; you're redder than a palace guard's tunic. What happened between the two of you?"

If possible, Maurynna's face turned even redder. "What do you mean, 'what happened'?"

"Don't deny it." Maylin folded her arms. "Rynna, when you talked about him you got all starry-eyed. And you kept smiling to yourself afterward. You're not planning to, to . . ."

"Have a dalliance with him?" Maurynna scowled like a storm about to break.

Maylin counted her breaths. One, two, three . . . She reached ten before the danger passed. The anger melted away, replaced by a look of bewilderment.

"I don't know. He's—he's . . . There's just something

about him," Maurynna said. "That's the best I can explain it—even to myself. I don't even know his name; he didn't tell me. He's a Yerrin noble; I saw his clan braid." She rose to her knees and blew out the rushlight. In the sudden darkness she confessed: "He kissed me when we were in the hold."

Maylin groaned. This was worse than she'd feared. "Rynna—have a care!" she pleaded. She waited until the sounds of Maurynna putting herself to bed ended. "If he's a Yerrin noble and working the docks now, then he must be an outcast and in disgrace. Are you really willing to risk everything you've worked for for him? Please; don't throw your life away. Tell me you won't."

The silence stretched on and on. Maylin fell asleep waiting for a reassurance that never came.

Seventeen

Harn crept along the hall. He had no fear of a squeaky floorboard betraying him. The thick, patterned carpets muffled every footstep. He paused outside the Dragonlords' bed chamber.

Damn their arrogance. Because they'd not let him accompany them, he'd had to spend the evening chafing in the house under the watchful eye of the house steward. He'd had no chance to follow. He wondered what they'd spoken of; the younger Dragonlord had left without coming back. The other two had looked disturbed and retired right away. This might be his only chance to find out what had happened.

The other servants were all below. He hoped none of them came upstairs. He had no duties to take him up here, no plausible excuse ready. Still, he had to take the risk. His lord was interested in anything the Dragonlords did or said.

He pressed his ear against the thick oak door. At first all he heard was muffled, indecipherable mumbling. Then the mumbling resolved itself into two voices that became clearer; it seemed the Dragonlords had moved closer to the door. Harn caught the name "Sherrine." He strained to hear.

The man spoke now. "Do you think Linden will be able to stay away from her now that he knows?"

A heavy sigh, and the woman said, "I don't know. I hope so. Best not to take him to task over it, though. You know how stubborn he can be. Maybe the other girl will distract him."

Harn rocked back on his heels, surprised. *Why would the young Dragonlord suddenly want to stay away from Lady Sherrine? My lord and the prince will not be at all pleased. And who is the "other girl"?*

He resumed listening in time to hear Kief Shaeldar's voice again and the sound of someone pacing. "To tell you the truth, I trust Linden; I think he'll be strong enough not to risk them both. And this matter *is* between them. I've interfered as much as I feel is right. Gods; I wish the Lady were here. This is a dangerous situation for a fledgling Dragonlord. . . ."

Startled, Harn gasped. From inside the room he heard the pacing stop. At once he jumped up, running lightly down the hall in the opposite direction. His stocking feet made only the faintest sound on the thick carpet.

As he turned the corner, he heard the door to the Dragonlords' chambers open. Kief Shaeldar called out, "Is someone there?"

Harn swore. He ducked into one of the unused bedrooms. His heart pounded as he leaned against the door, listening. There were no pursuing footsteps. He went slack with relief.

Damn! The tales of the Dragonlords' acute hearing were true, it seemed. Once more thing to tell his lord, Kas Althume.

He grinned. Althume would be well pleased with this night's work of his. To think Lady Sherrine was a new Dragonlord! What irony. The mother deep in the machinations of the Fraternity, and the daughter—

The daughter was one of the enemy.

As soon as all in the house slept, he'd take a horse and set off. News like this couldn't wait.

"What was it?" Tarlna asked as Kief shrugged and shut the chamber door once more.

"I thought I heard something. Must have been my imagination; still all agog over Linden's news, I guess. Imagine— the first new Dragonlord in six hundred years!"

"But is she?" Tarlna mused as she twined a curling strand of hair between her fingers.

Kief frowned. "What do you mean?"

"Think. Even before Linden's birth, there were fewer and fewer Dragonlords sensed with each passing century. No one thought it too odd at first; such ebb and flow has happened before. But was it in truth the beginning of this famine of Dragonlords?

"We know none of the elders sensed this girl; not even any of the truedragons did. How many others like her have there been? And how can we be certain she's the only one since Linden?" She watched her soultwin, saw him catch her meaning.

His eyes went wide. "Good gods. There could have been a thousand—ten thousand!—of them. . . ."

"And since most of our kind die before we're old enough to Change, we wouldn't know about any of them," Tarlna said. "So the question remains: is this girl truly the only one?"

Eighteen

Linden spent a miserable night tossing and turning, his mind running in circles. In the grey hours before dawn, he finally gave up the battle. He dragged the quilt from the foot of the bed, wrapped it around himself, and went to sit on the windowseat.

His eyes were gritty with lack of sleep. He rubbed at them. The glass was cold on his forehead as he rested his head against the windowpane. He stared outside, listless, drained.

Kief was right. His soultwin was in danger from him. For her safety, he had to forgo what he wanted and the desire he'd seen in her eyes. Yet already the urge to join with her tormented him. Rathan was quiescent now, but how long would that last? He knew he'd not be able to stay away from her, not completely. But would seeing her, talking to her, make it easier or harder? Everything in him cried out for her.

Gods, but this was not going to be easy. He shifted. The quilt fell away from his shoulder; he ignored the chill against his skin. The sky outside was lighter now with the first peach and apricot shades of approaching dawn. He yawned, wondering if he could get an hour or two of sleep before the servants came to fill his bath.

He looked over at the bed. No—it wasn't worth the effort to get up. He settled back.

All at once Rathan lashed at him, driving him mad with desire. The raging passions of a mating dragon scorched him as Rathan urged him to seek his soultwin, join with her. Linden cried out in torment. Breath by slow breath he pushed the draconic half of himself back. Rathan subsided, his sullen rage burning like a hot coal.

Linden's temper was no better. He couldn't shake off Rathan's black fury. He threw the quilt back onto the bed and snatched up a pair of breeches. He hauled them on, then threw open the door.

"Aran! Gifnu's bloody hells—where's my bath?" he bellowed. He heard squeaks and yells of surprise from the servants' quarters. Moments later two frightened young serving men tumbled half-dressed into the dim hall. They stared at him, bleary-eyed with sleepy surprise.

"Well?" he demanded. A small part of his mind scolded him for taking his temper out on the servants. He throttled it. "I want my bath and breakfast—now!"

Aran, the house steward, stumbled into the hall, his hair sticking up every which way. "Now, Dragonlord? But—"

"Now, blast it!" He slammed back into his room. The servants twittered outside, astonished at the change in their easygoing Dragonlord. Then came the sound of running feet as they hastened to obey.

He couldn't wait any longer. He mindcalled Kief. The elder Dragonlord was inclined to surliness at first.

Kief, Linden said, trying to still the turmoil in his mind. *I'm sorry to wake you.*

Kief's black mood vanished. He said sympathetically, *Rathan's after you, isn't he? Would you like us to delay the meeting until this afternoon so that you can start looking for your soultwin? I wish for your sake we could dispense with it altogether today, but . . .*

Linden went limp with relief. Kief was giving him what he needed before he'd even asked. *I understand. Just give me the morning. I have to at least start looking; I feel as if I'll lose my mind if I don't.*

I can give you until midday, Kief said. Then, faintly, as Kief withdrew from the contact: *Luck to you, little one.*

Linden whispered, "thank you" to the air. He reached out with his mind again. *Otter? Otter, I need your help.*

Otter's reply was so clear that Linden suspected the bard was already awake. *Now, boyo? It's barely after dawn.*

Now, Linden said.

I'm on my way.

* * *

Although the draconic rage had subsided, Linden was still in a foul mood. For no matter how carefully he carried his harp while in dragon-form, he always managed to break a few strings on it. To distract himself until Otter arrived, Linden had decided to restring the instrument.

It was a mistake. The cursed strings would *not* go right. The new ones kept slipping, fraying his already shredded temper even more. He forced his touch to remain delicate.

The door creaked a little as it opened slightly. He snarled, "What?" but there was no answer. Instead, it opened wider. He didn't bother looking up. Just let Aran get within range and he'd blast the man for his temerity, entering without leave.

"My, my—aren't we in quite the temper this morning?" a dry voice said.

"Huh? Otter!" Linden jumped up, almost dropping his harp. "Oh—yes, I suppose. Oh, gods, but I'm glad to see you!"

Otter regarded him with a speculative eye as he shut the door. "You had me fooled about that. And they're tiptoeing around out there, boyo. What in blazes did you do? And why?"

The bard settled himself in one of the chairs, neatly flipping his long, iron-grey clan braid out of the way. "Give me that before you break the pegs, you big ox. Between your mood and your strength you're going to destroy a fine instrument."

Grateful, Linden dumped harp and strings into Otter's lap. For a moment he watched Otter's practiced fingers make quick work of the stringing before sitting back down in the windowseat. "I'm not in a foul mood."

"Re-e-e-ally?" Otter drawled. "I never would have guessed—what with waking me up at first light and your loving greeting just now."

Linden laughed; he couldn't help it. "Very well, then. I guess I am being rather a wretch this morning, aren't I?"

Otter snorted. "No 'rather' about it, Linden—I'd say 'definitely' myself. So—what is this all about?'' He played a few notes on the harp. "Beautiful instrument."

"Thank you," Linden said. He hesitated, unsure how to begin.

As if to give Linden time to collect himself, Otter looked around the richly furnished sleeping chamber. "Very nice," the bard said, "if a bit overdone for my tastes. And how do you like it yourself?"

Linden shrugged. "Too ornate, but it gives me privacy. I didn't fancy the river estate I was offered. Too big; I would have felt lost in there by myself. When I said I'd prefer a private house to the castle quarters I was offered next, the owner volunteered this one for my use. Do you intend to continue staying with that merchant family? I thought you would stay here."

Otter grinned. "Maurynna will throw me off the *Sea Mist* if I do. Gods help me, boyo—forty years I've known you and this is one of the few times I've seen you blush!"

Linden mumbled something and stood up. For some reason the encounter with Harn last night had made him uneasy. He'd learned to pay attention to such feelings when he was with Bram and Rani. That was how mercenaries stayed alive. Feeling a little foolish, he went to the door and looked up and down the hall. There was no one in sight. He shut the door and went back to sit down across from Otter.

"Trouble?" Otter said, sitting up straighter.

"I don't think so—just an odd feeling." He hesitated a moment, then plunged in. "I need your help. The ship's captain—Maurynna, you said?—would she know who was unloading her ship? After I talked to you yesterday I wandered down to look at it. Now I need to find the leader of the crew of dockhands that was working there."

"Dockhands?" Otter looked perplexed. "But why? Did he steal something from you?"

"She," Linden corrected. The wild elation filled him again. He said softly, "It's over, Otter—my waiting." He watched realization dawn in Otter's eyes, joy spread across the bard's face.

"Oh, gods. Linden, you're not jesting, are you? No, of course not; not about this. Thank all the gods she's come at last." Otter's eyes looked suspiciously bright. "What's her name?"

Linden groaned. "I never found out. If I had asked hers, I would have had to tell her mine. Do you think your friend the captain will be at the ship now? I—I'd like to begin looking."

"I should think you would! Shall we go now, or do you have a council meeting this morning?" Otter said.

"No. The meeting's been put off until midday."

Otter set the harp aside and stood up. "Let's be off, then. Your lady may even be back there this morning to finish the job if it wasn't completed last night. If not, we'll start looking for her. And if we can't find her, we'll ask Maurynna. She'd be delighted to help you any way possible."

Linden bounded to his feet. "Done," he said.

"Rynna! Don't walk so fast, please. My legs aren't as long as yours," Maylin said crossly. "We'll be there in plenty of time."

She was annoyed. Maurynna had a ground-eating stride. But she and Kella took after their mother: little and plump, "like partridges," as Father said. There was no way she could comfortably keep up with the pace Maurynna was setting.

Especially in this weather. The heat was oppressive, the air so humid it was hard to breathe. Merely walking quickly made her sweat. With luck there would be a storm before long to clear the air.

Maylin had no intention of arriving at the Processional red in the face and puffing like a grampus. Kella, riding on Maurynna's shoulders, had no such worries.

Maurynna slowed down. "I'm sorry," she said.

She sounded so apologetic that Maylin was mollified. "No harm done. And I do understand, but I would feel silly fainting from the heat at his feet as he goes by. With my luck Lady Sherrine would be with him again; she has been on occasion."

Maurynna asked, "Who's Lady Sherrine?"

"Just the most beautiful of the young women at court." Maylin looked around before continuing in a lower voice, "And a flaming bitch. She buys most of Mother's woods lily perfume—which is a good thing, because that scent is so strongly associated with her, no one else at court buys it. They don't want to be thought competing with her, I guess. Luckily a few wealthy merchants buy the rest. But *gods* is she a proper pain to wait upon."

Kella giggled.

Maylin continued, "Gossip is that she's the one he's chosen for a dalliance, which shows remarkably little taste on his part, I think. Still, I daresay she's taken care that he's never seen that side of her. And Kella, don't you dare tell Mother I said that about Lady Sherrine."

Kella nodded. "I won't. But if she's so mean, then why does he have a dally . . . dally—" Her face contorted. "What *is* a dally-thing?"

Maurynna smiled. "Dalliance, gigglepuss. It means they're—"

Amused, Maylin waited to see how Maurynna would get out of this one.

"Keeping company together," Maurynna finished. "And as to why, because he must be lonely. He's the only Dragonlord without a soultwin."

"But why is Linden Rathan lonely? Doesn't he have any friends? What's a soultwin? And why are there Dragonlords?"

Maurynna reached up and tugged a lock of Kella's hair. "What, gigglepuss? Don't you know how Dragonlords came about? No? Where's that wretched bard when you need him? He ought to explain this."

Maylin shrugged. The pace had quickened once more; Maurynna in her eagerness was walking faster. Maylin hadn't the heart to complain again. So she kept her reply short and concentrated on not getting too out of breath. "Went out very early. You tell her—else no peace."

Maurynna said, "Listen well, then, small stuff. Long, long

ago, people lived in small tribes and clans, and there was peace between them.

"But one shaman—in what would become Yerrih someday—sought knowledge in places and ways that were evil. And he grew ambitious. Maybe a demon got into him, I don't know, but Red Deer Bearson wanted to rule over all the land and there was bloodshed where before there had been peace. Then he tried to get by magic what he couldn't get by war. But the working went awry. Wild magic stalked the land and times were evil indeed. Even the truedragons were caught by it.

"But one good thing came of it all. Somehow the wild magic caused the first Dragonlords, and who do you think the first one was?" Maurynna asked.

"Who?" Kella demanded.

"Red Deer's own son, Fox, who became Fox Morkerren. His father tried to use him, but he rebelled against the endless wars. He and his soultwin Morga Sanussin stopped Red Deer after a great battle, and then began the long work of rebuilding the peace that had existed before. Fox Morkerren promised that never again would a Dragonlord make war, that they would instead seek to avert it, and that in this way the Dragonlords would serve humankind.

"He and Morga were so wise and just, that the leaders of the tribes and clans pledged themselves in turn to accept the young Dragonlords' counsel, and to honor Dragonlords. And so it has gone to this day, that the Dragonlords are called in when there is need."

"Oooh," said Kella. "I like that story. Will you tell it to me again sometime?"

"Tell you what, gigglepuss, I'll get Otter to tell you; he does it much better. And as for what a soultwin is, well, a Dragonlord is born when a dragon soul bonds with a human one before birth. Then the souls divide, and each Dragonlord has a soultwin, the person with the other halves of the two souls. All the Dragonlords have a soultwin—all except Linden Rathan. That's why he's called the Last Dragonlord."

"That's sad. He's nice," Kella said. "I'll be his friend. Do you think he'd like that? I already wave to him whenever I can and he waves back. He called me 'kitten.' ''

Maurynna smiled. "I think he'd like you for a friend," she said. Then, her voice tight with excitement, "Look—we're almost there."

They were near the end of the narrow street that gave on to the great avenue known simply as the Processional. Dotted along its length by trees, the avenue stretched from the palace through the heart of Casna, ending in the part of the city where the highest ranking nobles lived.

A single stately elm graced the corner they approached. One of the city guard loitered in its shade.

Taking pity, Maylin said, "Go on—I know you can't wait any longer."

Maurynna swung Kella down. "D'you mind walking, sweetling?"

"Race you," Kella offered.

"You're on."

Maylin shook her head. "You're going to run in this heat? You're mad."

Maurynna laughed but got on her mark. Kella jumped up and down, then screamed "Go!" at the top of her lungs. The little girl set off as fast as her short legs would carry her. Maurynna jogged just behind.

Following at a pace more suited to the heat, Maylin watched the laughing racers. Kella reached the tree first. Maurynna spoke to the guard standing in its shade.

Uh-oh; why aren't there any people lining the route today? Not everyone's gotten jaded about the Dragonlords.

The guard was shaking his head. Maurynna's shoulders slumped. Then she and Kella started back at a slow, dejected walk.

Maylin stopped. "What's wrong?" she asked when they reached her.

"The guard said that the meeting's been postponed until midday," Kella piped.

"Oh, no." Maylin looked at her cousin and read the thought in her eyes. "Rynna, I wish we could wait with you, but Mother does need us. But if you want to . . ."

Maurynna shook her head. "I'm tempted, but it would be silly to stand here for candlemarks. No, go on to the shop. I think I'll go to the ship."

Maylin tried to catch her eye, but Maurynna wouldn't look at her, just turned and walked away.

"Poor Rynna," said Kella.

"I feel bad," Maylin said. "Getting her hopes up like this, I mean. I wish she were coming with us." *She's going to look for that dockhand; I just know it. I hope Otter introduces her to Linden Rathan soon. Because if anything can distract her from that wretched fellow, it will be meeting him.*

She shook her head; there was nothing she could do. "To the shop, gigglepuss."

Anstella sat at her desk, pleased with the delay even as she wondered at the reason for it. She had much to do.

First an anonymous letter to Merchant Farell, reminding him of his promise to contribute a purse of gold to the Fraternity's cause, and hinting, if he delayed much longer, that certain evidence regarding his daughter's illicit dalliance with that young guardsman would somehow find its way into the hands of his elderly, wealthy, noble—and insanely jealous— son-in-law. The same son-in-law who was pouring money into Merchant Farell's faltering business.

Then, perhaps, an equally anonymous note to the uncommitted Baron Gracien, to say it would be most unfortunate if Beren should win the regency; for the duke would surely discover that the bandits Gracien was charged to hunt down paid a tithe to be left alone—and not to the crown.

Yes, that would do for now. Anstella opened a drawer, then pressed a certain knot in the wood with her thumb and twisted. The false bottom slid back and she took out two of the spelled sheets of parchment Althume had prepared for her. As soon as the messages were read, the ink would fade, leaving a once-more blank sheet of parchment, and no evidence.

She smiled, took up a quill pen, and began to write.

*   *   *

Aside from a few sailors working on the deck, there was no activity at the dock where the *Sea Mist,* lay rocking gently at her mooring. The water glittered in the sun. Gulls swooped overhead, their raucous screams loud in the early morning quiet.

Otter shook his head. "Bad news, boyo."

Linden said hopefully, "They haven't started yet? We'll have to wait for them?"

"They're done. See how high the ship is riding in the water? She's empty. The dock crew must have moved on to another ship."

"Ah, damn," Linden said. Disappointment filled him. "I should have known this would be too easy."

Otter clapped him on the shoulder. "We'll find her—you'll see. I've a good feeling about this."

Linden smiled wanly. "I hope you're right."

"I know I am. Let's work our way along the river. At least it's a bit cooler here by the water. So—north or south?"

"North," Linden said, thinking of the cool, clean air of Dragonskeep. "We'll try north."

By the time she reached the *Sea Mist,* Maurynna was sorry she'd chosen to walk. She should have gone back to the house and taken one of the horses.

Hindsight sees all, she told herself. *Now if I can only last long enough to get into the warehouse.*

The building rose before her, cheerful with the Erdons' silver dolphin painted on the doors. She pushed the heavy door open, grateful for the dim coolness inside, and staggered to a crate. She sat with a thump. Wiping her forehead, she announced to all within earshot, "Sailors should not walk— not in this heat, anyway."

The clerks working nearby chuckled. One said, "No one should, Captain. Times like this I envy you sailors the open sea."

Danaet came out of the office. The clerks bent over their tally slates once more. "I thought I heard your voice, Captain Erdon. Could I talk to you—in the office?"

Mystified, Maurynna followed the stocky factor. *Captain Erdon?* From Danaet?

Once inside the office, Danaet carefully closed the door behind them. Something told Maurynna she was not going to like this.

Blunt as ever, Danaet went straight to the point. "Some of the dockhands were gossiping, Rynna—about you and that big blond worker, the way you two were looking at each other—and the way you looked after you were in the hold with him. Who is he?"

Maurynna's face grew hot. "I don't know. I thought you might—Jebby sent him. She'll know." She looked away, unable to meet Danaet's angry gaze.

"I asked Jebby; she tried every dock she could, but couldn't find anyone to send."

For a moment Maurynna was too surprised to speak. "What! But if she didn't send him—"

"Then he's not a member of the Dock Guild. And you know how they are about non-guild taking work from them. They might refuse to work here, and then where would we be? I only hope he didn't get the full wages—"

"He didn't get any at all," Maurynna said. She nodded at Danaet's astonished face. "I thought Jebby had sent him, that he was guild, and was going to pay him the same as any of the others. But he disappeared, long before I paid the workers. He never got anything, let alone full wages."

Grimacing, Danaet pulled the chair out from the desk and plumped down into it. Maurynna found another chair and did the same.

Danaet swore. "That's bad. I think he's a thief, then. What better way to learn what's worth stealing than to unload it? No doubt he also took a long look at the locks and such while he was here."

That infuriated Maurynna. "Danaet, whatever he was, I know he wasn't a thief. He was rarely even near the warehouse—he was by my side practically every moment."

"So I've heard," Danaet said dryly. "But I still think he's a thief. Gods, girl! How do you find these people for friends?

This one's likely as bad as that Flounder or whatever his name is. And if he isn't a thief, are you out of your mind, making eyes at a dockhand? He's well below your station. Probably outcast from his clan. Damnation, you're a member of one of the most powerful merchant families in the Five Kingdoms—an aristocracy of its own, even if these jackasses of Cassorin nobles think otherwise. Do you really want to set tongues wagging that you're dallying with a common dockhand?''

Maurynna gritted her teeth and stood up. Only the knowledge that Danaet spoke to her this way because the factor truly cared gave Maurynna the strength to bite back the angry words crowding her tongue.

''You're wrong about him. And I'll do as I see fit, thank you.'' She relented at the hurt look on Danaet's face. Sighing, she crossed the office in two quick strides. She bent and hugged the factor, saying, ''Danaet, please don't worry. I have to find him again, that's all. There was something odd. . . . Believe me; I do know what I'm doing.''

Danaet sighed. ''I hope so, girl. I don't want to see you hurt or lose your ship. But don't bother looking at any of the other docks, Rynna. He's nowhere to be found here at the riverfront.''

Maurynna paused by the door. ''How do you know?''

Danaet sighed again. ''I asked Jebby to look for him; I knew you'd want to find him again, and I didn't want you going from dock to dock. It wouldn't be fitting. And there's some out there that'll kill you for the gold in those bracelets.

''My word of honor on it—he's not working any dock today. And no other crew has ever seen someone even close to that description.''

Nineteen

"Three docks now, boyo," **Otter** said, "and we still haven't found her."

They guided their horses through the teeming streets of the waterfront. To Otter's amusement, now and again someone would jerk around as they took another look at Linden. Invariably the person would shake his or her head, certain that a Dragonlord couldn't be down at the docks with the common folk.

There were merchants, well-fed and glossy, sailors with the rolling walks that spoke of long months at sea, and a myriad of others, some respectable, some Otter never wanted to meet in an alley at any time, all walking slowly and complaining of the heat. Only the street children had the energy to run. One urchin dodged under Otter's horse's nose, causing him to pull up for a moment.

He wiped the sweat from his forehead. The air was so thick and heavy he felt as if he was breathing under water. He'd never known Casna to have such hot, humid weather. With luck there would be a storm soon to break it; at least he'd be on dry land this time. In the meantime, he looked with longing at every tavern they passed. But Linden had only a few candlemarks to look for his soultwin before it would be time to go to the council meeting. He'd not ask the Dragonlord to waste a moment by sitting in a tavern.

To distract himself from the heat and his thirst, Otter asked, "Will you tell her when you find her?"

Linden shook his head. "Too dangerous. I had wanted to court her, claim her as my soultwin, but Kief reminded me of the danger."

Otter's ears pricked up. This was something he'd never

known about Dragonlords—and thanks to Linden, he probably knew more about them than any truehuman alive. "Danger?"

"Yes. It sometimes happens that two Dragonlords—two *full* Dragonlords—will destroy each other when they join. You see, the soul-halves merge for a brief time, then separate once more. If they don't . . ."

"Wait a moment. 'When they join?' As in bedding?" At Linden's nod, Otter complained, "Then what's all this about some mystic ceremony? You mean it's just a matter of— Boyo, I can't put that in a song! At least not one that can be sung anywhere else than a tavern. And how much else about Dragonlords is a smoke tale?"

"No one at Dragonskeep knows how that story started. But it suits us. The less some truehumans know about us, the better," Linden said.

"Ah," said Otter, understanding, "of course. Yet if you can't claim her, that's going to be a bad time for you, isn't it?" He bit his tongue before adding, *You were never very good at celibacy*, and smothered a grin.

Linden's groan nearly made him repent his levity.

When Linden entered the council room, the other Dragonlords looked eagerly at him. He shook his head and took his seat. Then he sighed.

Damn, but this was going to be a long *long* meeting.

Twenty

*"**Are you certain about this**, Kas?"* said Prince Peridaen as he made ready for the mysteriously delayed council meeting. "I can hardly believe it; it's incredible. Your man is reliable?"

"Yes," Althume answered. "Harn and his brother Pol have been with me for years. Harn heard the older Dragonlords speak of a fledgling Dragonlord—a woman. From what he said, I think the new one is Linden Rathan's soultwin. For some reason they don't think he should join with her. And they're hoping 'the other girl'—whoever she is—distracts him from her for the time being."

Peridaen stood before the mirror in his quarters at the castle, adjusting the set of his tunic. "Don't the stories say that the joining of soultwins involves a ceremony? Perhaps it must be done at Dragonskeep."

Althume considered. "Very likely. The forces involved must be considerable; there would be wards at Dragonskeep against their raging out of control. The place is ancient and full of magic." He picked up Peridaen's heavy gold necklace of rank from the table and slipped it over the prince's head. "Think of it, Peridaen: the Fraternity's own Dragonlord as spy. How ironic."

"Could the fledgling really be Sherrine? She doesn't seem to have a Marking," said Peridaen.

"Perhaps not all Markings are noticeable. I wonder; if Linden Rathan suddenly stays away from her—Will Anstella come here before the council meets?"

An oddly patterned knock sounded at the door. Peridaen covered his eyes and said, his voice deep and mysterious, "Let me see—the mists are parting. Yes! Anstella will be here before the council meets." He went to the door and opened it.

Anstella of Colrane entered. Peridaen greeted her with a light kiss and shut the door again.

Althume chuckled. "Very good, my lord. Even *I* need a scrying bowl. You've missed your calling."

Peridaen grinned. "I'll leave the magery to you, Kas."

Anstella looked from one man to the other. "You two look uncommonly pleased with yourselves. It can't just be this little reprieve. Has something happened?"

"If we're right, you'll be pleased as well, my dear," Peridaen said, slipping his arm around her waist. "Kas?"

"Anstella, is there anything unusual about Sherrine? Aside from her extraordinary beauty," the mage said with a bow to the source of that same beauty.

Anstella acknowledged the compliment with a smile and a nod. "Such as?"

Althume shrugged. "A birthmark or some such thing."

A slight sneer curled Anstella's lip. "Why, yes, she has. A wine-red birthmark—like Linden Rathan's—on her lower back. So?"

Althume saw Peridaen smile. It was the smile of a hungry wolf. He knew his own matched it. "Just like Linden Rathan's, eh?"

Then Peridaen frowned, saying, "It may mean nothing; there are many people who have birthmarks like that and aren't Dragonlords. After all, the other two—their Markings don't match."

The mage interrupted, "But the Markings do, Peridaen. Think. They're both physical deformities. Maybe soultwins' Markings match up somehow." He slammed a fist into his palm. "There's so much we don't know about them, so much they keep hidden! Damn!"

His face cleared. "But if Markings do correspond, then that means Sherrine is the fledgling. And I'll wager anything they do. It would follow one of the Laws of Magic—that of Correspondence."

"What?" Anstella cried. Her face went white. "Sherrine—a Dragonlord?"

Peridaen laughed. "Indeed, my love. But I'm afraid your lovely daughter is about to lose her Dragonlord lover for a bit. In fact, I hope so. It will confirm what we suspect. But tell her not to grieve; it won't be for long."

"She'll have all of time to be with him," Althume said. "But don't tell her; not yet. That would complicate—"

"No!" Anstella shouted. "No! I don't believe it. It can't be true. You're lying." She looked wildly from one man to the other, her breast heaving.

Before Althume could speak, Peridaen took Anstella's hands in his own, holding them until they stopped shaking. There was a wild look in the eyes that stared up at the prince.

"We will not speak of this right now," Peridaen said gently. "We'll give you time to accustom yourself to this. And remember: this will help the Fraternity."

Althume watched tensely as long moments passed. Then, with a barely audible "For the Fraternity," Anstella was once more the self-assured Baroness of Colrane. Only her breathing, rapid and light, and the deathlike pallor of her face betrayed her now. "It can't be true," she said, but her voice was quiet now, if still tight and brittle. "You'll see. But let us speak of other things." Once more she looked to Peridaen, her eyes beseeching him.

"Kas," the prince said softly.

The mage nodded briskly. "If either of you can see a way to it, I need another delay in the council. A day or so if possible."

"Another?" Peridaen asked with a sigh, falling into the pretense that nothing was amiss. "Much more and the Dragonlords will notice something's in the wind, Kas."

"It can't be helped. The translation is difficult."

"What is it?" inquired Anstella, sounding almost like herself. She eased her hands from Peridaen's.

Althume smiled again. "A bit of this, a bit of that. And something that I hope is much more than an old tale."

Anstella tossed her head, once more the imperious baroness, and slid her arm through the prince's. "Not very helpful. But I've had Duriac working on Chardel for the past tenday, Peridaen. He said last evening that it would take very little more to goad the old fool into attacking him."

The mage nodded as the other two turned to leave. "Good. Tell him to save it for one of the actual council meetings. Might as well get the full benefit of it."

Peridaen paused in the doorway. "You mentioned Harn's brother before. Have you yet had any word from Pelnar from him?"

Althume said, "Not yet. The last from him was that Nethuryn has gone into hiding. Don't worry; Pol will hunt him the length and breadth of Pelnar if necessary. He'll bring us what we need."

Peridaen nodded; he and Anstella continued on their way.

As the door shut behind the two Cassorins, Althume locked his fingers together and stretched out his arms, cracking his knuckles with satisfaction. Yes, home to continue translating the only copy of Ankarlyn the Mage's grimoire known to have survived destruction by the Dragonlords. And to ponder the problem of Anstella, Baroness of Colrane.

Twenty-one

Somewhere beyond the high garden fence a nightingale sang. The night was hot and sticky, the heavy air filled with the scent of the roses that grew along the fence. A thin crescent of waxing moon, horns up, rode low in the sky. It wasn't enough for what Maurynna wanted.

She leaned over the edge of the well. Blackness thicker than the night lay below her. According to some of Otter's tales, if one caught the moon's reflection in water, tossed silver to it and wished, that wish would come true.

A coin lay in her hand. But try as she might, there was no angle from which Sister Moon's pale face rippled in the unseen water below her.

Ah, bother—it's likely for the best. With my luck that only works for Yerrins—those were Yerrin legends, after all—and I'd have just thrown away good money. Still—

She held out the coin. Before she could change her mind, she dropped it into the black opening. Long moments later she heard a soft, musical *plink* as it hit the water.

"That was silly," she said into the well.

Behind her a deep voice asked, "What was?"

Her heart jumped. She knew that voice. Before she could turn, strong arms caught her. She let him hold her, leaning back against her dockhand as he nuzzled her ear. Her hands came up to cover his.

Her fingers touched the ends of the sleeves covering his wrists. To her surprise, they were dagged. She found that odd; it was a style long out of fashion. Curious, she explored further, nearly gasping at the thick, nubby fabric under her questing fingers.

It was Neiranal mountain silk. Uncle Kesselandt had shown

her a bolt of it once, the only bolt he'd ever been able to buy. Produced in the mountains that the Dragonlords ruled, they were tithed most of it. Whatever extra there was, was usually snatched up by royalty and high-ranking nobility.

Her dockhand did well, then, despite being outcast. Or was he still in good standing with his clan and had been amusing himself by slumming? She hoped not; he'd likely think of her as no more than a distraction.

He laughed softly, his mouth against her ear. "If you only knew how I've been looking for you this day." His cheek rested against hers.

A warm glow filled her at his words. "And I looked for you. But what are you doing here? If my aunt knew that one of the dockhands—"

"Why should she object to another one?" He sounded puzzled. "You—"

So he was a dockhand after all. The knowledge relieved her. She pushed the question of how he could afford Neiranal silk from her mind.

She said, "I'm not one of the dock workers. I—I didn't want to say anything when I realized that you thought I was. I was afraid that you'd . . ." She was too embarrassed to finish.

"Shy off?" There was a wealth of understanding in his voice. "No, I wouldn't have. But if you're not a dockhand, then what are you? And what in blazes is your name, anyway?" His hand came up to stroke her cheek.

"Maurynna Erdon. I'm the captain of that—"

He shook with silent mirth, then laughed aloud. "Oh, gods! And here I was going to have Otter ask you to search for—yourself!" Still laughing softly, he nibbled at her ear.

Otter? How does he know Otter?

Confused, she tried to turn in his arms. His arms closed tighter, pinning her to his broad chest. She turned her head.

He kissed her—or as much of her mouth as could be reached. "You looked for me? Even though you're a ship's captain?" he asked.

"Yes," she admitted. "I did."

He was silent a moment. Another kiss, and he said, "I've something to confess as well, Maurynna."

The way he spoke her name was like a caress. She savored it.

He continued, "I'm not a dockhand either."

With that he released her, stepping back at the same time. As she turned she was blinded by a blaze of light. She blinked, wondering where he'd suddenly gotten a torch.

When she could see again she was amazed to see a small ball of fire hanging in the air between them. Tearing her gaze from this wonder, she stretched out her hand to him.

And stopped, gasping. He stood before her with a wry, wistful smile.

Though she had never seen them before, she knew the clothes he wore only too well. Hadn't Otter described them a hundred times or more?

Black tunic, breeches, and boots. A belt of linked silver plaques hung around his waist. Although he stood with his hands by his sides so that the silk lining of the wide dagged sleeves was hidden, she knew it would be the red of heart's blood. A band of silver embroidery, two fingers wide, trimmed the square-cut neck of his tunic.

"Are you mad?" she gasped, horrified. "That's the garb of a Dragonlord! If you're caught impersonating one, the gods only know what will happen to you!"

He smiled as his fingers came up to touch something around his neck: a heavy silver torc of rank. The ends were dragon-heads; their ruby eyes glittered in the light from the ball of fire.

She felt light-headed, as though she'd stood up too quickly from lying down. "Oh dear gods. That's coldfire, isn't it? You—you're . . ."

"Linden Rathan." He said quietly, "I apologize for the deception. But sometimes . . . Sometimes I want to be accepted for myself." A sudden wry smile. "I was afraid you might—shy off."

She came to herself then. "Your—Your Grace," she stammered. She plucked at her skirts to make him a courtesy.

"No!" He caught her hands. "Please—no," he said. "Not between us. Never between us."

He reversed his grip on her hands and brought them up so that they met behind his neck as he gently pulled her closer. Moving as if in a dream, Maurynna went to him. His arms went around her waist.

"And you must never call me 'Your Grace' again, Maurynna," he said. "Only by my first name."

She looked up at him, still unable to comprehend this was real. "Linden," she said. "Oh gods, I don't believe this."

He kissed her then. And again and again.

If she dreamed, she hoped she wouldn't wake for a long time—if ever.

But the strong, solid warmth of him was real. So was the dry voice that came out of the darkness.

"I see you two have already introduced yourselves," Otter said. "And I take it, Linden, that you've found your 'dockhand.'"

Twenty-two

I'm not sure I believe this, Otter said in Linden's mind. *It's just too much like a bard's tale.*

And you a bard, Linden replied, laughing silently. *Have you no faith? Those tales have to come from somewhere, after all. To think I sat through that wretched meeting and she was so close . . .*

He twined his fingers through Maurynna's. He knew he was grinning like an idiot, but he didn't care. To finally find his soultwin after so long without hope . . .

"You should go in and meet the rest of the family," Otter said. "It will set Maylin's mind at ease."

"What do you mean?" Maurynna asked as Linden said, "Who?"

"Maylin is Rynna's cousin." Otter folded his arms across his chest. "Almost as soon as I went in there looking for you, Rynna, she dragged me off to one side and demanded that I talk some sense into you. Seems she's very upset about some lowly dockhand you're mooning over—"

"Ot-*ter*!" Her tone was pure outrage.

Linden slid an arm around Maurynna's shoulders. "We should reassure her, then. But I think, Otter, that it might be a kindness to warn them first."

Otter's face lit in a mischievous grin. "I can't wait to see Maylin's face. She was rather . . . eloquent on the subject of dockhands who look above themselves."

Otter strolled off to the house, humming as he went. Linden turned to Maurynna. "We'll give him a bit of time, then go in. Do you think Maylin will mind now?" he teased as he rested his cheek against the top of her head.

"I don't think she'll believe this. I don't," Maurynna said, her voice shaking.

"Don't worry, love; you've time to get used to the idea." *Centuries' worth.*

Almost as soon as Otter walked back into the house Maylin pounced and dragged him into the front room.

"Well? Did you find her? And did you talk some sense into her?" she demanded. She eyed him suspiciously. "You weren't gone for very long. Certainly not long enough to argue with Rynna."

Before he could answer, Maylin's mother Elenna entered, Kella clinging to her skirts. "Talk what sense into Rynna? Maylin, what is happening? Your cousin has either had her head in the clouds or has been moping about as though she's lost a friend—or worse. And don't think I haven't seen you scowling at her, either."

Otter wondered how a woman who looked as much like a tiny bird as Elenna did could sound so stern. Seeing Maylin's dilemma—should she tattle on her cousin, or face her mother's anger—Otter decided the time had come to set the stage.

"Maylin is worried because Maurynna's suddenly become enamored of a dockhand she met. I daresay she went looking for him today, didn't she, Maylin?" the bard said. He ignored Maylin's hiss of outrage at his betrayal.

Elenna's eyebrows nearly disappeared into her grey-threaded brown curls. "Dockhand?" She turned her gaze upon her older daughter. "You knew of this and didn't tell me?"

Maylin set her lips in a stubborn line and glared at Otter.

"It so happens that her, ah, 'dockhand' was searching for her," Otter continued. "I brought him here and they found each other out in the garden." *Which is no more than the truth.*

"Otter," Elenna said, and her tone threatened to flay the hide from his back and salt the wounds, "you should know better than that. If word should get back to Kesselandt and the others, Maurynna could well face a great deal of trouble, even to losing her rank as captain. The Erdons are well above dalliances with common dockhands. I'd best have a word with the girl and send that upstart on his way.''

Otter stepped in front of Elenna and caught Maylin as she tried to get past him. ''Oh, but Elenna—this is a most uncommon dockhand. I think it would be well if you set out a bit of food—bread and cheese, that's homelike and he'll like that—and that fine ale you brew to make him welcome.''

Elenna eyed him. ''In-*deed*?''

Otter nodded, enjoying himself. ''My word as a bard on it. Come; I'll even help you and Maylin lay the table in the front room.''

As he helped Elenna and Maylin set out mugs of foaming ale and bread and cheese, Otter refused to answer their increasingly frustrated questions. ''You'll see,'' he said as he dodged Kella bearing a stack of plates in her arms.

But when he heard the door open, Otter relented. Best to warn them lest one of them faint from the surprise. ''The man Maurynna met while unloading her ship is no dockhand. He'd simply gone down to look at the ship I came in on. He was amused by her mistake and didn't tell her otherwise. He's Linden Rathan.''

''What!'' Elenna gasped, one hand flying to her mouth as the sound of boots could be heard in the hall.

Kella's mouth formed an *O* of surprise.

''It can't be!'' Maylin said in a fierce whisper. ''He's dallying with Lady Sherrine of Colrane!''

Now it was Otter's turn to be surprised—and concerned. ''What?'' he said in unconscious imitation of Elenna.

Maurynna's voice drifted in from the hall. ''I think they're in here; I heard voices.''

Maurynna appeared in the doorway. She glowed with happiness; Otter thought he'd never seen anything so beautiful. The look in her eyes caught at his heart and woke the beginnings of a song.

Linden looked in over her shoulder. ''You're the two I

wave to every day,'' he said, surprised, as he followed Maurynna in.

A small whirlwind flew past Otter. Linden bent and swept Kella up.

''Hello, kitten!'' the Dragonlord said in delight. ''I'm glad to finally meet you and your sister at last.''

Otter hung back. *It would sound too much like a herald announcing him if I introduce him. This way is better,* he thought as Linden greeted the women of the Vanadin family, laughing and informal, Kella perched on one arm. He smiled as he noticed how the Dragonlord's free hand found Maurynna's at every opportunity, even after they sat to eat.

The conversation, stiff at first, relaxed as the Vanadins accepted Linden as one of their own. They talked for many a candlemark. To Maylin's, ''How did you meet?'' Otter said, ''I found him camping during my journeyman's trek.''

Linden smothered a laugh. ''So you did, Otter—and none too pleased to share the space with a bumpkin, I remember. Give over, man, and stop denying it. It was all over your face that first night.''

''Gods help us, boyo, can you blame me for thinking that? More than six hundred years and you've still got that wretched mountain accent!'' Otter retorted. ''At least you were a good audience.''

''So I was. Lleld still wishes she could have seen your face when you found out, you know,'' said Linden.

''I can imagine,'' Otter said. ''She'd still be laughing.''

Maurynna asked, ''Who is Lleld?''

''Lleld,'' said Linden, ''is, as they would say in the mountains, 'a right little hellion' of a Dragonlord.''

Otter continued, ''She's little—as tall as a child of some ten years or so—and takes great, and perverse, delight in calling Linden 'little one.' ''

Maylin laughed. ''You? Little?''

''It's the traditional endearment for the youngest Dragonlord,'' Linden said. ''Lleld uses it every chance she gets.'' He turned to Maurynna and said gently, ''I'm enjoying this too much to leave, but leave I must. We all have business to attend to tomorrow, and I've kept all of you from your sleep for much too long."

Linden transferred the sleeping Kella from his lap to her mother's arms. Then he and Maurynna walked slowly into the hall. Otter stayed behind in tacit agreement with Elenna and Maylin.

Gods, but it must be hard. To find the other half of yourself at long last—and to turn away and leave her, even if it is only for the night, Otter thought as their footsteps retreated down the hall. He listened to the silence, broken occasionally by soft whispers, waiting for the sound of the door.

When he heard it, he reckoned the time he thought it would take Linden to mount up and ride a short distance. All around him the ladies of the Vanadin household talked excitedly. When he judged the time right, Otter "nudged" Linden.

Maylin said something that leads me to believe you're in the midst of a dalliance, boyo, he began when Linden mindspoke him, feeling his way delicately.

I was, but I was not the only man Sherrine was dallying with, so no harm done.

The answer sounded surprised but not angry. Heartened, Otter gathered his courage and plunged on.

So she was right about who, as well. Ah, boyo, there may be trouble of this.

More surprise and now consternation. *What do you mean? Do you know Sherrine?*

Otter remembered not to shake his head. *Not personally, but I know of her. Sherrine's a Colrane, and they're all fiercely proud. Gossip at court has it that she's had dalliances galore and boasts that no man has ever cast her aside.*

Meaning she's always been the one to end them? She and I spoke of this, Otter, and.I warned her she might not be the only one. She understood and accepted it. Indeed, and here Linden's mindvoice filled with chagrin, *she quite tartly pointed out that the same applied to her. As I said, she's been dallying with someone else as well all along. So I don't think there will be any trouble; stop worrying.*

Otter sighed. *I hope you're right, boyo; I truly hope you're right.*

Twenty-three

The old mage sat on a stool before the fire, stirring the pot bubbling on the hob. He brought the wooden spoon to his bearded lips and sipped carefully. The black-and-white cat wove a pattern between his ankles.

"It's done now, Merro," the old man said. "Needs a bit of salt, but it'll do."

"Mmrow," the cat answered.

Nethuryn stood up slowly, groaning at the stiffness in his joints and back. "Ah, Merro, Merro. I'm too old for this running. I think it's here we'll stay, my boy, come what may. We'll do well enough here, eh?"

The cat stretched up and danced snowy white forepaws against the old man's knee. "Mmm-row!"

"Patience, little greedy-guts." Running his fingers through his long white beard, Nethuryn muttered, "Where did I put those bowls? Ah! There they are."

He shuffled painfully across the room, fetched two wooden bowls from a shelf and went back to the simmering stew pot. He ladled some into a bowl—careful to equally divide the few bits of meat—and set it before the fire. Merro ran up and crouched before it, white paws tucked under himself, pink tongue lapping delicately.

"Careful now! It's hot. But there's naught like tender young coney in a stew, is there, my lad? Eat up."

Leaving the cat to enjoy his supper, Nethuryn filled the second bowl and carried it to the table. He broke off a chunk of the brown bread already there and sopped up some of the broth with it. He chewed slowly, examining by the glow of the single rushlight the one room of the cottage that was their new home.

"It's not what we're used to, is it, Merro-lad? But we should be safe here—we and *that*." He nodded at the small chest resting on the shelf with the only other pot, more bowls and a wooden dough trough flanking it on one side and a clay jug on the other. The word "spices" was crudely carved into its face.

Nethuryn tore his gaze from it. Perhaps he should have given it up when he first knew Kas wanted it. But he didn't trust young Kas. Oh, no; not at all. There was something about the coldness he remembered in his former student's eyes that made Nethuryn's flesh creep.

Too old, too slow now. My magics are nearly gone. If only I had never revealed to Kas that I had the cursed thing. But what's done is done and it should be well hidden here, he told himself as he ate his stew. *And Merro and I are warm and comfortable.*

For the first time in tendays he let himself relax. The little cottage *was* comfortable, the stew before him rich and savory with herbs from the garden, and Merro had the woods around to hunt in. They would do well enough.

Nethuryn drank the last drop of broth from the bowl and sat tired but content, watching the cat clean his whiskers. He fell into the light doze of the very old.

A crash of thunder and a terrified yowl from Merro brought him awake. Nethuryn struggled to his feet, confused and frightened. A storm? But there had been no sign of a storm earlier.

A second crash. It took Nethuryn precious moments before he realized that what he'd taken for thunder was the sound of the door being kicked open. He raised his hands to begin a spell, but it was too late. The door flew open, its latch shattered. A man filled the opening. Something in the man's hand flashed in the fire's light, then streaked through the air.

Nethuryn fell back into the chair, fingers clutched around the throwing dagger buried to the hilt between his ribs. Recognizing the man, he gasped, "Pol—Kas couldn't have told you to—" He still didn't want to believe the worst.

"Be quiet, old fool. You shouldn't have made me hunt you

down,'' the stocky man snarled. But the feral glee in his eyes told Nethuryn that Kas Althume's servant had enjoyed the chase—and lusted for the kill.

The knife a fire in his chest, Nethuryn could only watch helplessly as Pol ransacked his meager belongings. The man tore the bed apart first, then wrenched the door from the clothes cupboard with a powerful heave. Nethuryn fought for the strength to form a spell, but neither hands nor voice obeyed him. Indeed, it was all he could do to breathe now. Merro pressed against him, mewling piteously.

Pol worked a methodical way through the room; Nethuryn suspected he enjoyed the destruction he wrought. He even tore out whatever walls he could, seeking a hiding place behind them.

At last Nethuryn managed to gasp, ''Not here. Buried it.''

Pol sneered. ''The hell you did, old man. You would never have given it up so easily. You should have, long ago, when your magic first began to fail. Now where is it?''

Nethuryn whimpered, as much against the pain of the truth as that of the knife. He was dying; he knew it. There were many things he was sorry for in his long life and creating what lay in the little chest was not the least of them. He'd been a fool. He should have destroyed it or given it into the keeping of a more powerful mage whom he trusted. Yet how to give up what had cost him so much pain and toil? But perhaps—just perhaps—if he kept silent until the end, Pol would think he really had gotten rid of the thing and would go—

The sight of Kas Althume's minion standing before the shelf filled with the homely kitchenware wrung an involuntary protest from Nethuryn.

Pol looked over one burly shoulder and smiled. ''Am I, then, 'hot' as they say in the children's game?'' he mocked. ''Why, Nethuryn, I believe I am. Look how your eyes are starting from your head—or is that just death? But clever, old man, to hide it in the open like this. Had you not squealed like a pricked pig, I should have wasted more time seeking for it in a hundred secret places—for it is in here, isn't it? Ah, I thought so.''

Big hands closed over the crude little chest; Nethuryn stretched out his own hand. ''No—please. Kas doesn't understand how danger—''

Pol turned swiftly and slapped the hand aside. ''Fool; my lord understands more than you ever did. He knows what power is and how to take it—as I take this.'' He stood, thick legs apart, and opened the chest.

Through the rushing in his ears, Nethuryn heard him murmur, ''Who'd have thought the old bastard so clever?'' as Pol tossed packets of spices to the floor. Then a deep ''Ah!'' of pleasure and the assassin lifted something the size of a large apple from the chest.

Nethuryn stared at the jewel that Pol held aloft. It drank in the flickering light from the fire and let it fall dripping to the floor in icy blue flashes. Nethuryn grew colder as the light in the stone waxed brighter. Merro fled yowling into the night.

''Of course—it's feeding on you, isn't it, Nethuryn? You're dying so it's drinking your soul. How kind of you, old man.''

Pol turned the glittering stone from side to side, admiring it. ''My master will be well pleased indeed. A soultrap jewel already charged with the soul of one who opposed him.''

Nethuryn's dimming gaze followed the jewel's shining path. Its light filled his eyes. He saw the jewel blaze in final triumph, despaired, and died.

Twenty-four

Maylin stumbled bleary-eyed down the stairs early the next morning. Only long familiarity with her route kept her from falling.

Tea. She needed a mug of good, strong tea. That was the only way to cope with two candlemarks' worth of sleep. *I wonder if Maurynna ever got any. I certainly wouldn't have.* She yawned as she stepped off the bottom step and swung one-handed around the newel post. Her bare feet slid against the stone tiles as she shuffled down the hall to the kitchen.

She cocked her head as she passed the office and heard voices. *Good gods! 'Prentices who don't have to be rousted out of bed? What are we coming to?* she thought with drowsy amusement.

A quiet, deep-voiced laugh banished all thoughts of tea from her mind. *That's not an apprentice!* She gathered up her nightgown, spun on one heel, and ran back to the office. The door was slightly ajar. Gingerly pushing it open a little farther, she peeked around the edge.

Maurynna and Linden Rathan stood with their arms around each other. He was saying, "It can be done, then? You won't mind the sail?"

Maurynna answered, "It's an easy one; I don't think my crew will mind at all. Let me think a moment. . . . Hm, the tide should be right two mornings from now to—"

The door swung farther open under Maylin's hand—which she had not meant it to do. Not at all. She stood revealed in the doorway, wishing the earth would open up beneath her.

Maurynna and Linden Rathan jumped apart, but relaxed when they saw it was her. The Dragonlord slid an arm around Maurynna's shoulders. He was also, Maylin saw to complete her humiliation, trying to hide a smile. Maurynna just looked surprised.

"Your—Your G-Grace," Maylin stuttered. "I'm sorry; I didn't mean to—" A sudden revelation struck her dumb. *How* right *they look together.*

"No harm done, Maylin," Linden Rathan said. "But there is one thing I wish to make clear right now—"

Maylin braced herself for a well-earned tongue-lashing.

"There's no need for such formality. It makes me uncomfortable. Please, may we dispense with the titles? They'll be awkward—especially on the picnic."

Baffled, Maylin echoed, "Picnic?"

He had, part of her bemused mind noted, an utterly wicked little-boy grin. "Yes. We're all going on a picnic: Otter, Maurynna and I, you, Kella—and Prince Rann."

Linden arrived at the palace well before the day's council session was to begin. One of the servants met him as he crossed the great hall.

"Your Grace," she said. "You're here very early today. Is there anything you wish?"

"Will Duchess Alinya be awake yet?" he asked.

"Yes, my lord. She usually rises early and breaks her fast in her chambers. Do you wish to be escorted there?"

"Yes." A sudden thought struck Linden. "And please send someone to ask Healer Tasha to attend us in the Duchess's chambers."

A short while later he was following the servant through the maze that was the palace of Casna.

"Get back on board with you and that crew of lunatics? What was that you said to me once—'I may be mad but I'm not stupid'?"

Maurynna couldn't help laughing at the expression on the bard's face. "Otter, it will be perfectly calm weather—I promise you. If not, we won't go. It's as simple as that."

Otter crossed his arms over his chest. "No."

"But you must go. It won't be any fun without you."

That drew a derisive snort from the bard. "As if you'll notice whether I'm there or not as long as Linden is."

She hoped her face wasn't as red as it felt. "Prince Rann will be disappointed. Linden told me he was so excited when he heard you were coming to Casna and might sing for him."

She watched Otter visibly waver at the appeal to his professional pride. At last the bard said, "Oh, very well. But only because I'd hate to disappoint the boy."

Linden nibbled a seedcake and politely ignored Duchess Alinya and Healer Tasha as, their heads close together, they discussed his proposal. It wasn't easy because of his acute hearing, but on the whole he managed with only catching a word or two.

At first both women looked doubtful. Then he heard "sunshine" and "do him good." Alinya looked thoughtful at that, but not convinced. "Sea air" came next, but even that was not enough to sway the duchess.

Linden grew nervous. What if Alinya refused? While he outranked her and could force the issue if he wanted, it would not be politic.

Then Tasha whispered something that settled the debate. Alinya said, "Very well, then, but only under that condition. And let it be a surprise, else the child will make himself sick with excitement."

The women turned back to him. "Dragonlord," Healer Tasha said, "we have decided that this would be of great benefit to Prince Rann. There is, however, one condition: I go as well."

Thank the gods. "Healer Tasha, if you hadn't suggested it, I would have insisted upon it. Welcome to our picnic."

Maylin stopped on the corner, going over in her mind what else she needed to shop for and wondering when she'd wake from this mad dream. Dragonlords and orphaned princes, indeed! Once again she reminded herself it was quite real.

And her shopping was almost done. She looked into her basket. The bulk of her purchases would be delivered the night before the picnic. The basket held only a few special things that she didn't trust anyone else to pick out for her: the two little crocks of honey, lemon balm and rose, so tasty with bread; a hard little loaf of the whitest sugar she could find; a whole nutmeg; the small parchment packets of cinnamon and cloves, even pepper and saffron. She winced at the cost of the last two; she had bargained the spice merchant to a fare-thee-well, but the price still offended her frugal merchant soul—even if she spent Linden's money and not her own.

Linden. It felt odd to call him that, even in her own mind. She turned her attention back to the contents of the basket. There was, she decided, still enough room for one last little thing. But what?

"Maylin!"

Maylin looked around at the sound of her cousin's voice. She had no trouble spotting Maurynna above the mostly Cassorin passers-by. "Hello—have you spoken with your crew already?" she called as the taller girl worked her way through the crowd.

"Yes," Maurynna said when they stood together. "They're curious as cats, too. Every last one of 'em volunteered to go. I didn't tell them much, just enough to whet their appetites, else the word would go out through the taverns and we'd have half of Casna at the dock to see the fun. I'm glad I met you. If you're finished, we can walk home together after I give my family's greetings to Almered."

Maylin snapped her fingers. "That's it! Candied ginger."

Maurynna scratched her head. "Candied? . . . "

"Never mind. I'd forgotten the Assantikkan quarter was near here." Maylin shifted the basket to her other arm. "Almered has candied ginger. I want to see his silks, as well. Mother promised Kella her first silk gown for the Winter Solstice celebrations if Father's trip went well, and Almered has some of the best silk I've seen. Shall we?"

"You say it's as if we never told her?" Althume said as he slipped the chain with the amethyst pendant over Peridaen's head.

"Just so. If I mention it, it's as if she hasn't heard me," the prince said. A worried frown creased his brow. "I've seen her do something like this before, but never to this degree. It scares the hell out of me, Kas."

The mage considered Peridaen's words. "It is odd—but I've seen its like before as well. Don't force her to admit it, Peridaen. This may be the best thing."

Peridaen fingered the jewel hanging around his neck. "I hate to say it, but . . . I think you're right. Otherwise—" He abruptly cleared his throat. "Damn, I'm going to be late for that council meeting."

"You wished to see me, Anstella?" Lord Duriac asked.

Anstella looked up from the ivory lucet she held in her hands. As Duriac joined her on the marble garden bench, she carefully wrapped the silken cord she was weaving around the horns of the lyre-shaped tool and stowed it and the ball of thread in an embroidered pouch at her belt.

"I did," she said. "A delay is needed. Goad Chardel to the breaking point today."

"In the council?" Duriac asked in some surprise.

"Where better? And talk to the others; see that they're ready to join in."

"It's not much more than a candlemark until the council meets," Duriac objected. "That doesn't give me much time."

Anstella shrugged. "That is not my concern. I have told you what is needed and I expect it to be done." She stood up and smoothed her skirts. "Now go; there's not much time and I have other things to do."

I found her! Linden exulted to the other Dragonlords as they entered the room ahead of the members of the council.

Thank the gods, came the heartfelt chorus. *How?* Kief asked. *What is her name?* Tarlna demanded.

She isn't a dockhand after all. She's the captain of the ship. Her name is Maurynna Erdon and I met her when Otter brought me to her family's house. We'd thought to enlist her help since she knows the waterfront.

Oh, what a tangle, Tarlna said, a laugh behind the words.

Linden nodded. *Worse than a bard's tale. There's a favor I need to ask, but before I do, let me say that I have Duchess Alinya's and Healer Tasha's approval for this.* He quickly outlined his plan to them. *So I'd like to cancel the council meeting for that day.*

Kief frowned at that. But all he said was, *We'll see, Linden. We'll see.*

Although he was Assantikkan and did business in the Assantikkan quarter, Almered al zef Bakkuran had a shop in the Cassorin style rather than an open stall in the bazaar. It was a large shop, a treasure chest of an amazing variety of goods, and smelled wonderful.

Maurynna loved to visit it whenever she was in port. As she and Maylin entered the open door, she called out, "Greetings, cousin," in Assantikkan.

At first she thought the place empty. Then the tall, rangy figure of Almered rose from behind a counter. His dark face lit with delight. "Maurynna! I am so glad to see you!"

He came around the counter, hands outstretched to her, the amulets and beads in his long braids clicking together. She took his hands and they kissed first one cheek, then the other in the traditional greeting.

"You look wonderful, my dear. And what are these? You have made captain since the last time you were here? O, luck, luck, indeed! You must come to Pakkasan's *tisrahn*. And Maylin! I almost didn't see you behind Maurynna. You must come as well, and your father and mother if they are able to. Let me fetch Falissa; she will want to see both of you."

Before they could get a word in Almered disappeared behind the embroidered hangings at the back of the shop.

"Whew!" Maylin said. "Quickly, before he gets back: what's a *tisrahn* and what did you say when we came in?"

Maurynna said in an undertone, "A *tisrahn* is a coming-of-age ceremony in Assantik. They're huge feasts that are meant to bring luck and acknowledge the youngster's new status as an adult. This one's for his nephew. It's an honor to be invited to one. Guests are often chosen for the 'luck' they can bring.

"I greeted him as a cousin. It's the usual greeting for people you know well, though there might be truth to it for the two of us. Remember, one of my great-something grandmothers was Assantikkan and our Houses have been allied for many, many years. Hm—I wonder . . ." she said as Almered returned with his wife.

When the second round of greetings was over and the small talk out of the way, Maurynna said, "Almered, I know that this is not the way it is usually done, but—There are two friends of mine who would enjoy seeing a *tisrahn*. One is a bard—"

"Bards are lucky," Almered murmured. "Very lucky. Of course he is welcome. Doubly so since he is a friend of yours. And the other?"

"The other." Maurynna cleared her throat, suddenly embarrassed. "Ah, well, the other . . ."

Almered and Falissa exchanged knowing glances.

"Soooo—this other one is someone very special to you, then, Maurynna?" Almered said with a sly wink. "May we meet him before the *tisrahn*?"

"Stop it," Falissa ordered. "You are making the girl blush."

Maurynna ignored Maylin sniggering behind her hand by the wall where the bolts of silk were displayed. Revenging herself for the amused innuendo of Almered's tone, Maurynna said, "Let me say this about him: he may well be the greatest bringer of luck to ever attend a *tisrahn*."

She almost laughed aloud to see her "cousin" eaten alive with curiosity. "And yes, if I can I shall bring him here before then so that you may see for yourself. Maylin, do you still want that candied ginger?"

Tempers were running high throughout the council chamber this day. Linden shifted uneasily in his seat, trying to watch everyone at the same time. A dozen petty squabbles had broken out at once and every one of them threatened to explode.

Kief swore aloud in disgust and stood. Those nearest him gasped; Linden swiveled around to stare at him in surprise. He'd never known the slender Dragonlord to lose his temper so publicly.

It happened the moment he took his eyes off the council. In that instant one argument spilled over into physical violence. He looked back to find Lords Duriac and Chardel exchanging blows, falling over other members of the council, intent by all appearances on killing each other. Linden bellowed, "Enough!"

While it didn't halt the fight in progress, it was enough to stop any others from joining in. Linden pushed a way through the paralyzed councilors and seized each man by the neck of his tunic. He yanked them apart so hard he heard their jaws snap shut, then held them dangling above the ground.

"He struck me first!" Duriac sputtered.

The fire in Chardel's eye was in no way dimmed because there was a good foot of air below his feet. "You greasy little pimple. You've been at me this past tenday or more—don't think you didn't deserve this."

"That will be quite enough, my lords," Linden growled, looking from one to the other. "Do you understand me?"

Both men mumbled something that Linden took as agreement. He set them down none too gently.

In the sudden silence that followed, Kief spoke. His voice shook with suppressed anger and disgust. "I have sat in judgement, my lords and ladies, at least half a dozen times in my long life. And never—*never!*—have I been witness to such an unseemly display as this. Did I wish to see brawling, I would go to the worst tavern I could find—not here.

"I hereby adjourn this meeting; we will not meet again until four days from now, to give tempers a chance to cool. If this should happen again, I will have the offenders removed from these sessions—permanently. I am not jesting. I have that right and I will invoke it. Think well upon that." He stared stony-faced at the Cassorin nobles who filed past him like chastened schoolchildren as they left the room.

Linden watched from the side of the room, neither moving

nor speaking, legs braced wide, arms folded across his chest. He'd wanted the holiday, but he'd not wanted it to come this way. He waited until the last truehuman had left before he joined his fellow Dragonlords.

"I don't understand," Kief was saying to Tarlna. "I've never had anything like this happen before. You'd think between all the foot-dragging in this council, and now this, that the very gods were against us finding a solution."

"Or at least a quick one," Linden said without thinking. And wondered where the thought came from.

Twenty-five

Hooves clattered on the cobblestones outside, shattering his concentration; Althume looked up from the grimoire in front of him and listened. Though he could not make out any words, he thought he could recognize Prince Peridaen's voice. He shut the ancient leather-bound tome and waited.

Soon enough he heard laughing voices approach the study. *Something went right, by the sound of it, and about time.* The mage laced his fingers together and stretched his arms out, cracking his knuckles.

Peridaen and Anstella burst into the room without ceremony. "Oh, the look in Chardel's eye," Anstella said, trying to catch her breath. "Duriac is lucky indeed the old war dog didn't have a dagger with him."

Peridaen slipped an arm around her shoulders. "Kas, you have more time. Four days' worth, in fact, courtesy of Duriac's acid tongue—and Chardel's temper."

Althume smiled fiercely. "Excellent! Excellent!"

"There should have been even more fights—Duriac had spoken with the others," Anstella complained, "but when Linden Rathan yelled 'Enough!' it took the heart out of them. I've never seen him so angry. Luckily, the one fight did the trick. But I shall still have words with them." The fire in her eyes boded ill for someone.

The mage made a small noise of contempt. He had no use for snivelers who were so easily cowed. Couldn't the fools see the Yerrin Dragonlord was nothing more than one of those big soft men, more brawn than brain, who could be twisted around the finger of a clever girl like Sherrine? Bah. No wonder the Fraternity hadn't succeeded before this.

"But it's not a gambit we can use again," Peridaen said.

"Kief Shaeldar has threatened to remove any future transgressors from the deliberations on the regency. While it would also remove some of Beren's supporters, we don't have enough of our own to lose them that way. We need them to sway uncommitted councilors to our side. But still, it's four days' grace."

"It's a beginning. We'll get more time as we need it." Althume ran his long, thin fingers over the grimoire before him. "If this continues as it promises to, we'll be able to offer our Dragonlord guests a most . . . interesting visit."

Twenty-six

The first rays of the rising sun came through the window and spread fingers of light on the tiled floor and across the foot of the bed. A toy soldier, standing guard in its nest formed by the blanket tossed aside in the night, basked in the new day's warmth. The door to the sleeping chamber opened and a slender figure slipped in. The wolfhound on the floor by the bed raised its head but bayed no alarm. His tail thumped the floor.

The young woman carried a small dosing bottle in her hand. Going to the open window, she emptied its contents into the rain gutter below. Then, with a swiftness born of long practice, she extracted a flask from its hiding place in the clothes cupboard and filled the bottle once more, wrinkling her nose at the faint sour, mousey smell. Some of the potions didn't smell so bad, but this one! Unfortunately, it was also the usual one. She shook the flask gently before replacing it.

Nearly empty. I shall have to ask the steward for more. I wonder what's in it—but I daresay it's safer not to ask. Enough to know that it pays me well. And enough to know that it's not a poison.

She went to the bed, nudging the dog aside with a foot. The dog heaved itself to its feet and lumbered to one side.

"That's a good boy, Bramble," the young woman whispered as she sat on the edge of the featherbed and gently shook the thin shoulder that was all she could see above the sheet. "Rann? Rann, dear—time to wake up and take your tonic."

A querulous, sleepy grumble was her only answer. She laughed softly and slipped an arm around his shoulders and eased the boy up.

Rann blinked up at her, rubbing the sleep from his eyes. "Don't want to, Gevvy," he complained. "It tastes awful."

"That's how you know a medicine's good," Gevianna replied firmly. "The worse they taste the better they are. Come now; wake up a bit more and drink it down. I'll make sure there's extra honey for your porridge if—"

The sound of voices and the door opening in the outer room cut her off. Rann came instantly awake, bouncing onto his knees on the bed next to her. Gevianna gripped the small flask in suddenly trembling fingers. She recognized the voices.

So did Rann. "Healer Tasha!" he called. "What are you doing here?"

The door to the sleeping chamber opened and Healer Tasha poked her head around it. "Up already, Prince Rann? Good. Ah, Gevianna—has he had his tonic yet?"

Gevianna licked dry lips and shook her head. She didn't trust her voice.

"Good—very good. I don't think it would go well with what I have for him today," Healer Tasha said as she entered, bearing a steaming mug in her hands. Her two senior apprentices followed her.

"What's that?" Rann asked suspiciously.

Gevianna gathered her wits as the Healer approached the bed. She stood up and moved out of the way. Feigning a nonchalance that she didn't feel, the young nurse set the dosing bottle on a nearby table as if it had no importance. To her relief neither Healer nor apprentices took any notice.

Healer Tasha said, "This, my fine young lad, is a sovereign remedy against seasickness. It's ginger tea."

"Seasickness?" Rann stared at the mug. "Am I to go on one of the barges today?" He sounded half sick with fright.

Gevianna's stomach turned. Was the boy to go the way of his mother, then? It was one thing to give him a potion to keep him quiet, but this was murder.

And she would be expected to go with him. She who was even more terrified of water than the young prince was. She clamped a hand over her mouth.

She couldn't let it happen. She didn't want to die. Even if

it meant the ruin of her family, she couldn't let them kill her and the boy like that. Oh, gods, she would have to tell them. She would have to tell them everything . . . The thought made her ill.

Healer Tasha sat on the bed by Rann and hugged him one-armed, balancing the mug in the other hand. "No, love, no one expects that. This is a proper ship, with a real captain and crew. It's a surprise Dragonlord Linden Rathan thought of for you. He went through a great deal of trouble to arrange it, so I hope you will go."

Rann's eyes were huge in his thin face. "He did? And it's a real ship? Will it have sails and banners?"

The further his spirits rose the deeper Gevianna's sank. The thought of going out onto the river was bad enough, but the sea! She leaned on the table for support and squeezed her eyes shut.

"It will certainly have sails, and I imagine it will have— Gevianna! Girl, what ails you? You look about to faint."

Gevianna opened her eyes to find Healer Tasha peering intently into her face. She moved her lips, but no sound came out. She'd come so close to ruining everything and for nothing. . . .

"You're white as salt, child," Healer Tasha said. "Let me guess—you're terrified of sailing, aren't you? Ah, well—it's not as much of a problem as it might be otherwise. You'll just stay here. I will be with Rann and—"

A fear stronger than that of the bottomless sea tore through Gevianna. "Oh, no! I must go with Prince Rann."

Gods help her if she didn't go along to spy on whatever surprise the Dragonlord had thought of. She had no wish to explain how she'd been left behind to either Baroness Colrane or—worse yet—the prince's cold-eyed steward from whose hand came the potions nowadays.

"Drink the tea now, Rann; it must be cool enough," Healer Tasha said over her shoulder. Gevianna saw him take a cautious sip then drink eagerly. Then the Healer's full attention was back on her.

Through the buzzing in her ears Gevianna heard Healer Tasha say, "No. You will not come with us. I forbid it. I already have Rann to look after; I won't have the time for another patient. Nor will the ship's crew. Rann will be well taken care of today, Gevianna. You've nothing to worry about. I prescribe a day of rest for you and an infusion of lemon balm for your nerves."

Turning to her apprentices, the Healer continued, "Quirel, Jeralin—you two are in charge while I'm gone. I want one of you to look in on Gevianna later today, is that understood? If she is no better, add hops and skullcap to the lemon balm for another infusion."

The apprentices nodded. Then one—Quirel—pointed to the table behind Gevianna. "Shouldn't we take that with us, Healer? It wouldn't do to have someone else drink it by accident."

Gevianna clenched her skirts to keep from slapping the Healer's hand away as the older woman reached for the flask. What if the Healer or one of her apprentices opened the thing? One sniff would tell them it was not the original tonic. What would happen to her then? She thought she'd go mad with terror.

But Healer Tasha merely handed the flask to Quirel, who tucked it into the basket he carried. She said, "Leave it in the workroom."

Gevianna gasped, suddenly realizing she'd forgotten to breathe. Healer Tasha gave her a queer look.

"Help me get Rann dressed, Gevianna, then take to your bed. Quirel, make up that infusion with the hops now. Add a little syrup of poppy to it."

She had to watch as, a short time later, an excited Rann bounced out of the room with Healer Tasha. When she tried to follow, Jeralin caught her and Quirel forced a mug into her hands. They made her drink while she fought a battle with her stomach to keep it down. Defeated, she handed the empty mug back, already feeling the soporific effect of the hops and poppy.

She did not struggle as Jeralin led her to her little room to one side of Prince Rann's chambers. She only prayed that Baroness Colrane would understand. And that Healer Tasha never opened the flask.

Twenty-seven

Linden waited at the bottom of the old garden. The gelding pranced under him; he quieted it without thinking, looking to see if Healer Tasha and Prince Rann were coming yet. The two guards with him sat their stolid beasts in silence. One held the reins of a fourth horse.

One moment the garden was empty; the next Rann appeared around the corner of a hedge, towing the ginger-haired Healer along behind him. He pulled free and ran to Linden. "Dragonlord! Do you truly have a surprise for me?"

Linden leaned down and caught Rann's hands as the boy jumped. He swung the child up to sit on the horse behind him. Small fingers dug into his belt. "I do, Your Highness. Do you fancy a picnic today?"

One of the soldiers helped Tasha onto the spare horse.

Rann, sounding a little confused, said, "I thought I was going for a sail."

Linden led the way out of the gardens and through the little-used postern gate that Duchess Alinya had told him about. "You are; the picnic is on a beach that I found when I was in dragon form. I thought of you when I saw it."

The thin arms hugged him. "You did? Truly? And you'll be sailing with us?"

Linden smiled. "Truly. I will meet you at the beach itself, though I will sail back with you. I've something else to do first. Healer Tasha will take you to the ship. It's called the *Sea Mist* and the captain is . . . a friend of mine. Her name is Maurynna Erdon. You must promise me that you'll listen to whatever she or her crew tells you when you are on board the ship."

"But I'm a prince," Rann said.

"You are a prince here in Cassori," said Linden. "But on board a ship the captain is the ruler. And the crew know more than you do, so you'll listen to them as well. If Captain Erdon told me to do something, I'd do it right sharply, my lad. At sea she would outrank me."

He let Rann digest that bit of information as they rode through the waking city. "Promise?" Linden asked when they reached the small green near the merchants' quarter.

"I promise."

"Good. This is where I leave you. Corrise comes with me; I've a job for her. Will you ride with Healer Tasha or Captain Jerrell?"

Even Tasha laughed as Rann lunged for the guardsman. When Rann was settled in his new perch, Linden backed his horse away, Corrise following.

"But Dragonlord—aren't you coming on the picnic?" Rann called as they rode away. His voice trembled.

"Yes, but remember—you'll need a guide." Linden winked at the puzzled boy. He brought the gelding around in a prancing pirouette and set off at a canter, the young guard following.

Maurynna paced the dock before the gangplank. Now and again she cast an expert glance at the water. Her last passengers had best come soon; the tide had turned and was running out to sea. Master Remon lolled on a nearby stanchion, splicing a bit of rope as he waited.

"Captain," said he, "you said you don't know where this beach is?"

"That's right. I just know it's well east of Casna. But don't worry, Remon; we'll have a guide."

"But who, Rynna?" Maylin called from the deck. "None of us has ever been there."

Maurynna shrugged. Before she had to answer she heard the sound of horses approaching. She went to meet them.

Two riders trotted between the warehouses and onto the dock. The first was a soldier, the second a woman Maurynna guessed to be in her forties. The woman looked tired as though from long worry, but smiled when she saw the ship. For a moment Maurynna wondered where the prince was, then noticed the thin arms clasped about the soldier's middle. The woman stopped her horse and dismounted.

"Healer Tasha?" Maurynna asked.

The woman nodded as she went to the soldier's horse and helped the little boy down. "The same. You are Captain Erdon? Then, Captain, may I present His Royal Highness, Prince Rann."

Maurynna went down on one knee to inspect the child for whom Linden had made such plans. He was smaller than Kella, even though she guessed they were the same age, and frail. His brick-red hair hung in bangs over eyes that watched her warily.

"Your Highness," she said, "I'm very pleased to meet you. Linden spoke fondly of you." *Poor little mite; there's hardly anything to him. Some good salt air will be just the thing.*

The big brown eyes blinked slowly, once, twice. "You're the captain, aren't you? Linden Rathan said that I'm to listen to whatever you tell me. He made me promise."

Maurynna silently blessed Linden for his foresight.

Another blink. "You called him Linden, not Dragonlord or Linden Rathan."

Maurynna nodded solemnly. "I have his permission, Prince Rann, as do my cousins and Bard Otter Heronson."

Prince Rann's gaze dropped to study his toe digging into the dock. "Then please call me Rann."

Why, I believe he wants to be as much like Linden as he can. "Thank you, Rann. And we must board now; the tide is turning. Come meet my cousins—Kella's just your age."

Rann dashed up the gangplank. Maurynna gestured Healer Tasha to precede her, then strode onto the deck, eager to feel her ship come alive beneath her feet again.

Time to begin their adventure. "Cast off! Take her out to sea for us, Master Remon."

* * *

They were free of the Uildodd and standing out to sea when the questions began.

"What are we doing, Captain? Why are we stopping here?"

Maurynna turned from giving her orders to find Healer Tasha and Rann standing behind her. The little boy gazed up at her, waiting for an answer.

Master Remon called down from the quarterdeck, "The lad's got a good question, Captain. And where's this guide you promised us?"

"You'll see, Remon. This is called 'standing by,' Rann; we turn the *Sea Mist*'s bow into the waves, lower our sails, and toss out our grapnel anchor—it's shallow enough here. As for why, everyone, we're waiting for our guide who will join us out here."

The first mate scanned the horizon. "No other ships in sight, Captain. Are you certain of this?"

"Very, Master Remon. Linden Rathan promised us one. You'll see." And she would say no more to their questions as they waited.

Duke Beren couldn't believe his ears. "Rann is *where*, Alinya?" he exploded.

The old duchess looked up from her embroidery. She stared at him for a long, frozen moment. "Do not take that tone with me, young man. You heard what I said: Rann is at this moment on board a ship and on his way to a picnic. It was a surprise arranged by Linden Rathan for him."

"What do you know about these people you've entrusted Rann to?" Beren asked. "And where did they go to that they needed a ship?"

"A beach somewhere to the east, Linden Rathan said, that was too far for Rann to ride to. As for 'these people,' Linden Rathan knows and trusts them. Surely you do not suspect a Dragonlord of ill intentions?"

Beren said grimly, "Who went with the boy?" *Not Beryl, that much is certain. She'd have found a way to get word to me. That sly piece of goods Gevianna must be with him. Dam-*

nation! I'm certain the girl's in Peridaen's pay. If only I could prove it. Peridaen. Oh, gods. Did Peridaen go? The boy's certain to have an "accident" if so.

Instead of answering, Alinya said coldly, "Beren—just what is the meaning of these ill-mannered questions?"

He knew that glare; he'd get no more answers from her. With a brevity bordering on rudeness, Beren made his farewell.

He met Tev outside of the old duchess's chambers where the captain had been waiting for him. The man saluted and said, "My lord?"

"Gather your men, Tev. We ride to the hunt." *And may there be a quarry at the end of it.*

Twenty-eight

"Gods help us! Look up! Look up!" the sailor in the crow's nest shouted, pointing into the sun.

Maurynna caught Otter's eye and grinned. Although she knew what to expect, she looked up into the sky like everyone else, shading her dazzled eyes against the glare of the sun. The arching blueness was empty.

Then she saw him.

A huge red dragon dove at the *Sea Mist* like an arrow out of the blazing sun. The circling gulls made way, screaming their indignation as they hastily retreated.

Cries of mingled surprise, fear, and delight rose from the deck of the *Sea Mist*. Kella and Rann shrieked in excitement and the sailors cheered as they realized who the dragon was. Closer and closer he came, wings spread wide, his scales glittering like rubies.

For one terrifying instant Maurynna thought that Linden had misjudged his flight. But a heartbeat short of crashing into the ship he veered up, skimming over the top of the masts. The Erdon banners snapped out straight as he passed. Those who had thrown themselves to the deck stood up again, sheepishly fending off the good-natured teasing of the others.

"Show-off," Otter muttered.

Maurynna laughed in sheer delight. Let Linden show off; she could watch him all day, every day. She'd never dreamed of anything so beautiful. He turned and circled the ship. Everyone, passenger and crew alike, watched him, entranced.

A stray thought popped into her mind. She said to Otter, "Raven will be furious when I tell him about this."

Otter laughed. "He'll never forgive his father for sending him to fetch that wool from the highlands!" He rubbed his beard. "Poor Raven. Poor us when we tell him."

She watched Linden balance on the winds more gracefully than any albatross she'd ever seen. Then he sideslipped through the air and veered east. Maurynna sang out, "Hoist sail! Dragon ho!"

The spell was broken. "Dragon ho!" the crew echoed, laughing. Some of the sailors swarmed up the rigging; others pulled up the anchors holding the ship steady in the waves. The sails bellied out in the gentle wind and the *Sea Mist* rode the waves once more. As the ship got under way, Linden flew slowly along the coast.

Maurynna had never seen her crew work so eagerly. Even the *Sea Mist* seemed to know something wonderful was happening; the small ship took the waves as lightly as a dolphin, joyous and free, alive with the magic of having a dragon for a guide. Any moment now they would sail into a bard's song where brave warriors and enchanted castles awaited them. She knew they would all treasure this voyage—short as it would be—for the rest of their lives.

Near to bursting with happiness, she took Rann's hand and said to the others, "Shall we watch from the bow?"

"Good idea," Otter said, and took Rann's other hand. Together they helped the young prince walk the rolling deck. Tasha followed, walking carefully. Maylin and Kella brought up the rear, negotiating the deck with ease.

"Ah," Maylin said smugly to Maurynna's puzzled look, "we Vanadins are born with sea legs."

Maurynna snorted. "A good trick that, seeing as how the Vanadins have always been dirt huggers," she teased.

But Maylin just smiled, refusing to be baited.

They lined the railing along the bow. Rann looked nervously down at the waves as Otter lifted him so that he could see over the rail.

"Don't worry, boy—ah, Your Highness. I won't let you fall," Otter said.

Rann frowned.

Maurynna hid a smile at Otter's slip of the tongue. Then she stared out over the sea, watching the easy rise and fall of

Linden's wings as he flew above the turquoise water, listening to the conversation around her with half an ear.

"You nearly called him 'boyo,' didn't you, Otter?" Kella said. "Like you call Linden."

Rann said, "You call Linden Rathan 'boyo'? He lets you?"

"I'd wondered about that, Otter," Maylin said. "It's odd, you know. Leaving aside the question of his rank, he's much older than you."

The bard answered, "Yes indeed, Prince Rann, Linden lets me call him 'boyo.' And as for your question, Maylin, it's what I called him when I first met him; remember, I had no idea who he was then. It's become a joke between us now."

A silence, and then Rann said, "Bard Otter, would you call me 'boyo,' too?"

"As you wish—boyo," said Otter gently.

Maurynna turned in time to see the bard ruffle the little prince's hair. The boy grinned, revealing a missing front tooth. *Just like Linden indeed.* She looked away to hide her smile and was once more caught in the magic that was the Dragonlord's.

"I wonder," she said half to herself as she leaned on the rail, "what it must be like to fly. To cast yourself onto the wind and soar away." She wished she could. But that was for Dragonlords, not for the likes of her.

Still, she thought wistfully, *it must be wonderful.*

As if by chance, certain of Prince Peridaen's supporters drifted away from the group of musicians playing in Lady Montara's gardens. The prince himself stayed, listening with apparent enjoyment to the music arranged for his entertainment this day.

They gathered by a large topiary peacock as they had been ordered to. Some looked bored—or tried to; others openly fidgeted, looking nervously about, shifting from foot to foot, breaking twigs from the leafy bird and shredding the leaves as they waited.

When the contagion of unease had spread throughout the whole group, Anstella decided it was time. None of them would meet her eyes as she wandered artlessly among the topiary zoo, drawing ever closer.

At last she joined them. One or two faces blanched. Someone had the poor judgement to speak first. "Anstella—"

Her gaze raked them like a snow cat's claws and her voice dripped acid into the wounds. "Silence. I hope the lot of you can do at least that correctly."

They shrank into themselves.

"You were sent word that, once Duriac and Chardel came to blows, you were to provoke even more disturbances. Instead you meekly obeyed a Dragonlord—one of those you are sworn to destroy!—like the sheep you are. And all because he raised his voice. Gods help me, if he'd shouted 'Boo!' would you have all died of fright?" she sneered.

"He outranks us," someone said. Others murmured agreement.

Anstella snapped, "Only because cowards like you allow it! Most Dragonlords weren't even born noble, let alone royal; who are they to dictate to us? Truehumans should be ruled over by truehumans—not creatures born of an unholy and unnatural perversion of wild magic!"

She surveyed her victims, letting them writhe under her silence as they had under her scorn. When she judged the moment right, she said, "The *next* time . . ."

She turned and walked away.

Linden flew easily along the coast, enjoying the feel of the ocean air rippling over his scales, looking back now and again to make certain he didn't out-distance the *Sea Mist*. But the ship sailed bravely after him. She was a pretty little thing, he thought, with her blue sails and silver-and-green banners. The stylized eyes painted on her bow gave her a knowing look, though whether by design or chance, one "eyebrow" arched higher than the other so that the *Sea Mist* also had an air of being somewhat surprised.

The hot sun on his back felt good. And soon he would be with Maurynna once more, this time far from the prying eyes in Casna. A pity that they couldn't be here alone. Ah, well;

it was likely for the best. He hoped Rann would enjoy this day; he doubted the boy had ever had a chance to do something so spontaneous.

He's likely never had much chance just to be a boy.

He flew on for more than three candlemarks before the curve of the headlands came into view. Below him waves crashed white-crested over rocks beneath the surface; the *Sea Mist* would have to stand well out to sea. But there were gaps between the rocks where the water ran smoother. He studied them, finally picking out one that looked more than wide enough for the ship's boat.

He balanced on the wind, holding his position before the opening, and reached out for Otter's mind.

Here. Tell Maurynna that there is a way here for the ship's boat to pass. The ship itself should not come any closer, though.

She's already said as much, boyo; remember, she can read waves the way you can the winds. The crew is making the gig ready now. Is there really a beach in there?

Yes. I think Rann will enjoy this. A pity you can't sing up a merling or two for him. He felt Otter laugh in his mind and let the contact fade, concentrating on keeping his place above the break in the rocks.

He watched the flurry of activity on board the *Sea Mist*: sailors loading baskets into the boat, then finally the boat—not "boat"—"gig," *Otter called it*—itself being lowered over the side. Some of the sailors slid down the lines at bow and stern to the waiting gig. Two of them caught the lines, keeping the small vessel close alongside the *Sea Mist*. A third steadied the end of the rope ladder tossed down from the bulwarks above as the rest took up stations at the oars.

Then one by one the picnickers climbed down. Maurynna came down first, as confident as any of the sailors. Maylin was next, a little slower, but without hesitation. Otter's descent was slow and cautious; he looked nervous as he made his way to his place. As soon as he was seated the bard unslung his harp case from his back and clutched it to his chest as if he feared the waves would snatch it from him. Both

Kella and Rann came down on the backs of sailors who scrambled back up the ladder after depositing their precious cargoes. Healer Tasha came last of all. She descended slowly and carefully, but when she took her seat she smiled, as though proud she'd made it without falling overboard.

The one flaw in his plan finally made itself known to Linden. Cursing himself for an idiot, he mindcalled Otter.

Tell Maurynna to mark where the passage is below me. I've just realized that I can't stay in dragon form much longer. I daren't Change when she's too close—the gods only know what might come of it. It might even be enough to trigger a too early First Change because we're soultwins.

He watched as Otter spoke with Maurynna and wondered what excuse the bard gave her for the sudden change in plans. Then Maurynna stood up in the gig, and, shading her eyes, studied the coast. After a few minutes she sat once more and the gig cast off from the *Sea Mist;* he took it to mean that she had plotted a course and wheeled away.

He crossed the cove quickly, straining to keep as much distance as possible between them. Even before his claws touched the white sand he initiated Change. Moments later he landed, human once more.

Gods, but it was hot. He stripped off his tunic, then, as an afterthought, his boots and linen stockings. Dressed only in breeches, he waded along the beach, impatient for the others to arrive. To distract himself he looked for seashells to give the children when they landed.

At last the gig hove into sight. He watched nervously as the sailors threaded a way through the rocks jutting up from the water like fangs, Maurynna calling directions from the bow. Oar stroke by steady oar stroke the small craft drew closer.

When they were nearly to the shore the sailors shipped the oars, jumped into the surf, and ran the gig up onto the shore. Linden caught Rann as the excited prince hurled himself out of the gig.

"Easy there, lad," he said, laughing, and swung the boy onto his shoulders. He helped Kella next, then Maylin and

Tasha. Otter handed him the harp and clambered out.

As he returned the harp, a burst of activity swirled around him and he lost track of Maurynna. Sailors ran back and forth bearing mysterious armloads of poles, canvas, and ropes as well as the expected baskets of food and drink.

The mystery was quickly resolved. Minutes later an awning shaded a section of the beach. As the sailors hammered in the last few stakes, Maurynna appeared at his side, saying, "I thought we might want a bit of shade, so I had the lads bring along an old sail. Not all of us are used to so much sun."

He caught her hand and squeezed it gratefully. Thank the gods she'd thought of that; it wouldn't do to bring Rann back burned redder than an apple and sick with too much sun. As for him, he hadn't had to worry about such things since he'd Changed for the first time. He'd forgotten others had to.

He released her hand when he noticed her crew slyly watching and nudging each other. He heard one whisper, "Remember that dockhand I told you about? That's 'im!"

Best not to set too many tongues wagging. A glance told him she'd noticed the grins as well; her cheeks were red under her dark tan.

"Off with you," she told her crew sternly. "We'll signal when we're ready to return."

The sailors saluted and shoved off into the surf. None of them bothered hiding their smiles now. Maurynna glared at them until they were beyond the breakers.

Linden rested a hand on her shoulder for a moment. With a wink, he said, "Let's get the food into the shade. Then we can enjoy ourselves."

She blushed even more as he led the way to the awning.

The children scampered through the foam the dying waves cast up upon the sand. Their voices carried back on the breeze, excited and happy, calling to each other over every new shell. Maylin and Tasha trailed along behind.

Linden paused as he arranged the driftwood for the fire to bake the sweet tubers Otter had insisted on bringing along.

"They're getting along wonderfully," he said. "I'd hoped that would happen."

Otter handed him another stick. "I think Rann's put aside being a prince because he's seen you not being a Dragonlord out of legend. He wants to be just like you, I think."

Maurynna looked up from wrapping sweet tubers in seaweed. "You noticed it, too?"

The firewood arranged to his satisfaction, Linden sat back on his heels and asked, "What do you mean?"

"He asked that we call him just 'Rann' when he found out that you gave us permission to dispense with your titles." Maurynna gathered the slippery tubers in her arms; Linden hastened to help her, letting his fingers slide over hers. Together they arranged them by the side of the fire pit.

"And he asked me to call him 'boyo.'" Otter chuckled. "Damn well the worst case of hero worship I've ever seen. Don't look so embarrassed! There are worse things he could aspire to—though I can't think of 'em right now."

Linden muttered something rude under his breath for the jibe, but was flattered by their words. "I like Rann. He makes me think of my step-son, Ash," he said without thinking. He invoked the spell to start the fire; it blazed up under his hand.

Maurynna gasped. "What? Your—your . . ."

Linden mentally kicked himself. He couldn't have come up with a worse way to tell her of his past life if he'd tried. "I was married once, Maurynna—a very long time ago. After we'd put Rani on the throne, Bram hadn't the heart to keep up the mercenary company without her. Anyway, his father needed him; his brother, the heir, was mortally ill. We disbanded. Bram returned to his father's hall and I to mine. My father arranged a marriage between me and a young widow with a son. Her name was Bryony; her son's name was Ash.

"It went well enough at first. Bryony and I were content with each other and I came to love Ash as my own. But . . ."

He looked away. Even with all the intervening centuries, the old humiliation still burned, the remembered taunts still cut deep. *Mule.* Studying the cliff wall, he said, holding his voice steady with an effort, "But Dragonlord and truehuman can't breed. Of course, neither I nor anyone else knew I was a Dragonlord at that time. All we knew was that I couldn't get her with child. So, after three years, she repudiated our marriage oath." He took a deep breath. "It—it was not an easy time for me. She was not kind about it. Neither were many of my kin."

Silence followed his words. Otter, of course, already knew about it. He wondered what Maurynna would think.

She put all her heart into one word. "Bitch."

He studied her. The odd-colored eyes blazed with anger. *My soultwin doesn't think any less of me—so why should I care what a woman six centuries dead thought?* To his surprise the realization banished the pain any thought of Bryony had always brought him. He sighed with long overdue relief and shifted around so that he could rest an arm around Maurynna's shoulders. All he dared was a quick, hard hug. "It's a long time over."

Otter said, "I think the coals are right for the sweet tubers, Linden. Why don't you put them in?"

Linden poked a finger among the blazing coals. He looked up at a choked-off exclamation from Maurynna. One hand was clamped over her mouth and her eyes bade fair to pop out of her head.

Oh, gods. He'd gone and startled the hell out of her again. Otter, blast him, was laughing as if his sides would split. Belatedly Linden realized he'd been tricked. His hand still in the coals, he said, "Maurynna-love, it's all right. Truly it is. It's not comfortable—think what it feels like to stick your hands into *very* hot water—but it's bearable and I'll take no harm from it. Fire can't hurt me."

She swallowed hard. The hand came down to clench at her chest. "I—I know that. It's in the stories. B-but to see it—" She shivered.

Fuming, Linden made holes in the glowing embers and tucked the seaweed-wrapped sweet tubers into them. "I ought to make you do this, you wretch," he growled at Otter.

"What? And have me burn my fingers so that I can't play when we've finished eating? Tchah. That would mean I'd have to sing to your playing. And I'll wager anything you've not been practicing much of late.''

Linden grinned. ''No, I haven't. Anyway, I'd much rather have you do the harping while Maurynna and I loll about watching you. Right, love?'' he asked with a wink.

She was, he decided, lovely when she blushed.

To Maurynna the day passed like a dream. Walking along the beach, chasing the happy children through the waves foaming along the sand, or playing hide-and-seek among the rocks—and Linden Rathan by her side almost every moment.

It was the most perfect day of her life, yet—Linden had seemed to hold back, to avoid being alone with her. And now the gig had been summoned from the ship; this day would soon be only a memory.

So she had taken this last walk alone and out of sight of the others. She leaned back against one of the tall rocks that rose so abruptly from the shore, one foot braced against it, and closed her eyes.

Well and well, she hadn't really expected that he'd continue as he'd started in the hold of the *Sea Mist* and the garden, had she? After all, he dallied with the most beautiful girl in Cassori.

Well, yes—I did hope that, she thought. Her mind answered, *Silly girl. Why should he—*

A shadow fell across her. She jumped, alert once more.

Linden stood before her. He was fully dressed now, ready for the trip back to Casna.

She waited. His hands came up, slowly, as if against his will. Hardly able to breathe, she stood trembling as he cupped her face between his hands.

All he said was ''Maurynna.'' Quietly, like a prayer.

It was enough.

Twenty-nine

A harsh yell shattered the moment. Maurynna gasped as Linden spun around and sprang away with a speed no true-human could match. Stumbling in the soft sand, she ran after him.

As she came around the rocks, the sight that greeted her made her stop in shock. Ropes dangled from the top of the cliffs, twitching like snakes as armed men slid down them.

Linden yelled "Maurynna, Otter—clear the beach for me!"

That broke her momentary paralysis. She raced to where Maylin and Healer Tasha were snatching up the children. Otter came from the other direction. "To the water's edge!" she yelled. "Get to the water's edge!"

She risked a glance at the men on the ropes; they were nearly to the beach. Would Linden have time to Change?

Then she was upon the others and pushing them toward the water.

Linden looked over his shoulder. Maurynna and Otter, the latter now carrying Kella, Maylin and Tasha, bearing Rann, stood knee-deep in the foamy surf. Their faces were stark with fear. Beyond them he could see the ship's boat pulling for shore. It would never get here in time.

He turned back to watch their attackers with a wordless snarl of frustration. Without thinking, he'd ordered the beach cleared to give himself room to Change.

And that was the one thing he couldn't do. Not with Maurynna only yards away. Yet he had little chance in human form, unarmed as he was, if enough men rushed him. To defend Rann—and he had no doubt that's who these men were after——he would have to take the risk of Changing.

He had only moments to decide. If the men reached him in the middle of Change and thrust a sword into the mist he became he would be unmade; and that would be far worse for Maurynna.

Tormented by indecision, he hesitated too long and the choice was made for him. The first men reached the packed sand at the foot of the cliff. But to his surprise, instead of rushing him, they simply steadied the ropes for those coming after them. One even saluted him.

Now Linden realized he recognized some of them; he'd seen them at the palace, wearing the scarlet of the palace guard. What was their game here?

His answer came when Beren slid down. Pulling leather gloves from his hands with impatient fury, the red-haired duke strode across the intervening beach and planted himself before Linden. Aside from the customary belt dagger for eating, the man was unarmed. Though still wary, Linden relaxed a little.

"I've come to take my nephew home," Beren snarled. He glanced over Linden's shoulder and a perplexed look shot across his face. His eyes darted from side to side, and the look of puzzlement grew.

"Up that?" Linden said in derision, jerking a thumb at the cliff, even as he wondered at Beren's puzzlement.

Their eyes met. For a moment Linden thought the man would strike him. But Beren controlled himself after one abortive movement; the only sign of his temper now was the clenching and unclenching of his big fists.

"Any way I have to," Beren said with quiet anger.

Another voice answered before Linden could. It spoke with an anger that matched the duke's.

"Only over my very dead body, will you take that boy, my lord."

Healer Tasha marched past Linden. She looked ready to explode with wrath. "Have you any idea what a ride that long will do to Rann, my lord?" she said, her voice shaking with fury.

Beren didn't answer that. Instead, to Linden's surprise, the duke looked up and down the beach once more and asked, "Where's Gevianna? She must be here. And did Peridaen come?"

"Gevianna," Tasha snapped, "is sleeping in her bed after being dosed with syrup of poppy."

"But Ber—," interrupted the duke, then shut his mouth with a snap.

Tasha went on, "The thought of a trip by sea upset her badly, and since I was coming along, her services were not needed. As for Prince Peridaen, my lord, I have no idea where he is. And Rann is *not* going with you. It would not only undo all the good this day has done him, it would exhaust him to the point of a serious relapse. As his Healer, I will not allow it."

She folded her arms across her chest. *And that is that!* the gesture said.

Beren rubbed his chin. "So neither Peridaen nor Gevianna is here," he said as if to himself. "Still," he said, hand dropping to his side once more, "still, Rann comes with me."

"No," said Tasha.

"Yes," said Beren. He raised a hand as if to summon his men.

Time to take a hand in this. It was not something Linden relished doing; no one liked having his authority challenged by an outsider. If Beren hadn't hated him before this . . .

"No," Linden said with quiet finality. "Rann does not go home with you, my lord Duke. He returns on board the ship with the rest of us and under Healer Tasha's care."

Beren's face turned brick red with fury. The man wasn't stupid; he knew what was coming next.

"Dragonlord's orders," Linden said.

Beren's lips drew back in a snarl, baring strong white teeth. One hand even darted toward his belt dagger. Linden braced himself for an attack.

Then Beren turned on his heel and strode back to his waiting men, and Linden knew he'd made an enemy.

Thirty

The old solar was quiet so late in the afternoon. The round room was high up in a tower that jutted out from the oldest part of the palace. Few people cared to take the time to seek out the old-fashioned solar now that the new, larger one was the favored gathering place of the ladies of the palace. All of which made this room perfect for a summer afternoon of solitude.

Long, narrow lancet windows marched along the outer walls looking out over the river far below. One could trace the line of the river, moving widdershins from window to window. At the last to overlook the brown waters of the Uildodd, the sea began, revealing itself as a silver flash along the horizon to the south.

The last of the sunlight streamed in through the westerly windows, illuminating the oak planking caught in their spear tips of light. Sherrine sat curled up in one of the chairs scattered around the room. She watched the patterns of light and shadow in their advance across the honey-colored wood of the floor. She was glad that no one had ever thought to cover it with tiles. The oak had a warmth that tiles lacked.

Best of all her mother never came here. Sherrine bit her lip at the thought of her parent; of late, her mother had been acting, well, oddly.

Always acid-tongued, her mother had outdone herself the past few days. Sherrine clenched her fists as a memory of her mother's taunts echoed in her mind.

You think you're special because of your Dragonlord lover? Bah! He'll find better—it won't be hard.

You are flawed. Never forget that. You're flawed and it makes you worthless.

Where's your precious Linden Rathan, little fool? Perhaps he's come to his senses; who'd want you with that hideous birthmark splashed across your back? It must have made him sick to look at; the mere thought of it makes me ill.

Sherrine had made the mistake of pointing out that Linden Rathan himself had the same kind of birthmark. It had simply sparked her mother into a vicious tirade the likes of which Sherrine had never dreamed possible. Inured as she was to her mother's constant insults, Sherrine had run from the room in tears.

And then there was the fear that she saw now in her mother's eyes when they lit upon her. A fear that came from the soul—

No. She'd no longer think about such things. They did not exist.

She would think only about *now*. How the solar was warm and she was pleasantly drowsy. It was enough to sink into the soft cushions, awaiting Tandavi's return from her post outside the council chamber. The surprise holiday from the meetings had been tedious. She was glad they'd resumed. Linden always appreciated her company after a particularly trying day.

She wondered if he would return with her servant. Surely by now he'd fulfilled his obligation to his Yerrin friend and could join her for a late dinner tonight. She smiled, knowing what was sure to follow.

And, of course, she would do her best to get more information from him. After all, she mustn't forget her reason for this dalliance. She stretched with the languorous ease of a cat. This was more pleasure than business—just the way she liked it.

As she settled herself again, Sherrine heard laughing voices approach. She rolled her eyes at the amount of giggling. It gave her a fair idea of who was about to disturb her sanctuary: Niathea and her flock of featherheads. She wondered if they'd been asked to leave the other solar for being too noisy; it had happened more than once.

They burst through the wide doorway as Niathea declaimed, "My dears, I tell you I saw—"

"Hello, Niathea," Sherrine said, her voice pure honey. She despised the girl and had no compunction about showing it.

Niathea stopped short in surprise, her mouth hanging open, red-brown curls tumbled in their usual disarray. Her face was shiny with perspiration. The others gathered behind her like a flock of chicks hiding in the safety of their mother's shadow.

Sherrine longed for an apple to pop into that open mouth. Niathea had such piggy little eyes it needed only that final touch to complete the resemblance to the traditional Winter Solstice boar's head.

And it would silence the intolerable twit.

Sherrine readied one of the many barbs she held in reserve for those who annoyed her. The words died on her tongue as she saw the sly looks the girls with Niathea now slanted from the corners of their eyes at each other. More than one hand came up to hide a smile. Some didn't bother; their smirks sent a warning chill down her back. They fanned out around Niathea as if jockeying for a view of some spectacle. Worse yet was the look of patently false sympathy that Niathea arranged on her face.

Sherrine's mouth went dry. Something inside her cowered as Niathea's eyes gloated. She wanted nothing more than to run from the solar, hands clapped over her ears. She'd die before giving the cow that satisfaction.

So she remained seated and even smiled. "Yes, Niathea?" she drawled. "I can see that you're simply dying to tell me something—which I no doubt already know. But if it will give you pleasure . . ." She breathed an exaggerated sigh.

Niathea's face turned an unbecoming shade of brick red. For a moment her face contorted as if her words choked her. Then the smile was back and so venomous that Sherrine regretted baiting her. Niathea advanced, stubby-fingered hands clasped to ample bosom. The others followed her like ravens ready to descend on a battlefield.

Niathea cooed, "Oh, Sherrine—you poor dear. To think!

That Linden Rathan would *do* such a thing! I'm so sorry.''

Sherrine's blood turned to ice. She said, more sharply than she'd meant, ''What do you mean?'' She bit her lip; she must have more control of herself than that—or Niathea would be spreading the tale far and wide.

Niathea blinked innocently. ''Why, you don't know? Oh— the cad! That he would let you think that he was yours alone!'' She brushed an imaginary tear from her eye.

Sherrine squirmed. The other young ladies of the court believed that only because she'd taken pains to hammer it into their dull heads, thinking it might eliminate competition. To an extent her ruse had worked. Now it was coming back to haunt her.

After an eternity, Niathea said, ''I was in the merchants' district yesterday with my lady mother. We were looking for silk—I'm to have a new gown of Assantikkan silk.''

Oh, get to it! Sherrine thought. She'd forgotten how Niathea could dawdle all around the point of a story. ''How nice,'' she murmured.

''We were trying to decide between the green and the violet silks when, from the back room, comes the merchant and this great *horse* of a Thalnian woman—Thalnian women are so tall, don't you think that's ugly? Though she was slender, I'll give her that. Anyway,'' Niathea said, warming to her tale, ''she was low-born; I could see that at a glance. She was as brown as a sailor—that's exactly what I thought: 'brown as a sailor'—and don't you know that the merchant's apprentice who was helping us said, 'Good day, Captain—' '' Niathea faltered. She bit her lip, thinking, then waved a hand, saying, ''Oh, I can't remember the name; who cares about a Thalnian sailor, anyway?''

The look she flashed at Sherrine from under lowered lashes said that she thought at least one person certainly would.

Sherrine made no move. She couldn't have if she'd wanted to—not now.

Niathea's lower lip jutted out. It seemed that she wasn't getting the reaction she wanted. She continued, speaking faster and faster, ''The sailor talked to the merchant a bit, I don't know what they said because they spoke Assantikkan, and there was laughter coming from the back room. She called to the people there. I glanced at them when they came out: another girl who looked Cassorin and two Yerrin men—one a bit older than us, the other a greybeard wearing a bard's torc. The merchant switched to Cassorin and kept saying what an honor it was.

"At first I didn't pay them any mind, not really. Why should I? They were commoners. I didn't bother about them until the younger man talked—he sounded familiar. He said something about wanting to see shadow puppets or some such thing. But he kept his face turned away so that I almost didn't recognize him. After all, I've never seen him when he wasn't wearing the formal regalia. He wasn't even wearing his torc of rank.

"They all talked a bit more with the merchant, something about a feast, and they were all laughing together."

Niathea stopped and heaved a great breath as if she'd run through her entire tale without breathing once. She looked down, folded her lips over a smile, and said, "I'm so sorry, Sherrine dear."

Sherrine nearly laughed aloud. *This* was Niathea's great tale of woe for her? She smiled at Niathea and thought how pleasant it was to disappoint the poisonous little bitch.

Sherrine raised her eyebrows. Letting her amusement color her voice, she said, "My dearest Niathea, I already knew about Linden's bard friend and that he would be spending time with him. He spoke to me of him some time ago. So you see, there is nothing in your little story for you to be . . . upset . . . about."

*But who are the women—especially the Thalnian? I don't like the way Niathea looked when—*Sherrine cut off the thought. She continued as if instructing a particularly simple child: "The bard is Otter Heronson, as you would have known if you—"

Gone now was any pretense at sympathy. "She—the sailor—called him Linden," Niathea said in triumph. "They all did, but you could hear the caress in her voice when *she* said his name. And he didn't stop her—oh, no. When they were outside the shop, he held her back a moment and kissed her before they went off down the street after the others. And he put his arm around her shoulders.''

Niathea's lips curled in a cruel smile. She pushed the sweaty curls back from her face and leaned forward, her face only inches away.

Sherrine pressed herself back into the cushions.

Niathea's eyes blazed and venom poured forth from her tongue like a river that had been dammed for too long. ''All along you've been gloating because Linden Rathan chose you, lording it over the rest of us, bragging how he was yours alone. Not anymore. You've been thrown over for a great horse of a Thalnian—a sailor, no less—as sunburned and calloused as any peasant behind a plow.

''I saw the way he looked at her, Sherrine. You've lost him—forever.''

She had no memory of leaving the solar. Only of mocking laughter chasing her.

Tandavi found her stumbling through the halls. The servant's slim arms caught her, held her tightly.

''My lady! What's wrong?'' Tandavi cried.

Sherrine wiped her eyes. For a moment she stared at Tandavi without recognizing her. Then she collected her wits and whispered, ''What answer did Linden Rathan give you?''

That answer would tell her whether Niathea lied—or whether she had indeed lost him. When Tandavi didn't speak right away, Sherrine shook her. ''Tell me!''

''H-he—he looked annoyed, said he had another engagement, my lady, the friend he'd told—Ow! My lady!'' Tandavi clutched at her wrists.

Sherrine numbly watched the blood well up in the furrows her nails had dug on the girl's arms. The pattern of red against white skin fascinated her.

''Oh, gods, Tandavi—I'm sorry. I didn't mean to . . .'' She came to herself abruptly. Oh, gods indeed—she must be more shaken than she thought, apologizing to a servant.

Tandavi gulped in surprise. "It's no matter, my lady," she sniffled. "But what's wrong—?"

"Nothing. Be quiet. Let me think." Sherrine leaned back against the cold granite wall of the narrow hallway, glad that few people came to this older section. The fewer who saw her like this, the better. She pressed the heels of her palms against her eyes, willing herself to calmness.

She would not give up Linden without a fight. That was unthinkable; her pride would not allow it. Even if her rival had been noble-born, she would not have stood meekly aside. But that she should be cast aside for a commoner!

And there was her mother. Sherrine could already hear Anstella gloating: "Little fool—can't you do anything right? He threw you over for a sailor?"

An image of calloused hands, brown against Linden's fair skin, came to her mind. She saw them running down his back. . . . She ground her hands into her eyes, banishing the picture. She must think this through.

First, she had to find out her rival's name. But how? She could hardly search the docks looking for a Thalnian woman who captained a ship.

How, how, how?

"Gerd Warbek." Sherrine dropped her hands. Surely the merchant knew who the captains were or knew how to find out. It might take him a few days, but Warbek would find out for her; the man would do anything to keep the patronage of the Colranes.

She pushed herself off from the wall. "Oh, yes; he's the person to ask. Come along, Tandavi. I've business with Master Warbek. And then with a certain Thalnian sailor."

Thirty-one

"It's wonderful up here!" Linden said. "You can see for miles."

Maurynna smiled wryly at him from her own perch. They sat on the topmost yard, on either side of the mast; each had an arm wrapped around it to steady themselves against the gentle sway. It was one of her favorite places to sit and think whenever the *Sea Mist* was at dock. "Stop teasing. You know you can get much higher than this yourself and see much, much farther."

He grinned back, looking like an unrepentant and utterly wicked little boy. "True. But the company isn't as good. Or as beautiful."

"Linden!" Pure pleasure suffused her. But blast it all, judging by the sudden heat in her face, she knew she was—

"Especially when you blush like that."

"You are even more of a tease than Otter is, do you know that?" she demanded. Then, more softly, "But thank you, anyway."

He stroked her face lightly with the fingers of his free hand. "Maurynna-love—I meant that. Truly. Every word."

She kissed the palm of his hand, thinking, *This is a dream. It has to be a dream. This can't be happening to me.*

But the hand that now caught her free one was big and warm and strong. He laced his fingers through hers. She was content.

They sat together without speaking for a long time. It was a comfortable silence, with a closeness in it that Maurynna treasured, hoarding memories against the time this idyll ended with his return to Dragonskeep or her departure for her next port.

Then Linden sat up straighter and pulled his hand away. "Look—there's one of the royal barges sailing up the river." He pointed.

Blast. Her fingers felt lonely already. Stifling a sigh, Maurynna shaded her eyes against the evening sun and looked.

Sure enough, she picked it out immediately from all the other vessels plying the Uildodd. Banners of the royal scarlet fluttered at its bow and stern, and the wood of the rails and cabin was gilded where it wasn't painted scarlet. To her eyes it looked both dumpy and gaudy, like an overweight and over-painted whore.

Still, the thing was solidly built. Gajji must have been wrong. . . . Following the thought, she mused aloud, "That must have been some storm that day."

Linden picked up her meaning as though he read her thoughts. "You mean the day Queen Desia drowned? No, it wasn't. At least, that's what I was told."

Frowning in puzzlement, Maurynna said, "I was told the same—and by another sailor. So why did that barge sink?"

Linden looked at her and shrugged. "Even that was too much for it? The water came over the back end, I heard."

"Stern," Maurynna corrected absently. She shook her head. "No, Linden. I know ships: Those barges wallow like pregnant cows in the water, but even they shouldn't dip their sterns low enough to founder in a small following sea—and that's all it was, Gajji said."

"Then why? . . . " Linden asked. He turned his head to watch the barge once more, as if he might find his answer there.

"I don't know," Maurynna said. "But it's very, very odd."

Linden started to say something, but a shout from below interrupted him.

"Hoy, up there! Did you two forget we're to have dinner tonight with Almered and Falissa?" Otter stared up at them, hands on hips. Even foreshortened as her view of him was, Maurynna could see the toe of one boot impatiently tapping the deck.

She clapped her hand to her mouth; she *had* forgotten about dinner. "Oh, dear."

She looked down at herself. Patched tunic and breeches, and Linden not much better; they'd worn their oldest clothes to clamber about the *Sea Mist*'s rigging while she taught Linden what was what. Though he still said "rope" more often than not, he was learning fast.

No, these clothes wouldn't do at all. "I must go home and change," she said.

For a moment a startled look filled Linden's eyes. Then he blinked and said, "Oh! Of course. So must I. We'd better hurry."

She was already swinging down from the yard and clambering down the rat lines as fast as she could. "Indeed."

Moments later her feet hit the deck with a thump. She sprang aside to make room for Linden, who was right behind her. Otter, she saw, was already properly dressed.

He'd also had their horses brought right down to the dock. "Hurry," he urged them, running for his own horse.

Linden tossed her up into her saddle and vaulted into his own. He leaned over and gave her a quick, hard kiss, then wheeled his horse away. "Otter, come with me, why don't you? Tell me how Rann was when you left him." His ugly pied gelding danced under him, impatient to be off. "I'll be at the house soon," he called to Maurynna. "Until then, love."

"Until then, Linden," she said, her heart singing at the caress in his voice. He smiled and rode off, Otter close behind.

She watched him a moment before setting heels to her own horse. She hadn't much time.

Maurynna paused halfway down the stairs, Maylin and Kella a few steps behind her. She cocked her head at the noise outside. Horses—was Linden here already? True, he'd said he'd hurry, but this was faster than she'd expected. Her heart beating faster in anticipation, she gathered up her skirts to run the rest of the way.

The door burst open and one of the apprentices, Gavren, dashed in, forgetting to shut it again. His face was white. He stood at the bottom of the stairs and waved his hands at her. "Go back," he gasped, then disappeared into the back of the house.

"What? Isn't that Linden? Maylin, what—," Maurynna stopped in confusion.

Maylin pushed past her. "Wait here," she ordered.

Maylin ran down the stairs and peeked out the door. Whatever she saw there made her pull hurriedly back, using language Maurynna didn't think her cousin even knew. She dashed back up the stairs. "Not Linden," Maylin puffed. Her eyes were wide with fright. "Rynna, go—"

"If you kneel, you can see out the door," Kella whispered. "Not very well, but enough."

Maurynna joined the little girl in peering between the banisters. Maylin fluttered for a moment then settled beside them.

From her vantage point Maurynna could see Aunt Elenna's back. Her aunt had one arm raised; Maurynna guessed she held a torch.

Just beyond Aunt Elenna was a woman on horseback. Of her, Maurynna could see only her skirts and hands. One hand held a riding whip, tapping it incessantly against the pommel of the saddle.

The courtyard was brighter than could be accounted for by one torch. Maurynna remembered the other horses she'd heard, the ones she'd assumed were Linden's escort. By the jangling of harness they were still out there. Add to that the fine fabric of the skirts she could see and this must be a noblewoman and her escort, the latter carrying torches among them.

Maurynna heard the woman say, "Once again—where is this Maurynna Erdon? Send her out, or I'll have my guards look for her." Her low, husky voice was menacing.

Maurynna had a sinking feeling that she could guess which noblewoman was asking for her. She asked Maylin, "Lady Sherrine?" At Maylin's nod, she continued, "And she wishes to . . . speak with me?"

"Yes." Maylin's voice was barely audible. "Get back up the stairs, Rynna. She hasn't seen you; Mother's keeping the torch between her eyes and the door. She can't see beyond it.

"Go on; we'll get rid of her—tell her you're at the docks. A fine lady like her won't go there, especially at night. Hide until Linden comes. This tangle is of his making; he started it when he dallied with her. Let him sort it out."

Outraged at the suggestion, Maurynna began, "I've done nothing wrong that I should hide like a thief. And I certainly won't run from—"

Maylin, cuddling the frightened Kella against her, snapped, "Oh, don't be an ass, Rynna—you don't know what she's like. The Colranes are chancy to cross. And Lady Sherrine is a bad one—Mother hates it when she or her mother the baroness come into the shop. She says their business isn't worth it."

Maurynna raised her eyebrows. That her practical aunt was so ready to do without a baroness's patronage told her much about the Colranes. She wavered, not sure of what she should do: retreat or confront this woman? If only her rival for Linden's affections weren't noble. . . . She cursed softly, wishing this were happening in Thalnia. Her status as a member of House Erdon wouldn't help her here in Cassori—not against a noble.

"Go!" Maylin pushed her up the stairs.

"You've no warrant from the palace guard or the Watch," she heard her aunt say as she went up a step or two.

"I need none," was the reply. "Guards!"

Maurynna heard the guards dismounting and turned without hesitating. She gently pushed Maylin to one side, stepped around Kella, and strode down the stairs to the door, her head held high. She'd not be dragged out like a common criminal.

Maylin thumped down the stairs behind her, muttering, "Of all the pig-headed, stubborn . . ."

Gathering her skirts in one hand, Maurynna, with Maylin treading on her heels, made a dignified descent of the three steps to the courtyard. She stepped around her aunt and crossed the few feet to stand before Lady Sherrine. "I understand you are looking for me, my lady," she said.

She waited in the pool of light cast by the torches. The darkness beyond was impenetrable. In the silence that followed she had time to notice how warm the night air was, the lingering sweetness of the roses that climbed the walls of the house. The cobblestones were hard and cold through the thin soles of her indoor shoes.

Lady Sherrine said nothing for a long moment, then: "You are Maurynna Erdon, captain of the *Sea Mist*?"

"I am." Maurynna looked the noblewoman straight in the eye. *Remember—you're not in Thalnia. To this woman you have no rank.*

They studied each other in silence. Though she took care to give no outward sign, her first sight of her rival shook Maurynna badly. Even in the poor light of the torches Lady Sherrine's beauty was astonishing.

Look at her, sitting straight as a mast in the saddle, Maurynna thought. *She's like something out of a bard's song made real, beautiful as a song of autumn.* She looked at the delicate hands gripping reins and whip and thought of her own work-roughened fingers.

She wondered what color Sherrine's large, slightly tilted eyes were. *No doubt hers will match, not like mine. She's perfection, pure and simple,* Maurynna thought with despair. *No wonder Linden chose her for a dalliance—and how did I ever think that I might take him away from her? Now I know why he's never even hinted that I stay the night with him.*

Maurynna felt like a fool. But she would never give this woman the satisfaction of knowing that. *Even if Linden has been toying with me, she has no right to look at me as if I'm something out of the gutter.* She stiffened her spine.

"My lady, you asked for me and here I am. You have said nothing. Am I to conclude then that you require nothing further of me? If so, I—"

The whip snapped against the saddle and was still. The horse snorted in surprise.

Lady Sherrine spat, "While I know you are nothing more

than a diverting little amusement to him, I require you to stay away from Linden Rathan, you sneaking little money-grubber. How dare you look so high above yourself?''

Because I'm a starry-eyed idiot, Maurynna thought. Then she reminded herself that Linden had sought her out, not the other way around. A tiny flower of hope bloomed. She said quietly, ''With all due respect, my lady, isn't this up to Linden? He—''

The horse leaped forward. Maurynna dodged to one side barely in time to avoid being knocked down. She heard Aunt Elenna and Maylin scream and the harsh cries of the guards. Hands—she thought they were her aunt's—tried to catch her, but she stumbled from their grasp.

Lady Sherrine raged, ''You dare to use his name? He is 'Dragonlord' to the likes of you, gutter rat!'' She brought the palfrey around in a tight, rearing curve.

Time slowed down. Every moment stretched out forever; Maurynna saw everything with a terrible clarity. She was frozen in place just as in her worst nightmares. The scent of woods lily nearly overwhelmed her.

The lash of the whip across her face broke her paralysis, the thin tip raking her eye. She screamed; it felt as though a dagger fresh from the forge slashed across her eye. She nearly fainted.

Someone caught her as she fell to the hard cobblestones and lowered her to her knees. She thought it was Maylin. She cradled her face in her hands, fighting the faintness. Warm blood welled between her fingers and ran down her hands. Somewhere behind her Kella began crying hysterically.

Maurynna swallowed hard. She refused to be sick in front of Lady Sherrine. Instead she concentrated on the uneven hardness of the cobbles beneath her, on Maylin's fierce, obscene summation of Lady Sherrine and just what she could do with herself. She thought hazily, *Good thing she's speaking the Thalnian I taught her.*

She heard Lady Sherrine gasp, heard a male voice she didn't recognize say, ''You've gone too far, Lady. Best we get you home.''

She looked up out of her good eye. Lady Sherrine was staring down at her, horrified.

The whip dropped from the noblewoman's fingers. One of her guards reached for her horse's reins. Lady Sherrine nodded. Her lips moved soundlessly. The tilted eyes never left Maurynna's face.

Out of the night beyond the torches came a deep voice as sharp and dangerous as a sword.

"What in the bloody nine hells is going on here?" Linden said.

Thirty-two

Leaving his escort in the street, Linden pushed his horse through the brown-and-gold-clad guards filling the Vanadins' little courtyard. Otter followed close behind. What were Sherrine's men doing here? A chill crawled down Linden's spine.

The men fell back before him in the wavering torchlight. One guard held the reins of Sherrine's palfrey. The man dropped them and edged away, leaving Sherrine alone.

She brought her horse around to face him. Her eyes were huge in her face; she looked close to fainting. "I didn't mean to," she whispered. "Truly, I—"

Linden's breath froze in his chest. Something had happened to Maurynna. And Sherrine was responsible. He jumped down from the saddle.

Sherrine was wise; she didn't try to stop him. He ducked past the palfrey.

Maurynna was on her knees on the cobbles. Her hands held one side of her face. Blood covered them. Even as he watched, drops trickled over her bracelets and splashed on the stone.

He stood like one turned to stone. He didn't trust himself to move. If he did, he would lose control and likely kill someone in his fury. Sherrine had dared to harm his soultwin!

Then he was at Maurynna's side with a speed that brought gasps from the watchers. Gently he eased her from Maylin's arms. She came to him, resting her head on his shoulder. Her sobs were barely audible.

"Oh, gods," Otter said from behind him. "What happened? Who—?"

Maylin, her face salt white, spat out in Thalnian, <<Who do you think did it? The sweet-faced bitch who sits there, of

course! She came here, no warrant—none but her bully-boys!—and called Maurynna out. Then she laid Rynna's face and eye open with that whip.>> She pointed to the cobble-stones behind him.

Linden looked over his shoulder. A riding whip with a daintily carved handle of bone lay on the cobbles. Its tip was stained with blood. Sickened and burning with rage, he said, "Guards—take your lady home. Lady Sherrine, you will at-tend me at my residence at the fourth candlemark past dawn tomorrow. Go."

Elenna came forward. She cradled a sobbing Kella against her shoulder. <<Mind your tongue, stupid girl—what if one of her guards understands Thalnian and tells her what you're saying? Now tend to Maurynna; I've got to calm Kella down or she'll have nightmares all night long.>> She held out a folded pad of cloth and a long narrow strip of fabric that Linden suspected were torn from her undergown.

Maylin subsided, looking sullen as she took the makeshift bandage. Her mother went into the house. Linden moved aside, watched Maylin arrange the pad over Maurynna's eye and tie it in place.

"Thank you," Maurynna whispered, her voice tight with pain. Her fingers gripped his tunic convulsively.

The ring of hooves on cobblestones told him that Sherrine was leaving—unpunished. She'd harmed Maurynna and he could do nothing. He was cold and sick and frustrated at his helplessness.

Maylin jumped up and ran to the gate, watching the riders disappear. Then she spun around, fists clenched at her side and yelled, "You let her go! You're a Dragonlord—do some-thing!"

Otter, calm her down—please! She's upsetting Maurynna.

"Maylin, be quiet," Otter snapped. "You don't know what you're talking about." He led her back, Maylin protesting every step.

Linden said, *My gods, but she's a fierce one for such a little thing, isn't she?*

Otter chuckled in his mind. *Isn't she, though? I don't think*

*it's a good idea to harm this one's family. For a moment I
thought she'd go for Sherrine.*

So did I, and that would have been very bad. Linden
cradled Maurynna against him and called, "Captain Jerrell—
send some guards after Lady Sherrine. See that she goes to
her home and no other place. Have them watch the house;
she is not to leave until tomorrow morning. If she does not
come out at the appointed time, bring her to me."

The captain snapped out an order; some of Linden's escort
split off from the group and rode after Sherrine.

Otter and Maylin reached him, the bard holding Maylin
tightly around the shoulders. Maylin dropped to her knees.

"What are you going to do about this? How will you pun-
ish Sherrine?" she demanded.

His answer was as bitter as wormwood on his tongue. "I
can do nothing," he said. When Maylin protested, he said,
"If Maurynna wishes redress, she must seek it through Cassorin law. And I do not think she will find it."

He clenched his jaw and said in Otter's mind, *My soultwin
is attacked and I can't see the one responsible brought to
justice. Sherrine should be punished for attacking a Dragonlord. But because I can't say anything, Cassorin law will slap
Sherrine on the wrist—if even that!—and send Maurynna
begging.*

Otter said, *You're right of course. You can't even act too
upset—someone might wonder why you care so much. What
are you going to do now?*

Linden considered. *That wide avenue leading to the palace—the Processional. It's big enough for me to Change.
Then I can use my Healing fire—*

Otter made a strangled sound. *Are you mad? Gods, this has
rattled you worse than I thought! Remember what you said
the effect might be if you Change so close to Maurynna—
you, her soultwin.*

Cold sweat ran down Linden's back. *Gods have mercy—
you're right. I don't know if I could control Rathan; he would
call to the dragonsoul within her. And that might kill her.
Thank you, Otter.*

The bard nodded.

Maylin said, "Stop ignoring me. Why should you care for Cassorin law?"

Shaken by how close he'd come to endangering Maurynna, Linden lost his temper. He shouted, "Don't you understand? I'm one of the Givers of Law. That's what being a Dragonlord means—not that I can take revenge where it pleases me. We're the servants of humankind, not their rulers. I can't flout a country's laws because I don't like them. I can't even give myself the satisfaction of calling out a champion of Sherrine's in a duel. I may not Challenge; I may only act as a champion."

Linden bit his tongue. Was he mad, talking of Challenges on Maurynna's behalf? Neither Maurynna nor Maylin was stupid. Gods, if he wasn't careful he'd be blurting out why he'd even thought of such a thing.

He said, "Now stop talking nonsense and tell one of my guards to bring me my horse. Maurynna needs a Healer. I'm taking her to the palace."

He stood up with Maurynna in his arms. "Love," he whispered, "don't worry. You'll be fine."

"I—I hope so," Maurynna said. "And please stop fighting over my head as though I weren't here. It's giving me a headache."

But she laughed a little through her sobs, so Linden knew she wasn't angry. He squeezed her gently. "It will be better soon," he said, and sighed. It hurt not being able to help his soultwin himself.

A soldier brought his horse and held it. Linden handed Maurynna to Otter, mounted, and took her back. He settled her against himself. "Comfortable?" he asked.

"Well enough," Maurynna said. Her voice shook. She fiddled with the pad over her eye. "There."

He wheeled his horse around and rode through the gate. He halted long enough to allow his escort to form up around him once more. The globes of coldfire he'd called up earlier bobbed in the air above them.

Otter ran up beside him. The bard said, "Do you want me to stay with the family?"

"Yes," Linden said. "That way I can send word to them through you as soon as Maurynna's Healed." Then: *I'm not sure I trust Sherrine not to take some sort of revenge on the family once the shock wears off. She might think twice if a bard's here. And try to talk some sense into Maylin, will you? Or the next time I show my face here she'll throw something at me.*

Otter grinned and blew a kiss at Maurynna. *I wouldn't doubt it. She's as bad as a Yerrin about kith and kin. I'll talk to her.*

Linden pushed his horse to walk as fast as it could. Maurynna trembled in his arms. He pulled her closer. Her hands clutched again at his tunic. "Not much farther," he whispered against her hair, reassuring himself as much as her.

With the escort surrounding them like shadows, they rode quickly through the streets of Casna, golden coldfire lighting the way like a dozen tiny suns. The only sound in the warm night was the ringing of hooves on stone.

They reached the avenue where Linden had thought to Change. He shuddered at how close he'd come to endangering Maurynna. *Thank the gods for Otter's cool head,* he thought.

At last the palace loomed before them. "Corrise, ride ahead and have them open the gates," he ordered. One shadow broke away from the others and galloped off.

The gates swung open as they approached. More soldiers in the scarlet of the palace guard waited to take their horses. Linden dismounted, swinging his leg over his horse's neck and sliding along one hip to the ground. He ignored the questions peppering the air and strode into the palace.

When they were inside, Linden called to the first servant he saw. "Where is Healer Tasha?"

The surprised man said, "She is attending Prince Rann in his rooms, Your Grace."

"Take me there."

The servant bowed and set off through the maze of the palace halls. Linden followed close on his heels.

Maurynna lifted her head. She peered around her and shook her head. "Linden, will Tasha be allowed to attend me? I know how the Cassorin nobles feel about merchants. Since she's the personal Healer of the royal family, they might refuse—"

"They won't," Linden said shortly. "Or they'll have me to deal with. Don't worry, love."

She rested her head against his shoulder again, but trembled harder than ever.

Gods, she must be terrified. Can she sail half-blind? It would kill her, I think, to be chained to the land. If only I could tell her that even if she loses that eye she'll have the freedom of the wind someday. He set his jaw and steadily walked on.

After far too long for Linden's peace of mind, the servant stopped before a wide oak door. The two guards on either side stared curiously but made no move.

"Announce me," Linden said.

The man nodded; he knocked once, then pushed the door open. "His Grace Dragonlord Linden Rathan seeks Healer Tasha, my lord, my lady."

Linden entered. He nodded to the surprised faces staring back at him. Rann sat on the floor with Healer Tasha and his nurse Gevianna. Toy soldiers surrounded them.

Duchess Alinya was just rising from a chair by the fireplace. The wolfhound behind Rann scrambled to its feet. Through a half-open door in the far wall Linden could see a canopied bed, its covers already turned back.

Tasha jumped up. Though her faded ginger hair was pulled back in its usual severe bun, wisps of it had escaped to frame her face. They made her look oddly young and vulnerable. But when she spoke, her voice was crisp and sure. "What happened? Put her down here and let me look at that eye." She pointed to the cushion she'd vacated.

He said to Duchess Alinya, "This is Maurynna Erdon." To Tasha, "A whip caught her across the eye." Linden snapped his teeth shut on the words and set Maurynna down on the cushion. He knelt beside her, supporting her against his chest.

The duchess came to stand by his side. "Captain Erdon, I assume, with those bracelets? You're young for it; you must be very good."

"She is indeed," Tasha said as she undid the bandage. Her voice was steady and cheerful. "Very well now, let me have a look at that eye. Yes, yes, I know—the light hurts, doesn't it? Don't pull your head away—that's it. I'll be quick, I promise. Rann, dear, get out of my light, or the next tonic I give you will be truly awful."

"But I want to *see*," Rann complained, peering over Tasha's shoulder. "Maurynna, does it hurt? You're bleeding all over *everything*."

"Bloodthirsty little monster," Duchess Alinya said mildly. "Gevianna?"

Gevianna scooped Rann up and carried him away, ignoring his protests. Because he could think of nothing else to distract the boy, Linden tossed the young prince a ball of scarlet cold-fire. A yelp of delight told him the ploy had worked.

Despite her promise to be quick, Linden thought that Tasha's examination took forever. The Healer *hmmm*ed and *tsk*ed, and muttered under her breath as she turned Maurynna's face this way and that. He realized at one point that Maurynna's nails were digging into his hand. He cradled her fingers.

At last Tasha sat back on her heels. She said cheerfully, "Not as bad as I'd feared. The eyelid took the worst of it; the pupil wasn't touched at all—just the white of the eye was scratched. You must have blinked at the right moment. All the blood is from the cuts on your forehead, lid, and cheek. Frightening, but nothing serious."

Linden went limp with relief. Maurynna squeezed his hands one last time. He asked, "Can you Heal it?"

"Yes; I'll want to clean it first, though. Gevianna, would you bring my kit, please? As luck would have it, I made up an infusion of goldenseal today for Lady Corvy; there's still some left."

Gevianna delivered the large leather pouch. Tasha rummaged through it, saying, "This will hurt, Maurynna, but you must try to hold still." She paused, looking at Linden. "Would you help, Dragonlord? You'll need to keep her from moving."

"Of course," Linden said. He stroked Maurynna's cheek lightly. "I'm sorry."

"I understand," Maurynna said, shielding her face from the light. "It's the best way."

He slid behind her. One arm went around Maurynna's waist, pinning her arms to her sides, holding her against his chest. With his other hand he drew Maurynna's head back against his shoulder and held it there, his hand firm against her forehead. She shuddered once, then relaxed into his arms.

Tasha held up a small bottle in one hand. "Ready?" the Healer asked.

Before Maurynna could answer, Tasha dribbled the infusion over her eye. She whimpered and struggled a little. Linden tightened his grip.

If only we were linked, he thought, *I could ease this pain for her by taking it upon myself.* Then, bitterly: *Had we been linked, this never would have happened. I would have known the moment she was uneasy and could have gotten there in time to prevent this.*

The infusion ran in rivulets down Maurynna's face, washing away the drying blood in streaks. It dripped lukewarm and rusty brown onto his arm.

"There—good enough. Now for the bad part, I'm afraid," Tasha said. She shook back her sleeves, revealing the tattoos on her forearms. "Have you ever been Healed before, dear?"

"Yes," Maurynna said. "I broke my arm once falling out of a tree."

Tasha smiled. "Then you've been through worse, though this will be bad enough. Dragonlord—hold her steady." She covered Maurynna's eye, forehead, and cheek with her hands and closed her own eyes. For a few moments Tasha breathed deeply as she invoked the Healing trance. Linden looked down at her hands.

A blue-green haze surrounded them. Maurynna cried out; once again he held her tight. The haze darkened. Tasha's breathing became heavy. Then the haze disappeared and Tasha opened her eyes. She pulled her hands away from Maurynna's face.

"How does the eye feel now?" Tasha asked.

Linden let Maurynna go and eased himself around to kneel before her. She blinked, looking this way and that, her lips parted in surprise. Despite the runnels of dried blood streaking her face, Linden thought she'd never looked so beautiful.

"I can see perfectly!" Maurynna said. She smiled; Linden couldn't tell whether it was more from joy or relief. "I was so afraid. . . ."

He hugged her. "It's all over now, sweetheart. Let me tell Otter." Resting his cheek against her hair, he called, *Otter? Are you listening?*

Boyo—do you have any other foolish questions? Otter snapped. *Of course I am! How's Maurynna?*

Completely healed. The eye is fine. Hm—wait a moment. . . .

Otter's sigh of relief rang in Linden's mind as he pulled back enough to study Maurynna's face. He ran his thumb along the line of the healed cut across her cheek. She tilted her head in question at him. *There won't even be a scar; there's just a thin pink line that will fade in a few days.*

The bard said, *I'll tell her family; they've been frantic. You'll bring her home soon?*

Linden said regretfully, *Yes. No doubt she'll be sleepy in a short while.* And he ended the contact before Otter picked up the thought that he would far rather bring Maurynna to his house than hers.

He came back to find Maurynna and Tasha staring at him. He smiled and said, "Your family won't be worrying anymore, love. I told Otter you're well."

"Thank you," Maurynna said. Her eyes said much more.

And he had to bring her back to her family—and leave her there? He sighed.

Gevianna approached, bearing a basin of steaming water and some cloths. Rann clung to her side like a burr, cradling the coldfire against his chest. She said, "We can't let you go covered in blood like this, my lady. Let me help you."

Linden pulled back enough to let Rann's nurse kneel by Maurynna. Before he could take a cloth and help, Duchess Alinya spoke.

"Dragonlord—may I have a private word with you?"

He jumped, feeling guilty. He'd forgotten she was in the room. "I'll be back," he whispered in Maurynna's ear.

Alinya gestured to the door of Rann's sleeping chamber. He followed as she slowly made her way to the other room. Once there she said nothing, but looked back through the half-closed door. Linden followed her gaze.

Gevianna and Tasha had finished with Maurynna. Now the three women sat on the floor with Rann. The boy held his coldfire in one hand; with the other he pointed at the toy soldiers as he directed his "generals" in their placement. Linden smiled as Maurynna solemnly galloped a mounted fighter across the tiles. The wolfhound lay thumping its tail.

The duchess's soft voice interrupted his revery. "She's your soultwin, isn't she, Dragonlord?"

He spun to face her. "What do you—?"

The old woman cut him off with a gesture. "It's the way you look at her and she at you. It's the same way Kief Shael-dar and Tarlna Aurianne look at each other. Yet you've made no announcement. Why?"

Linden said, "Because she doesn't know. And she mustn't; if she tries to force early Change, she could kill herself."

Alinya made the sign to avert misfortune. "Who did this to her?"

"Sherrine. Had I known about Maurynna, I would never have dallied with her. Fool that I am, I never thought the girl would do something like this. I had made it clear to her—I thought—that she might not be the only one." He picked up a toy soldier that had not joined the muster of its fellows and turned it over and over in his fingers.

Alinya said, "Sherrine is not the sort to take defeat grace-fully, Dragonlord. Bad enough that the ending of your dalli-ance was not of her choosing. But that she should lose a

Dragonlord lover to a Thalnian commoner would be very bitter indeed.

"Sherrine," the duchess added, "can be a fool. Like too many Cassorin nobles. They refuse to see that power may rest with others besides the nobly born."

Linden raised an eyebrow. "Oh?"

Alinya smiled. "When I was a girl, Dragonlord, my parents and I lived for a time in Thalnia with my mother's foster sister. I know how powerful their great merchant families are—some might as well be noble, such as the Erdons. Yes, I recognized the name. If Sherrine had looked beyond her prejudices, she would have realized that Maurynna was no common trader. The only way someone as young as Maurynna could have her own ship is with the backing of vast resources—the kind that merchant princes control. But Sherrine sees what she wants to see."

Linden grunted in embarrassment. Just as he'd seen what he'd wanted to see in Sherrine: a lighthearted companion for a while, with no hearts broken on either side when it came time for parting.

Alinya looked into the other room again. She said, "May I give you some advice, Dragonlord? Take your soultwin back to her people—and stay away from her."

Linden first reaction was fury. Then common sense prevailed. Alinya must have a reason; he would hear it.

He followed her gaze. The wolfhound held Rann down with one paw while washing his face with a very large, pink tongue. Rann sputtered and beat the dog with a small fist. The wolfhound ignored him. Tasha and Gevianna tried to pull the dog off, but were laughing too much to help. Maurynna was yawning; the weariness that often followed a Healing was setting in.

"Why?" Linden asked at last, surprised at how calm he sounded.

"Because, I am sorry to say, the Fraternity of Blood may not be the old nurse's tale that many people think; there are whispers that some misguided fools have resurrected it here in Casna. I believe those rumors have some substance behind them.''

''There have always been a few grumblers who have fancied themselves as bearing the mantle of the Fraternity,'' Linden said. ''And aside from the odd madman trying for a Dragonlord's life, that is all they do: grumble.''

Alinya studied him, her old eyes clear and calm. ''I have spent my life avoiding the dances of power in Cassori, Dragonlord, but I have not closed my ears. I . . . hear things. And I am very good at adding two and two, as the saying goes. I truly believe that this incarnation of the Fraternity *is* dangerous.

''If it becomes known that the girl is precious to you, the Fraternity could well strike at you through her. The more you are seen together, the more chance that someone else will see what I saw tonight. Are you willing to take that chance with your soultwin's life, Linden Rathan?''

''They didn't attack Sherrine,'' Linden pointed out.

''True,'' Alinya replied. ''But Sherrine is noble and her mother a favorite of a prince. Likely they dare not strike so high; not yet. But Maurynna . . . She has no such protection and is a foreigner to boot.''

The old woman rested a wrinkled hand gently on his arm. ''I'm sorry, Dragonlord. I know how long you've had to wait. I can't truly comprehend that amount of time, but I can imagine it. But this is only until you can leave Cassori and take her someplace safe with you.''

''I could take her under my protection,'' Linden said, more out of stubbornness than because he believed it.

''Bah! Why not have the heralds cry the news of the best way to hurt you? Can you stay with her every candlemark of the day to protect her? And she's not stupid—or her family would never have trusted her with her own ship. How long before she adds two and two—and comes up with five? Yet you say she must not know what she is.'' Alinya tapped her foot.

Linden looked around at the little-boy clutter of the sleeping chamber. He nudged a leather ball by his foot. It rolled across the floor to rest under a table covered with glittering stones, brightly colored feathers, and seashells from the picnic. He tossed the soldier he still held into an open chest of toys.

It was foolishness; nothing but moonshine. Alinya was imagining things. The true Fraternity of Blood had been destroyed long ago.

But he couldn't take the chance.

Maurynna rode pillion behind Linden as they journeyed back to the house. She was having trouble staying awake now, dozing off only to be jerked into consciousness once more at some change in the horse's gait.

"Wrap your hands in my belt, love, and go to sleep if you want," Linden said. "I won't let you fall."

Grateful, Maurynna did as he said, resting her head against his broad back. His clan braid tickled her nose, but even that wasn't enough to keep her awake now. She slept until they reached the house.

She woke enough to get down from the horse. Linden helped her inside. She was vaguely aware of her aunt and cousin converging on her, then retreating at something Linden said. All she could do was yawn, it seemed; she hadn't even the curiosity to wonder why he led her to the front room.

She came out of the sleepy fog pulling her down when he suddenly held her tight, nearly crushing her, and just as suddenly released her and stepped back. She blinked up at him, surprised.

"Maurynna," he said, taking her hands. "I'm sorry. Gods, I can't tell you how sorry, but—we will not be able to see each other again."

Thirty-three

Maurynna snapped awake at Linden's words. "What?" was all she could say. "But why?"

"Because it's too dangerous for you. I can't subject you to another attack. We won't be able to meet again—not until this is over, and likely not in Casna."

His hands were warm around her own that had suddenly turned icy. She pulled them away.

"I don't believe you," she said, confused and hurt. "Who would attack me? Lady Sherrine again?"

He started to say something, then stopped. A moment later he conceded, "No, I don't think Sherrine would—"

"Then who? Did anyone attack her for keeping company with you? Don't tell me your dalliance was a great secret."

He shook his head impatiently. "Of course it wasn't. Blast it, Maurynna—be sensible. Sherrine has her rank to protect her. You're both foreigner and commoner. Cassorin law—" He paused and tried to capture her hands once more. She wouldn't let him. "Cassorin law would be against—"

She turned to stare at the wall, her mind fastening on the word "commoner."

"It's because I'm not noble, isn't it? Have you come to your senses, then, and decided to look to your own station for . . ." Her voice broke. She said through tears, "Lady Sherrine said that you could only be amusing yourself keeping company with a commoner. She was right, wasn't she? You've never asked me to stay with you; *she* did, and many times, didn't she? What was the point of it all, Linden? Were you truly just amusing yourself?"

She could hear his teeth grind from where she stood but refused to look at him.

"Don't be stupid—you know that isn't it. I wouldn't do that—"

Maurynna turned to face him squarely and cast her pride into the dust. "Then take me home with you tonight," she said quietly.

He looked away. "I—I can't," he whispered.

Hot tears slid down her cheeks. "Then go. Go to your Lady Sherrine, Linden; she's beautiful. Not like me, with my mismatched eyes and calloused hands."

She turned her back on him once more and leaned her forehead against the cool paneling. "It shall be as you wish, Your Grace. Indeed, I never want to see you again," she lied. "Go."

He did not come to her as she had hoped he would. He stood for a long time behind her; out of whatever rags of pride she had left, Maurynna held back the worst of her tears until she heard him leave. When the door slammed, she slid to the floor and cried.

The next thing she knew Aunt Elenna and Maylin were fluttering around her like frantic partridges.

"What's wrong, Rynna?" Maylin asked over and over.

"Hush, girl, don't badger her," Aunt Elenna said. "She's simply tired from the Healing and the shock of everything that's happened. It sometimes takes people this way. Come, dear heart, try to stand. You'll feel better in the morning."

No, she wanted to say. *I won't be better in the morning. How can I be?* She tried to find the words to tell them how her world had collapsed around her, but only more tears came. Giving up—for she cared about nothing anymore—Maurynna let her aunt and cousin hustle her up the stairs to the bedroom. Once there she stood quietly while they drew off her gown and shift and replaced them with her nightgown as though they dressed a doll. She had stopped sobbing by now, but the tears still fell from her eyes.

She remembered seeing Maylin's worried face above her as they put her to bed and drew the sheet up under her chin. Then Maurynna closed her eyes and shut out the world. They tried to make her talk to them. She refused. In the end, when she turned her back and curled into a tight ball, they blew out the rushlight and left her alone in the darkened room.

How could he? Maurynna grieved. *I thought—I thought perhaps . . . Damn it, I was right—it's sometimes better to let a dream stay a dream. I wish I'd never met him.*

She cried herself to sleep, still lying to herself.

"Was it bad, boyo?" Otter asked.

They sat in the dining hall of Linden's city house. On the table between them rested a jug of wine and two goblets. A single candle lit the room. Aside from their quiet conversation the house was silent; the servants had been dismissed for the night.

Linden rested his elbows on the inlaid wood and buried his face in his hands. "Beyond belief, Otter. I feel as though I've torn myself in two, and I know what's between us. She won't understand why it will hurt so much. Ah, gods help me—the look in her eyes . . ." He squeezed his own eyes shut as if that would blot out the memory.

"Did you tell her what you feared? What Duchess Alinya told you about the Fraternity?" the bard said as he filled the goblet in front of the Dragonlord yet again. "Hang it all, boyo, but I wish you could get drunk."

Linden drank half the wine at a gulp. "So do I. Roaring, stinking drunk; then I could forget for a little while. And no, Otter, I didn't tell her that. She wouldn't have believed me. Most people think they're nothing more than a myth, something for bards to hang a tale on. It would have sounded like an excuse to put her aside, and a bad excuse at that."

"So instead you gave her no real reason." The bard sighed. "If it would make you feel any better, I don't think it would have helped even if you'd told her. She's fought off pirates and robbers; some half-legendary bogeymen wouldn't make her blink. She'd be determined to prove you wrong. Our Rynna, if you haven't guessed by now, is a stubborn one."

Linden was too sunk in his misery to rise to the wry bantering in Otter's voice. He didn't even raise his head from his hands. "She said she never wanted to see me again."

Otter blinked in surprise. "How—Can she truly want that? Doesn't the soultwinning mean that you two can't get along without each other or some such thing?"

"No." Linden finished the rest of his wine and held the goblet out to be filled again. He rested one cheek against a hand and swirled the wine around, staring morosely into it. "No, not every soultwinning is like that. There are degrees. Most are no closer than a very close truehuman couple might be; it's as if the souls, while still recognizing the bond, have also grown independent of each other—much as truehuman twins have their own lives.

"And there are a few—very few, thank the gods—that cannot stand each other."

"How can that be, boyo? Not to care for the other half of yourself—how?" the bard asked, surprised.

"Have you never met someone who hated him or herself, then, Otter?" Linden asked. "Think."

"Ah," the bard said, nodding. "I remember now. You're right."

Linden continued, "Some are very close, like Kief and Tarlna. It's a hardship for them to be apart for great lengths of time." Pain filled him; for a moment he couldn't speak, then said bitterly, "I had thought that Maurynna and I would be like that."

He fell silent, reliving his happier memories of Maurynna. The most recent kept pushing them aside to haunt him. The candle was shorter by nearly a finger's width before Otter broke the oppressive quiet.

"I think you will find your bonding is like Kief's and Tarlna's. You said earlier she won't understand why it hurts so much. I think she's hurting, boyo, hurting and striking out with it. And you're the natural target, like it or not."

"May the gods grant that you're right, Otter," said Linden.

The bard snorted. "Of course I am. Have you ever known me to be wrong?"

Linden couldn't help a smile at that, though a wry and halfhearted one it was. "Remember that mountain bumpkin you thought you'd found?"

*　　*　　*

Sent home under guard as though she were a common criminal. And for what?

Sherrine paced her room. "For what?" she said aloud. "Teaching the little gutter rat proper manners? How *dare* she call Linden by name? It was her fault—*her* fault, not mine!"

But you didn't have to blind her. That was excessive.

"It wasn't! She deserved it. Anyway, it was an accident."

Her linen nightgown billowed as she roamed through darkness broken only by a single candle beneath the mirror. Her bare feet pattered against the cold tiles. Back and forth, back and forth, she swept, convincing herself with every step that she had done nothing wrong.

She detoured, snatched up the lavender headache bag from the table by the bed and resumed pacing. She inhaled deeply, but for once the fragrance had no power to soothe her. The memory of how the guards refused to look at her, their eyes sliding over her as if she were too foul to contemplate, came back.

"It was her fault, not mine. I didn't mean to cut her eye, but she shouldn't have provoked me." She stopped before her mirror. She asked her reflection, "She did provoke me, didn't she? Lowborn slut, casting her eyes above herself. Who does she think she is, trying to take Linden away from me?"

As if from the image facing her came a thought: *And is Linden blameless? After all, he sided with her—"attend me at my residence," indeed! How dare he treat you like a common thug?*

Sherrine shook her head. "He'll see what a mistake he made. He'll see I'm right. I know I can convince him."

Can you? Or was Niathea right? You've lost him. A pity Althume doesn't have a love potion for a Dragonlord.

"Althume," Sherrine breathed. "Of course. If Linden won't see reason, I'll speak to Althume. Not even a Dragonlord can treat me this way for the sake of a lowborn trull like that."

She shredded the bag in her fingers. Tiny dried purple flowers cascaded over her toes. She crushed them beneath one heel; the sharp scent of lavender filled the air.

"How dare he treat me that way...."

Thirty-four

Gevianna listened at the door to Rann's sleeping chamber. The boy had taken forever to fall asleep this night; the excitement of the young sea captain's injury and his unbounded delight in the scarlet coldfire had conspired to keep the boy awake much later than usual.

But now there were no longer any mutterings from the room; Rann had evidently finished whatever bedtime story he sent himself to sleep with most nights. She eased the door open. Still no sound.

Good. Now to see if my idea will work. She went in quietly.

The boy lay sprawled across the bed. He snored, tiny, child-sized snorts and snuffles. She pulled the sheet he'd kicked aside over him once more and smiled. The boy was an endearing little mite. If only things had been different. . . .

But she was not here to gaze fondly upon her charge. What she wanted bobbed a handsbreadth or two above the foot of the bed, lighting the dark room with a faint crimson glow.

She undid the ribbons that held the little sewing basket to her belt. Pulling lid and bottom apart, she crept up upon the coldfire as craftily as though she hunted a timid rabbit. The coldfire did not retreat at her approach. She reached out slowly, carefully . . .

A moment later it was hers. If she held the basket up to her eye she could see the red glow through the tight weave, but otherwise it looked like an ordinary round basket of the sort many of the castle women used to hold their embroidery needles and threads. She tied the ribbons to her belt once more. She would have to be quick about her errand; by Duchess Alinya's orders, Rann wasn't to be left alone.

Let us see if this is enough to redeem me in the baroness's eyes, she thought as she left Rann's chambers and made her way to Prince Peridaen's. She bit her lip, remembering the tongue-lashing that had been her lot for missing the picnic.

The farther she journeyed from Rann, the more nervous she became. If someone should find out she'd gone . . . *I hope that I don't have to search all over for Prince Peridaen's steward.*

She rounded a corner and saw one of the servants she'd been told she could trust to run errands. *Thank the gods.* She called, "Ormery—I need a . . . favor, if you please."

Ormery came alert at once; he had recognized the sentence and its phrasing. Without further ado—and with a great deal of relief—Gevianna gave him the sewing basket. "Please give this to Prince Peridaen's steward. I must go back."

Her errand done, Gevianna ran back to the young prince's chambers.

"Rann?" she called softly as she let herself in. No answer. She sent up a prayer of thanksgiving to the gods as she sat down. No one was the wiser for her absence.

"Gevvy? Where's my coldfire?"

The sleepy plaint brought Gevianna into Rann's chamber the next morning. "Is it gone? I guess it burned out in the night. I'm sorry, Your Highness. But come along now; it's time for your tonic, Rann, dear."

Thirty-five

Sherrine held herself stiffly erect as she rode into the court-yard of Linden's residence. She looked neither to the right nor to the left, ignoring the speculative glances of the groom who came to take her horse, the servant who helped her to dismount.

So no doubt the tale of her falling out with Linden was known to all Casna by now. Her jaw clenched at the thought of the servants gossiping amongst themselves and the news sent flying to the ears of their masters and mistresses. She would wager Niathea laughed herself sick even now.

Drawing a deep breath as she approached the front door, Sherrine made herself walk with a measured dignity. But happier memories flooded her and nearly broke her resolve. Blinking away tears, Sherrine swept through the door as the house steward opened it.

"Good day, my lady," he said. Like the others, he did not look directly at her. "If you will follow me, please, His Grace will join you shortly."

He led her to a room that she'd never seen before, small, with only a few chairs and a desk, and left her there. Not a comfortable room, or even an intimate one despite its size. It had the impersonal air of a place used only for work, where one went over the household accounts or some such thing, and then left for more congenial surroundings.

She stood in the center of the room and clenched her fists. It was an insult to send her here. Dragonlord or not, how dare he? And all for the sake of a common trull who dared look above herself! Her breath caught in a sob. Perhaps, just perhaps, she could convince Linden that it was all a mistake. She could forgive him his angry words last night, the humiliating summons to attend him, cursing herself even as she thought it. To humble herself so would not be an easy thing. But surely he felt some of what she did.

The door opened quietly behind her; as if the thought had summoned him, Linden entered the room. She cast a quick glance over her shoulder, one designed to melt him with its mute appeal. But even as she turned, she guessed the game might already be lost.

The Linden that towered over her was not the one she knew, indulgent and easygoing, as ready to laugh at himself as at a witty remark. This new Linden was cold and withdrawn, more imperious than any king—the Dragonlord she had been taught to hate.

But she still had a mission—and her heart—at stake in this game. She would play until the end.

"Linden," she said. The tremor in her voice was real, as was the tear that slid down one cheek.

Yet the ice did not melt from the grey eyes. "My lady Sherrine," he said. "Perhaps you will explain your actions of yesterday evening to me. I thought we had an understanding that neither of us was bound to the other. I have not interfered with your other private doings—yet you dared interfere with mine."

She was frightened by a rage she sensed being held in check, though Linden did nothing more than stand, big hands tightly gripping his belt, staring down at her.

"She is only a commoner," Sherrine began feebly, her pretty words and wit fleeing before his silent fury. "She has no rank. Surely—"

"Rank? Do you truly think that excuses your actions, my lady? The other man you have been dallying with—"

Sherrine stopped herself a moment before blurting out that there had been no other man; it was only a tale to throw him off the scent if he became suspicious of any necessary absences. If she was to have any hope of winning him back, she must remain silent.

Linden continued, "Is his rank equal to mine? No. But I did not hunt him down as you did Maurynna.

"And do you truly think rank matters so much to Dragonlords? Almost all of us began life as commoners—"

Startled, Sherrine said, "What do you mean? Surely you were all royal, or at least nobly born before—"

His harsh laugh cut her off. "Royal? Nobly born? What fool's tale have you listened to, Sherrine? There are only two of us now alive who were born noble, girl—I'm one. And yet, had I come before you in that rank as a truehuman, you would have scorned me. My father was lord of his holding, true—by virtue of squatting on a tumbled-down keep no one else wanted. He also took to wife the sister of the High Chief's mistress, she who bore Bram. In the eyes of the local people it gave him standing. To you and the rest of the rank-proud Cassorin nobility I've met, he would have been nothing more than an upstart peasant.

"Dragonlords are born farmers and merchants, slaves and traveling entertainers, peasants and charcoal burners; we are the children of fishermen and of weavers. We live those lives until we Change. And we remember them. Perhaps that is why the gods destined us to be the arbiters between nations—we think first of the common people, not of the pride of kings and queens."

Sherrine was horrified. She had always assumed that the Dragonlords came from the ranks of those gifted by the gods with the right to rule. That entire countries would accept the counsel of a peasant's brat, that a king would bend the knee to a, a—"Slave?"

Linden nodded, smiling grimly. "Tarlna was one. And Kief was the son of potters. Very good potters; he's still proud of them."

He turned away. "I had thought you saw past the rank to the man, Sherrine. It was my mistake—but you made someone else pay the price.

"And there is nothing I can do about it. A Cassorin would never have stood up to you. But Maurynna is Thalnian; like my own countrymen they speak their minds. By Cassorin law you were entirely within your rights to strike her. She is, as you said, only a commoner—but that means nothing to me.

Yet as a Dragonlord, no matter how I feel personally about Cassorin law, I must uphold it. As a man, I can only tell you that it is ended between us. We could have parted friends; you chose otherwise.''

Desperate now, Sherrine was ready to try anything. For the sake of the Fraternity she must not lose her hold over him. She did not want to know what her mother would say to this. And there was the small matter of her heart.

She caught his sleeve; he pulled away. "Linden, please. Forgive me. I cannot bear to lose you.''

Gods help her; it was the truth. Never had she lost her heart before. How had he brought her to this pass? She continued, the words rushing forth like a mountain stream, "I'll pay a wergild to the girl—as much as though she were royal! I'll— I'll even apologize to her. Just say—''

"No, Sherrine. There is nothing between us now, and there will never be again. I do not repeat my mistakes.''

The cold finality of his words was like a slap. Sherrine felt the blood drain from her face. Her heart was a lump of ice in her breast. So—he would truly cast her aside for such a little thing? For the sake of some lowborn wench? How dare he!

She stared at him, saying nothing. Her rage refused to let her speak lest she say too much. Then she turned and stormed out of the room, wrapping cold fury around her like a cloak.

The spy had disturbing news.

Althume sat behind his desk in the study of Prince Peridaen's city home, playing out his role of steward. He inclined his head to the man before him, a man who looked well dressed if not prosperous, a man who would excite no suspicion as he moved through the layers of society in Casna. "Go on,'' the mage said.

"Like I said, m'lord, one of my mates was part of the young lady's escort yesterday evening. Said she went to some merchant's house to call out an upstart wench who'd been making eyes at the big Dragonlord. Slashed the girl across the face with her whip, the Lady Sherrine did. Maybe blinded the wench, Narin said. That's what upset him so, y'see; it's one thing to strike the girl, but blinding her was summat else, and all just because the Dragonlord's got a roving eye. Narin didn't think that was fair-like.''

The spy paused a moment to eye the sewing basket as if surprised at finding it on the steward's desk. He continued, ''So, anyway, who comes riding in at that moment but Linden Rathan himself. Narin said he'd never seen anyone so angry. Not that the Dragonlord yelled or anything; just got cold as ice to Lady Sherrine and looked like the lord of storms. He told her to attend him the next morning at the fourth hour past dawn and sent her away like a whipped scullery maid.''

''It is now well after the third hour,'' Althume said coldly. ''Why didn't you bring this tale to me sooner?''

The man shifted uneasily. ''Have some pity, m'lord,'' he protested. ''I didn't run into Narin at the Spotted Cow until well after midnight, and he was drunker than a drowned pig in a beer barrel by then. It took a long time to get all the tale out of him. He rambled something awful, m'lord, he was that upset about the merchant girl. And then I couldn't find you this morning till you came back here.''

Althume did not look at the innocent-appearing chest behind him—the chest that had arrived from Pelnar this very morning. ''I had business to attend to elsewhere,'' he allowed. His fingers itched to open the chest once more and gloat over its contents. He schooled himself to unnatural stillness.

''That's what they told me when I came by earlier. So I went and watched Lady Sherrine's house for a while to see if aught unusual went on. I was curious-like to see if she'd obey the Dragonlord's summons, or to see if he'd go and patch things up with her. Don't think he did, 'cause the grooms was getting the horses ready and they and the other servants standing about looked worried. Daresay they're afraid their mistress will take it out on them when she gets back.''

''So she intends to obey the summons,'' Althume murmured. He steepled his fingers before his face and thought. This was an opportunity not to be wasted. As chancy as a toss of the dice, but it seemed the very gods played on his side for this round. He'd been pleased enough with the unexpected gift from Rann's nurse. That Sherrine should have a falling-out with Linden Rathan at the same time a certain precious cargo had arrived might give him the time he needed. Once more the mage resisted looking over his shoulder.

Things happen in threes, the old wives said. A soultrap jewel, Dragonlord coldfire to charge it with—and now this. Did he cast the dice the gods gave him?

Yes. He opened the drawer, pulled out a small bag of silver pennies, and tossed it to the spy, who snatched it out of the air with greedy glee.

"Go," the mage said. "You've done well. For the Fraternity."

"May their blood flow." The man returned the ritual answer and bowed himself out of the room.

Althume listened to the man's footsteps fade as he decided which course he should take. The girl might think she had fooled everyone into believing that it was for the Fraternity's sake that she dallied with the Dragonlord, but Althume knew better. He had seen the way she looked at Linden Rathan when she thought no one watched. The girl was infatuated with the big Dragonlord.

Althume did not know Sherrine herself well, but in the course of his unnaturally long life he had run across many like her—men or women whose love could turn to hate with an angry word. She would be hot for revenge if she could not talk her way back into Linden Rathan's bed. How ironic that she didn't know that all she had to do was wait until she'd Changed.

He went to the cabinet at the other side of the room. Taking the key from a silken cord around his neck, he unlocked the carved doors and removed the silver scrying bowl and the bottle of black ink hidden inside. He set the bowl on a nearby table and filled it. A moment later, having invoked the spells, Althume leaned over the bowl, trying to make sense of the hazy, distorted images that came and went.

But the magic that surrounded the Dragonlords defeated him; he caught only one clear glimpse: Linden Rathan's face tight with cold anger. Althume involuntarily started back from the fury in the grey eyes that seemed to look into his own.

"Well and well and well," the mage said softly. "It seems I underestimated you, my good Dragonlord, didn't I? You're not as soft as I had thought. There is indeed steel beneath that easygoing exterior—yet even the finest steel may be broken. But how to talk Lady Sherrine into helping destroy you?"

Thirty-six

The journey along the Processional had never seemed so
long. Kief and Tarlna rode beside him; as they chatted gaily,
Linden tried to think how to tell them what had happened.
And ahead was the tree where Maylin and Kélla always
waited to wave at him. He wondered if they'd be there today.
He rather doubted it. Still, he stretched up in the saddle and
searched the crowd.

To his surprise they were in their usual spot. His heart
lightened; perhaps Maurynna had realized that he was concerned only for her safety and had talked some sense into
Maylin. He smiled and raised his hand before he realized that
Kella was not waving and giggling as she always did. The
child sat in her sister's arms, watching him with wide, sad
eyes, then turned her face away. That hurt him more than
Maylin's glare, which bade fair to flay the skin from his back.
A moment later they disappeared into the crowd.

Linden took up the reins again with both hands and set his
lips.

*What was that about, Linden? Your new kinswomen seem
furious with you,* Kief said, astonished. *There was enough
venom in that look to fell a dragon.*

*That was to let me know what they think of me after last
night—Maylin's idea, I think. For such a soft-looking little
thing, she's as fierce as a snow cat.*

Is something wrong between you and your soultwin?

He sighed. The moment he'd been dreading had arrived.
*Ah, well—yes. Although Sherrine and I had an understanding,
she took exception to my keeping company with Maurynna.*
Once more the cold fear at seeing Maurynna's bloodied face

rocked him. He didn't realize how strong the image was until Kief's shocked exclamation rang in his mind.

Gods help us—did she lose the eye?

Linden said, *No, thank the gods; it looked much worse than it was.* He quickly told Kief and Tarlna, who had picked up her soultwin's distress and was demanding an explanation, all that had happened the night before.

And earlier this morning I spoke with Sherrine. It was not . . . pleasant. I think I've made an enemy of her; she was furious that I took the part of a "commoner" against her.

Oh, aye—a "commoner" who just happens to be a fledgling Dragonlord, Tarlna said in disgust. *These Cassorins and their obsession with rank. By their own law Sherrine should be the one punished.*

Kief observed, *That "obsession" is a sword that cuts both ways; it's what allows us to do our duty.*

It is still an insult to Dragonlords, Tarlna insisted.

With no way to seek redress, said Linden bitterly. *And Duchess Alinya was right; it would be folly to call more attention to Maurynna by continuing to see her—at least for now.*

Especially if she's correct that some troublemakers fancy themselves the Fraternity reborn, Kief said. *I wonder—could she be right?*

Even if she is, they'd need a powerful mage to be truly dangerous. Have you heard any rumors of such a one? Tarlna pointed out.

No, Kief admitted.

And thank all the gods for that, Linden added.

The Processional climbed the gentle hill leading to the palace. Linden stared sourly at the granite walls rising before him. The last thing he wanted was to sit through another interminable council. The first person to annoy him would get his head snapped off.

Once again Kief spoke in his mind. *While I sympathize with you, I must admit that I always thought it would have been best if you'd stayed away from your soultwin until she's Changed. I take it that this estrangement means you will not be going to that coming-of-age feast with her?*

Linden groaned aloud. The guards riding alongside darted surprised and concerned glances at him; he ignored them.

Gods help him, he'd forgotten about the *tisrahn*. He shouldn't go; best to make the break clean until he could get away from Cassori, and seek Maurynna in whatever port she sailed to next. He thought, *I've lasted more than six centuries without my soultwin. Lonely, yes, but I made do. Why is the prospect of a few more tendays such hell?*

There had to be a way.

Inspiration dawned. Keeping his mindvoice carefully diffident, Linden said, *But if I don't go, I dishonor my host, Almered. And that will dishonor House Erdon, my new kin— Almered's family is leagued with them. After all, if Maurynna and Almered's jests are more than that, he's also kin—if somewhat distant. I'm Yerrin, Kief; I can't insult family that way. You know that.*

With your first Change you became Dragonlord before Yerrin, Kief pointed out.

All the more reason to behave in an honorable manner, Linden said. *So I shall go to the* tisrahn. He looked over at the older Dragonlord.

Kief's glare rivaled Maylin's. *Someday, little one, that stubborn streak of yours will get you into trouble.*

Linden grinned as they rode into the courtyard. *It already has, my friend, and no doubt will again. But not this time, I think.*

"Your Highness—here are the accounts you wished to see," Althume said as he presented himself, estate books cradled in his arms, to Prince Peridaen in the latter's study.

Peridaen looked up from the supper he and Anstella were just finishing. "Ah, good, Kas. We're finished, Yulla; you may clear the table. We'll need plenty of room for these books."

Peridaen leaned back in his chair, smiling benignly at the servants as they scurried to do his bidding. Althume waited humbly by the empty fireplace. Anstella looked amused.

As soon as the last servant had left, Prince Peridaen dropped his pose of affable royalty. "Now what, Kas? I daresay you've already heard Sherrine's made a pretty mess of this. Seemed the whole wretched council couldn't wait to tell us about it this morning."

"I knew the little fool couldn't do it right," Anstella said scornfully. "A very pretty mess, indeed, this is."

Althume set the books down with a thump. "On the contrary, it's to our advantage—for, you see, there's been a slight change in plans. I've spent the past few hours looking over a manuscript that Pol brought back with him along with the soultrap jewel. It's made up of certain notes of Nethuryn's from long ago. With those notes, my translations of Ankarlyn's tracts should prove much easier.

"I also found, among the notes, a recipe for a drug that bears a notation that it is of Ankarlyn's devising. I would dearly love to put it to the test on one of the Dragonlords. Were one of them under its influence, I would be able to question him or her to my heart's content. And the crowning jest is that afterward they wouldn't remember what happened to them."

Anstella laughed. "How deliciously ironic."

Peridaen grinned like a schoolboy with a pouch full of stolen apples. "I like that. Do you intend to try it?"

"I would love to, but there is one slight problem with it," Althume admitted with a wry twist of his lips. "Judging by the ingredients, it would be quite bitter and very odd tasting. I'm afraid it would be noticeable in a meal."

Peridaen stroked his beard. "So concealing it in food is out. Hm. That is a problem. Could one of the Dragonlords be overwhelmed and forced to take it?"

"Possibly. I was thinking along the same lines," Althume said.

An amused laugh made both men turn to Anstella.

"Men," the baroness said an amused tone, as if she spoke of an entertaining—but rather backward—pack of puppies. "Always thinking force is the answer to everything. Think, my lords; think. There is indeed something such a drug could be hidden in.''

Althume looked to the prince; Peridaen shrugged his ignorance.

''What?'' the mage asked, nettled that Anstella had found an answer so easily to the problem.

Anstella smiled. ''What is expected to be bitter? A farewell cup, of course.''

Annoyed, Althume exploded, ''For the sake of the gods, Anstella, are you thinking of Sherrine and Linden Rathan? Do you honestly think he'd accept any such thing from her after what she did to that girl?''

''*I* wouldn't,'' Peridaen said. ''And neither would Linden Rathan; the man's not stupid.''

Now Anstella fairly purred. ''But he would—if there were witnesses. Think! He's a Dragonlord. He can't afford to look mean-spirited and petty, can he? Especially over some commoner. And petty he would look, did he refuse a cup offered in . . . sincere repentance.

''No, my lords, take my word for it; if Sherrine offers him a farewell cup before a goodly number of the nobles of Cassori, Linden Rathan will drink it even if it chokes him.''

By all the gods, she was right; so simple an answer . . . Althume smiled like a wolf.

''Anstella, that's brilliant,'' Peridaen said. He caught her hand and kissed it. ''Absolutely brilliant. But where would there be such a gathering of witnesses? Sherrine can hardly burst into the council.''

''Not the council, Peridaen,'' Althume said. ''But there could be an occasion. . . .'' He caught Anstella's eye.

The baroness nodded and smiled slightly. ''Just so; I think we have the same idea, Kas. Leave it to me. Can you be ready on short notice? I may not be able to give you much warning.''

''Yes. Once the drug is compounded, it simply needs to be dropped into a cup of wine. The beauty of this is that, in itself, it is not magical. There will be no risk of warning

Linden Rathan that way. It merely sets the stage for the spell to follow."

"Good," Peridaen said. "That just leaves Sherrine. I'll order her—"

"No," Althume interrupted. "Don't. Not yet. I want her to do this of her own free will, if possible. If her heart's not in it, she might well warn him. I want her to come seeking help from you."

"But how to get her to want to do it?" Peridaen objected.

Anstella's smile turned from mysterious to pitiless. "Leave that to me as well." She glanced at the time-candle. "In fact, if you will excuse me, my lord, I believe I shall pay my daughter a visit this evening. I'm certain she needs . . . comforting this night."

With that, Anstella rose gracefully; Peridaen stood as well. He escorted her to the door where they exchanged a brief kiss.

When she was gone, Peridaen returned to his seat and poured out two goblets of wine. "Do you think it will work?" He pushed one goblet across the table.

"Likely better than trying to overpower someone Linden Rathan's size would," the mage admitted as he joined the prince at the table. He drank.

"So—what else is involved in this change in plans you mentioned?" Peridaen asked.

"I still intend to use the soultrap jewel, but not quite as we planned. You've heard the legend that Ankarlyn enslaved a fledgling Dragonlord?"

"Of course. But it's just a legend, Kas."

"I don't think so—not anymore. And I'll know for certain if I can question Linden Rathan."

Peridaen frowned. "And if it is true about the fledgling? You intend—"

"To enslave Sherrine, of course. As a member of the Fraternity, she should be prepared to lay down her life. It may not come to that."

"This isn't something that can be done quickly, is it?"

Peridaen asked, an odd note in his voice. "That is, you weren't planning on doing it tonight."

"No. The soultrap jewel will need to be charged," the mage replied. "That will take time." He wondered at the look of guilty relief that flashed across the prince's face.

"Isn't that dangerous—to begin your ceremonies again?" said Peridaen. "Could the Dragonlords sense them?"

"A chance I'll have to take. But I'm confident that I'll be too far away for them to detect."

Peridaen shuddered. "You'll be at that place again?"

"I will. It's warded and has long been dedicated to such workings. There's a considerable amount of innate power already there, and that will aid in charging the jewel. And once it's charged . . ."

Althume shrugged and watched Peridaen narrowly as the prince struggled with the idea.

"Ah, gods, I wish there was some other way. I don't know how I'll face Anstella after this." Peridaen buried his face in his hands. "I don't like this."

"We must all make what sacrifices we can for the Fraternity. And are you so certain that Anstella will be upset? There seems to be little love lost between mother and daughter," Althume said.

Peridaen's head snapped up at that. "Don't be a fool," he exploded. "However it looks, and however much Anstella derides the girl, she is still a mother. I've never been able to understand what is happening between them or why it's like that. But I do know that if anyone else dares insult Sherrine— even if they're simply echoing something she just said— Anstella will be at their throats like a mother bear defending her cub. Twisted as this bond may be, it is still that of mother and child, and that is a thing even a mage would do well to fear. If you value this scheme of yours, don't tell her what you plan."

His royal patron's anger startled Althume. Peridaen had never spoken to him in that way before. So, then. It would be well to tread softly here. He forced into his voice a sympathy he didn't feel. "I'm sorry. I didn't realize that. And it pains me to think that I will cause your lady such grief. But you must see that this is a gift from the gods themselves, Peridaen. We'll never have a chance like this again.''

"I know." Peridaen stared at the table. He suddenly looked tired beyond measuring. "I know. But didn't Ankarlyn kill that fledgling?''

"Only indirectly. Ankarlyn made clumsy use of his fledgling once the man had Changed—a mistake we won't repeat. The enslaved Dragonlord's soultwin killed him, then committed suicide herself. If we play this game well, neither Linden Rathan nor any other Dragonlord should know what has happened."

"May the gods will it so," Peridaen said heavily. "*If* we play the game."

Alone at the long table in the dining room of the Colranes' city house, Sherrine picked at her food, pushing it around the plate. The mere thought of eating turned her stomach. She shoved the plate aside.

"Take it away," she snapped at the serving maid.

An instant later the offending meal was whisked away. The maid fled the room. Sherrine heard murmuring. No doubt the servants were discussing this latest bit of temper, curse them.

Now what? She stared at her hands as she twisted the rings on her fingers. The long, lonely evening—and lonelier night—stretched out before her.

So lost in her thoughts was she, that at first she didn't heed the sudden babble of voices at the front of the house. Then—

"Oh, gods—*no!*"

Sherrine stood up, gripping the edge of the table with both hands. Not her mother. Not on this day of all days.

Her mother swept regally into the room. Sherrine pushed away from the table and forced herself to stand upright.

One beautiful eyebrow rose in a disdainful arch. "I knew you'd fail. But not quite so spectacularly, I must admit. Thrown over for a *saflor,* of all things."

Sherrine stiffened. The door behind her mother was still open and, though her mother did not raise her voice, from past experience Sherrine well knew the carrying power of her mother's jibes. Judging by the sudden silence throughout the rest of the house, every servant in the place was eavesdropping. And Sherrine had no illusions that they would keep silent for love of her; the tale would be spread throughout the noble houses of Casna by tomorrow night.

"Thrown over for a *sailor*," her mother repeated, "and then dismissed like a thieving steward—all for the sake of some low-born wench. And you took it meekly, didn't you?"

The words were bitter enough, but the worst was the amused disdain and contempt that dripped from her mother's voice. And she could find no words of her own to fight back with. She despised herself for her weakness.

"Outsmarted yourself, didn't you, this time? Thought you were so clever and never saw that Linden Rathan was just amusing himself until something better came along." Her mother shook her head, smiling scornfully. "And there's not a thing you can do about it, is there?" she taunted.

Sherrine turned her head away from the hateful truth. There was nothing she could do. She was powerless.

"I knew all along this idiocy of yours would fail. The likes of you would need sorcery to catch a Dragonlord," her mother said with a final sneer. "You're a disappointment to me, girl; you always have been. Bah, I've no more time to waste on you."

On the last cutting words her mother gracefully gathered up her skirts and departed. Sherrine stood trembling, unable to move, feeling as if her soul had been torn apart.

Then her spirit rebelled. She had not needed sorcery to catch Linden! Not the first time!

But she would if she were to snare him again. And she thought she knew where to find such magic; she might be powerless, but she knew of one who was not.

She would give Linden one last chance. And then . . .

And then he'd see he could not treat her so and escape unscathed.

Thirty-seven

The morning light poured through the window. Cursing under his breath, Althume bent over the ancient manuscript. The script was crabbed and blotted, the language archaic where it wasn't in an unknown tongue altogether. At last he threw down his quill pen in frustration.

Time. He needed more time, damn it. From the little he'd translated, it could be done. But he needed the entire ceremony and spells, not just this piddling bit he had so far.

Most frustrating of all was that he knew how to gain the time he needed, but for it he needed a certain accomplice. He wondered how long it would be before she sought either her mother or Peridaen's aid for revenge. They, of course, would send her on to him. He did not relish the thought of her knowing him for a mage, but that could not be helped.

He just hoped it would not be long—or that Peridaen would be forced to order her aid.

He was still lost in thought when the house steward opened the study door. "My Lord Steward, Lady Sherrine of Colrane asks to see you."

Before he could reply, Sherrine entered the room, head held high, eyes glittering with fury. For a moment Althume, too surprised to stand or speak, merely stared at her. By all the gods, what had Anstella said to the girl last night? And why straight here? He knew that Anstella would not have divulged his secret. Not without his permission.

It took a frown from the house steward to bring him back to his assumed role. He rose and came around the desk, hands extended. "My lady—you honor me. Herrel, send for tea," he ordered as he guided Sherrine to a chair, "and then see that we are not disturbed."

As Herrel closed the door Althume finished for his benefit, "How may I be of service to you, my lady?"

The latch dropped. Althume listened a moment to be certain that the house steward was not eavesdropping at the keyhole, then dropped his mask of obsequious servant. "So, you've failed."

Sherrine hissed in anger. "Only because Linden took the side of a lowborn slut. I even offered to pay her a wergild."

Althume waved a hand. "Spare me the details; I already know them."

A dark flush crept up the girl's cheeks.

"However, may I say that I sympathize with you? Who would have thought that a Dragonlord would have become so angry at such a little thing. It's not as if the girl was noble." *But if, as the other Dragonlords seemed to think, having you in close proximity to Linden Rathan was too dangerous, this was a clever ruse on his part to have you keep your distance, my little fledgling.* "Still, the fact remains you did not get very much useful information for all the time you spent with Linden Rathan."

"Should I have handed him a list and said 'The Fraternity of Blood would like the answers to these questions, my lord'?" Sherrine retorted. "The man is not stupid. I asked him as much as I dared. If I had more time I could get even deeper into his confidence." She tossed her head. "Get me that time, Althume."

The mage leaned back in his chair and steepled his fingers before his face. Audacious chit—he had to grant her that. He had no doubt she had suggested the dalliance for her own pleasure; she had not the strength of purpose to discomfit herself for the Fraternity. And here she was demanding he help her reconcile with Linden Rathan as if he had nothing better to do.

But what did she think a mere steward could do? Or did she know more than she'd let on so far?

He said with a touch of irony, "Time is something we are all in need of, Lady Sherrine. And how could I, the humble steward of Prince Peridaen's estates, get you more time with Linden Rathan?''

"Let us end this farce—*steward*. You are no more a servant than I. You are a mage—and a powerful one, I would wager.''

Althume allowed a tiny smile to cross his lips. "Very good, my dear. How did you guess?''

The corners of Sherrine's mouth quirked up but it was not a smile. "I am not stupid, my lord mage. Not at all. I know how to *see*, not merely *look*.''

Amused now, Althume asked, "And what do you want of me?''

She came directly to the point of her visit. Althume approved; he had no time to waste on maidenly vaporings and false modesty.

"Prince Peridaen once jested about a love philter for Linden Rathan. I want one. Once he accepts me again, I can continue gathering information. Indeed, if the philter causes him to become entirely besotted with me, I could be more daring in what I asked him.''

"Alas," said the mage ruefully. "As much as I hate to admit it, it cannot be done. Oh, don't think I didn't research it; Peridaen stung my pride with his assumption that it wasn't possible. Unfortunately he was right. You will have to find your own way back into Linden Rathan's bed.''

Her nostrils flared, but Sherrine betrayed no other sign of anger. "I—His servants turned me away not a candlemark ago," she admitted.

Good, Althume thought. As if to himself, he mused aloud, "How odd you should mention time before. Time, time, time; exactly what we—Prince Peridaen and I—need.''

"Why?''

The question was a mild surprise. "Hasn't your mother told you of the most recent development in the council?''

Sherrine's laugh was crystalline and unamused. "We judged it best to have as little contact as possible while I dallied with Linden as she faced him across the council table. That way Beren's supporters could not so easily claim undue influence. A plan, I must say, that suited me quite well.''

Still, she should have kept you apprised of which way events were turning. Ah, Anstella—clever as you can be, in so many ways you are a fool. A pity Peridaen took up with you instead of your daughter.

He said, "The Dragonlords seem to be favoring Duke Beren's claim. While it would make things very easy indeed for us if they gave the throne to Peridaen, even if they don't there may be another way to win this battle. But for that I need time to study certain ancient manuscripts. And from what I have already gleaned from those same manuscripts, my lady Sherrine, while I cannot make you a love philter, I can promise you a certain amount of revenge for this insult."

She dropped her gaze to the bejeweled hands lying in her lap, studying the fingers twisting the rings that adorned them. Long lashes veiled her eyes, leaving the mage to wonder what went on behind them.

Then once again her gaze met his. As Sherrine twisted a lock of auburn hair, she asked, "Will you tell me what you plan?"

He shook his head. "You will know only what you need to for your part in this. And you will not like some of it, but it is necessary."

She considered that. Her lips parted in a tiny, cruel smile. "Will it be painful for him?"

"Yes. Very."

The beautiful hazel eyes lit with the thought of vengeance. "It is no more than he deserves. I am yours to command, my lord mage."

"Good. First we set the stage. . . ."

Thirty-eight

Staring morosely at the ship's charts before her, Maurynna listened to the bustle of the Vanadin household. Aunt Elenna called out orders to 'prentices, Maylin chivvied Kella along to hurry and eat, servants passed to and fro on their various duties. One peered into the front room where Maurynna sat. After one glance at the face that looked back at her, the girl mumbled an apology and disappeared after a last disapproving look at the oil lamp still burning.

Maurynna took the hint. No sense in wasting oil now that it was light. She blew out the lamp and forced herself back to her task. It was something that truly needed to be done, she told herself.

In truth she'd come downstairs long before dawn so that she could be miserable in private. Her eyes were hot and dry and no doubt red and swollen to boot; she'd spent the better part of the past few candlemarks crying, heartsore, and furious with herself for it.

Just forget about him, cold reason told her over and over.

But try as she might, no matter what she forced her mind to, the image of Linden came back to her, haunted her waking and sleeping.

Cold reason tried again. *He's not worth all this even if he did walk straight out of a legend. Forget him.*

"I can't forget him," she whispered, admitting defeat. At least, she thought, it will be a long, long time indeed. "Damn you, Linden Rathan."

The clamor of hooves on the courtyard outside cut through her fog of misery. Her heart jumped in panic; the last time she'd heard that sound, she'd nearly been blinded.

And this time, Maurynna knew, Linden would not come to her rescue.

She made her shaking legs carry her to the door to the hall. There they rebelled and would take her no farther; she leaned against the doorframe, listening as more horses crowded into the yard.

Little Aunt Elenna swept past her to the front door, apprentices carried along after her like leaves in a wind. Her head held high, Elenna flung open the door and planted herself squarely in the entrance, arms crossed over her chest, barring the way as surely as an army.

"My Lady Sherrine," she called, and Maurynna clenched her fists in mingled fear and anger. How dare that noble bitch come back here to threaten and harass her and her family again? Surely Linden had forbidden her this—or had he bothered?

Elenna went on, her voice colder than Maurynna had ever heard it. "What means *this* visit?"

"Is Captain Erdon within? I would speak with her," a low, husky, and all too well-remembered voice answered.

Maurynna laid her hand on her belt dagger. The beautiful Lady Sherrine would not have it all her way this time, she vowed. Maylin pushed through the crowd of apprentices to her side.

"Rynna, it's not what you think; there are packhorses among her guards, and blue ribbons hanging from her horse's bridle," Maylin said, grabbing the wrist of Maurynna's knife hand with surprising strength.

That took a moment to penetrate. Astonishment swept away all other emotions before it. "What? What do you mean?" Her hand fell from the dagger.

Maylin's odd-colored gaze met her own, her eyes dancing with mischief. "Wergild is what I mean. I'll wager you anything the Lady Sherrine is paying you wergild."

"Me? Pay me—? Here in Cassori?"

At home in Thalnia, yes; there she would fetch a wergild from near all but the royal family itself. Not as much as, say, her Uncle Kesselandt or some of her other uncles and aunts, but a fair amount to be sure. She was an Erdon and that family was one to be reckoned with.

But here in Cassori?

She wanted nothing from Lady Sherrine save to be left alone. Or perhaps that lady thought that her money-grubbing merchant's soul would forget Linden at the sight of some tawdry goods. Damn her to every hell known, then.

Yet . . . *I almost wish it were so; it would be easier than wanting him so much.*

Or had Linden ordered this? The thought infuriated Maurynna and broke her paralysis with the force of a boom swinging wild in a gale. She strode to the door. Aunt Elenna turned at her coming and, after one quick glance, yielded the battle-field.

"Get Bard Otter—quickly!" she heard her aunt say to one of the servants.

Maurynna stepped into the hot, unrelenting sunlight and stood on the front step, as straight and proud as the *Sea Mist*'s mainmast, hands clenched at her side. She met Lady Sherrine's eyes without flinching.

As if Maurynna's coming were a signal, Lady Sherrine placed her hand in that of the guardsman standing at her palfrey's head and dismounted. It was, Maurynna thought in the back of her mind, the same horse Lady Sherrine had ridden the other night; if Raven were here, he would know for certain—he recognized horses the way she recognized ships. She had an instant's regret that her oldest friend wasn't here to guard her back.

Now the Cassorin noblewoman stepped daintily across the cobbled yard. Maurynna went to meet her.

They stopped a few paces from each other. Afoot, Lady Sherrine had to tilt her head back to meet Maurynna's gaze. Maurynna said nothing; merely stared down at the beautiful woman as coldly as she could.

They were joined by Otter. He also held to the silence, but from the corner of her eye Maurynna saw that his bard's torc was no longer hidden by the neck of his tunic as it usually was, but proudly displayed for all to see. Well and good, then;

he would stand witness for her in this. She looked back to Lady Sherrine, still waiting. Let her enemy make the first move.

She nearly cried out at that move. For Lady Sherrine swept her a courtesy, one that would have lent grace to the Dawn Emperor's court in Assantik, where the intricate dance of the courtiers was a thing of legend. Maurynna heard gasps of surprise from those around them.

She almost missed the noblewoman's words; there was an odd roaring in her ears and her head spun.

"Bard Otter Heronson, will you be witness for what I do this day? Thank you."

Now a man dressed in Colrane livery came forward. He held a roll of parchment tied with the blue ribbon of peace in one hand.

Her steward, Maurynna guessed, with a listing of the wergild. As witness, Otter held out his hand; the man laid the roll in his palm and retreated once again.

"Captain," Lady Sherrine continued, "I humbly beg your pardon for my actions the other day. My rash temper could have blinded you; I rejoice that Linden Rathan could get help for you. Again—I apologize."

The low voice was husky with . . . shame? Regret? Maurynna was not certain. But the single tear that slid down the pale cheek told her that Lady Sherrine was indeed in the grip of some strong emotion. Did she truly love Linden? If so, Maurynna almost felt sorry for her.

Almost. But Lady Sherrine was still not forgiven.

"Please, accept these humble things as my wergild to you. I was wrong and this is the only way I may make amends to you."

One slender hand gestured gracefully at the waiting packhorses. Maurynna wondered if this woman were capable of making any movement that wasn't graceful. She wished the elegant Lady Sherrine would go away; the woman made her feel like a packhorse herself.

As if she read Maurynna's mind, the noblewoman said, "I

realize my presence is . . . disagreeable to you, so with your acceptance, Captain, I will withdraw.''

Maurynna looked to Otter, who slid the ribbon from the parchment and studied it. The bard was well-schooled in the art of hiding his feelings, but Maurynna saw the sudden widening of his eyes. Nor could he hide a quick, wondering glance at the packhorses. His gaze flickered to meet hers and he nodded slightly.

So; it was to end here and now, this war between her and Lady Sherrine. Maurynna drew a deep breath and schooled her voice to a serenity she didn't feel. ''I accept your wergild, Lady Sherrine, and say that from this day forth there shall be no further quarrel with you by me or my kin.'' The ritual words tasted foul on her tongue.

And worse was yet to come. She forced herself to hold out her hand, palm up. After a moment's hesitation, Lady Sherrine placed her own on top. Maurynna looked down at the dainty hand, so white and soft against her own tanned and calloused one. The contrast was sharp as a blow.

Otter looped the blue ribbon loosely around their joined hands. With her free hand Maurynna took the parchment tally from him, signaling her formal acceptance of the wergild.

The final words were bitter as aloes. ''Let this offering wash away whatever ill will lies between us.''

She pulled her hand away as quickly as she decently could. Lady Sherrine did the same. The ribbon fluttered to the ground.

''Thank you, Captain,'' Lady Sherrine said. She raised her hand in an imperious gesture. The guard led her palfrey up and she mounted once more.

The guards by the packhorses began unloading their charges. Maurynna watched, appalled; somehow it had not seemed like so much when distributed between the animals, but when piled together in the little courtyard, it quickly became a daunting amount.

For the sake of the gods, what was the woman thinking of? Was it truly a guilty conscience? Or did she think she could buy her way back into Linden's affections? Maurynna glanced at Lady Sherrine.

For a moment Maurynna thought she saw a small, secret smile play over Lady Sherrine's mouth. But no; it must have been a trick of the light, for the noblewoman, her beautiful hazel eyes downcast, said humbly, "Again I thank you, Captain Erdon. Farewell."

The palfrey wheeled away and clattered over the cobbles and out into the street. The guards, with packhorses trailing behind, followed their lady. A moment later they were gone, leaving only the scent of horses and leather hanging in the hot air; then, like a ghost, came a seductive whisper of woods lily, gone as soon as it danced across the senses.

Hardly knowing what she did, Maurynna walked to the pile. She stared at it in a daze. Otter joined her.

He gazed at the parchment in his hand. "You must admit that she's made amends handsomely. Have a look." He held the sheet out to her.

"I don't want this," she said dully.

A hand passed in front of her and snatched the parchment from Otter's hand. "Oh, Rynna—don't be an ass. She owes you far more than this, the bitch," Maylin said, appearing from nowhere.

"Maylin!" Aunt Elenna scolded.

"I'm sorry, Mother, but it's no more than the truth and you kn—gods have mercy! Mother, look at this!"

Maylin and Aunt Elenna put their heads together over the listing of the wergild, exclaiming and calling each other's attention to various things, their excitement growing with every item. Maurynna left them to it.

I don't want this, she thought, feeling empty inside. *Any of it. If only—*

She turned away and walked blindly back into the house.

"Very well, then, if you won't be sensible and keep any of it for yourself, then trade the wretched things! They're yours and not the Family's; you could turn a tidy profit from all of this!" Maylin fumed.

They stood now in the front room where the opened bundles of Lady Sherrine's wergild lay scattered across table, desk, chairs, and floor. Maylin was gesturing at the various piles with one hand as she spoke; the other held a carved box.

She continued, "Some of these things are exquisite, like this box." Her fingers caressed it.

Maurynna shrugged and said, "Then keep it and whatever's inside. It's yours."

Maylin's jaw dropped. Then she said, "I can't, Rynna! Look at it! I'm certain it's jade and . . ." She cradled it against her. "Do you really mean it?" she said softly. "It's the most beautiful thing I've ever seen."

"I mean it. It's all yours."

Maylin looked down at her new treasure. "Just look at the carving on it; so intricate, a bird of some sort, rising from a fire."

"What?" Aunt Elenna said sharply. "Let me see that."

Maylin handed the box to her mother. While the older woman studied it, running gentle fingers over the carvings, the two cousins exchanged puzzled looks. Maurynna had no more idea than Maylin what the box was, though something teased at the back of her mind.

A bird rising from a fire . . .

Ignoring all questions, Aunt Elenna opened the box; her eyebrows shot up nearly to her hairline. She carefully removed something from the box and gingerly nibbled the tiny thing. Then she shook her head in wonder. "I don't believe it," she whispered. "But that's all this could be. Maurynna, this is a princely gift." She fell to studying the box once more, shaking her head in wonderment.

Gods help me, Maurynna thought, too stunned to speak. *What could it be?*

At last Aunt Elenna sighed. "I still don't believe it," she said. "This alone would have been wergild enough—more than enough, Rynna. At least from a baroness's daughter to the likes of our kind." Only a trace of bitterness came through the words.

Once more the cousins' eyes met, this time in frustrated

anticipation. *I'm going to scream*, Maylin mouthed, hands yanking at her curls.

"So what is it, for pity's sakes?" Otter asked from where he helped Kella poke among some bolts of silk.

"What? Didn't I—? Brown peppercorns from Jehanglan. Near a half pound's worth, I'd say."

"What!" Otter exclaimed. "Good gods!"

Maurynna felt as if the wind had been knocked out of her. Jehanglan—the Kingdom of the Phoenix far to the south! A land half a fable and wholly mysterious.

The box alone, being Jehangli jade and work, would have been enough. But add to it that kingdom's famed brown peppercorns, fragrant, flavorful, numbing to the tongue instead of hot as pepper from Assantik was, and so rare as to be worth their weight in gold, and one had a princely gift indeed.

She was glad she'd given it away.

All at once she had to sit down. This was all too much, too unexpected.

And she wanted none of it. She did not trust the fair Lady Sherrine.

"Well, then, boyo—that's the whole of it," Otter said as they walked among the topiary animals in the garden behind the townhouse, safe from eavesdroppers. "Did you order Sherrine to do it?"

Linden shook his head in mute astonishment as he had all during Otter's tale. "No. In Cassori it's likely no wergild would have been assessed against Sherrine even if Maurynna had been blinded. Not to a merchant. I couldn't insist. Not without making people wonder. And Maurynna accepted it?"

"She did. Even to the 'washing away' of all ill will that stood between them and binding her kin to end the quarrel as well." Here Otter paused a moment and tugged at his beard. "Good gods—that means it's binding on you, too, doesn't it?"

Still boggled by the size of Sherrine's wergild to his soul-twin, it took Linden a moment to realize the full import of Otter's words. "Oh, for—Yes. Yes, it does."

Otter went on, "Maurynna's wondering why Sherrine did it. She doesn't trust her, of course." He grinned.

Linden smiled rather distractedly in return. A good question, that; why did Sherrine do it? He said, thinking aloud, "My guess is that she did it to show me that she truly was sorry—but it changes nothing."

He remembered something from their last, painful conversation. "She did offer to pay a wergild as if Maurynna were royal," he said.

Otter laughed quietly. "Did she? To a mere merchant? Interesting; she must have been desperate to convince you of her sincerity, hoping you'd take her back. Very desperate, indeed. The Colranes are not noted for openhanded generosity.

"Ah, well, one has to allow that she certainly did pay a royal wergild," Otter continued. "And of her own free will. One fit for a king or a queen or . . ."

He paused, then finished in an ironic drawl, "A Dragonlord."

Thirty-nine

The five days since she'd seen Linden felt more like forever. Maurynna ran fingers over the fading line on her cheek. "I hate him," she whispered.

Danaet looked up from her tally sheets. "What? Did you say something, Maurynna?"

Maurynna swung her legs and jumped down from the stacked crates she'd been straddling. "No. Are you almost done?" She walked all around the sacks Danaet was working on and back again.

"No, I'm not. I've no intention of rushing the valuing of this wergild of yours. And will you please sit still? You've been hopping up and down all day. It's making me nervous when it isn't making me tired."

Maurynna muttered something under her breath and gently kicked a crate by her foot. The markings on the box declared it from her least favorite Thalnian cousin's ship. She kicked it again, wishing Breslin were here to fight with. She was in the mood for a good, rousing, knockdown, drag-out argument—and since she couldn't fight with Linden, Breslin was just the man for it.

"I hate him," she said again.

Danaet raised her eyebrows. "While I admit Breslin is as personable as a stoat with the toothache, I would have thought that a bit extreme."

Maurynna shook her head impatiently. "Not Breslin; he's just annoying."

"Then who—? Ah. Never mind. I think I can guess." Danaet sighed. "I don't know if his being a Dragonlord is any improvement over being a dockhand, you know that? Both ways he's trouble. And if you don't stop moping around here, you'll drive my clerks mad. They never know when you're going to pop up and snarl at them. You had Leela in tears yesterday.''

Shocked and contrite, Maurynna stopped pacing. "I did? Oh, gods—I'm sorry, Danaet. I wasn't angry at her—truly I wasn't. It's just—I'll tell her I'm sorry."

"I sent her off to play messenger for me today. I wasn't having her subjected to any more of your moods. Maurynna, I hate to say this, but will you please go somewhere else until you're fit to speak to again?" Danaet pleaded.

That stung, badly. Maurynna drew herself up. "I will. I apologize. I hadn't meant to make anyone else miserable." She spun around and walked out of the warehouse.

The bright sunlight hurt her eyes. *Where to go?* Nothing appealed to her. Wandering the streets and byways and just looking at the varied peoples who came to Casna was usually one of her favorite things, but not this time. All she had to do at her aunt's house was look out a window into the garden and she'd be in tears. And she was through crying for Linden.

Her last haven lay before her. Maurynna watched the *Sea Mist* roll gently on the swells and felt sorry for herself.

An instant later she came to a decision. She'd hide on board her ship, absolutely wallow in her misery and get it out of her blood once and for all. Feeling more cheerful in an upside-down sort of way, Maurynna trotted up the gangplank. Her crew saluted her warily. They looked relieved when she went straight to her cabin.

She collapsed onto her bed. *Guess I have been a raving bitch.* The thought made her giggle and the giggle dissolved into tears. She buried her face in her pillow and cried.

It was a long time before she finally felt at peace. She'd had a chance at her dream and it hadn't quite worked out. So be it. She curled herself around her pillow and fell asleep, spent.

Some time later a soft voice woke her. Maurynna thrashed on the bed, her eyes gritty, trying to identify who had called her, and rubbed the sleep from her eyes.

"*Captain* Erdon is it now? Haven't we come up in the world. Still know your old friend Eel?"

"Lord Sevrynel!"

The Earl of Rockfall turned in the saddle at the sound of his name. He blinked in surprise when he saw who had hailed him; he and the elegant Baroness Anstella of Colrane moved in very different circles. "My lady?" he said doubtfully.

But it seemed she had indeed been the one who had called him. For she guided her palfrey—a lovely animal, Sevrynel thought with pride; the mare had come from his stables—alongside his horse. She smiled at him.

For a moment Sevrynel forgot to breathe.

"My lord," she said, "may I congratulate you? Lord Duriac was just telling me about your new brood mares. He said they were some of the finest animals he'd ever seen."

Sevrynel straightened his stooped shoulders with pride, too pleased at the compliment to wonder why in the world Lord Duriac would be discussing horses with Anstella of Colrane. "That they are," he said, beaming. "Royal stock of the Mhari line, direct descendants of Queen Rani's own mare."

Anstella gazed upon him with awe. "Truly? You are, of course, going to have one of your famous gatherings to celebrate their arrival, aren't you?"

"My lady, what a lovely thought! I believe I shall. It would welcome my royal ladies properly.".

"And all the more so if you invited the Dragonlords. I'm sure they would be most interested—especially Linden Rathan." A hint of sadness overshadowed her beautiful face.

Now why—Oh. Oh, dear. Sevrynel suddenly remembered something he'd heard about. . . . *Oh, dear.* Flustered, he said, "Um, do you really think—?"

"Oh, yes. Why, according to the legends, he would have seen Queen Rani's mare, wouldn't he?"

That decided Sevrynel. He simply *had* to have Linden Rathan's opinion on his new beauties. And the Dragonlords had already attended one or two of his other little gatherings and had seemed to enjoy themselves—especially Linden Rathan when he'd been shown the stables.

He'd do it. "Baroness, I thank you for such a lovely thought. I shall set it in motion immediately. And, my lady, will you and Prince Peridaen also honor me with your presences?"

"My lord, we wouldn't miss this for the world. When will it be?" Anstella asked with flattering eagerness.

Sevrynel thought a moment. "Tomorrow," he said. "It shall be tomorrow."

"Perfect," Anstella said.

Maurynna gaped at the figure standing in the doorway. "Eel? Is that really you?"

A preposterous little man bounced into the cabin, resplendent in a wildly patched jerkin and tunic, the colors of which would have hurt Maurynna's eyes if the patches hadn't faded into decent drabness. Despite the heat, Eel, as always, wore a grimy cap. He swept it off, revealing a fringe of grey hair around a shining pate, and bowed as elegantly as any court dandy. "It is, indeed."

She sat on the edge of her bunk and laughed. "Where have you been? I expected you to show up long before this."

"I was in Balyaranna, working the big horse fair up there, but the pickings were lean. Everyone who can be is here in Casna to see the Dragonlords." He cocked his head like a motley, bright-eyed robin. "So I came back. The Watch have better things to do these days than watch me. And the crowds here are simply lovely. Easy pickings, every last one, bless 'em." He sat down at the table.

Maurynna joined him. With one of the lightning movements she'd come to expect from the old thief, Eel reached into his bulging belt pouch and came up with two ripe peaches in one hand. An instant later a tiny knife appeared in the other; he began peeling the peaches.

She watched him, chin resting on one hand. She was fond of the slippery little Cassorin thief; she'd once saved his neck for him. *Probably the only time in his life he was innocent,* she thought. Since then he'd done her many little favors. But she liked him most of all because he made her laugh.

And gods knew that she could use that now. He cut the peaches into precise sections with the little razor-sharp blade he used for relieving unsuspecting victims of their belt pouches, and prattled about the country yokels who were now sadder and wiser—and poorer—thanks to him.

By the time she'd finished her peach, Maurynna was laughing heartily at one of Eel's many stories.

"Whinnied like a horse, he did, when he realized his ring was gone. 'Whe-e-e-e-ere's my ring?' he kept whining. 'Whe-e-e-ere? Whe-e-e-ere?' Annoying he was, so I—"

Maurynna held up a hand; she'd caught the sound of boots crossing the deck.

A voice called out, "Rynna?"

"In here, Otter," she answered.

Eel half rose as if to flee; Maurynna motioned him back to his seat.

Otter ducked through the doorway, blinking as his eyes adjusted. "I hope I'm not interrupting."

She waved Otter to a chair. It seemed she was going to have a party whether she'd planned it or not. "No. Otter, this is Eel, a friend of mine. Eel, this is Bard Otter Heronson. He is," she said, fixing Eel with a stern eye, "a very good friend as well as a bard."

Eel grinned and tapped his long, nimble fingers together before his face. "Understood, O Captain." He jumped up for another of his elaborate bows. "I'm very pleased to meet you, Bard Otter, and desolate that I didn't bring another peach to share—but alas! I didn't know I'd have the honor of your company."

Otter, Maurynna thought, did very well at hiding his smile. "The honor is mine, good sir. I merely came to deliver a message to Rynna."

She froze. There was only one person Otter would carry messages for—at least, she hoped so. If he bore a warning from Aunt Elenna that dinner would be late, or some other piddling news, she'd tie him to the anchor and go fishing for whales. She waited breathlessly for the bard's next words.

"I saw Linden today. He said that he would still like to go to the *tisrahn* with us. He feels it would dishonor Almered and his nephew not to, and might cause you to lose face with them."

All the old hurt came back in a rush, growling like a black dog in her ear. She snorted. "As if someone as high and mighty as he would care about that." Yet mixed in with the hurt was a rushing excitement at the prospect of seeing Linden again.

Eel's gaze darted from one to the other of them.

Otter pressed his lips together. "Rynna, don't be stupid. It's for your own safety that Linden has—"

Eel interrupted, "Linden? Do you mean Dragonlord Linden Rathan?"

"Yes," said Maurynna. "Unfortunately. He and Otter are old friends."

Otter ignored her and said to Eel, "Maurynna knows him quite well, too. They met when she mistook him for a dock-hand and ordered him to unload her ship."

Eel's jaw dropped. Maurynna said, "I do not know him well. And it wasn't quite like that, Otter."

"No? I believe your words were 'Get your ass over here and earn your pay,' weren't they? He did a good job of it, I heard. Earned every copper you didn't pay him."

Eel's eyes threatened to pop from his head and roll about the floor like marbles. "You did? He did? You didn't? Oh, my. Oh, *my*!" the little thief gasped and went off into peals of laughter.

Maurynna divided a scowl between thief and bard. Would she never hear the end of that wretched mistake?

At last Eel stopped laughing. He said, "The evening crowds to see the Dragonlords should be gathering soon. Must be there when they do. Fare thee well, beautiful captain and honored bard. I'll wave to your Dragonlord for you, Rynna m'dear." And with another flourish of his dilapidated cap, Eel was out the door.

Otter, bless him, waited a decent interval before he burst

out laughing. "What an odd little duck. And since he's no Yerrin to bear a name like that, I'd love to know how he got it. Just what is he?"

"A thief," Maurynna answered. "And a very good one, too. That's why I warned him off you. He won't bother my family or friends. I did him a good turn once. Pointed out the real thief to the Watch when he'd been falsely accused of robbing someone's belt pouch."

She pushed one of the peach pits around the gimballed table. "Linden will really go to the _tisrahn_?"

"Yes. He made a commitment. He will honor it. Maurynna—he wants to go. And not because of the shadow puppets, either."

She didn't believe that. Not at all. But that didn't stop her fool heart from singing. Yet all she said was, "Give him my thanks. Not only would I have been shamed before Almered but also House Erdon."

"That's all?" Otter asked as he stood up to leave.

She wouldn't look at him. She'd betray too much if she did. "That's all."

Three days until she could see Linden again . . .

Otter walked out, then stuck his head back in the cabin. "You're not the only one hurting, Rynna. He misses you as well," the bard said and was gone.

Her breath caught at his words. It couldn't be true—could it? But Otter wouldn't lie to her; not about something so important. Hope blazed up in her heart.

"Please," she whispered. "Please let it be true."

Forty

Another frustrating council. By the gods, why did Lleld have to be right about this, too, Linden thought as he rode home, recalling her warning that regency debates were boring.

Deadly dull is what he'd call them. If he never had to sit in judgement again, the happier he'd be. Of course, it didn't help that he begrudged every moment until he could see Maurynna again. If only the ceremony were tonight instead of the day after tomorrow.

At least he was free for the rest öf the day now. Of course, what would he do with himself now that he couldn't see Maurynna? He heaved a sigh and saw his escort exchange sympathetic—and amused—glances.

Hmm—this wouldn't do. He remembered what gossips soldiers could be. He'd been one. Ah, well—they were nearly home and he could go sit by himself in the garden.

But when they reached the house, Linden saw with annoyance that a servant in the brown-and-gold of the Colranes waited in the courtyard. *Now what?* he thought angrily as he dismounted.

Though visibly nervous, the man approached and held out a note. "Dragonlord, I bear a message from the Lady Sherrine and am to wait for a reply." He hastened to add, "If Your Grace wishes, of course," when Linden scowled at him.

Linden took the note with no good grace and held it in his hand, debating whether to read it now or later. Then he reflected that later meant this fellow would be hanging about half the day at least. Linden broke the seal and quickly read the contents.

Just as he thought. Another apology from Sherrine and a plea for reconciliation. By Gifnu's hells, didn't he make himself plain enough that day? And did she really think that the wergild, lavish as it was, could erase what had happened?

In a rare fit of ill temper, he crumpled the note and cast it aside. To the man, he said, "Tell your lady that the answer is 'no.' And tell her that it will not change. No, leave him."

The last was snapped at the groom who'd come to take the gelding.

"My lord?" the woman said in surprise.

"I'm going for a ride. Don't bother gathering the escort, Jerrell. I'd rather be alone."

Wise man that he was, Jerrell forbore to protest. Linden swung back into the saddle and wheeled the gelding around. He dug his heels in; the horse snorted and jumped. As he exploded through the gate, Linden nearly collided with a rider in Rockfall's blue-and-orange. But the gelding dodged nimbly and they were off.

As he rode through Casna, Linden wondered where he might go. Then he remembered the stone circle and the peace he'd felt there. That decided him; gods knew he needed some of that right now. Once more he set off for the sea cliff road.

Linden lay in the shade of the trilithon, chewing on a blade of grass. The gelding, bare of saddle and bridle and hobbled nearby, cropped the coarse grass that grew among the standing stones.

He'd been right to come here. Once again he'd felt the magic resting in the stones fill him, washing away his anger. Drowsy now, he let his mind drift where it would.

Images of Maurynna . . . Of course, he thought with a smile, what else? He refused to dwell on the last memory of her, when she'd sent him away. Instead he recalled climbing about the rigging with her as she'd shown him her ship. He began naming over the things she'd taught him: yard, shrouds, mizzen, boom—what did she call the ropes again? Blast; he couldn't remember—port, starboard, bow, and stern.

Stern . . . There was something about sterns . . . But his sleepy mind refused to supply it, and when he sought for it, he snapped out of his half-doze. He sat up and stretched.

He should probably start back soon, before Jerrell sent out a search party. Linden started to stand and then paused.

Jerrell. Well and well, his errant memory might not want to remember the proper name for ropes aboard a ship, but it presented him with something Jerrell had once said.

Something about another place of magic . . .

Straight inland from the stone circle as the crow flies, it's supposed to be, like it was deliberate. And whether it's real or just moonshine, no one goes near that part of the forest if they can help it. People just don't feel welcome there.

Even if it wasn't real, it would give him something to do—and an excuse not to return to Casna for a little while longer.

He scooped up the bridle as he straightened. Catching the gelding, he said, "So, gooserump—shall we see if Dragon-lords are welcome in this place that truehumans aren't?"

It was a hot and humid ride. And the fairther he got from the coast, the worse it became. But in the distance he could see the tall pines that made up this end of the forest. Linden urged the gelding to a canter. The sooner they were in the shade, the better.

He sighed with relief as they entered the cool of the woods. All around him the thick trunks of the pines towered straight and true to the blue sky above, bare for three or more spear lengths before the branches began. Underfoot many years' worth of pine needles muffled the sound of the gelding's hooves, save for the occasional crunch of a pine cone.

As he rode deeper into the forest the trees became smaller and closer together, and underbrush appeared. Nothing yet. He pressed on out of idle curiosity until the bushes became so thick that he decided to turn back. As he did, something caught his eye.

Linden halted the gelding before the tree that had claimed his attention. He whistled softly as he examined the parallel sets of gashes scarring its trunk. Tears of sap bled from the wounds. He touched one golden drop; it was still liquid. He absentmindedly rubbed the sticky resin from his fingers, the aromatic scent of pine filling the air.

"A bear? This close to the city?" he wondered aloud. *Not to mention a damned big one, too; those gashes are shoulder-height to me mounted.*

He remembered the boar that had killed Rann's father. It seemed the woods about the fair city of Casna bred very large animals indeed. He decided to push on a little farther.

After a short while dark patches of nervous sweat appeared on the gelding's neck and shoulders. It danced under him. Rather than risk an argument—and concerned at the flecks of lather he saw now—Linden rode back a short way. When the horse calmed, Linden tethered it once more and retraced his way on foot, pushing a slow and cautious way through the underbrush.

The deeper into the woods he went, the more uneasy he became. And now the short hairs of the back of his neck rose, the feeling was so strong. He could understand why no one wanted to come here. The feeling of repulsion was well-nigh overwhelming.

Yet weaving through it came a seductive call, something that beckoned him on. He followed it.

The woods ended abruptly. Linden stopped short between two trees, a hand on each, to study what he'd found. He had no doubt this was what he'd been hunting. Magic had been worked here—old magic, and dark magic. Where he'd felt the magical resonance of the stone circle as a pleasant hum, this made his bones ache. He set his teeth against it.

And only magic would account for the way the woods ended as if at a wall. Not even the underbrush penetrated the clearing before him; the edge was as cleanly drawn as though with a knife.

A slope rose before Linden; there seemed to be something on the top of the low hill. To either side the forest curved around the base of the hill. Everything was so patently unnatural it set his teeth on edge, from the ending of the forest to the precise cone shape of the hill. It shouted of magery. That so much effort had been taken spoke of the place's importance to someone.

But to whom? And why? Linden asked himself as he left the shelter of the trees.

At once the ache in his bones became worse. Clenching his fists, Linden set out to investigate his discovery.

First he circled the base of the gentle hill. The circle was large; almost large enough, he noted absently, for him to Change. Not that he would want to do so. The magic here was inimical to his own; the pain he felt now would be nothing compared to what he'd feel if he made himself vulnerable by Changing. He shuddered at the thought of it.

The grass carpeting the slope was short; it made him think of the lawns in the palace gardens. It seemed someone didn't fancy trudging through long, dew-laden grass to get to the top of the hill.

Definitely not some hedge-wizard, then—not that one would be likely to have the kind of power that's been used here. This is the work of a trained—and damned strong— mage. Yet a mage of that caliber usually attaches him—or her—self to a royal patron, and I've heard no talk of any mages in Casna.

That such a mage might be about—and hidden—did not bode well. *Bloody, bloody damn. Please don't tell me Lleld was right after all. Ah, well. Best look over the crown of this cursed hill; there seems to be something up there.*

Linden strode up the slope. The ache dug dark fingers into the very marrow of his bones now. The pain increased as he came closer to the summit; he had to stop and deliberately shut his mind to it. Yet there was still that seductive thread he'd felt before running through the pain. Linden ground his teeth and continued to the top.

The summit of the hill was flat, as though a giant sword had neatly sliced off the crown, and no grass grew upon it. It was empty save for a large rectangular stone that rested on a base of smaller, square-cut stones, rather like a tabletop. Linden eyed it as he circled the packed earth of the summit, careful to walk sunwise. He estimated the stone to be some seven feet long and a good yard wide; the top edge was nearly waist-high to him. The stone was smooth; too smooth to be natural, yet he could make out no marks from tools upon it.

It's an altar, said a voice at the back of his mind. *And old—very, very old.*

Linden had no doubts what this altar had been used for in the past. Sickened, he forced himself to go closer until he stood next to it.

The power within the altar beat at him. As he'd suspected, this was the focus of the dark magery that tainted this clearing. But even as it repelled him, the darkness called to him, honey-sweet, magic seeking magic. His will lulled, Linden stretched his hands to the altar.

From deep inside him, Rathan bellowed *No!*

He pulled back, disoriented by the sudden surge of his dragonsoul. But Rathan was right; he hadn't the magic to fight this if ensnared. He was no trained mage. He backed away until his feet found the slope, then turned and skidded and slid down the hill.

The altar called to him to return, trying to wind the threads of its magic through his, to bind him to it. Linden closed his mind to the stone's beckoning.

He was almost at the beginning of the woods when the stench of rotting meat assailed his nostrils. Cold sweat broke out on his forehead and back. Linden stopped short and spun around, looking everywhere at once. He knew that smell. All at once he was sixteen again and terrified.

Then Linden caught hold of himself and shook his head. *Fool! It's not Satha—it can't be! With your own eyes you saw him crumble to dust more than six hundred years ago. Either you're imagining that smell or it's some dead animal nearby.*

Still, he wished for his sword. If it *was* Satha, the undead Harper might recognize the blade, if not the wielder. After all, Tsan Rhilin had rested in the same tomb with him for the gods only knew how long before Rani had awakened him.

He waited, but the stench was gone. Not a dead animal, then, or he'd still smell it. Had he imagined it? He must have—he *had* to have imagined it. His mind refused to contemplate otherwise.

He was only a Dragonlord, after all—not a god. And even Dragonlords could still fear demons from their pasts. Linden turned his back on the clearing and ran.

By the time he reached the gelding, who was munching on a bush it could just reach, Linden had convinced himself that, if not a figment of his imagination, the stench was nothing more than some dead animal, perhaps even a kill of the bear who had gouged the tree. The gelding's feckless unconcern reassured him. Surely if anything were wrong this stupid beast would have ripped free and run for home.

Linden pulled as many leaves and twigs out of the gelding's mouth as he could, ruefully noting that he owed the groom in charge of the tack an apology.

"Nothing worse than a filthy bit, gooserump," he grumbled after he was back in the saddle. The very ordinariness of this problem soothed him. "And you've done a fine job of fouling yours."

He found a path that ran in the direction he wanted and turned the gelding onto it, recalling in his mind the lay of the forest and the lands between it and Casna.

It was imperative that he return to the city as quickly as possible.

Dusk was falling by the time he reached the city once more. As soon as he reached his house, Linden retired to his sleeping chamber with orders he was not to be disturbed. Still shaken by what he'd seen and felt in the woods, he threw himself into a chair and reached out with his mind.

It was barely a half-instant before the others answered; it felt like an age.

Linden? What's wrong? Where are you? Kief demanded.

Why aren't you here yet? Tarlna chimed in.

Confused, Linden said *"Here"? Where's "here"?*

Lord Sevrynel's estate, they both answered. Tarlna said, *It's another of his impromptu gatherings and this one was especially for you. It was to show off some new brood mares from Kelneth. Didn't the messenger find you?*

He remembered the rider in the blue-and-orange livery

earlier. *No, I was out riding. And hang Sevrynel and his gatherings! This is important. I've got to talk to you; can you two find somewhere private?*

He felt them withdraw slightly while they discussed the problem. Then: *Give us a few moments.*

He waited in an agony of impatience until he felt their minds again. *You're not going to like this,* he said.

Then he told them all he'd found.

When he finished, there was a moment of stunned silence. Then, so faintly he could barely hear it, Tarlna said, *Oh, dear gods—no.*

Are you certain? Kief said. The bleakness in his mindvoice told Linden the older Dragonlord was grasping at straws rather than truly doubting him.

As certain as I can be. But I'm not a trained mage; none of us are. All I got were impressions, really.

We'll have to investigate it further, Tarlna said. The force of her revulsion made Linden's flesh creep in sympathy.

I think I know how to, Linden said. An idea was forming at the back of his mind; he hid it from the others. He didn't like it but he could see no other way.

But Kief must have picked up something in his tone. *You're not planning anything rash, are you, Linden?*

No, Linden said, keeping a tight rein on his emotions. *I just want to fly over it in dragon-form; I suspect I'll be able to "see" more.*

You may well be right. When do you intend to do it?

After full dark. I don't want to take the chance of being seen. No sense in alerting whoever's responsible that Dragonlords are interested, is there?

Kief asked, *Do you want one or both of us to go with you?*

Ah—no, Linden said. *It would look suspicious if you leave suddenly. People will wonder why. It's best I go alone.*

So be it, Kief said at last. *We'll stay as a distraction.*

But Tarlna tried to argue him out of it. She desisted when he finally yelled at her, *Do you have any better ideas?*

No, she had to admit.

Neither do I, Linden retorted. *Now let me go; I want to rest and eat before I do this.*

The others withdrew reluctantly.

Linden wiped a hand across his forehead. Thank the gods he'd finally been able to break the mindspeech link; he didn't know how much longer he'd have been able to hide the full extent of his plans.

He just hoped he wasn't about to commit suicide.

"Where the blazes is he?" Peridaen whispered to Anstella as they watched the revelers milling about the Earl of Rockfall's great hall.

"I don't know," Anstella snapped back. "He should have been here by now. Look—there's Sevrynel talking to the other Dragonlords. Perhaps our answer is there."

"He doesn't look happy," Peridaen said, and drank. "And neither am I. I want this over with."

"Hush. Here he comes."

When their host drew near, Anstella beckoned to him.

"My lord," she said when he joined them, "isn't Linden Rathan coming?"

If possible, Sevrynel's stooped shoulders drooped a little more. "No, my dear Baroness. The other Dragonlords just had mindspeech with him. It seems that he had other business to attend to and never got my invitation. Oh, dear. And I did so want his opinion of my beautiful ladies. . . ." He half turned away, shaking his head in a distracted manner as he meandered off.

"Oh, for—" Peridaen began.

"Go tell Ormery," Anstella hissed in his ear, "and leave this to me."

With that, she broke away from Peridaen's side, knowing he would send the servant to warn off Sherrine and Althume. She would deal with Sevrynel.

She caught up to him and slid her arm through his. He blinked at her in surprise; before he could say anything, she smiled warmly at him, knowing well the effect it would have.

It did. The man looked as if he'd been pole-axed.

"Poor Sevrynel," she said, her voice low and husky and rich with sympathy. "I'm so sorry. But perhaps—just perhaps, you could do this again? I know Linden Rathan will be so sorry he missed this; Sherrine told me he thought very highly indeed of your horses." She squeezed his arm.

An idiotically happy smile lit Sevrynel's face. "Truly?"

"Truly."

"Hm. Let me think." He twisted one end of his sweeping mustache around and around a finger. "Tomorrow?" he murmured.

Anstella bit back a fierce grin of triumph.

"No, not tomorrow." He shook his head. "Tomorrow is Lady Telia's dinner and I'm attending. No, not tomorrow night."

He trailed off, muttering to himself. Anstella refrained from boxing his ears. But if they hadn't needed this fool . . .

Sevrynel said happily, "But the night after is free! I can do it then."

"My lord," Anstella said. "You've no idea how happy I am to hear that. How very happy."

She withdrew her arm from his. "The day after tomorrow it shall be. Until then—farewell, my lord."

Forty-one

Linden slipped out of the house late that night, saddled the gelding himself, and rode alone out of Casna.

It was more than a candlemark later before he found what he wanted: a large meadow with a stream so that the gelding could drink and eat, and another field beyond with enough room for him to Change—and far enough away that he wouldn't panic this idiot horse.

Long practice made quick work of settling the gelding. It immediately began to tear at the lush grass. Linden left it and jogged off. He refused to think about what he planned to do.

As he trotted through the long grass, memories of long ago returned. He'd done much the same thing on a hot summer's night centuries back while a member of Bram and Rani's company. Nor had the feeling of mixed excitement and apprehension dimmed with the passage of the years. He lengthened his stride and ran for the sheer joy of it, deliberately pushing away the thought of what was to come.

At last he stopped and looked back to see if he'd gone far enough. Linden nearly laughed to see how much ground he had covered. Throwing his head back and lifting his hands to the stars, he let himself melt into Change before he had second thoughts.

He reveled for a moment in the power of his dragon body, then leaped into the sky. Wing stroke after powerful wing stroke swept out and down as he spiraled up into the starry night. When he judged himself high enough, Linden stretched his wings out and hung in the air like a gigantic hawk. He took his bearings and angled east.

The air flowed over him like warm silk, soft and smooth against the skin stretching between the vanes of his wings.

Sister moon hung in the sky, watching him as he flew over the fields and meadows outside of Casna.

His sharp dragonsight pierced the night, searching for anything unusual. His long neck curved as he swung his head from side to side.

Nothing that interested him as a man—but something that caught his draconic half's interest: sheep. They were penned together by a hut at the edge of a field well away from the forest. This shepherd took no chances with wolves; he had obviously never considered dragons.

Linden dropped lower. His mouth watered at the sudden blast of rich, muttony scent from below—though the thought of gulping down raw sheep still in its fleece made him queasy. Rathan thought it a wonderful idea. *Absolutely not,* Linden said firmly. To his relief Rathan subsided. He just hoped he'd be able to subdue Rathan again later on.

The sheep bleated in terror as he passed overhead. No doubt the shepherd would be looking to see what had disturbed his flock and Linden had no desire to be seen in this form by anyone. He stretched his wings and flew faster.

In far less time than it would have taken him to ride there, Linden hovered high above the uncanny clearing in the woods. To his dragon eyes the place glowed with a faint but disquieting sickly green light. He nodded to himself.

So; he'd been right that he might see more in this form. Yet he was certain there was even more than this to see. He hoped he wasn't about to make the worst mistake of his life, gods help him.

He could just imagine what Kief would say. "Idiot" and "fool" would be the least—and politest—of it. Tarlna . . . Best not to think about what Tarlna would say. Even Lleld, known for leaping first and looking long afterward, would be appalled.

Linden deliberately relinquished control to Rathan.

The draconic half of his soul startled into full wakefulness. Linden greeted it from his new position as "bystander."

Wary, Rathan asked, *Is it time, then, humansoul Linden? Does thee wish to pass on?*

No, Rathan; I've not yet tired of this life. But there is something here that I do not fully understand and I think you would know more than I about such things.

If he'd been in control of their body, Linden would have held his breath. As it was, he waited in an agony of suspense. With rare exceptions, the dragon half of a Dragonlord's soul was content to wait until his human counterpart tired of life. But if Rathan decided that *his* time was now come, there was nothing Linden could do; Rathan was by far the stronger. He was used to light touches of Rathan's personality—such as the argument about fresh mutton—but this was well-nigh overwhelming. He prayed he'd not committed the gravest folly of his life.

Then thee is either very foolish or very brave waking me like this.

But there was a wry amusement behind the words that reassured Linden. It confirmed his long-held—and very private—belief that the dragons let their human counterparts rule for so long because the dragons found them entertaining.

Rathan continued, *Be reassured, humansoul Linden. I promise thee I will wait until my proper time. Now—what is this thing thee wishes to show me?*

Down there. Do you see it?

He felt Rathan contemplate the magical clearing.

Faugh! It is a vile thing, Rathan said in disgust. *It stinks of dark magery.*

Linden asked eagerly, *Of what sort?*

Though he grumbled, Rathan dropped lower and stretched out his senses to touch the magical resonance below. At first there was only darkness, then—

Mind-wrenching fear burned into Linden's consciousness, the mortal terror of a soul spiraling down into darkness as it was torn from life, screaming helplessly in agony.

His was that soul. He was the one lying bound upon the cold stone, waiting for the knife to plunge down. And now it was falling, seeking his heart—

Linden wrenched his mind free from the vision as Rathan flung them back and away, screaming in draconic rage,

burying Linden beneath his fury. Linden found himself shut
away within Rathan's mind, all his senses blinded, as though
he'd been wrapped in a blanket and thrust into a chest. He
knew nothing of the world outside; his world had narrowed
to this body and he was suffocating.

Rathan! Rathan—please! Linden begged as he fought to
stay alive in the fire of Rathan's anger. *You'll kill me!*

He felt the dragon draw in a deep breath, knew that Rathan
intended to wipe this foulness from the face of the earth. A
tiny voice at the back of his mind said, *No—the woods are
too dry; it'll spread everywhere, even to the farmers' fields.*
The realization frightened Linden into redoubling his efforts
to break into Rathan's consciousness once more. But it was
like beating against an iron door while bound hand and foot.

The great mouth opened; Linden felt the rumble of the
flames as they passed down the long throat.

With an effort that came near to tearing him apart, Linden
fought with Rathan for control of their body. He couldn't stop
the flames, it was too late for that, but perhaps—

As the great head snapped up, a huge gout of fire shot
harmlessly into the night sky like some strange shooting star.
Rathan bellowed, turning his rage on Linden.

Remember your vow! Linden screamed as the dragon's fury
consumed him. He writhed as Rathan tore at him. Gods help
him, he never thought to die this way.

Then—peace. For a moment Linden thought he must have
died. Slowly it came to him: he was alive. Barely.

Rathan said with sullen fury, *I remember my vow, humansoul. But I will also remember that thee stopped me from
destroying this sore upon the body of Mother Earth. I understand why, so I forgive it. But now I charge thee to see to
this foul thing's destruction. Does thee understand, humansoul Linden?*

I understand, Rathan, Linden said, weak and shaking.

One moment he was bereft of all his senses, held in thrall
by Rathan's power. The next Rathan was gone. Linden was
plunging headlong from the sky before he realized that he
once more controlled their body. Only the frantic beating of

his wings saved him from crashing into the ground. Shaken, he soared into the sky and drifted on the wind, numb with shock.

It was long before he came fully to himself. At first he was confused by the unfamiliar terrain below him. Then he realized that he'd drifted south and further east than he'd yet been. Below him was the shoreline.

Tall rocks marched along the edge between water and sand. But between them and the cliffs was a wide expanse of beach, wide enough for him to Change. He swooped down and began Changing while still in the air. A few heartbeats later he landed on booted feet, bending his knees to take the shock and staggering a little as the sand shifted beneath him. Then he was pulling off his clothes as fast as he could.

Linden ran down the beach and threw himself into the sea. Let the clean salt water wash away the taint of the sacrificial altar, the taste of his own mortality, the memory of the fear and pain; he wanted to be free of all of it. He battled the waves, letting them toss him this way and that, until he felt cleansed.

Gods, what a fool he'd been; he wasn't certain he deserved to come through that so little scathed. But he was thankful he had. He hauled himself out of the water, tired beyond belief. He dressed, feeling more at peace with himself, if not completely healed.

Once again he let himself flow into Change. But this time there was a hesitation to it, something he'd felt only a few times before when he was either ill or injured. It was his magic's way of telling him that he was not really strong enough to spend the necessary energy so freely. He would heed that warning; once back to man-form he'd not Change again for a few days at least.

Once aloft, he decided it would be easiest to follow the coastline until he found a familiar area. The updrafts from the cliffs would do much to spare his strength.

He tilted his wings and glided west along the coast. At one point he recognized the beach where they'd had the picnic. The memory cheered him a little.

Some time later he saw the standing stones guarding their headland. Wary but curious, he dropped a little lower.

The area of the headland around the stones glowed with a gentle silver light to his dragon eyes, the stones themselves brighter pillars of silver and gold. Once more he felt the humming in his bones; this time it was stronger, growing as he dropped lower. The magic here was like a balm to the seared and tattered edges of his soul. He glided over it, his wingtips almost brushing the tallest stones, grateful for the easing of the last of the pain and terror.

He gave the area of the clearing a wide berth and came down at last in the field near where the hobbled gelding waited. This time it was even harder to Change.

As he rode back to Casna, slumped in near exhaustion, Linden thought over what he'd learned. *Not very much, after all, and I don't like what I did discover. But who's responsible for the sorcery? Does it even have anything to do with the Fraternity? And what can three Dragonlords do against it, anyway? We're creatures of magic, not mages!*

By the time Linden reached the house once more he was shaking. He guided the gelding to the stables and sat for a moment, gathering the strength to dismount.

He told himself it was just reaction, that he'd be fine once he rested a little and ate something, had a bit of wine to restore him. Of course, if he couldn't get out of the saddle . . . He debated calling for a groom to help him. But if the grooms were sound sleepers, he'd have to yell loud enough to wake half the house; the fewer people who saw him like this, the better.

A figure detached itself from the shadows. Surprise lent Linden a brief surge of strength. He sat upright.

"Boyo," said a familiar voice in Yerrin, "where have you been and *what* have you been doing? You look like something the cat threw back."

Truth be told, he felt like something the cat threw *up*. Linden closed his eyes for a moment in relief. "Thank all the gods it's you, Otter. But what are you doing here? Wait—let me get down.''

With Otter's help, Linden dismounted without falling. Together they led the horse into the stable. Linden didn't argue when Otter insisted he sit and leave the horse to him.

''As for what I'm doing here, Kief mindcalled me earlier. Seems he was worried about something you were up to—though he wouldn't tell me what; very secretive, he was. But he and Tarlna didn't want to come here themselves because it might cause comment, their hanging about so late. But everyone knows we're friends and that bards are unpredictable creatures anyway, so it wouldn't seem odd if *I* did. Now—what in the world were you doing, you big idiot, to get yourself into such a condition?'' Otter waved the hoof pick threateningly at him before going back to cleaning the gelding's feet. ''And why is Kief being so cautious about being seen here?''

Linden rubbed a hand over his eyes. Gods, but he was going to have to sleep soon. But first he had to report to Kief and Tarlna, a thing he was not looking forward to. Nor did he relish telling his tale more than once. ''Let me get some food and wine before I fall down. Then I have to mindcall the others; I'll let you 'listen' in.''

Otter, in the midst of hanging up the gelding's tack, raised his eyebrows and asked, ''Will the others stand for it?''

''Have they any choice?'' Linden replied.

Somewhat restored by half of a cold chicken, bread, cheese, and a goodly amount of wine, Linden pulled his boots and tunic off and lay down on his bed. Otter pulled up a chair.

''Ready?'' said Linden.

''Ready,'' Otter replied as he tossed his cloak back from his shoulders. The bard closed his eyes and stretched his legs out.

''Very well, then.'' Linden closed his own eyes and reached out to Kief and Tarlna.

The speed with which they answered told him they'd been waiting for his call. And the annoyed apprehension he felt through the link told him in what state of mind that time had been spent.

This was not going to be pleasant.

Before they could do more than exclaim, Linden launched into his tale. He held nothing back, though he did try to mute the full effect of the victim's terror and what he himself had suffered from Rathan's rage; Otter was no longer a young man.

As he knew would happen, the moment he finished, the other two Dragonlords heaped violent recriminations upon his head. He stood it for a few moments, then bellowed, *Enough!*

In the shocked silence that followed, he continued, *Yes, I was a fool. We're all agreed on that. And no, I won't do it again. But what's done is done, and instead of wasting time and what little energy I have left this night, let us see what we can make of this.*

A moment of stiff silence followed. Then Kief said, *Very well, Linden. So what do we now know? First, that there is a mage of some power about.*

And that he—or she—uses blood magic, Tarlna added. *Linden—could you tell how long ago that . . .* Her mindvoice faltered.

I'm no mage to know for certain, but I do think someone was killed there not very long ago. Within a few months at the most; remember, what was left was nearly strong enough to catch a Dragonlord.

Tarlna said, *That would seem to indicate that it was fairly recent, else the power would have ebbed away, thank the gods. Dark magery is too volatile to sustain itself at such strength when stored like that, save in a soultrap jewel—or unless another mage the equal of Ankarlyn has arisen.*

Avert! Linden and Kief said at the same time.

Linden shuddered as though shaking off a nightmare. That was something he hadn't yet considered—didn't want to consider. Ankarlyn the Mage had been the worst enemy the Dragonlords had ever faced; though it was long before his time, the tale of how Ankarlyn had nearly annihilated their kind touched a chord in every Dragonlord. After they'd destroyed him and his following, the Fraternity of the Blood, the Dragonlords had hunted down every grimoire, every scrap of spell on parchment that Ankarlyn had written, and burned them. The thought that a single book might have escaped—or that another mage had been able to repeat Ankarlyn's spells—made him feel ill.

And the thought that such a mage might be working for the newly reborn Fraternity made his very soul tremble.

But we don't know that this mage is attached to the Fraternity said to be in existence here in Cassori, he said.

True, Kief said. *There have been, after all, no attacks on us. It could be some mage garnering power for his own ends and nothing to do with events here in Cassori.*

Just so, Tarlna said. *After all, it was not magic that caused the storm that sank the queen's barge.*

For some reason the mention of the barge made Linden remember Maurynna's amusing description of the ungainly vessels. "They wallow like pregnant cows in the water, but—"

Dear gods! he exclaimed, interrupting something Kief was saying. *Maybe we've been looking at it all wrong!*

What do you mean? the others demanded. This time even Otter, who'd remained discreetly quiet during the conversation, joined in.

We've always looked at the storm as the cause of the sinking, he said in a rush, lest the half-formed idea surfacing in his mind vanish before he could share it, *and wondered if it was mage-born. But the storm was the work of nature and nothing else. It wasn't even that bad of one, I've been told.*

He went slowly now, feeling his way through unfamiliar concepts and language. *But it wasn't the weather that made the barge sink. What caused that was her stern going under. Which it shouldn't have; another sailor told Maurynna that it was only a small following sea—he saw it. And she once remarked that, clumsy as the barges are, even they shouldn't dip their sterns low enough to founder in such a sea.*

Another conversation came back to him. *Gods, even Healer Tasha once said that the barge had weathered worse.*

A long, thoughtful silence followed his words. Then . . .

A storm might well be out of our mage's powers, Kief began.

But causing the end of a boat to dip just low enough for waves already there to swamp it . . . Tarlna continued.

Is well within the abilities of the mage that I sensed tonight, Linden finished.

And who benefited the most by Queen Desia's death? Whose way to the throne was made clear? Duke Beren. That same Duke Beren who had revealed time and again his antipathy to the Dragonlords. In his mind's eye Linden saw once more the duke's livid face as he and Linden confronted each other on the beach.

He let the other three follow his thoughts and felt their wordless agreement, then listened as Kief and Tarlna discussed what they could do, for they still had no proof the mage who used the altar was even connected with the queen's death.

All at once he couldn't stay awake any longer. *Please, I must sleep now.*

Understood. Rest well, Linden.

The others withdrew from his mind. Sighing, he let himself sink toward sleep.

A hand on his shoulder startled him awake. His eyes flew open; Otter was bending over him. Gods help him, he'd forgotten the man was still here! He began an apology.

The fury in Otter's eyes stopped him. Linden had never thought to see the bard so angry that words would fail him. He saw it now.

"Don't," Otter said, his voice tight and flat when he could finally talk once more, "you ever, *ever* do something like that again. Damn it all, boyo! We could have lost you!"

Linden began feebly, "But I had—"

Otter snarled, "And what would have become of Maurynna? Tell me that, you bloody idiot! Oh, ho—you'd forgotten that there's not just yourself to think of now, didn't you? Then you'd best get used to the idea and right quick, do you hear?"

There was no arguing. Otter was right; he'd been even more of a fool than he'd thought. The thought of what his death might have done to his soultwin sickened him.

Otter must have seen it in his face, for the bard straightened, a grim, satisfied smile on his face. He picked up his cloak from the chair and slung it over one arm. "No—you'll not be repeating that bit of arrant stupidity any time too soon." He paused at the door and said with rough affection, "Go to sleep, you ass. You're done in."

There was no arguing with *that,* either. Linden nodded and once more closed his eyes.

He was asleep even before the door closed.

Forty-two

During the noonmark break from the council meeting, Linden decided to wander out to the garden where Rann played when he felt well enough. Perhaps it would wake him up. He was still tired and feeling more than a touch mind-fogged from his adventure, even though he'd spent most of yesterday napping when he wasn't in the council. Kief and Tarlna had given up trying to discuss anything with him after he'd fallen asleep for the third time.

It would be a long, long time before he tried something like that with Rathan again.

But in a few candlemarks he would see Maurynna again. The thought lifted his spirits as nothing else could have done.

He turned the corner of the hall and saw the Earl of Rockfall coming toward him. He raised a hand in greeting, feeling a little guilty that Sevrynel had gone through all that trouble for him—and for nothing.

So when Sevrynel greeted him with, "Dragonlord! A moment, please!" he stopped.

"Yes, my lord Earl?" he said. "I'm sorry I missed your gathering the other day. Both Kief and Tarlna told me much about your new mares."

The little earl joined him. "I'm sorry, too, Your Grace," he said, sounding truly disappointed. "I would dearly love your opinion on them. Did the other Dragonlords tell you the mares are of the Mhari line?"

That caught Linden's interest as nothing else could have. "Indeed? Then I'm doubly sorry I missed them. Perhaps another time—" *Such as after we figure out what to do about this damned mage . . .* Moved by guilt—and too tired to think carefully about what he promised—Linden said, "I swear I shall attend your next gathering without fail, my lord. Will that do?''

Sevrynel beamed. ''Indeed it will, Dragonlord—for the next one is this evening!''

Linden could only boggle at him. Tonight? But—

The earl must have noticed his hesitation, for he waggled an admonitory finger, and with a roguish grin, said, ''Ah—remember! I have your sworn word, my lord. Tonight.''

And with that, the earl bowed and continued on his way. Linden stared dumbfounded at nothing, mentally berating himself for his careless tongue.

He had to go to that cursed gathering now; he'd given his word. And that would make him late for the *tisrahn*. Maurynna would have his head.

''Oh, bloody hells,'' he said, suddenly disgusted with the world.

Well and well, he'd just have to do the best he could. At least he had until moonrise to get to the *tisrahn*.

Maurynna paced back and forth in the upper hall, her shadow on the wall following her in the glow from the rushlights. ''Where can he be? Surely the council meeting ended hours ago. I can't see those fat nobles missing their suppers.''

''Will you stop,'' Maylin snapped. ''You're making me dizzy. And we can't wait any longer. The moon's going to rise soon. You're one of the sponsors—you have to be there on time. If we don't leave now—Someone's here!''

Both young women gathered up their skirts and ran to the top of the stairs. Maurynna paused at the first step.

Please let it be Linden!

Maylin crowded beside her. They spied as Merrisa, one of the young clerk-apprentices, answered the door.

But the man who stood there was not Linden. For one thing he was far too old. And he wore royal livery. He and Merrisa had a hurried discussion, then the apprentice disappeared down the hall. The cousins exchanged glances, puzzled.

''Do you think he's sent a messenger warning you to go ahead?'' whispered Maylin.

"Let's find out," Maurynna said and descended the stairs.

The man looked up at her, but beyond a polite nod paid her no attention.

"Sir," she said, her voice trembling. "May I ask your business here?"

He weighed his answer for a long moment. Then he said, "Prince Rann wishes Bard Otter Heronson to sing for him, young mistress. He's feeling poorly tonight and Healer Tasha thought it might help."

"Ah. There was—um, no other message?"

"No, mistress." The lined face was bored.

She felt a fool but had to ask. "None from Dragonlord Linden Rathan?"

Puzzlement replaced boredom. "No. All three Dragonlords left the palace early this afternoon to attend a dinner in their honor at Lord Sevrynel's river estate." He eyed her, no doubt wondering what mad fancy had taken her that she thought a Dragonlord would deign to send her private messages.

Maurynna retreated in bewilderment to stand with Maylin at the foot of the stairs. Otter came down the hall, arranging a cloak over himself and the harp case slung over his shoulder.

"I'm sorry I can't go with you, Rynna. I hope Almered will understand about a royal summons." He peered over the servant's shoulder at the sky outside. "You'd best leave now for the *tisrahn*—looks like rain," he said cheerfully. "Don't wait any longer for Linden; he wouldn't want you to be late. Likely he's still stuck in the council."

"But—" Maurynna began. Her words were lost as the bard rushed out, drawing the servant in his wake. "He's not," she finished to the oaken door that shut in her face.

She turned to Maylin. "A dinner? Why didn't he warn us, then?"

"Perhaps it was a sudden thing?" Maylin hazarded. "The gods only know the answer to that, but I do know this: if we wait for him to get back from the other side of the river, we'll miss the *tisrahn*. We must leave now, Maurynna."

Aunt Elenna stuck her head out of the office. "If neither

Otter nor the Dragonlord are with you, you girls are taking a
'prentice for an escort. It's too late for you to go unescorted.''
She looked over her shoulder and called, "Gavren, come
here! You're escorting Maylin and Rynna to this feast.''

Gavren, all gangly elbows and knees and bobbing throat
apple, came grinning out of the office. "Yes, Mistress Vanadin. I'll go round to the stable and get some horses.'' He
disappeared through the door at a shambling lope.

Maylin groaned. "Why Gavren, Mother? He'll eat everything in sight and laugh that horrible braying laugh of his.''
She shuddered.

Her mother shrugged unsympathetically. "So send him to
the servants' quarters when you get there. If he tries to get
more than his fair share of the food, don't worry—someone
will thump him. Besides, he's the only male apprentice here
tonight.''

The ring of horses' hooves on the cobblestones outside
announced Gavren's return. Maurynna numbly allowed Aunt
Elenna to fling a cloak over her shoulders. Without knowing
what she did, she kissed her aunt's cheek and followed Maylin out the door.

Somehow she was astride her horse, arranging her blue silk
skirts around her. The sense of emptiness and abandonment
astonished her as they clattered out of the courtyard.

Maylin reached over and patted her hand. "I'm sorry,
Rynna. If there's anything . . .''

Maurynna decided on a brave front. "It's all right, Maylin.
I didn't really think he'd come.''

"You did as I bade you?" Althume said.

"Yes," Sherrine replied. "Indeed, I don't think I've ever
eaten so much in my life as I have these past few days." She
laid a hand across her middle. She'd had to force every bite
of that meal down; she'd been so nervous about seeing Linden
again that her stomach had threatened to rebel with every
mouthful. "Why did I have to eat so much, anyway? You
never told me the first time.''

And she'd been too frightened to ask.

"To slow down the effects of the drug," Althume answered and held up a small parchment packet. "Once more—there is a servant named Joslin at Lord Sevrynel's estate. See that he is the one to prepare the farewell cup for you and give him this to add to it. A pity that it couldn't have just gone into his food."

"True," Sherrine said as she took the packet. She tucked it safely away in the embroidered pouch hanging from her belt. "Where are the vials?"

"Here."

Now the mage handed her two small earthenware vials. Both had wax seals, one brown, one white. "Repeat what you will do with these."

Holding on to her temper, Sherrine said, "The brown is an emetic; get away as soon as possible after I finish the cup and drink it when I'm alone. Then drink the white; it is the antidote to the powder." She looked down at the second vial and asked the second question she'd not dared to ask the first time. "Antidote? Is the stuff poison, then?" Gods help her, she'd no wish to *murder* Linden. Make him suffer, yes, but killing him had no part in her plans.

"No." The mage smiled slightly. "I've no more wish to kill Linden Rathan than you do, my lady. The potion will simply spare you the . . .unpleasant effects that he will suffer."

"As well he should," Sherrine muttered.

Hoofbeats sounded outside. Althume went to the window. Sherrine heard him grunt in pleasure as he raised his hand in salute to the rider outside. "That's the signal. Everything's set."

The mage turned back into the room and caught up his cloak from a chair. "Are you ready, my lady? Then it is time."

Indeed it was. Time for her revenge.

Linden excused himself from the group he'd been talking to. Spotting Kief across the room, he worked his way to the older Dragonlord's side.

"You're not planning to leave already, are you?" Kief demanded in an undertone.

"I most certainly am," Linden snapped. "This idiotic, last-minute affair has made me late enough. I will not dishonor Maurynna in the eyes of her family. Or myself in *her* eyes."

"I wish you'd reconsider th—Oh, bother; here comes Sevrynel, and he looks like a man with a bug in his breeches. I wonder what's wrong?"

Linden looked over his shoulder. Lord Sevrynel was making straight for them; Linden had seldom seen a man look so flustered and worried. Annoyed as he was at their host for the poor timing of this dinner—for he liked the man and had enjoyed the other impromptu feasts—Linden couldn't help feeling sorry for him. "Looks like one bloody big bug, too," he whispered.

Kief smothered a laugh behind his hand.

Lord Sevrynel fluttered to a halt in front of them. "Your Graces—Linden Rathan—Oh, dear. Oh, dear. I don't know how to tell you this. . . ."

A commotion at the door made Linden—and everyone else in the room, judging by the sudden hush—look in that direction. He nearly swore aloud.

For Sherrine, her proud face salt-white and streaked with tears, walked slowly toward him. Astonished murmurs followed her. Her eyes were fixed on him as if she were a storm-lost wayfarer and he a beacon.

And in her hands she bore a large silver goblet.

In a flash he knew what it was: a farewell cup. One that he had to share with her or look like the worst sort of petty bastard before all these nobles—for they, of course, had no idea of the true enormity of Sherrine's crime. Some he'd overheard even wondered why he'd been so upset for the sake of a commoner.

He would have to share the cup and publicly forgive Sherrine. Once more the girl had trapped him. This time he was not amused.

He waited for her, hands gripping his belt so hard it was a

wonder the heavy silver plaques didn't bend under the pressure.

Easy, Linden, Kief warned. *Don't do anything rash.*

When she reached him, Sherrine went down on one knee. "Linden," she began, her voice shaking with unshed tears. "Linden, I—I wanted to say I'm sorry. I had no right. You had made it clear that—" She looked away for a moment, then continued. "I know now that there can never be anything more between us. I just wanted to tell you that I am retiring to my family's estates in the country for the duration of the regency debate; I know that my continued presence is . . . painful to you. I leave tomorrow morning. But I wanted to share the farewell cup with you before I left. For a time we were happy, I think, and I would bid farewell to you and that time."

Linden studied the pale face raised to him. Sherrine's beautiful eyes were sad but hopeful. Now the murmurs from the watching crowd were sympathetic. He'd look like the rankest cad indeed if he refused the cup held out to him.

Still, he thought of doing just that. Then he remembered: the wergild. Maurynna's words ending the feud bound him as well. He wanted to snarl his frustration aloud.

"I will share that farewell with you, my lady," he forced himself to say instead.

Sherrine gifted him then with one of the most beautiful smiles he'd ever seen and stood once more. Raising the cup so that all might witness, she said, "Fare thee well, Linden. I would have you remember me more kindly than I deserve," and drank deeply.

As she presented the cup to him, he caught a delicate trace of her perfume. It brought back happier memories. A pity it had ended this way.

Linden raised the goblet to those bittersweet memories and said, "Fare thee well, Sherrine. I shall remember that we were happy. May the gods watch over you."

Approving nods and whispers greeted his words. The Cassorins had the ending they wanted.

He drank.

The wine was rich and strong. As was traditional with a farewell cup, it was spiced with overtones of both sweet and bitter, this one more bitter than most. Or was that only because he'd no wish to be drinking this one in the first place?

Blast the girl for doing this to him.

Licking his lips as he finished, Linden reflected he had never tasted quite that combination of herbs before, but then he'd never partaken of a farewell cup in Cassori, either. There was a faint metallic aftertaste to this one that sat harshly on his tongue.

I daresay they have their own traditional herbs, though I prefer the Yerrin or Kelnethi brews.

He returned the goblet to Sherrine. She raised it and turned the goblet over in the traditional ending. The few drops of wine left spattered across the white tile floor. They looked like blood, he thought, remembering Maurynna's wounds.

Sherrine made him a courtesy; a servant came up with her cloak. "Farewell, Linden. May the gods watch over you."

And with those words, Sherrine swirled the cloak over her shoulders and drew the hood up, shielding her face from the eager stares of those around her. Head bowed, she left the room.

Well done, Linden, Kief said in his mind. *I know how hard that was for you.*

Do you really, Kief? And now I am leaving.

He'd give Sherrine enough time to get well away and bid their host good-bye. And no one and nothing was stopping him this time.

Turning off the road into a thicket, Sherrine reined her horse in just inside the shelter of the trees. She fumbled desperately at her belt pouch for a moment before her nervous fingers found the vials they sought. With frantic haste she selected one, broke the brown wax seal, and gulped down the contents. Tossing the vial away, she dismounted and, after looping the palfrey's reins around a low branch, walked a short distance into the woods. She waited tensely.

But Althume was as good as his word. Her stomach roiled.

Sherrine fell to her knees and vomited forth the wine she had just shared with Linden. Spasm after spasm of nausea shook her, and the heavy supper the mage had warned her to eat followed the wine. Even as the tears streamed down her face she welcomed the sickness—else she would have fared far worse.

Linden would have no such reprieve. And it was no more than he deserved.

After what seemed an eternity of retching, Sherrine returned to her horse, one hand pressed to her aching stomach. The little mare snorted at the scents clinging to her mistress, but stood steady. With shaking hands, Sherrine untied the waterskin from behind the saddle and washed her face. Then she rinsed her mouth again and again, seeking to rid herself of the taste of wine and herbs that lingered on her tongue. Then she broke the white seal on the other vial and drank that one down.

She rested her head against the saddle for a few moments, then wearily pulled herself onto the palfrey's back. She could rest well this night. She had her revenge. Sherrine wondered how Linden was faring. And, turning her face up to the rain just beginning, smiled.

Linden grumbled as he swung into the saddle. First this ill-timed feast; now a blasted storm was brewing. He'd be lucky to get to the other side of the river before the rain began.

The gelding's hooves clattered on the cobblestones as Linden wheeled it around. A ball of coldfire burst out of the darkness at his eye level, momentarily blinding him. He spat out a curse and threw up a hand to shield his eyes.

Kief said, "Apologies, Linden; I didn't mean to blind you. Perhaps you should delay returning. You don't have a cloak with you; you'll be soaked if it starts—"

Mindful of the watching grooms, Linden switched to mind-speech and exploded, *Damn it all, Kief! A little wetting won't hurt me—I've fared far worse than that over the years. Don't think I don't know what you're trying to do. I know bloody well how pleased you are at our estrangement. But I was invited to this feast before that happened and I have every intention of going tonight. You and Tarlna have been delaying me ever since Sherrine left. You will not change my mind—understand that. And now I'm leaving whether you like it or not.*

Fat, cold drops of rain began to fall, first a hesitant spattering, then a steady downpour. Kief stood oblivious to it, looking up at Linden.

"Were we truly that transparent?" Kief asked ruefully.

"Yes," Linden snapped. "Now get out of my way. And get that damned coldfire out of my eyes."

The coldfire retreated to hover by Kief's shoulder. "Will you take some of our escort with you?"

Linden touched the greatsword slung across his back; ever since that scare in the woods, he'd taken it with him whenever he left the city proper. "Kief, I do know how to use this—remember? And you don't really think any footpad with even half his wits will be out in this rain to waylay travelers, do you?" *And that mage has made no move against any of us.* "Let your guards stay dry."

For a moment he thought the older Dragonlord would argue further, but Kief stepped back, bowing his head in acceptance.

Linden urged the gelding past Kief. He wondered if he'd be able to find the site of the *tisrahn* by himself; Maurynna had no doubt left for it long ago. He'd have to go soaking wet, as well. There was no time to spare to return home for dry clothes and a cloak. He'd not give her more excuse to be angry with him than she already had.

It was a long ride to the ferry and Linden didn't dare ask the gelding to gallop in the sloppy footing and poor light. As it was, the horse shied and snorted at the heavy rain and wind gusting through the tree branches. Linden thought he heard thunder far off in the distance. He pressed the gelding as much as he thought safe, but the trip was taking far longer than he'd hoped.

At last he was on the straight stretch of road that led through the little meadow to the ferry landing. He could make out the ribbon of darkness that was the Uildodd in the distance.

Damn! Looks like the ferry's on the other side, he thought. Since the way was clear, he urged his mount to a canter.

A short time later the gelding's hooves thudded on the wooden landing. Sure enough, the boat was gone. Linden set the ball of coldfire to hover high over his head; a distant "Hallooo!" told him the ferrymen knew they had a fare waiting. He wrapped his arms around himself, hunching his shoulders against the rain, and called up a heat spell. Once again he heard thunder rumble in the distance as he settled himself for the wait.

Linden licked his lips and grimaced. The taste of those herbs still lingered. Ah, well; the sooner he got to the *tisrahn*, the sooner he could get a cup of wine to clear that wretched taste from his mouth.

He smiled. And the sooner he got there, the sooner he'd see Maurynna again.

He hoped the ferry returned quickly.

Forty-three

The hot, humid air, thick with perfumes and incense, clung stickily to Maurynna. The rich aromas of roasting goat and pig wove through the more exotic scents, drawing them together in the tapestry of smells that Maurynna associated with her voyages to Assantik. All around her the crowd surged through the noisy darkness, laughing, chattering, and singing. Now and again ululations rose above the steady beat of the drums. She was suddenly homesick for the feel of the *Sea Mist* rolling beneath her feet, the sharp tang of the salt breezes blowing in her face, crisp and clean.

She wiped the sweat from her brow. Maylin appeared at her side; she said something that Maurynna couldn't hear over the clamor. Bending, Maurynna heard: "Let's get closer to the dancers! I can't see over all these people."

Though the last thing she wanted to do was wade deeper into the crowd, Maurynna hadn't the spirit to say no. She still couldn't quite believe that Linden had played her for a fool. So, with Maylin following on her heels like a dinghy behind its mother ship, Maurynna elbowed a way through the tightly packed celebrants to the center of the courtyard where the dancers performed around a bonfire.

If only I could have asked Otter to mindspeak Linden when he was first late. Though I don't think I would have dared.

She just hoped Linden wasn't with Lady Sherrine.

As they drew closer, Maurynna could hear the clashing of the tiny brass cymbals the dancers wore on their fingers. All around her people swayed and stamped their feet, mesmerized by the music.

The rhythm of the drums pounded in her bones now. Almost against her will, the deep boom, double-boom of the *daggas* set her feet moving. Weaving in and out of the *daggas'* heavy pulse were the sharper-toned *zamlas*, little brass drums with dyed goat hide stretched across them. Above the beat of the drums swirled the melody of the shrill pipes.

"Look at them! They're so graceful!" Maylin yelled up at her.

Maurynna grinned back, remembering her first sight of Assantikkan dancers. "Aren't they, though!"

She set her worries adrift on the music and enjoyed the dancers circling the bonfire. They twisted and turned, men and women, bodies impossibly serpentine, their arms echoing with movement the intricate melodies of the pipes, hips and feet following the drumbeats. Like everyone around her, Maurynna swayed to the music, stamping her feet in time with the dancers'.

One moment she was lost in the music. The next, the realization that Linden still wasn't there shattered her contentment. She went cold inside and looked around.

No, no bright blond head towered above the crowd. She tugged nervously on a lock of her hair. Where on earth was Linden? He should have been here long ago; Aunt Elenna would have given him directions. Surely he wouldn't dishonor Almered this way.

It's not like it's very far away from Aunt Elenna's. Or hard to find, either. A sudden thought made her feel very small. *Could he have forgotten? Just let him not be with Lady Sherrine.*

She wrapped both hands in her hair now, pulling until it hurt. She was desperate to leave, to go look for Linden. Which was stupid; she hadn't the faintest idea where to start.

Something cold stung her face. She looked up, wondering. A second fat, cold raindrop slapped her cheek. "Ouch!" she cried, and the scattered drops became a downpour.

At once the courtyard became a madhouse of activity. People rushed for the arcades lining the courtyard, servants ran everywhere at once, dragging tables laden with food and drink under shelter. The music ended with a discordant squawk as the performers joined the laughing rout.

Moments later Maurynna stood alone in the courtyard, staring up at the sky, oblivious to the soaking rain. The sense of urgency overwhelmed her.

Maybe he left word at the house.

She spun on her heel, mind made up. She joined the throng crowding the arcade, calling for her cousin.

"Here! Over here!"

Maurynna craned to see over the crowd; many of the Assantikkans were as tall as she. At last she caught a glimpse of a pale hand waving at her. She elbowed her way through the crowd.

Maylin—as Maurynna should have guessed—had managed to find a spot by one of the tables of food. She stood, smiling smugly between bites of a pasty filled with honey and dried fruit. "Want some?" she offered as Maurynna squeezed in next to her.

The sight of the sticky sweet turned Maurynna's stomach. "No! Maylin, I . . . I must leave. I can't—" Someone jostled between them; Maurynna pushed back to her cousin's side.

Maylin finished the pasty in three quick bites. "It's because of Linden, isn't it? Rynna, he may have been delayed at that feast. Maybe he had to talk to the other Dragonlords. Won't Almered be offended if you leave now?"

"Very likely, yes," Maurynna admitted. An elbow dug into her back; she shifted away from it. "But I'll have to risk that. I want to go home, in case—anyway, this crowd is driving me mad. If you don't want to go, you don't have to, you know. I'll leave Gavren to see you home."

Maylin sighed. "Don't be an ass; Mother would have my head if I let you go unescorted. Please don't tell me you're expecting to find a message from Linden waiting for you.

"Oh, don't glare at me like that, Rynna. You've been mooning about like a lovesick calf for days. We've been worried about you ever since the night Lady Sherrine attacked you and he said he couldn't see you anymore—for no good reason that I can see."

Maylin set her hands on her hips. "I know you've always loved the legends about him, and believe me, I can understand how exciting it was to meet him. I'm just afraid you're making too much of it. He didn't ask you to dally with him, did he? But he wasn't at all shy to ask Lady Sherrine to. Face it, Rynna—whatever his interest in you was, it wasn't that. You're a friend of Otter's, no more.''

Maylin's voice turned gentle. ''And I don't want to see you hurt over him. You're eating yourself alive, Rynna. You're . . . not like yourself,'' she finished with an uncertain, frustrated gesture.

Maurynna forced back angry words and hurt tears. When she could trust her voice, she said, ''Don't think I haven't told myself all that already, Maylin. Over and over and over. But I just''—the memory of the kiss in the garden filled her—''can't make myself believe it.''

''You're being a fool, Rynna.''

Maurynna said sadly, ''I know. But I can't help it. I can't explain it, either; I wonder if this is what being under a geas is like.''

Maylin threw her hands up. ''Oh, wonderful,'' she said, sticking her head out in the rain to glare up at the heavens as if holding the gods responsible for her cousin's madness. ''Now the girl's talking like a bard's tale!'' Her shoulders slumped in defeat. ''I don't suppose you'd be willing to wait for the rain to end? No, I didn't think so. Very well, let's be off. Besides, I forgot to set the bread dough to rise for tomorrow's baking.''

Maurynna swallowed. ''Maylin—thank you.''

With a grunt and a heave the gelding scrambled out of the ferry and onto the landing. It snorted at the hollow booming under its hooves and danced.

''Stupid creature,'' Linden said, keeping a firm grip on the reins as he led the horse to solid ground. ''You've done this how many times now? And has the dock opened beneath you yet?''

The gelding's rolling eye and rapidly flicking ears said, *You never know.*

Laughing, Linden tossed a coin to the ferrymen. ''And let's

hope I'm the last to drag you out on such a miserable night."

The younger ferryman caught the coin out of the air. The older one smiled, revealing stained and missing teeth.

"Thankee, m'lord. There's a nice bit of fire waiting in yon hut. Would 'ee like to warm up by it?"

Linden vaulted into the saddle. "No, thank you. I've already kept a lady waiting for me for too long."

The ferrymen laughed in understanding and ran for the hut. Linden urged the reluctant gelding into the mud of the road.

Once more he pushed it as fast as he dared; no sense in having it get caught in the mud and strain a hock or fall down. It was bad enough that the idiot animal shied and tried to bolt at each blaze of lightning and peal of thunder. He had to concentrate every moment on keeping it under control.

"Ah, Shan, Shan," Linden muttered. "If only you were here."

He kept his head lowered against the rain driving into his face, only looking up from time to time to gauge his progress.

They passed the clump of birches that marked the bend in the road, then the dead oak blasted in some earlier storm. The gelding trotted on, snorting nervously.

There was the big field stretching away to his right. That meant he was only a quarter mile or so from the city. Good; he'd be at the Vanadins' soon. Maybe Maurynna had waited for him. . . .

Movement flickered in the corner of his eye. He jerked his head around, searching the darkness.

Two horsemen were riding out of the woods at the far side of the field as if they had been waiting for him. And he was a rock lizard if they meant him well. Linden reached for Tsan Rhilin.

But before Linden's hand reached the hilt one of the men gestured. Pain exploded through the Dragonlord's body. He screamed at the sudden agony and half-fell from the saddle. Before he could claw his way back up, the terrified gelding slewed around and jumped sideways, flinging him to the ground, and made its escape.

Linden writhed in agony in the muddy road, each wave of pain worse than the one before.

She'd been a fool to think that he'd have left word at the house. Damn him to every one of the nine Yerrin hells; Dragonlord or no, he had no right to treat her this way and dishonor his invitation from Almered.

And Otter had said Linden Rathan wasn't an ass.

A wave of panic hit Maurynna. It was gone so quickly that she thought she'd imagined it. But an uneasy feeling lingered, and without thinking she was stripping off her gown and shift in exchange for breeches, tunic, and boots. She snatched up the belt with her sailor's dirk and made her way as quietly as she could downstairs.

Maurynna poked her head into the kitchen. Maylin was kneading dough.

"I'll be upstairs in a bit," Maylin said as she slapped and pummeled the floury mass.

"Ah, um—I can't sleep, so I thought I'd go over some accounts in the office." She cleared her throat. "Don't wait up for me."

Maylin blew a tendril of hair out of her face. "Oh, very well," she said, and went back to her dough.

Maurynna crept down the hall and tossed her cloak around her shoulders. She eased the door open and slid outside into the rain. She had to find Linden, damn him. But where?

Forty-four

Fire blazed through Linden as his muscles spasmed and
heaved. He thrashed in the mud. It felt as if acid ran through
his veins; had he been able to, he would have screamed. But
even that release was denied him. He could only grunt like
an animal.

Instinctively he tried to mindcall Kief and Tarlna. Pain
lanced through his skull; he nearly blacked out. It took everything he had to fight his way back from the edge of uncon-
sciousness.

Convulsion after convulsion wracked him. What was happening to him? He'd never heard of any illness like this.

A new fear stabbed him. Gods help him, what if he rolled
to land face down in the mud? He hadn't the strength to lift
himself; he'd drown.

As if that burst of panic were a signal, his thoughts became
chaos. Images tumbled over each other in his mind as his
consciousness ebbed away. A final memory flashed before his
mind's eye as if lit by lightning: Sherrine drinking, then offering him the goblet of wine.

Poison? The word echoed in his mind as he sank into darkness. *But how—how—how? . . .*

"Rynna—where are you going?"

Maurynna clenched her fists in frustration and stopped. She
should have known Maylin wouldn't believe her. "For a
walk."

Perhaps—just perhaps—her cousin would take the hint and
leave her alone.

Maylin caught up to her and snorted in derision, flour-
covered fists planted on hips. "At this hour? In the rain? You

must think me dim to believe that. What are you really up to?''

Maurynna bit her lip, wondering what story she could tell the younger girl. If she told her cousin what she planned, Maylin would likely drag her back to the house, yelling for her mother all the while. The words tumbled out anyway. ''To find Linden. Something's wrong; I know it.''

She nearly kicked herself for a fool. And the long, hard look Maylin gave her shredded her already frayed nerves a little more. Just as she couldn't stand it any longer, the other girl said, ''Maurynna—you're being an ass. What if you find out he's with someone else? But fool or not, you're not walking about alone in Casna after midnight. If you insist on this idiocy, I'm coming with you. Are you armed?''

Maurynna sighed and pulled her oilskin cloak enough to reveal the long, heavy sailor's dirk—almost a short sword— hanging from her belt.

''Good. Give me a moment. I want to change to breeches in case we have to run.'' Maylin dashed up the walk and eased open the door, slipping inside without a sound.

Maurynna waited, sick with worry, listening to the drip-splash of rain falling from eaves to cobblestones. Far off in the distance she heard the ominous rumble of thunder; another storm was moving in. She bit her knuckles. Something was wrong. She knew it. She *knew* it.

If only she knew what.

The door opened again; a shadow slipped out. Maylin trotted up to her, buckling something around her waist. To Maurynna's surprise it was a sword belt with a short sword in a worn sheath.

She must have made some exclamation, for Maylin said, ''It's Father's old one. And yes, I do know how to use it. Maybe I don't fight off pirates the way you do, but I sometimes ride with our pack trains, and bandits have been known to attack even well-guarded merchant trains. Now—which way do we go?''

For a moment Maurynna thought Maylin mocked her. But

her cousin was serious; it seemed her feelings were as good a guide as any for this fool's mission.

"I—I don't know exactly. But I feel . . . *pulled* that way." She gestured to the north. Thunder rumbled again, closer this time.

Maylin scratched her snub nose. "Not much to go on, but better than nothing. Lead on, Captain."

Forty-five

He woke up enough to realize that he was being dragged up the bank and onto the grass, though he couldn't open his eyes. Nor, try as he might, could Linden move a muscle to fight his captors. They were not gentle with him, but he had a small sort of revenge. Judging by the grunts and groans, as a dead weight he cost them a great deal of effort.

They hauled him across the wet grass well away from the road. The motion made his head spin again. Once more he tried to mindcall his fellow Dragonlords; once more his only reward was agony. There would be no help from that quarter.

"Far enough!" one man protested. "It's not likely anyone's going to come past in this storm."

"I'd like to get him under the trees," the other gasped. "But you're right. Gods, he's heavy; it would have to be the damned Yerrin."

They dropped him face-up to the rain. He was nauseated almost beyond enduring now. He sensed one of the men drop to his knees beside him and fought to gather what was left of his wits.

"Well met, Dragonlord," said a voice, coldly amused. "In a few moments—when you're able to answer them—I'm going to ask you some questions and you will answer truthfully. You have no choice, you see. And when this is over, you will remember nothing of this. Just that you were suddenly taken ill after you left the ferry."

Linden fought to move, but the paralysis was complete. Not even an eyelid flickered. He was trapped in darkness, helpless before these men. And terrified as he'd never been in his life.

After a long silence, the voice spoke again. "Very well,

Dragonlord—I think we're ready to begin." Then, triumphantly, "I can't tell you how long I've waited for this."

They stood in the rain-soaked darkness, their cloaks pulled tight around them.

"Where to now, Maurynna?" asked Maylin, sounding tired and resigned.

Maurynna rubbed the tears from her eyes. "I'm not sure—oh, hang it all, I just don't know. I know something's wrong, but I don't know which way anymore." Her voice rose, an edge of hysteria in it.

"Stop it!" Maylin snapped. "That won't help us! Think, Rynna, think!"

Maurynna caught back a sobbing breath. Maylin was right; breaking down wouldn't help them or Linden. Besides, she'd always despised girls who did just that at any excuse.

She concentrated on the smell of wet earth, the different sounds the rain made as it lashed against their cloaks, solid where the cloaks stretched tight across their backs, a hollow *thup! thup!* against empty fabric. She focused her mind on them until she had herself under control once more.

But she still had no idea which way to go.

"Very well, then," Maylin said, her voice falsely bright. "The way we started is as good as any, I'd say."

Numb with despair, Maurynna asked, "What is in this direction?"

Maylin stepped out at a brisk pace. Maurynna fell in beside her.

"All sorts of things. The goldsmiths' section, the spice merchants, things like that. If we keep going long enough, we'll fall into the Uildodd."

The Uildodd . . . Maurynna stumbled. Of course, of all the stupid—"Maylin—there's a ferry, isn't there? Where is it?"

"A bit north and west of here. Why—oh!"

"Exactly. Most of the nobles have estates on the other side, don't they? What if that's where that dinner was? He'd have to use the ferry to return."

They broke into a trot at the same time, Maylin in front to

lead the way. Maurynna fretted at slowing her pace to her cousin's shorter legs but had no other choice, despite the voice deep inside urging her to hurry, hurry.

He's breaking free of the spell!

Althume couldn't believe his eyes. The big Dragonlord should not have been able to move so much as an eyelid, yet Linden Rathan was raising a hand. Just barely, true, but it should have been impossible. "Damn it!" the mage said. There were still many more questions to ask. He thought quickly. "Pol—while I strengthen the spell, get the sword off him. I think we'll have a use for it."

While Pol worked the buckle of the greatsword's baldric free, Althume began the enchantment that would bring Linden Rathan under his control again. He ignored the rain, the thunder booming like war drums overhead, as he wove words and gesture in a magical pattern.

Lightning split the sky overhead. Pol jumped beside him and exclaimed, "My lord! 'Ware!"

Althume looked over at the road. Two cloaked figures were climbing the high bank. One held a blade. The mage swore in frustration; aside from the greatsword, which neither he nor Pol were skilled with, they were unarmed. He made an instant's decision. "Take the sword and run. We daren't face them." He jumped to his feet.

"But the antidote—"

"Linden Rathan will just have to take his chances." Althume reached down and yanked Pol to his feet. "Run!"

Forty-six

Maurynna could barely breathe now; the sense of fear, of *wrongness*, constricted her chest so that to draw a breath was torture. Linden was nearby; she knew it. And something was terribly, terribly wrong.

She broke into a run without thinking. Keeping to the grassy verge on the right side of the road, she avoided the worst of the clinging mud. Maylin yelled something but she ignored it.

From ahead of her and to the left came a muffled exclamation. She jumped down from the bank, running across the road, the mud sucking at her feet, turning every step into a battle. There was a dim light in the field by the road; by its uncertain gleam she could make out two men bending over something in the long grass.

No, not something. Someone.

Linden.

She drew her dirk. One of the men looked up just as a stroke of lightning lit the world. His hood fell back. He had a square, blocky face, with lips drawn back in a snarl of hatred.

Maurynna ran up the far bank of the road to firmer ground, Maylin not far behind. The other man stood up and hauled the square-faced one to his feet as she screamed a cry as harsh as a sea eagle's. She charged them, teeth bared, yelling a wordless challenge. Battle fury raged in her blood. At first Maurynna thought they would stand firm; half-berserk, she welcomed the fight. But they broke and ran for the trees instead. Moments later she heard the retreating thunder of horses' hooves.

Her momentum almost carried her past the still form lying

in the wet grass. Then she was on her knees beside Linden, gently raising his head, her dirk cast aside. A ball of cold-fire—the light she had seen—glowed weakly a foot or so above the Dragonlord's still form. His face looked waxen in its sickly light.

She gathered him into her arms. He lay a heavy, limp burden against her. Maurynna went half mad with fear, certain that he was dead. But then, with a gasping effort that nearly pulled him from her embrace, he breathed. She tightened her arms around him; holding him close, she begged, "Linden! Linden, what happened? What did they do to you?"

She thought he tried to speak, but no sound came. Maylin, slipping and sliding in the wet grass, dropped to her knees on the other side of Linden.

"What's wrong with him? Was he stabbed?" asked Maylin.

"I don't know. Help me look."

With Maylin supporting him, Maurynna slid her hand beneath Linden's tunic. But there were no wounds, nothing to explain his condition. His skin was clammy, but that was no more than to be expected in this weather. Or was it? Maurynna paused with her hand over Linden's heart. It hammered under her palm, its rhythm ragged and uneven. Was he ill, then? She could smell wine, but surely he wasn't drunk. Then, ever so faintly, she caught the scent of woods lily.

While she tried to think, she unpinned her cloak and wrapped it around the too-still Dragonlord. She took him back from Maylin to rest against her.

"Rynna, what—?"

Her frustration and fear overwhelmed her. "Maylin, hush! Let me think what to do!" Maurynna sobbed. She squeezed her eyes shut.

Think! Think! Think!

Her mind spun in circles like a child's top. Then came the memory of Healer Tasha's sympathetic face. Maurynna's panic fled before the thought of the ginger-haired Healer.

But what if this were some illness only Dragonlords get? Tasha could do nothing then. But a dragon's healing fire . . .

"Maylin—you've got to get the other Dragonlords. They'll know what to do. I'll stay here with Linden."

For a moment she thought her cousin would protest leaving her. But Maylin, bless her, stood and said, "Very well. I'll be back as soon as I can. Here—in case those men come back. It would just trip me."

The short sword fell next to Maurynna's leg. The next moment Maylin swirled the cloak from her shoulders and draped it over Linden's legs.

Before she could insist Maylin keep it, the younger girl disappeared into the darkness. Maurynna prayed the ferry was still running; with all the rain the river must be rising fast.

She pulled Linden closer, trying to warm him with her body, ignoring the rain soaking through her clothes. Cradling Linden's head on her shoulder and stroking his rain-drenched hair, she murmured encouragement as he struggled for each rasping breath.

"Hold on, Linden—please. Maylin will be back soon and she'll bring help. Please. Please," she begged in an agony of fear.

The ball of the coldfire sank closer to the ground. She guessed it would not leave unless Linden dismissed it—or died. Maurynna watched its feeble pulsing with dread, dying a thousand deaths every time the light flickered and threatened to go out. Each time it returned. But how much longer could it last?

Maylin ran along the bank of the road, her lips pressed against the pain of the stitch in her side. She could hear the river now, the murmur of voices, the thud of feet on wood. A sudden blaze of lightning showed her the ferrymen making ready to cast off.

Thunder rolled down the river valley, drowning out her cries. She shut her mouth so as not to waste her breath any more and ran harder. The moment the peal ended she screamed, "Wait! Wait!"

But the men didn't hear. The first stepped into the barge and took his place at one long oar. Maylin bit her lip and from somewhere found strength for a final burst of speed.

The second man cast the rope into the ferry and pushed off from the landing, jumping into the boat as he did. He looked around at the sound of feet on wood. The first ferryman half rose from his oar.

"What the bloody—?" he yelled as Maylin flung herself from the landing and fell sprawling in the bottom of the boat. The next moment the river caught the ferry and the men had to look to the oars or be swamped.

Maylin pressed her face against the boards and ignored the cursing above—and at—her, concentrating only on getting her breath back.

A kick roused her. She sat up, pushing her sodden brown curls back from her face, her lower lip jutting out in anger.

"Fool cow! Coulda fallen in the river an' been drownded!" the older of the two men snarled at her as he pulled on his oar. "Ought to charge you double for—"

"I don't have any money," she said.

The other man swore. "Gaw, Yattil, bloody little baggage thinks she be getting across for nothin', then? Ought to throw you in, you thievin' bitch, tryin' to cheat honest men!"

Maylin rolled out of the way of a second kick and came up on her knees. Then the temper that was so well hidden by the gentle eyes and round face blazed up. Whenever small, soft-spoken Maylin lost that temper, it startled whoever was its target. These men were no exception. They jumped, almost forgetting to row, when Maylin blasted them.

"How dare you!" she raged. "How *dare* you! Keep your hands off of me, you fools, and listen. Delay me and likely your thick heads will part company with the rest of you, do you hear? This is life or death for Linden Rathan."

The ferrymen gaped at each other. "What do you mean?" Yattil asked sharply. "The young Dragonlord went over a while back now—"

"That's right," said Maylin. "Someone ambushed him. My cousin is with him now. I'm going to get the other Dragonlords to help him."

Yattil stared at her as he rowed, obviously not believing

and not daring to disbelieve. Then, deciding to err on the side of caution, he asked, "What happened?"

Maylin took a moment to weigh how much she should tell, decided to leave Maurynna's premonitions out of the tale. She related her story between the peals of thunder. "We—my cousin and I—are friends of the Yerrin bard Otter Heronson, who is Linden Rathan's friend. Otter's staying with my family, the Vanadins. We're merchants."

The men nodded and looked relieved; they'd obviously heard of either Otter or her family. She was glad they didn't ask why Otter was staying with them rather than the Dragonlord. She hadn't figured out why either.

Before they could have time to think of objections, Maylin continued, "Linden Rathan was supposed to meet . . . When he didn't come, we went looking for him. Rynna and I found him not far from the ferry. Two men were bending over him. Rynna scared them off." Maylin paused, shuddering, remembering the rage in Maurynna's voice as her cousin had charged.

She scared me as well! I thought only dragons could be that fierce.

"Now I need to get the other Dragonlords. Linden Rathan is badly hurt or ill. They can help him."

The men looked at each other. Then Yattil nodded and they bent harder to the oars. Maylin doubted the old ferry had ever moved so quickly.

She crawled past the men to the prow and hunched there, cold, miserable, and scared, willing the far bank to come into sight. The rain stung her through the thin fabric of her tunic.

Gods help us, she thought. *Let him still be alive.* Then, from deep inside, *How in blazes did Rynna know something was wrong?*

She curled up tighter against the boat, weighing all the evidence and possibilities in her "orderly merchant's mind" as her mother had often teased her. For this would require a great deal of thinking—mostly to get around the fantastic idea lurking at the back of her thoughts.

* * *

As the storm moved closer, Maurynna prayed as she never had before in her life, not even as she had prayed by her mother's deathbed. She had been only a child then, too young to understand what death truly meant. Now she did. And the thought of losing Linden terrified her.

She pressed her cheek against his forehead. His breathing seemed a little easier now and he felt warmer. She dared to let herself hope.

He stirred in her arms. She tilted his head so that she could see his face. His eyes opened like a reluctant waker's: slitting open, shutting again, then the eyelids struggling to open fully. He stared at her with terror-filled eyes.

"Linden?" she whispered. "It's Maurynna."

Her heart nearly broke at the look in his eyes. Then recognition dawned in them. He whispered something she didn't catch.

"What? What did you say?" Maurynna said. "Linden, who did this to you?"

He spoke again. She bent her head to catch his words, but all she heard was "Questions. Ask . . . questions." Then he snuggled into her shoulder. The trust in the gesture made her forget how cold and miserable she was.

The next moment a spasm nearly wrenched him from her embrace and his breathing turned harsh and uneven once more. To Maurynna's relief, the fit subsided as abruptly as it began.

She rearranged the cloaks that he had dislodged, worried at how quickly he'd grown cold again. Once more she braced him against her shoulder and wondered if Maylin was across the river yet.

And still the walk to where the Dragonlords are staying. I hope she doesn't get lost.

The thought of delay frightened Maurynna so much she scolded herself for borrowing trouble. Maylin wouldn't fail her; all she had to do was be patient. The rumbling thunder mocked her as the lightning danced gaily across the sky.

By the third convulsive fit Maurynna had learned the signs preceding them: a short gasp for breath followed by a quivering rigidity in the muscles. Then the bone-wrenching shaking and desperate gasping for air.

Her arms turned heavy and leaden with the strain of supporting Linden's weight. And the fits were coming closer and closer together. Once more Maurynna slid a hand under Linden's tunic. She was no Healer, but the arrhythmic beating of his heart frightened her, now hammering like someone with a high fever, now skipping beats.

And Maylin still had to find the Dragonlords' estate.

Gods—please help us!

The boat pitched and rolled in the water. The silence of the ferrymen had a grim edge to it now. Maylin looked back as they struggled to keep the boat from shipping too much water. It strained against the thick rope it ran along as if fighting to be free, to seek the ocean not far away.

Stupid thing, Maylin thought to the boat as once more she strained her eyes searching the darkness ahead. *You'd not last the length of a sea chantey before turning turtle. Be happy with your river.*

It seemed they were barely moving at all now. Maylin cursed steadily under her breath and gripped the rail as if that would hurry the boat on.

A huge bolt of lightning tore the night apart. Maylin squeaked in surprise. But the sudden flare had shown her the landing not far ahead—and a rider waiting upon the landing.

She pressed her lips together. Whoever the servant was—he had to be a servant; no lord would forsake the comfort of his hearth this night—he could forget his original plans. She had more important things for him to do. She just hoped he wouldn't waste too much time arguing.

The landing was only a few feet away now. She rose to a crouch. The moment the prow thudded against the sloped landing she leaped from the boat.

"You! she cried. "Take me up with you! I must find the Dragonlords."

The cloaked and hooded rider made no motion.

Maylin stamped a foot in frustration. "Are you deaf, man?

Hurry!'' She scowled up at him, wondering if she could dump him from the saddle and take the horse. Not likely, considering her height. She'd have to bully him. ''You fool—listen to me!''

''I am,'' the rider said calmly. ''And if you are truly looking for the Dragonlords, why then—''

He swept the hood back from his head, and with the same six-fingered hand brought forth a ball of light from the air. He leaned down.

''You've found one,'' said Kief Shaeldar. ''Now—what is this about?''

Forty-seven

Maylin stared open-mouthed at Kief Shaeldar. Before she could gather her wits, he caught the ball of coldfire and brought it down to illuminate her face.

"I know you," he said. "You're the one with the little girl that Linden waves to each morning." Then, sharply, "Now what is this about? Be quick, girl, for I must cross the river."

He looked out across the Uildodd, frowning. It was plain he barely tolerated her delay.

Another bolt of lightning and a long, rumbling peal of thunder gave Maylin time to find her tongue. She said, "My— my cousin knows Linden Rathan. She knew something was wrong—I don't know how—but—"

He cut her off. "Your cousin? She 'knew something was'—Of course— Maurynna!"

Maylin nodded. All at once his entire being was focused on her with an intensity that frightened her. She spared a moment to wonder why Maurynna's name would invoke such a change in the Dragonlord, then poured forth her tale.

She had barely finished when Kief Shaeldar jumped down from his horse. He turned as if to run to the open area before the landing, and then stopped.

"Damn, damn, *damn!*" he snarled. "Not enough room to Change! Ferrymen—can you cross one more time?"

"If we hurry, Dragonlord—the river she's rising fast! But yon horse'll be too much weight."

With the speed of a striking snake Kief Shaeldar caught her up and set her upon the horse. Too surprised to protest, Maylin snatched the reins he threw at her. Before she could speak he had jumped into the ferry. At once it receded into the darkness; Kief Shaeldar's voice called out of the night,

"I hope you can ride, girl! Follow the coldfire."

Stunned, Maylin nodded, forgetting for a moment that he couldn't possibly see her. Or could he? The tales said that Dragonlords' eyes were sharper than truehumans'.

She looked up at the ball of coldfire as it revolved slowly in the air before her and swallowed hard. "Lead on, then," she told it.

The coldfire obediently drifted along the track. Maylin backed the horse and turned it. It seemed a well-mannered, willing animal; she hoped it wouldn't spook at the stirrups swinging loose against its belly. Small as he was compared to Linden Rathan, Kief Shaeldar was still much longer of leg than she.

But the horse seemed not to mind as it ambled along. Bereft now of her mission and its all-consuming urgency, Maylin suddenly realized just how cold, wet, and miserable she was. Each drop of rain seemed determined to slide down her tunic's neck. She hunched her shoulders and shivered. The night was vast and empty around her; only the coldfire seemed cheerful as it bobbed along.

She wanted to kick it; nothing should be that blithe on a night like this with all that was happening.

Maylin was half asleep and nodding in the saddle when she realized that what she had taken for distant thunder was in truth the pounding of horses' hooves on the road ahead of her. At first she thought that the group of riders drawing closer carried torches and wondered how they kept them lit in this downpour. Then she realized that the "torches" were more balls of coldfire. Her own guide abandoned her and raced to join the newcomers.

One rider stopped before her. The others formed a ring around her.

She looked into the glittering blue eyes of Tarlna Aurianne. At the Dragonlord's gesture, one of the other riders flung a cloak about Maylin's shoulders. She huddled into it gratefully, rubbing the fur-lined softness against her cheek. Another rider offered her a skin of wine. She drank, the hot spiced wine warming her as much as the cloak.

When Maylin returned the skin, Tarlna Aurianne leaned forward and studied her. Maylin shifted uneasily; she'd been teased too many times about the odd-colored eyes she shared with Maurynna.

But Tarlna Aurianne only smiled and murmured, "Yes, you would be kin. You have the look about you."

Confused, Maylin said, "Um—aside from the eyes I don't look that much like Maurynna."

Tarlna Aurianne's mouth quirked. "It's there for those that can see, child." She sounded amused. "You've done much for us tonight. The least we can do is offer you a warm bed and dry clothes. Come along."

The coldfire was barely glowing now. Maurynna ignored the tears and rain flowing down her cheeks and gently wiped blood from Linden's face. During his last fit—the worst yet—he'd bitten his lip. Fearing that he would bite his tongue next, she slashed a strip from the bottom of her tunic and forced the folded cloth between his teeth.

Could he have the falling sickness? she wondered. One of her childhood playmates had had it. *But Naille's fits never lasted this long that I can recall.* She wished she could remember more about it.

The muddy *plop-plop* of a horse's hooves on the road startled her. Linden's attackers were returning! She laid him down and grabbed Maylin's sword since it was closer. But her legs had fallen asleep; she fell as she tried to stand. Cursing herself for a fool, she knelt before Linden, teeth bared, determined to take at least one of them with her.

It wasn't until she was tucked into the most luxurious bed she could imagine, a hot brick wrapped in flannel comforting her cold feet, that Maylin remembered Maurynna had never said anything about meeting the other Dragonlords—just Linden.

Tarlna Aurianne doesn't know what Rynna looks like—so how could she know whether I have the "look" of kin or not?

Her earlier speculations from the barge bounded back into

her mind, clamoring to be noticed like a pack of unruly puppies.

I shan't, she told them firmly, *pay any attention to you.
You're nothing but moonshine.*

She turned them out again, rolled onto her side, and fell
asleep.

"Hallooooooo! Rynna! Rynna—are you there?"

She couldn't believe her ears. "Otter?" she screamed, wild
with relief. "Otter, is that really you?" She staggered to her
feet despite the pins and needles stabbing her legs.

She heard him urging the horse up the bank. Moments later
she felt the ground quivering under the flying hooves. "Here!
We're over here!"

The horse came to a sliding stop in front of her. Otter flung
himself from the saddle like a man forty years younger. She
fell into his arms, crying.

"How—how did you know?" she sobbed as she led the
bard to where Linden lay.

"Kief Shaeldar mindspoke me," Otter said grimly. "He
met Maylin on the other side of the river. I was on my way
home when he told me as much as he knew. He's on the ferry
now. Rynna—what happened? Who were those men?"

She shook her head as she knelt beside Linden again. "I
don't know." She controlled her sobs with an effort. "I
don't—Otter, help me get him sitting up again. It seems to
ease his breathing."

Together they arranged Linden so that he rested against
Maurynna's shoulder once more. When Otter tried to give her
his cloak, she shook her head. "I'm already soaked. Are you
certain Kief Shaeldar is on his way?"

Otter stretched a hand out to the coldfire, but drew it away
as though afraid he'd somehow hurt the feebly glowing ball.
"Yes. Seems he tried to mindspeak Linden, but could sense
only pain and blackness. That alarmed Kief so much he went
looking for Linden and met Maylin on the way."

The bard brushed a lock of wet hair from Linden's face.
"All we can do is wait, Rynna. And pray."

The knowledge that Otter now sat across from her on Linden's other side comforted Maurynna, even though she knew that he could do no more than she.

She remembered something. "Linden spoke once. He said to 'ask question.' Does that make any sense to you?"

Otter shook his head. "None whatsoever. You're certain? Hm—what could it mean?"

Suddenly the bard surged to his feet. His trained voice bellowed across the field, "Kief! Over here!"

Maurynna looked over her shoulder. A figure ran across the wet grass at a speed that few—if any—truehumans could match. A silvery ball of coldfire lit Kief Shaeldar's way.

He slid to a halt by them. "Let me see him," the Dragonlord ordered.

Otter stepped back. Maurynna clung to Linden, reluctant to let him go. She braced herself to argue should Kief Shaeldar order her away, but to her surprise he said nothing, simply took Linden's chin and looked closely into his face.

At last Kief Shaeldar sat back on his heels. "Black magery!" he spat. "Get back—both of you. I need room."

Before she could refuse, Otter grabbed her and dragged her back. "Don't be stupid, Rynna," he said when she struggled. "He needs room to Change!"

She went with him reluctantly. But it was Otter who stopped after only a few yards.

"Ah—Kief?" he said. "Do you think this is wi—"

"Get back, curse it!" the Dragonlord roared as he flung his cloak to the ground.

"On your head be it, then." The bard grabbed her hand and pulled her along until they reached the edge of the bank.

Maurynna clung to Otter as lightning flared and a red mist surrounded Kief Shaeldar. A second bolt revealed the ghostly figure of a dragon. Her head swirled. The crack of thunder that followed nearly deafened her. She cried out and shut her eyes. From a great distance she heard the squeal of a frightened horse and pounding hooves, then Otter's disgusted voice saying, "That tears it, Kief. That horse won't stop until the middle of next tenday."

But now she fell through an unending night. And there were voices in the darkness, great golden voices, more beautiful than anything she'd ever heard. But she couldn't understand what they said, and if she didn't, she'd die. She didn't want to die—not yet. She had to find out what the voices were saying to her. . . .

Forty-eight

"My lord? What will become of Linden Rathan?"

Althume glanced at the servant riding beside him. "I'm not certain, Pol. It is truly unfortunate that those travelers came when they did."

Pol grunted assent. Then, "Does Prince Peridaen know?"

"That the potion I gave Sherrine could kill Linden Rathan? No. A pity we had no time to administer the antidote, but there it is. If he dies, it will be awkward for us, true, but if the gods will it so—" He shrugged. "It will fall out as it will. I will not worry the prince with maybes and might-bes."

His only real worry was, if Linden Rathan died, how would it affect his plans for Sherrine?

Pain blazed through the darkness. Maurynna gasped and opened her eyes.

Why was she lying on the ground with Otter bending over her? Puzzled, she put a hand up to her stinging cheek and knew that he'd slapped her. He looked relieved and angry at the same time.

"I tried to tell you," he said to the brown dragon crouching over Linden.

Oh, gods, is she well?

The words were faint, like someone whispering up in the rigging. But they were inside her head. And she somehow knew she wasn't meant to hear them. Well and well; she'd not let on that she could.

And after everything I've said to Linden. He'll have my head.

The thought of Linden brought Maurynna upright, though

her head still spun. "Can you Heal Linden?" she pleaded. "You can, can't you? Your Healing fire—"

The voice spoke in her mind once more. This time it rang as loudly as a watch bell, rough with anger and fear.

I'm only a Dragonlord, not one of the bleeding gods! I'll do my best, but—

The great scaled head reared back. The mouth opened, revealing long, wickedly sharp fangs. Kief Shaeldar spread his wings slightly and drew a deep breath. Then he lowered his head once more. Blue-green flames rushed out past the deadly fangs and washed over Linden. Once, twice, three times the flames played over the stricken Dragonlord. After the third time Kief Shaeldar stepped back. His long neck and wings drooped.

Maurynna broke away from Otter and stumbled to Linden. Without thinking, she seized Linden's ball of coldfire. It burned a little brighter now—not much, but the light was steadier. And his color and breathing were better. For the first time she began to hope.

I must return the coldfire to Linden, Kief Shaeldar apologized. *It costs him energy that he can ill afford right now. I'm sorry; I know he'd like you to have it if possible.*

The big head dropped to her level, turned a bit so that one big eye watched her. Part of her mind noted that the iris was vertical like a cat's. She wondered why he cared for her feelings. The coldfire disappeared from her hands.

Help me pick him up; I'll take him back with me. Maurynna—take my cloak; it will be a long, wet walk.

Between them, Maurynna and Otter lifted Linden to the cradle formed by Kief Shaeldar's front legs. The brown dragon gently closed one six-clawed forefoot around Linden, holding him securely to the scaled chest. Then Kief Shaeldar rocked back onto his hind legs, doubled his long neck back on itself, and spread his wings.

"Come on!" Otter yelled, and pulled her away at a run. Surprised, Maurynna went without protest. She looked back in time to see Kief Shaeldar spring into the air, his neck snapping forward as if to cleave the sky above him, wings beating in short, powerful strokes.

She dragged Otter to a halt, ignoring the rain that beat against her face. The rush of air displaced by those wing strokes rocked her a moment later; she understood then why Otter had pulled her away. Any closer and they would have been knocked over.

Then the vertigo claimed her again and she was falling into forever. She dimly heard Otter calling her name, but was trapped inside her tumbling mind and couldn't answer. For one glorious moment she soared through the lightning-streaked sky by Kief Shaeldar's side; the next she spiraled into darkness.

Forty-nine

Althume stood as patiently as he could while the servant removed his wet cloak. The long, dripping bundle in his arms felt like both a prize and a beacon. But he schooled his expression as he had learned to over the many decades of his long life, looking neither guilty nor triumphant.

"No—I'll take this myself," he told the servant when the man offered to carry his burden.

The servant bowed himself away, saying, "Prince Peridaen is in his study."

Althume strode down the hall, cradling the sword wrapped in Pol's cloak against his chest. At the door to the study he pushed the latch down and elbowed the oak door open. To his relief, Peridaen sat alone before the fireplace.

"Where's Anstella?" Althume asked. He locked the door behind him.

Peridaen looked up from the chessboard he was studying. "With Sherrine; the girl looked like—what is that?"

With a flourish Althume swept the concealing cloak away. "Tsan Rhilin," said the mage. He looked down at the sheathed greatsword resting in his arms with the fierce pride of an eagle for its nestling.

"Good gods!" Peridaen stood, knocking his chair to the floor. "Let me see!" He crossed the intervening space in two long strides.

Althume laid the sword in the prince's waiting hands.

Peridaen studied the plain leather scabbard. "Hardly seems fitting for a sword out of legend, does it?" he said, fingering the unadorned straps. "And the sword itself—doesn't look as if it's magical." He half drew it from its sheath. "It simply looks to be a well-made, serviceable blade,'' he observed as he sheathed it once more.

''It isn't magical—not of itself, anyway.'' Althume wandered to the table and poured himself wine. ''There's some Yerrin legend about Sister Moon and the sword—its name means 'Moon Dancer' in archaic Yerrin.'' He drank a little, then finished, ''Supposedly Rani eo'Tsan took it from an undead Kelnethi harper—though I never understood how *he* came to have it—and gave it to Bram Wolfson.''

''And Linden Rathan had it of the Wolfson.'' Peridaen ran a hand over the hilt wrapped in twisted wire for a sure grip, the pommel of silver like a full moon. ''They were related somehow, weren't they?''

He seemed unable to tear his gaze away from the sword, plain though it was. Althume watched him with disdain. As loudly as Peridaen might prate of his hatred of the Dragonlords, he was still susceptible to the glamour surrounding them. It irked Althume that even as powerful a mage as himself needed the patronage of the nobility.

If only a mage could seize power as in those foolish tales. Such a pity that it would take more magic than any one mage could wield.

And who ever heard of mages agreeing long enough to league together?

''We've more important things than the sword,'' the mage snapped.

That broke the spell. Peridaen set the greatsword on the table. ''Gods, yes! Of course. It seems that there's no need to ask if your mission was at least partially successful. That you have Tsan Rhilin is proof that your spells worked. But why in the name of all the gods did you take it? That was a dangerous trick, Kas. And of the rest? Did you find out what we need to know?''

''Some.'' Althume pulled a chair before the fire and sat. He stretched his boots onto the hearth; in a few moments the steam rose from them. ''I'll give him this: Dragonlord Linden Rathan is one very strong-willed, stubborn bastard. He should not have been able to move while under the influence of the potion or to resist me. Yet he did both at the end. Still, I found out some things and had others confirmed.''

Peridaen retrieved his fallen chair. ''Such as?''

''Dragonlords cannot read minds—''

''Thank the gods,'' Peridaen murmured with a wry smile. ''Else we should all hang.''

''*I* would hang; *you* would be beheaded, courtesy of your royal birth. But as for the Dragonlords, while they cannot read minds, they can speak mind-to-mind with each other.

''And we can now lay to rest two of the causes of endless arguments within the Fraternity: Ankarlyn the Mage did indeed find a way to loosen the bond between a Dragonlord's souls. Unfortunately Linden Rathan had no idea how this was done, so he could not confirm what I have learned in my studies. We're on our own for that.

''But Ankarlyn's spells will work against them. It was proven once and for all by the successful mix of potion and spell that I used against Linden Rathan and further confirmed by his own words,'' said Althume.

''That's one cause laid to rest,'' the prince noted. ''What is the other?''

The mage smiled briefly. ''Why, that 'idiotic nursery tale' as some of the Fraternity's less enlightened members call it, of course—Ankarlyn's enslavement of a fledgling Dragonlord. This time Linden Rathan did know how that was done: using the blood of a Dragonlord—or one who has Dragonlord blood.''

Peridaen said slowly, ''One of my ancestors was the true-human daughter of two Dragonlords. And that means—damn it all, Kas, does it have to be the boy? I'm rather fond of him.''

Shrugging, the mage said, ''Rann is endearing enough, I'm sure, but will you let even him stand between the Fraternity and success? For if we do succeed, there are many that hesitate now who will flock to our banner, my prince. Will you cast that aside?

''Oh, gods.'' Peridaen closed his eyes and rubbed his forehead as if his head suddenly hurt him. "No, of course not. It's just . . . Sherrine *and* Rann?"

"The gods drive stiff bargains, my prince," Althume warned.

"I know. But this . . . I'll have to think about it, Kas," said Peridaen.

Peridaen's tone lit a warning beacon in the mage's mind, but he decided against pursuing the subject. Instead, he said, "Now, it may be possible to develop other spells to use against Dragonlords, but I'm not willing to spend the time. We can't drag out this regency debate for much longer, though I think we have a way to prolong it now." Althume leaned back in his seat and folded his hands across his stomach. "And there is a fledgling Dragonlord; I asked just to be certain. That seemed to frighten Linden Rathan; it was then that he fought the enchantment so hard that he came near to breaking it."

The mage raised his goblet in mock salute to the absent Dragonlord. "As I said, a stubborn and strong-willed bastard. I was amazed; I didn't think it could be done. The effort must have cost him dearly." He drained his cup and wiped his lips.

"I might have been able to subdue him again, but as bad luck would have it, two late-night travelers happened upon us."

"What! Who?" Peridaen demanded. "And did they see you well enough to recognize you?"

"I don't know; all I could see through the rain were two cloaked and hooded figures. By the same token, that would have been all that they could see as well. One charged us with a blade—whoever he is, he's used to using it. Rather than risk a wounding and awkward questions, I judged it best for us to get away." He held up a hand to forestall the question he knew Peridaen was about to ask. "Remember—neither Pol nor I were armed. The casting of spells that powerful will not tolerate the presence of cold iron. By the time the travelers found us, we had most of what we wanted—and that besides," the mage said, nodding at Tsan Rhilin lying on the table.

"Yes, *that*. And what shall we do with *that*? We can't leave it here. If one of the servants finds it—Blast it, Kas, you're taking too many chances! This wasn't in our plans."

Althume smiled one of his wintry smiles. "Plans are for changing, my dear prince. And stop worrying; this treasure will remain hidden until the proper time."

Low, urgent voices and the sound of people running up and down the hall woke Maylin. She sat up, startled by the thickness of the featherbed beneath her, the feel of finer linen sheets than any she'd ever known. Memory returned in a rush and she tumbled out of bed onto a richly carpeted floor.

Hiking up her borrowed nightgown so that she wouldn't trip, Maylin hurried to the door and ran into the hall. She was just in time to see Kief Shaeldar, water streaming from his clothes, reach the top of the stairs and turn into the hall. He carried Linden Rathan as if the big Dragonlord weighed no more than a child. A bevy of servants draggled behind him like lost chicks. One caught her eye; a blocky-faced man with a hard expression.

Didn't I see him somewhere tonight? No; I couldn't have. He's not been out in the wet. Then, *My gods—Dragonlords are strong, aren't they? No one as small as Kief Shaeldar has any business being able to carry someone of Linden's size that easily.*

Any other time the image of Linden's long legs dangling over Kief Shaeldar's arm would have been funny. But not tonight. Maylin ran down the hall as the door to one of the bedrooms opened.

"In here," Tarlna Aurianne said from inside the room. "Hurry."

Maylin caught only a glimpse of Linden's face as Kief Shaeldar hurried into the room. She reached it in time to have the door shut in her face. For a moment she debated knocking. But whatever grace being Maurynna's cousin earned her, she didn't think it stretched that far. So she turned and dragged her feet back to her room.

This time the big bed felt lonely; she wished Maurynna,

her mother, or even Kella, were here with her. She tossed and turned, pounded the pillow, counted sheep—but nothing would drive away the memory of Linden's face: still, slack, and grey, with dried blood crusted around his lips.

Fifty

Three desperate faces looked to Tasha for answers she didn't have: the Dragonlords Kief Shaeldar and Tarlna Aurianne, and Linden Rathan's friend, Otter.

"Can you help him, Healer?" Kief Shaeldar asked.

Tasha shook her head. "Your Grace, you told me that you used a dragon's Healing fire on him and it did little good. How can a truehuman Healer do any better? Especially with so much time gone by; if only I could have crossed the river last night. All I can tell you is that he looks to have been poisoned, unlikely as it seems. And if you're right that there was magery involved . . ."

She spread her hands helplessly. It was a feeling that she was all too familiar with these days and heartily sick of. "The best I can do is to try to counteract the symptoms with herbs and make him as comfortable as possible."

For the first time since Tasha had arrived at the river estate, Tarlna Aurianne spoke.

"Will he survive?"

Tasha drew a deep breath. "I don't know. I truly don't know—and the odds aren't on his side. Nearly a day since you brought him here and there's still no change."

The bard bowed his head and walked a short distance away. Tarlna Aurianne turned to the comforting embrace her soultwin offered. They clung together.

"I will try my best," Tasha said.

Kief Shaeldar nodded. "We understand, Healer. And we thank you. He's a stubborn pain in the ass at times, but we're very fond of him anyway," the Dragonlord said with a weak smile. "May the gods help you save him."

May they indeed, she thought as she left them in the hallway and returned to Linden Rathan's sickroom.

Globes of coldfire—left there by the other two Dragonlords—stood sentry at the four posts of the bed. Still unnerved by the idea of grabbing something her instincts clamored would burn her, Tasha caught one of the balls gingerly and directed its light onto Linden Rathan's face.

His skin had the grey, waxy look of a corpse. Only the slight rise and fall of his chest reassured her that he still lived. She released the coldfire; it drifted back to its place.

Once more she sat by his bed and attempted to puzzle out what exactly was wrong with Linden Rathan. If only he could tell her what had happened to him. All anyone was certain of was that two men were involved—and that only because the young sea captain and her cousin had seen them.

Who were those men? And what did they do to Linden Rathan? Did they poison him? His symptoms suggest it. If so, how did they overpower a Dragonlord? And what did they use?

But she had no more answers for this Dragonlord than she did for her young prince. All she could do was wait. And hope.

"By all the gods, Kas, what did you do to him?" Peridaen demanded. "Rumor has it that Linden Rathan's dying! What was in that cursed potion?"

Althume watched the agitated prince stride from one side of the room to the other for a moment before answering; all the while Peridaen yanked at his beard as if trying to pull it out. "The potion should not prove fatal, I don't think, even without the antidote."

That brought Peridaen to a dead halt. "Antidote? This thing was deadly enough to require an antidote and you didn't give it to him? What were you thinking of? What if he dies? We'll have Dragonlords turning the country inside out looking for answers. Why didn't you give it to him? And why didn't you tell—?"

Weary of the flood of questions, Althume broke in, "Because you're sometimes unwilling to take necessary risks.

And as for why I didn't give him the antidote, remember the two travelers? It was leave Linden Rathan there to take his chances or be caught. I don't need to tell you what *that* would have meant. The man's as healthy and strong as the proverbial ox; he should pull through. I'm more worried about the aftereffects. It is likely he will be severely depressed, perhaps even suicidal. A pity we can't warn the other Dragonlords, but one can't have everything.

"And if he does die—by his own hand, or because of the potion—we might well lose Sherrine," the mage continued. "I have no idea what losing a soultwin would do to a fledgling." He shrugged. "If so, we return to the original plan."

Peridaen eyed him. "Since when had we decided to abandon it? Take care you don't overstep your boundaries, Kas. I have not yet decided that we shall attempt to enslave Sherrine. Do nothing else to involve *or* endanger the girl, do you understand?"

Althume was beginning to understand all too well. "Of course, my lord."

Maurynna woke up with a pounding headache. She sat up carefully, holding her head in her hands; it felt as if mad smiths hammered behind her eyes, and her stomach was none too steady.

"How are you feeling, dear?" her aunt asked.

Maurynna took a chance and cracked her eyelids open. "Like I've been flogged from one end of the *Sea Mist* to the other with belaying pins. My head hurts," she complained.

"Some meadowsweet tea might help with that," Aunt Elenna said. "Now that you're awake I'll get you some. Are you hungry yet?"

"No!" Maurynna said, swallowing hard.

Elenna got up from her chair. "You will be later. But the tea will be best for now." She hesitated in the doorway on her way out. "Are you certain you're well enough to be left alone?"

Rubbing her temples, Maurynna said in surprise, "Of course I am. Why shouldn't I be?"

"Do you remember coming home?"

She had to think. "No," she admitted. "Or going to bed." She squinted at the window. The curtains were drawn, but she could see a faint light outside. "It's almost dawn, isn't it?"

Aunt Elenna shook her head. "No, dear—it's twilight. The *tisrahn* was last night. You were barely conscious when Otter brought you here. Then you fell into a sleep we couldn't rouse you out of all day long."

Maurynna gaped at her. For the first time she noticed the tenseness in Elenna's voice, the fatigue in her aunt's face. "I—I don't understand."

"Neither do I. You kept muttering about 'golden voices' in your sleep. At first I thought that perhaps you had whatever made Linden ill, but Otter assured me that wasn't the case. What it was, or what he thinks it might be, he wouldn't say."

"How did I get home? Otter couldn't have carried me. And where is he? And Maylin?" Maurynna asked, trying to think despite the pounding in her skull. "Have you heard anything about Linden?" She clenched her fists and squeezed her head between them as if that would still the smiths' hammers, and tried to remember what she'd dreamed.

"Oh, gods, Rynna—I'm sorry. I forgot about your headache; I'm too tired to think straight anymore what with everything that's happening. If you and Maylin ever worry me like that again, I'll—Let me get that tea for you," said her aunt as she hurried away.

Maurynna leaned back against the wall. She was in Maylin's bed and not the pallet on the floor, she noticed. *I wonder if Maylin's back from the other side of the river yet?*

A short while later she had her answer. Maylin entered bearing a mug and pushed the door closed with one foot.

"Drink this first before I answer any questions," Maylin said. "Mother's orders."

Maurynna knew better than to argue. As quickly as she could, she gulped the scalding tea. By the time she finished, the headache had changed from excruciating to merely painful. "Maylin, tell me everything before I go mad. Where did you sleep last night? Did you see Linden?''

"I stayed at the Dragonlords' estate. And, yes, I did see Linden when Kief Shaeldar brought him in. Rynna, I'm sorry, but—he looked awful. They wouldn't let me see him this morning when I asked. Everyone went about looking frightened. I saw Healer Tasha come out of his room at one point and she looked grim. I don't think she even noticed me; she called for a basin of heated water and went back in.''

Maurynna closed her eyes and tried not to cry, but the tears leaked out anyway. She searched inside herself; after all, hadn't she known somehow last night that Linden was in trouble? But she found no answers there. It felt like pushing against a locked door. "And where's Otter in all this? And what's wrong with me?''

"I passed Otter on the road as the Dragonlords' guards were escorting me home. He didn't stop to talk; he just galloped past, riding hard for the estate. He looked tired. And we don't know what's wrong with you. From what Otter said, you took sick as the two of you were walking home. Don't you remember?''

"No." Maurynna brushed the tears from her face. "I don't. Tell me.''

"He carried you as long as he could, he said, then by the grace of the gods found his horse and Linden's. I guess that they stopped running once they'd found each other and felt safe together. Somehow he got you onto Linden's horse, tied you into the saddle and brought you home like that. You kept talking about 'soaring through the storm' and other strange things.''

Maylin fell silent, studying Maurynna as if she were some new type of bird never before seen. Maurynna squirmed under the intent gaze.

Maylin asked, "How did you know something was wrong with Linden?''

Maurynna shrugged uncomfortably. "I just did. I don't know how.''

Maylin's reply came as a surprise. "Good." And she would say nothing more.

Fifty-one

Having finished the tale explaining Linden's absence from the *tisrahn* five days ago now, Maurynna sat in the back room of Almered's shop and slouched wearily in her chair. It was the first day she'd felt strong enough to go out.

Or wanted to. She couldn't go on like this for much longer, both worrying about Linden and angry with him. Had he had any intention of truly going to the *tisrahn*? The remembered scent of woods lily as he lay in her arms nearly turned her stomach. Once more the black mood that had nearly engulfed her the past few days threatened to swallow her. She shook it off.

"So I'm sorry I didn't come sooner, but I kept waiting and waiting for Otter to come back. The other Dragonlords had sent orders that I was not to try to see Linden, you see. Otter would send notes back to us but, hang it all, it's not the same as talking to him. His wretched messages were so brief and guarded that there was really nothing in them. So for nearly a tenday I've been sick with worry.

"Otter came back this morning for a little while and we got into a fight. I tried to make him see sense about something and he would have none of it. And when I asked him if the rumors were true—that Linden's dying—he denied it, but I don't think he knows for certain either." She slammed her fists against her thighs. "I don't know anything and I need to *know*, damn it!"

Almered caught her hands and made soothing noises. "I understand. This is not an easy thing for you; there is something special between you and this Dragonlord. And I wish I could help you, to say the thing that will give you comfort, but I do not have those words," he said, his accent thicker than usual with his anxiety. He finished sadly, "All I can do is listen."

She smiled a little. "Thank you for doing that."

"Are our Houses not as kin? Whether we share blood or not, you are my cousin, my little sister—I have said so. So I listen. But I also have questions."

His apprentice entered bearing a tray. Maurynna sat a bit straighter when she saw what was on it. There was a squat ceramic teapot and two cups in the Assantikkan style, the cups low and without handles, meant to be cradled in the hands so that the warmth of the tea comforted the drinker both inside and out. All three were in the pale blue glaze that was so prized in Almered's country; intricate designs in gold leaf swirled over their graceful curves. She was no expert, but she thought she recognized the style of the artisan whose wares graced the emperor's own table. Almered had brought out his best, a subtle reassurance that he bore her no ill will over the *tisrahn*.

She accepted the steaming cup offered her, sniffed, and smiled. The best tea service to honor her and homely chamomile tea to soothe her. She waited until the apprentice left once more before asking, "And what are these questions?"

"I have heard differing stories as to what happened the night of the *tisrahn*, but all agree that Linden Rathan's assailants were disturbed by two, maybe three or four men. Men—not young women. Why? One would think the palace and the other Dragonlords would wish to honor you for saving his life."

"Under other circumstances they would, I think." She sighed. "But because they don't know who attacked Linden or why, the other two seem to feel that Maylin and I might be the next victims if it's nosed about we were involved. At least that's what one of Otter's little messages said. And that's why I'm not allowed to see him; they think someone might put two and two together."

Almered fingered one of his braids, nodding to himself. "Ah; the truth will go no further than this room, then. And

I am glad they are so cautious. But it must be hard for you, yes?''

"Yes," Maurynna agreed, her voice shaking. "I want to see him, Almered. I must see him. Why can't they understand that?''

Suddenly her doubts returned; she slumped in her chair once more. Despite all of Otter's reassurances to the contrary, had Linden been with Lady Sherrine? If not, where had that trace of perfume come from? Someone else entirely?

Remembering what Maylin had told her her first morning in Casna, she doubted it. No one else at court used that scent. The only other customers for it were some women of the wealthy merchants' class.

But no merchant, no matter how rich, had an estate on the far side of the river. Therefore Linden had to have been with Lady Sherrine.

Perhaps she shouldn't be anxious for Linden but hating him instead.

Healer Tasha entered the chamber where Otter sat talking quietly with Tarlna and Kief.

"I think he'll be able to answer some questions now," she said. "For the first time he was able to really understand what I said to him and reply sensibly. But you won't be able to stay for long. Also, don't tell him at this time about Tsan Rhilin. The shock would be very bad for him. He's still quite ill.''

Kief and Tarlna quickly rose. Otter stood more slowly. "May I," he asked, "see him as well?"

He held his breath while the two Dragonlords exchanged glances and, no doubt, arguments in mindspeech. At last Kief shrugged.

Tarlna said, "Yes. You know better what the girl said."

Leading the mystified Healer, they trooped through the halls until they came to Linden's room. The scarlet-clad soldier before the door—on loan from the palace's own elite guard at Rann's tearful insistence—opened the door for them and stepped aside.

"Healer," Kief began.

"Dragonlord, I will wait out here. I trust that you will not upset my patient, but be warned that if you do, I will order you to leave. And please don't stay too long and tire him. He's weak."

He's weak.

The words chilled Otter. He followed the Dragonlords into Linden's room. *Boyo—how could anyone as big as you be "weak"? You must have been as strong as the farm bull even before you Changed. I can't believe—Oh, dear gods.*

Linden sat propped up by pillows. From the way he sagged into them, Otter doubted Linden capable of sitting up without their support. His color still wasn't good and he'd lost a great deal of weight. Cheekbones, nose, and jaw pushed against the skin drawn tight over them. Somehow his condition hadn't seemed so bad when he was sleeping.

But worse yet was the dullness in his sunken eyes. All the sparkling liveliness that made him Linden was gone. Only the merest shadow was left.

Both Kief and Tarlna stopped short and cursed softly at the sight of him. Gathering his courage, Otter passed them and sat on the edge of the bed. Linden regarded him with no sign of interest. Otter felt the bed behind him sink as the soultwins took places at the foot of the bed.

"Boyo," the bard said. "Can you tell us what happened to you?"

Linden hesitated long enough before answering that Otter wondered if he'd understood. Then, "No."

Just "No," as if Linden had no interest in what had been done to him.

Kief tried next. "Do you remember the two men? Were they attacking you?"

Linden blinked a few times. "Two men? I don't know," he said, his voice falling.

Time for a gamble. Otter leaned forward. "Maurynna said that when she and Maylin found you, there were two men bending over you. You seemed to be unconscious."

A tiny spark appeared in the grey eyes at the mention of

Maurynna's name. Otter nodded encouragement, and then nearly pulled his beard out as it disappeared the next moment. Linden sighed and began smoothing the sheet tucked around his waist.

"I don't remember anything, and I'm sorry, but I don't really care. I just want to . . . sleep."

Otter didn't care for the sound of that. Not at all. He slewed around to exchange desperate glances with the other Dragonlords.

Go on, Kief said.

Tarlna said, *Mention Maurynna's name as much as possible; it seems to be the only thing that catches his attention.*

Otter licked his lips and began, "You were at Lord Sevrynel's, do you remember? And you had to leave to meet Maurynna."

Linden stopped picking at the sheet and frowned. "I left there," he said slowly. "Yes. I do remember that. I was angry because, because—"

The brief moment of animation was failing. Otter hurriedly filled in, "The *tisrahn.* You were late for the *tisrahn.* Don't you remember that? Maurynna had invited you. It was for Maurynna's friend Almered's nephew." He wondered how many times he could work Maurynna's name in without Linden noticing the ploy and ceasing to react.

The spark of interest was back. "That's right—the *tisrahn.* I didn't want Maurynna to be any angrier than she was, so I hurried."

The words tumbled out one after the other now. Linden pushed himself to sit up straighter; Otter winced at the sight of the Dragonlord's powerful arms shaking with the effort of supporting his weight even this little bit.

"The ferry was on the other side. I remember that. I had to wait for it."

Now to introduce Maurynna's mad idea. Otter shook his head a little, remembering their conversation—hells, their fight—earlier.

"What do you mean he was poisoned?" Maurynna had demanded.

"We don't know that. That's only speculation on Healer Tasha's part. His symptoms seem to suggest—," Otter tried to explain but was cut off.

"Then she did it, that bitch."

At first he'd thought she'd meant the Healer. "Tasha?"

"Of course not! I mean Lady Sherrine. She was with Linden at some point; I smelled her perfume."

"I just told you she was! She appeared at Lord Sevrynel's that night."

"Then that's when she did it. Somehow she slipped something into that blasted farewell cup," Maurynna insisted.

"In front of half a hundred people? And then drank that same poison herself? Give over, Rynna," he'd retorted in exasperation. "The girl's too bloody fond of herself to be suicidal."

"Then she met him somewhere else and tricked him into taking it," said Maurynna.

He'd ridiculed the idea. It wasn't long before they were yelling at each other, followed by Elenna threatening to throw them both out of the house. Since he'd had to return here anyway, Otter exited in a grand huff, but Maurynna had not relented. Indeed, up until the last moment she had insisted she was right, screaming down the stairs after him, "You mark my words, you stubborn wretch—she did it to him!" as he'd walked out the door.

Damn good lungs on that girl, he thought to himself now. *Too bad she can't carry a tune.* Aloud, Otter said, "Did you meet Sherrine again after you left the dinner?"

"No. No, I waited alone at the ferry." Linden fell back among the pillows once more. "Oh, gods—I'm so tired. Please . . ."

Kief said, "If you wish to rest now—"

"Wait." Otter held up a hand, remembering something. "Just one more thing. Linden, while we were with you in the field, Maurynna told me you'd spoken once, but that she couldn't understand what you meant. It was something about asking questions. Could those two men have been questioning you?"

"Gods help us," Kief muttered. "I never even thought of that. I thought they were only after—" He broke off.

Linden struggled upright once more, the lethargy replaced by horror. "I don't know! What if they did? And if so, *what did I tell them*?" he shouted, fighting to get out of bed.

Otter caught Linden's shoulders and pushed him back against the pillows. That he could do it told Otter just how weak Linden was.

The door burst open; Healer Tasha hurled herself into the room, flask in hand, apprentice close behind. "I knew this would happen," she said grimly. "Get out, all of you. Now!"

They retreated before her wrath. Otter paused in the doorway to watch as Healer and apprentice expertly subdued their patient and forced whatever potion they had down him.

Tasha looked over one shoulder and snarled, "I said 'get out,' curse it, and I meant it. Do you want to kill him?"

Almost lost behind her tirade, Otter heard Linden whispering in despair, "Dear gods—what did I say? What did I betray about us?"

Otter shut the door, unable to bear any more.

Fifty-two

Sherrine ambled through the garden of her family's country estate. As she walked, now and again she would select some unlucky flower and pluck it from its stem, only to shred it in her fingers and cast the fragrant remains upon the ground moments later.

She had never been so bored in her life.

"And all because of that stupid little bitch," she told her latest victim, a tall spire of foxglove, as she tore the blossoms from its stem. "How dare he take her part."

And I don't care that it was best to play out the charade of "retiring" to the country. I shall go mad if I have to stay here much longer.

Even as a child she'd hated coming here. She much preferred the excitement that was Casna. She threw down the foxglove.

"My lady! Where are you?" a voice called from the other end of the gardens.

"Here, Tandavi," she called. "Beyond the lilacs. What is it now?"

"Your lady mother," Tandavi called as she ran through the garden. She stopped before her mistress and finished with a gasp, "She wishes to see you—immediately!"

Sherrine clenched her fists. What right had her mother to sneer at her now? She'd done what was needed—and done it well. Indeed, she was the only person who could have played the part.

She was about to send Tandavi back with a blistering message when a thought struck her and she stopped short.

Her mother thought this country retreat as boring as she did. Not even for the pleasure of deriding her would her mother journey all this way from Casna; not even if she had a thousand reasons and a pocketful of gold for the task.

So why? . . .

Sherrine caught up her skirts and ran. Tandavi gave a startled yelp as her mistress passed her and hurried to catch up.

Sherrine found her mother waiting in the front room of the house. She entered, and after a pause to catch her breath, deliberately made a hurried, ungraceful courtesy. "My lady mother?" she said, waiting.

Her mother said not one word about her clumsiness. That alerted Sherrine as nothing else would have.

That, and the queer look in her mother's eyes.

"You are well these days?" her mother asked, an odd note in her voice.

"Indeed, madam, I am quite well—if somewhat bored," Sherrine replied cautiously.

"You have taken no ill effects from—"

Her mother did not finish the sentence, but Sherrine knew what she meant.

Puzzled, she said, "No. None at all, I assure you." For the first time she noticed that her mother still wore riding garb, and that the garb was filthy; her mother hadn't even bothered to bathe and change clothes before summoning her. Add to that the lines of fatigue in her mother's face, as if the other woman had ridden hard to get here, and one had a mystery indeed.

The next words came hard; Sherrine vowed long ago to never ask her mother for anything, and she'd kept that vow. But she had to know. . . .

"Mother—what is this all about?"

Moments passed in silence. When the baroness spoke at last, the words came in a bleak monotone. "Linden Rathan may be dying. And I . . . feared that . . ."

The room spun. Sherrine put out a hand; her mother caught it and led her to a chair. Half-swooning, Sherrine sank down into it.

"Dear gods," she whispered. This was no plan of hers.

Make Linden suffer, yes—but to kill him? No. No and no and no.

A surge of anger cleared her head. Had that bastard of a mage known this might happen? She bit her lip. If Linden died, Althume would pay.

Fifty-three

Prince and steward rode through the city, their escort following behind. The streets were quieter than usual despite the crowds that had poured into Casna for both the upcoming Solstice celebration and a chance to see the Dragonlords. It seemed the threat of Linden Rathan's death and the renewed possibility of civil war had dampened everyone's spirits.

"Eerie, isn't it?" Peridaen said as he graciously acknowledged the bows of a trio of men, clerks by their dress. "With this many people there should be much more noise."

Althume nodded, looking around. "Interesting that even these cattle should sense something is happening. Ah—I almost forgot. A messenger arrived this morning with a letter for you while you were in your bath. My guess is it's from Anstella." He dug into his belt pouch and brought out a folded and sealed square of parchment.

Peridaen took it and dropped the reins to lie on his horse's neck. He read, nodding to himself as he did. "Good," he said. "Anstella sends word that Sherrine is well." He took up his reins once more.

"Of course she is," Althume said. "I gave her an emetic to purge her stomach and the antidote to be certain the potion would not affect her. And since she was also on the other side of the river when I invoked the second part of the spell, she was quite safe; the potion was only the first part."

"I see," said the prince. Then, after a long silence, "Kas—what was in that stuff that made Linden Rathan so sick?"

Althume smiled. He knew Peridaen had been working himself up to this question for days. No doubt the prince's reaction would prove amusing. "Among other interesting things, *keftih*," he said. "Quite a lot of it, in fact."

Horror. Disgust. Finally panic. "Damn it all," Peridaen managed to say at last, "what if you're caught with it? You know what the penalties are for possessing that filth—it's used only for the blackest magery." His face was pale.

Althume did something he rarely did: laughed in real amusement. "And what did you think a soultrap jewel was, Peridaen? White magery? Why boggle at *keftih* if you condone the use of that? We're fighting a war. We use whatever we must.

"But don't worry. I've taken precautions; it's stored somewhere far from your chambers. I have delivered to me only what little I need at a time." *And you haven't guessed for what yet, have you? I wonder when that acorn will drop, my squeamish prince.*

Fifty-four

Tasha snapped out of her doze as a hand gently shook her shoulder. She blinked up at Quirel.

"Go get something to eat and drink," her apprentice urged. "I'll sit with him for a while."

The Healer yawned. "What time is it?"

"Nearly midnight. But there's bread, cheese, cold meats, and ale left out for us in the kitchen. I didn't bring anything here because, well—" He wrinkled his nose.

She nodded. The thought of eating in this sickroom with its odd odor was not appealing. She heaved herself to her feet. "I'm not really hungry, but I could do with a walk around, so thank you. There's been no change."

He nodded and took her place by Linden Rathan's bedside.

Once out of the room Tasha leaned against the wall, trying to make up her mind what to do next. She should eat. But walking helped her think. And she desperately needed to do that; she was running out of ideas to help Linden Rathan. She suspected the only reason he was still alive was a deep-down stubborn will to live. But even that couldn't keep him going much longer if she couldn't cure whatever ailed him. So she would prowl around and think. Maybe something would come to her.

Althume strode a spiraling path up the hill in the clearing, chanting as he walked, holding the chest containing the soul-trap jewel before him. Pol followed, a torch held in one hand, a limp form slung over his other shoulder. The tiny procession wound its way, moving widdershins, to the altar crowning the flat hilltop.

The mage laid the chest at the head of the altar and opened

it. Pol dumped his burden down less ceremoniously. A muffled grunt of pain escaped it.

"Careful, Pol," Althume admonished. "You don't want to break the lad's neck now; that would be a waste."

He leaned over to examine the victim's bonds. Excellent; they were still tight. No chance that this one would work his way loose as the last one did. That one had almost gotten away; indeed, would have if he hadn't turned back screaming at the sight of the *dragauth*.

"You tie a better knot than your brother," he said as he yanked the hood from their victim's head. The boy, he saw with approval, was gagged.

Pol chuckled.

Althume caught the boy's chin and turned his face from side to side. The lad looked to be twelve or thirteen, pretty for a boy. Althume thought he could guess how Pol had captured him—not that the mage cared. "You're certain no one will miss him?"

"Yes, my lord. He's naught but a common whore peddling his ass down by the docks. His sort disappear all the time."

Whatever drug Pol had given the boy was wearing off. Wide, terrified eyes stared at Althume as the boy tried to scream despite the cloth cutting into the corners of his mouth.

The mage smiled thinly. "Thought you'd been taken up by a gentleman at last, did you? How sad. But you're about to do the best thing you could with your miserable little life, boy. You're going to help us defeat the Dragonlords," he said as picked up the soultrap jewel with one hand and drew the dagger from his belt with the other.

The boy threw himself against his bonds. Pol shoved him down again and held him.

Althume began the chant of sacrifice.

You'd think that storm would have cooled everything off, Tasha thought as, still seeking inspiration, she wandered the vast lawn that separated the house from the road. *It's as hot as a—*

"Dear gods" she yelled. "That's it!" She ran for the house.

Maurynna let herself into the house quietly, not wanting to wake up her aunt or cousins. She hadn't meant to stay at the warehouse this late, but what with one thing and another, talking to Danaet, and straightening out problems, the evening and too much of the night had slipped away. Besides, it kept her busy and didn't let her think about Linden or her newest problem—at least not too much.

Someone stirred in the front room. "Rynna?" a sleepy voice said.

She stopped, astonished. "Otter? What are you doing here? I thought you were still at the estate," she whispered. A possible reason struck her. "Otter—please; Linden's not . . ." Her voice failed.

"He was still the same when I left." The sleepy bard appeared in the doorway, rubbing his eyes. "I think either Kief or Tarlna would have mindcalled me if anything had happened, so don't worry."

She sagged against the wall, weak with relief. "Thank the gods."

"Duchess Alinya sent word that Rann was making himself sick with worry, so I was sent off to cheer the boy up. Tell him stories, sing to him, that sort of thing." Otter gave his eyes a final rub and shook his head. "Feh. I hadn't meant to fall asleep waiting for you."

"Oh." Maurynna suddenly felt awkward, remembering the last time she'd seen Otter. "That's all right."

By the way he looked at her, he remembered as well. "How are you faring these days? I've been worried about you, too."

Maurynna brushed aside the thing that worried her when she wasn't thinking about Linden, saying only, "Well enough. Thank you, though." She wondered how to frame an apology for the things she'd said. And would he even accept it?

But before she could speak, Otter said, "Rynna, don't say

a word. It's all past.'' His eyes twinkled with a mischievous light. ''Besides, it would ruin my 'I told you so'; I'd feel like a lout, then.''

Maurynna gaped at him.

''Linden did not meet Sherrine again that night. He rode alone to the ferry. And I think if she'd had whatever felled Linden, she'd be dead by now. Yet we've had no such word.

''It had to be those two men you and Maylin saw. Somehow they overpowered Linden and forced him to drink whatever it was. You said they were bending over Linden when you first saw them, yes? Perhaps they were giving it to him even then.''

Maurynna shook her head. ''No. You're wrong. It was Sherrine. I don't know how, but she did it.''

''Dear heart, are you certain you're not blaming her because of what she did to you and Linden?'' Otter said, cradling her hands in her own. ''Please—let's not fight over it again, Rynna. We've been friends for too long.''

''Oh, very well,'' she conceded. *But I'm right, damn it.*

Otter continued, ''While Linden is still angry with Sherrine for the way she trapped him into publicly forgiving her, even he believes her innocent of any part in this.''

The more fool he, then. Gods above, why is it men think a beautiful woman can do no wrong? Maurynna thought acidly. She sat, fuming. They'd never know the truth; Lady Sherrine would never confess willingly. And by Cassorin law, the only crime a noble could be tortured for was treason. She supposed that the attack on Linden might be stretched to fit that; he was, after all, here to sit in judgement and avert civil war at the behest of the Cassorin council. But as surely as she knew the sun would rise tomorrow, she knew Linden would never demand that; he had no stomach for torture.

If only the other Dragonlords would insist. If only *she* could insist. . . .

And then it was happening again, just as it had this afternoon. The voices that she had previously heard only while dreaming called to her waking mind, pulling her into herself. One soared above the rest, a sweet voice like the singing of a flute; it spoke to her, enticing her, promising her the freedom of the sky and the songs of the winds.

She heard Otter call her name, but she couldn't answer. And now his voice came from farther and farther away as she sank deeper into her mind. Soon she would be lost in the voices, unable to hear him at all.

And there was nothing she could do about it.

Althume ran blood-streaked fingers over the soultrap jewel. It glowed beneath his caress with a faint, pulsating light as it drank in the blood. He regarded it fondly, like a father with a favorite child.

"A beautiful thing, is it not, Pol? And so useful a tool for a mage. For it stores not only souls—the magic of life—but any sort of magical energy for a bold mage to make use of. And the beauty of it is, once it reaches a certain threshold, it can be used to leech a soul even from a distance, without killing its victim—at least, not right away."

Pol continued pulling the clothes from the body sprawled across the altar. "And has this one reached that point, my lord?"

"Almost, Pol, almost. Catching Nethuryn's soul within it was a masterly stroke. And using the Dragonlord's own coldfire a deliciously ironic touch, don't you think? A few more like this and we're ready for the next step in my plan."

He ceased his contemplation of the bloody jewel to note Pol's progress. "Done? Good. We'll burn them in a few minutes. But first let's give my pet a treat."

The mage drew a small bone whistle from his belt pouch and trilled a note upon it. Pol picked up the body and came to stand by him.

They waited.

Crackling bushes were their first warning of the *dragauth*'s approach. The second was the foul stench of rotting flesh on the night breeze.

One moment the edge of the clearing was empty; the next a towering figure appeared, man-shaped, but standing nearly eight feet tall. Althume regarded this child of his magery with pleasure. Not every mage had the skill to construct a *dragauth*, even if he had the courage to sacrifice the necessary flesh. Althume had had both. He rubbed his thigh, absently running his fingers over the ridged scar.

The *dragauth* raised its hands. The torchlight glinted on razor-sharp claws capable of disemboweling a man at a single stroke.

"Give it to him," Althume ordered.

Pol stepped forward and flung the boy's body. It flew through the air like some ghastly travesty of a bird. The *dragauth* snatched it before it could hit the ground.

As he watched his pet eat, Althume couldn't help chuckling as a thought came to mind: *Whatever would poor Peridaen say to* this?

He called to her, but the other voice was far sweeter and more seductive—and frightening. She wanted to follow Otter's voice out of this madness, but the singer in her head was far more powerful. She wasn't even certain who she was anymore. Maurynna or . . . Another name danced at the very edge of her mind and vanished like a wisp of fog in sunlight. Then—

Pain. She welcomed it even as she cried out. She concentrated, anchoring herself to it, using it as a beacon to bring herself to safe harbor. The golden voices retreated, the flute-like one last of all.

Her eyes cleared. Otter knelt before her, shaking her.

"Rynna! Rynna—listen to me. Please!"

Trembling, Maurynna focused on the bard. "Otter?" she said uncertainly.

He sat back on his heels. "Thank the gods. Rynna—what happened to you? One moment you were talking to me, the next—"

"There were voices—beautiful voices—calling to me. I've been dreaming them, but earlier today, and now. . . . Am I going mad?" she sobbed, terrified.

"No. No, you're not. It's just—you're just upset about Linden, that's all. The two of you are . . . very close, after all, and, well—you're just upset," Otter fairly babbled. "That's all, Maurynna. Things will be better soon. Truly.

"But if it happens again, tell me!"

Servants bearing loads of sheets and firewood came in, set their burdens down, and left to fetch more. Tasha directed others as they folded blankets on the floor before the fireplace.

"That's right; make it up good and thick. I want him well separated from the cool tiles. That should do. You—put that pile of sheets down here. And make certain those windows are shut tight."

The other Dragonlords came in, dodging servants rushing out on Tasha's orders. They looked as though they'd dressed in haste; Kief Shaeldar wore only breeches. Tasha had no time to feel sorry the noise had awakened them.

"What on earth?" he asked.

"It's as hot as—" Tarlna began in complaint.

"A steam bath in here," Tarlna finished in triumph. "And it will be hotter yet. If I can't purge Linden Rathan of whatever's poisoning him, or cure it, I'll bloody well sweat it out of him."

Kief Shaeldar and Tarlna Aurianne looked at each other. Tasha braced herself for an argument; Dragonlords or no, this was *her* patient and she would brook no interference from the two standing before her.

"You don't need all this," Kief Shaeldar said, waving at the firewood. "We can help. We're yours to order, Healer."

"Done," Tasha said, relieved. "Quirel—send the servants away. We're ready to begin." At the lift of Kief Shaeldar's eyebrow, Tasha said quietly, "He may talk in delirium, Dragonlord. I assume that there are things you might prefer the servants not hear."

Just as quietly the Dragonlord said, "Thank you, Healer."

When the door shut behind the last servant, Tasha said, "I need a good blaze, Quirel; I want this room as hot as possible. Dragonlord, they told me you carried Linden Rathan to the house, so I know you can pick him up. Would you please lay him down here?" She shook out a sheet and arranged it over the pallet of blankets. "I plan to wrap him in these, changing them each time one is soaked with the poisons he will—I hope—sweat out. If this doesn't work . . ." She didn't want to think about that.

The others nodded and set to work. Tarlna Aurianne and Quirel laid the fire; the Dragonlord set the wood blazing with a word. The sudden blast of heat made Tasha sweat. She gasped as Tarlna Aurianne held her hands in the leaping flames and whispered an incantation under her breath. Her mind screamed that the Dragonlord's flesh would be burned from her bones, but Tarlna Aurianne withdrew her hands unscathed by the blaze. Now the fire burned twice as hot as before, yet did not consume the wood any faster.

"I trust," Tarlna Aurianne said, "that this will do."

"Yes," said Tasha, fervently wishing that modesty didn't prevent her from removing her tunic as a panting Quirel was already doing with his. "Your Grace, we're ready for him here," she said to Kief Shaeldar.

He flipped the blankets back from Linden Rathan and gently picked up the tall Dragonlord. Tasha marveled at his strength; Linden Rathan was no little weight, and Kief Shaeldar was a small man.

She helped him arrange Linden Rathan on the makeshift bed and with Quirel's help wrapped the ailing Dragonlord in the first sheet. Tasha noted with satisfaction that there were already a few beads of sweat on Linden Rathan's forehead. She wiped it away with a cloth, and, prompted by a sudden impulse, sniffed the linen.

The odd smell that permeated the sickroom was stronger, concentrated in the fabric. It was a sour, mousey odor that niggled her memory. *Where have I smelled this before?* But the answer eluded her. Aloud she said, "I think it's working, though it's too soon to be certain. Quirel, make up some catnip tea. If he can drink that, it will make him sweat even more."

There was nothing to do now but wait and see if her idea worked. The room grew hotter; Tasha felt the sweat running down her back, trickling between her breasts. Tarlna Aurianne twisted her long blond hair up into a knot and fanned her face with a hand. The men were barely more comfortable; their chests glistened in the firelight.

Now and again the others would get up and escape to the relative coolness of the hall, but they would quickly return as though their absence somehow might hurt Linden Rathan. But Tasha stayed by his side, taking his pulse, touching the sheet wrapped around the still form. It stayed depressingly dry.

"More wood on the fire," she ordered.

Quirel grimaced, but obeyed her.

The room grew unbearable. Tasha could hardly breathe for the heat, but there was no change in her patient. She began to despair.

A little longer; it's worth trying just a little longer.

But nothing changed.

She was ready to give up when it happened. One moment the sheet under her hand was dry. The next it was soaking and the sour smell overpowering. Though it would cool the room, she didn't stop Kief Shaeldar when he staggered, gagging, to throw open a window.

"What is that?" he gasped.

"I don't know," Tasha replied. "But I've a feeling that's what's making him so ill. Get that sheet off him; I want a fresh one."

It seemed that Linden Rathan's body had suddenly determined to throw off the poison holding it in thrall. He twisted and turned under their hands, tried to push the sheets away as they changed them, muttered things in a language Tasha didn't recognize but the other Dragonlords seemed to, and sweated like a lathered horse. At times he regained consciousness after a fashion and Tasha forced him to drink as much tea as he could—or would—take.

It was after dawn when Tasha realized that the strange odor was abating. The sheet that Quirel cast to one side smelled of honest sweat now, not noxious substances. She dared to hope a little.

That hope soared when Linden Rathan opened his eyes

long enough to ask, "Where's Maurynna?" and fell into a natural sleep the next moment.

Tasha grinned. "He must be on the mend if he can think of his lady-love at a time like this."

The other Dragonlords answered her with relieved smiles of their own.

"Shall I return him to the bed?" Kief Shaeldar asked.

"Yes, please. And you, Your Grace," Tasha said to Tarlna Aurianne, "can you make a fire go out as easily as you can make it burn?"

Tarlna Aurianne nodded and passed a hand through the flames. At once the fire died down to a bed of glowing coals. Then she put a hand to her forehead and drooped as if suddenly tired. An instant later she shook her head, looking a little surprised.

Tasha sympathized. She was exhausted herself, more from strain than anything else. Despite only knowing him for a short time, she liked Linden Rathan. Tarlna Aurianne had known him for—how long? Centuries, at least. The thought of his possible death must have terrified the other Dragonlords.

Not to mention what losing the big Dragonlord would have done to Rann. Tasha dug her fingers into her thighs at the thought. If she ever found out who had poisoned Linden Rathan—and, by extension, put Rann into danger—she'd do everything in her power to bring them to justice.

Fifty-five

He's better, Kief reported. **But** *Healer Tasha says he's more depressed than she'd hoped he'd be by now.*

You think he's still worried about what he might have given away? Otter said, relieved at Kief's continuing messages, but worried himself at the lingering depression now that the crisis was past.

Likely. How is the girl faring?

Otter grimaced as he continued pulling on his boots; Kief's mindcall had come in the middle of dressing. *You're not going to like this,* he said, and detailed Maurynna's "attacks." *It's happening every day now; sometimes twice a day or more. And there's been a new twist lately: her senses become unnaturally sharp. Sight, sound, smell, taste—all threaten to overwhelm her. Then, moments later, it's over.*

Gods help me; this may be the result of Changing so close to her. Linden will throttle me if anything happens to the girl.

Hm—the first episode did happen that night, but maybe . . . Could this simply be a sign of impending First Change? Otter asked.

He felt Kief withdraw from his mind and guessed the Dragonlord was mulling over what he'd said. He used the time to shrug into a tunic and find his belt where it had lost itself under the bed. Then Kief was back.

Perhaps. First Change does take some of us that way. Many Dragonlords have no inkling that something is happening to them. There's simply a sudden, overwhelming urge to find an open area and then it—happens. For an unlucky few, there are dreams and visions frightening enough to make them think they're going mad. I think Linden might have been one of those; Lleld would know. She was with him when he first Changed. While it does not necessarily mean that Maurynna would follow his pattern, that may well be what's happening to her.

Especially, Otter said, *if their bond is a very close one, perhaps?* He shuddered, wondering what it must be like to be caught in such a waking nightmare. *Which I think it is, so the timing of this may simply be coincidence.*

True, said Kief.

Otter smiled. The Dragonlord sounded like a schoolboy who'd been let off an anticipated whipping. Which, if Kief was responsible for hurting Maurynna somehow, would likely have been the least Linden would have done to him. *Will he see me yet?*

No. He wants no one. And I'm worried. . . . Then, abruptly, *Thank you for keeping watch over the girl. I'll mindcall you again should anything change.*

Alone in his mind once more, Otter stared unseeing at the whitewashed walls of his tiny attic bedroom in the Vanadins' household. He did not like this. He did not like this at all. Linden ambushed and nearly dying; Maurynna terrified she was falling into madness.

What else is going to go wrong?

Fifty-six

The day was hot and sticky. Maurynna tugged at her tunic, pulling the linen away from her back. Despite the heat, she walked easily alongside Otter, matching his long strides as they made their way through the crowds thronging the marketplace and milling through the streets.

"Have—have you received any other word about Linden?" she asked as casually as she could.

Otter shook his head. "The last was two days ago. Kief mindspoke me; he said Linden is still the same as he was the other times. Depressed, won't see anyone, hardly eats. It's not like him at all, Rynna. They haven't even told him yet that Tsan Rhilin's missing. Afraid of what that would do, I suspect. But Kief doesn't realize that with all the practice I've had mindspeaking with Linden, I can sense more through a mindlink than most truehumans."

They dodged around a troupe of street jugglers. Maurynna dug into her belt pouch and tossed a copper to the tumblers' boy as he passed around a wooden bowl. She tugged at her tunic again.

"I've a good mind to take the *Sea Mist* out just to get away from this cursed heat," she grumbled. And to run away from her worries. But they'd simply hunt her down.

Said Otter, "And I'd be tempted to go with you."

Before Maurynna could reply, a ruckus ahead claimed their attention. Since she was taller than most of the crowd, Maurynna had a good view.

From what she could make out of the swirling melee, someone's horse had gotten loose and was raising merry hell. She saw another horse, this one with a rider, spin around, throwing its rider to the ground. Members of the Watch appeared as if materializing from the stone and wood of the buildings lining the street. A ringing neigh assaulted her ears and she suddenly understood.

"Someone's stallion got loose," she said with a little snicker. "May the gods help the poor owner when the Watch catches up to him." She looked to Otter for amused agreement.

Instead the bard stood rooted in place. "That horse sounds famil—Oh, no. I don't believe it. It can't be!"

The stallion neighed another challenge.

Otter grabbed his beard with both hands. "Gods help us— it is!" he groaned, and started running.

Maurynna stared after him. Then she was pushing through the laughing crowd in Otter's wake. Someone snatched at her, angry at his rough handling by the bard and determined to take it out on someone. She pulled herself free and burst through the press into the suddenly clear street a heartbeat behind Otter.

He ran toward the soldiers of the Watch that had surrounded the amorous stallion. All the while he called "Shan! Shan!" his trained voice rising above the buzz of the onlookers.

Maurynna followed hard on his heels, still mystified. The humid air was heavy in her lungs. She felt as if she was breathing water.

How did Otter know this horse? Her puzzlement increased as the stallion looked over at Otter and neighed what could only be a greeting—though how she was so sure of that she couldn't have said.

She noticed that the guards circling the stallion looked nervous and wondered why they feared a horse. Then she remembered Raven once telling her only a fool tried to come between a loose stallion they didn't know and his mare. "There are neater ways of committing suicide," he'd said.

So why hadn't this Shan charged the soldiers in his path?

Two of the Watch were helping the mare's rider to his feet. The mare called to the stallion. She plainly relished his advances; her rider seized the reins from the guard holding her.

He cursed and howled in a voice surprisingly shrill for such a heavy man.

"I don't care who owns that stinking animal! I'll have damages of him! This is a pure-bred desert mare—I'll not have her defiled by the likes of, of—that!" The curls of his foppishly dressed beard trembled with indignation.

"That" danced within the ring of the soldiers as he returned the mare's calls. He dodged the hands grasping at his mane, letting them come just so close then jumping back as if he played a game. Even Maurynna, who knew ships better than horses, admired the fire and grace of his movements and the mischievous light in his eye. She wished Raven could see this beauty. His owner must be frantic at his loss.

Yet it was obvious the horse hadn't been cared for of late. Burrs and twigs wove themselves through the knots and tangles of the long mane and tail. And his coat, though glossy, hadn't met with a brush for far too long. The powerful legs, thick as sturdy oak saplings, were coated up to knee and hock with mud.

One of the soldiers held a rope halter in his hands, trying unsuccessfully to coax the big stallion to lower his head so that it could be slipped on. The man held out his hand as if he had a bit of carrot or apple, all the while making the soft hissing sounds Maurynna had heard grooms using to their charges.

"You won't catch him that way, you ninny," Otter cried. He skidded to a stop just short of the line of guards. He bent, hands on knees, trying to catch his breath.

Maurynna stopped beside him. Her own chest heaved in the humid air.

"Is this your cursed horse?" the captain of the Watch demanded of the puffing bard.

Otter shook his head. "Know him, though," he said between gasps. He straightened. "Gods, but I'm getting too old to run like that! For pity's sake, will you put that halter away? I tell you, it won't work." He wiped the sweat from his forehead.

The mare's rider pushed up to confront Otter. Maurynna

could see by the torn and dusty remains of his fine clothing that he was a noble. She felt sorry for the stallion's owner. This fellow looked the sort to take ill any affront to his dignity.

The man drew himself up to his full height—well below Otter's shoulder—and shrilled, "Who owns this flea-bitten nag then? Out with it, or I'll have you flogged!"

Maurynna's fists clenched at the threat. She longed to hit the man, noble or not. How dare he threaten a bard—and Otter, at that!

The stallion's scream of rage beat upon their ears. He stood now, teeth bared, one eye fixed on the noble, and the look in that eye promised murder. Then he sank down on his haunches and raised forehooves over a handbreadth wide a short way from the ground. He looked like a statue carved from onyx; utterly beautiful—and deadly.

A breathless hush fell over the crowd. Even the mare fell silent.

Maurynna's mouth went dry. Ignorant as she was of anything but the most basic riding skills, even she recognized what that stance portended. Any moment now the stallion would hop forward and strike. A blow from those hooves would crush a man's skull like a walnut. And she had no doubt who was to be the victim.

The soldiers scattered like leaves. The noble backed away on shaking legs. He stopped short as he fetched up against his mare.

Only Otter stood firm. He said, "I think not, my lord." Then, to the horse, "Easy, Shan. He'll do no such thing—I promise you."

To Maurynna's astonishment, the stallion dropped to stand with all four hooves solidly on the cobblestones. He snorted.

"Coo!" she heard someone whisper. "You'd think the bloody animal understood him."

"He did," Otter said. "Don't try to catch him again; he'll stand there until I tell him otherwise. And as for *you*," and Otter looked down his high-arched nose at the noble, "flog a bard, would you?'' He pulled aside the neck of his tunic to reveal his bard's torc.

"Likely stolen, that torc! You're not—'' the man shrilled.

"Ah—Lord Duriac,'' the captain began.

Unable to keep silent any longer, Maurynna said, "He is a bard—and friend to Linden Rathan, as well!'' There. Let the pompous ass choke on that. She no longer cared about bringing the wrath of the Cassorin nobility down on her head.

He nearly did choke. The Watch moved back as one as though disassociating themselves from someone fool enough to threaten a Dragonlord's kith.

The bard said, "This is Shan, Linden Rathan's Llysanyin stallion. How he got here from Dragonskeep I don't know. Do you understand what Llysanyin means, my lord?''

Otter's voice rose and fell as if he chanted a lay in the Yerrin High Chief's hall. "Strength and speed beyond your dreams, for the Llysanyins are the children of the west wind from the land of the star-kindred, the land beyond the sun. East they came to bear the Dragonlords in a time lost in the mists of the past.

"And *that* is what you nearly had covering your . . . 'pure-bred desert mare,' '' the bard finished in a slow drawl.

The noble fell back. A greedy light filled his eyes. He dropped the mare's reins. "I, ah, that is—if it would please the young Dragonlord . . .'' He beckoned to Shan.

No doubt, Maurynna thought. *And it would please you even more, wouldn't it, you selfish pig.*

Shan stepped forward, his neck arched at a proud angle. The mare raised her tail in invitation as she looked coquettishly over her shoulder at him.

Otter laid his hand on Shan's neck as the stallion passed him. "No, Shan.''

Maurynna gasped as the big head whipped around. The stallion's ears were pinned back and his teeth snapped at Otter's wrist.

Otter didn't flinch. "Linden has been ill; very ill. He's still far from well. It would do him good to see you.''

The big horse turned his back to the mare, his entire being

intent on the bard. It wrung Maurynna's heart to see the proud stallion trembling like a foal. He lipped at the front of Otter's tunic. Without thinking, she went up to him and stroked the deep sloping shoulder, saying, "He's better now, Shan; truly."

Shan rolled one eye to look at her. She saw his ears flick back and forth. To her delight Shan turned his full attention to her. He snuffled her, snorting softly. He sounded surprised, even confused.

Otter laughed quietly. Then, catching hold of the stallion's long forelock, he said, "I'd like to speak to you alone a moment if I may. Don't worry; you'll be seeing more of her later."

The soldiers fell back before him as he led Shan to one side. The plump lord sputtered, "But—but—but!" The mare looked insulted.

Maurynna sighed. She was sorry Otter had taken Shan away. No doubt he'd now take him to Linden. Somehow she'd felt drawn to the big horse. And to see one of the fabled Llysanyins! Her fingers itched to untangle the thick black mane and tail.

She waited with the soldiers, watching man and horse. Shan had dropped his head; Otter whispered into his ear. Now and again Shan nodded as if listening intently. At one point the stallion's head shot up. He looked over to where she stood and then back at Otter. Now Otter nodded; the stallion hopped and nickered in excitement. The bard laughed. A few more minutes of urgent whispering and the two returned.

Otter said to the noble, "Do you still wish to seek damages, my lord? If you have been injured in any manner, I'm sure Linden Rathan will be more than willing to make it up to you."

At a low growl from the crowd, the noble hastened to say, "Not at all, my lord bard. Though if you could see your way to asking him . . ." The man winked and bestowed an oily grin upon the bard. He licked his lips nervously as the angry rumble continued.

Maurynna warmed at this sign of the crowd's regard for Linden—then remembered she hated him.

Didn't she?

And the sun will rise in the west tomorrow and seagulls will fly backwards, she told herself. *At least be honest with yourself if with no one else.*

Otter coughed, hiding a smile behind his hand. "Of course. Perhaps when he's better." To the captain he said, "And you, Captain—are you satisfied? I can assure you there will be no repeats of this. Shan wishes only to see his master as soon as possible."

Shan nodded, his mane and forelock flying.

The captain considered for a long moment. "If you'll take responsibility for him and see that he gets to the Dragonlord, my lord bard, I've naught to say against it." The man looked up at Shan, awe written across his face. "Daresay the Dragonlord has been missing him, him being a Llysanyin and all." The captain blushed and ducked his head. "I remember the tales from when I was a sprat, y'see—I always liked hearing about the Dragonlords' horses the best."

Otter smiled. "And rest assured that they're true, Captain. But I shan't be able to take Shan to Linden Rathan myself. I've—ahh—I've a prior engagement." Otter winked at Maurynna.

She gaped at him. He'd said nothing to her about—

"But this young lady will. She's Maurynna Erdon, captain of the *Sea Mist* from Thalnia. She's also a close friend of Linden Rathan's," Otter finished.

Looking dubious, the captain glanced quickly at her wrists; the sight of her captain's bracelets seemed to reassure him. He nodded. "As you wish, m'lord bard."

Maurynna tried to speak, but only a squeak came out. Then she found her voice and said, "Otter, are you mad? I'm not a good enough rider for a horse like Shan! And there's no saddle or bridle. He'll throw me in an instant!"

And as for telling the captain of the Watch she was a friend—a close friend—of Linden's! . . . She fumed in silence; the Watch would only arrest her if she kicked Otter.

Shan shook his head even as Otter said, ''He won't throw you, Rynna. And all you'll need to do to guide him is tell him which way to go. Bring him to Linden, Rynna. It's what Linden needs more than . . . almost . . . anything.''

Maurynna wondered at the sudden sly tone in Otter's voice, but Shan lipped at her hair, distracting her. Her fingers moved to the stallion's forelock without conscious thought. As she untangled a twig she asked him, ''You've understood everything we've said, haven't you?'' At Shan's nod, she continued, ''You do understand that I'm a sailor, not a rider—and I've never been on a horse as big as you.''

She swallowed hard as she looked at how far Shan's back was from the cobblestones. *Seventeen hands if he's an inch,* she thought, remembering more of Raven's lessons. If she fell, it was a long, long way down.

She'd refuse. This was madness. But Shan rubbed his soft muzzle against her cheek as if to reassure her, and the thought of seeing Linden again made her heart beat faster. Wasn't that what she'd been wishing for all this time?

Shan settled the matter by nudging her to his side. His look said as plain as speech, ''Mount!'' Between Otter and a guard pushing and pulling, Maurynna found herself straddling the stallion's broad back. She clutched a handful of mane as Shan slowly and carefully turned, Otter steadying her.

The captain dug into his belt pouch and pulled out a square of parchment. It bore the wax impression of the Watch's seal. He said, ''This pass will get you by any other companies you may run into, lass. They might think you're trying your hand at horse thieving, riding with no tack.''

Maurynna reached down to take it and nearly slid from Shan's back. Otter caught her and pushed her up. She gulped as she realized how close she'd come to falling.

''Oh, gods,'' she whispered, looking down. The ground looked even farther away than she'd thought it would. And she felt horribly insecure without a saddle. Moving with painstaking care, Maurynna tucked the pass into her belt pouch. ''Please walk slowly, Shan,'' she quavered.

The stallion whickered in answer. He stepped out at a

gentle walk. The crowd melted before them. Nervous as she was, Maurynna still noticed the envious awe in many of the faces looking up at her. Then the full wonder of it all dawned on her. She rode a Dragonlord's horse!

Remembered childhood daydreams of galloping across flower-strewn meadows on a Llysanyin welled up in her mind. She sat up a bit straighter.

Otter called after her, "He's got a lovely canter, Rynna. When you get to the river road, ask him to—"

Her knuckles turned white as she clenched the bit of mane she held. "Otter," she yelled, not daring to turn around, "I really will keelhaul you if you give him any ideas!"

She set her teeth as Otter's laugh floated on the humid air behind them. Shan made a noise deep in his chest. She swore it was a horse's chuckle.

"Linden," she gritted, "this is all your fault. I don't know how, but it is!"

Shan "chuckled" again.

Maurynna thanked all the gods that Shan was sensible about the ferry ride. When they'd reached the dock, the Llysanyin had stepped down the ramp and onto the ferry like an old hand. Now he stood quietly beside her, hooves braced wide, while she pulled twigs and leaves out of his mane and cast them into the river sliding past.

"A pity I can't brush out the feathers on your feet," Maurynna told him.

Shan blew down the neck of her tunic.

"Stop that. It tickles," she said.

"Hunh," Shan grunted. "Hunh, hunnh."

Maurynna studied him. "I wish I knew what you were trying to say." *And I wish I knew what Linden is going to say.* Going to him like this made her uneasy; he'd been so adamant that they part company. Well and well, she'd just blame Otter. This was, after all, his brilliant idea.

Still, she'd be the one Linden yelled at. And not much longer till then; the far shore was coming up fast.

"Do you think he'll be angry?" she whispered into the stallion's ear.

"Hunnnh," Shan replied.

"Here, Shan," Maurynna said. "He's staying here."

Shan neighed and turned off the shady road so sharply that she came close to falling off. Before she could he'd slipped back under her. She could feel him trembling with excitement. She set him to cross the parkland between the road and the estate house at a diagonal, making for the stables behind the far side of the manor.

For that matter, she was shaking as well. She sighed. If only she could break free of this desire of Linden. Then, all at once, she couldn't wait to see him again.

"Canter, Shan!" she cried, before she could regret trying it barebacked.

Shan's ears flicked back at her. Then he surged forward so smoothly that Maurynna felt no jolt. To her surprise the motion felt akin to the rise and fall of a boat on the sea. Maurynna stretched her legs as Raven had taught her; toes turned in and heels down, and sat as tall as she could. She laughed aloud, wondering why she'd been afraid. She had no need of a saddle on this wondrous beast.

They raced across lush grass that looked soft enough to sleep on. This close to the river the air was fresh and cool with a hint of violets. Trees dotted the great expanse of green. Every time they passed beneath one and came back into the sunshine Maurynna blinked at the sudden brightness.

Shan moved so lightly she hardly heard his hooves striking the ground. The wind of their passing blew her hair back. It was so like one of her dreams she wanted the ride to go on and on.

But now she could see the stables. People were gathering in front of them, eyes shaded to watch the rider who disdained to come along the estate road. She tugged on Shan's mane. He swerved in a gentle curve and slowed.

That proved to be her undoing. One moment she was riding in a waking dream, the next she lay flat on her back in the thick grass. She blinked up at Shan, not even sure how it had happened. He snuffled her apologetically.

She didn't think she'd broken anything. She stretched her limbs one at a time. No, everything worked. And it hadn't really hurt to fall on the grass. She thanked the gods it hadn't happened on the cobbles of the stable courtyard.

She rolled onto her stomach and stood up. As she dusted herself off the first of the grooms reached her.

"Bloody hell, girl—did you hurt yourself? And what do you mean by riding across—" the man said.

She cut him off. "I'm Captain Maurynna Erdon. This is Linden Rathan's Llysanyin stallion, Shan. Our mutual friend Otter—you know of whom I speak, don't you? The Yerrin bard."

The moment she said "Llysanyin," she saw awe replace anger in his face. Though he nodded as she spoke, the groom never took his eyes from Shan after that.

Maurynna continued, "Shan traveled by himself from Dragonskeep. Otter and I ran across him in the city; Otter asked me to bring him to Linden Rathan. As you can see, Shan is rather a mess."

Shan snorted and seized a lock of her hair.

"Ow! Stop that! You are a mess, Shan, even if you are a beautiful mess. Do you really want Linden to see you like this?" She batted at his nose.

Shan forbore tugging as he considered that. He dropped her hair and shook his head.

"Gaw!" the groom said, his eyes huge.

"Then please go with the groom. I'll tell Linden you're here." She rubbed Shan's ears. To the groom and the others now standing a respectful distance behind him, she said, "Remember, this is no ordinary horse. Don't try to halter or tie him—I don't think Linden Rathan would be pleased by that. If you need Shan to do anything, just tell him. He can understand everything you say."

"Gaw!" the groom said again. An excited buzz rose from the group behind him.

Shan raised his head and lipped at her cheek. He stepped

lightly away from her and strode toward the stables. The grooms fell in around him like an honor guard.

Maurynna watched them until they passed the wide doors to the stable. Then she looked up at the manor house. Rows of blank windows stared back at her. She wondered if Linden Rathan's chamber was on this side of the house. Had he seen Shan's arrival? Was he even now on his way?

Not bloody likely. Face it; you're going to have to go in and tell him yourself. And you do want to see him again, she told herself. *Even if he was a wretch to you, you want to see him. No pride; no pride at all.*

Why did she have to want Linden so much? Maurynna squared her shoulders and set off before despair could claim her.

A rapping at the chamber door woke Linden from a fitful doze. He sat up and shook his head, trying to clear the fog from his mind.

Was his bath ready? He vaguely remembered servants passing through, bearing ewers of steaming water to the bathing room. He'd only closed his eyes for a moment. . . .

He must have fallen asleep again. Damn. He'd truly meant to get up today. Another hazy memory came back: one of the servants shaking him, telling him his bath was ready. But the effort to rise had been too much.

It still was. He curled up once more into the welcoming softness of the featherbed.

The knock came again. "Go away," he called, sinking back into greyness.

Louder and sharper came the knock this time. He heard muffled voices arguing in the hall.

"I said 'go away,' blast it," he snarled. A tiny flare of anger smoldered in the greyness. When he felt up to it, he'd find out who the impertinent servant was and—

A booming thud filled the room as the door reverberated from a kick. An angry voice said, "The nine hells I will. Curse you, Linden—open this door right now!" Sounds of a scuffle followed.

Linden shot upright. "Maurynna?" Oh, gods—what was she doing here? Snapping out of his funk, Linden threw himself out of the bed and snatched up a pair of breeches from the floor. As he pulled them on he heard Maurynna cry out. He yelled "Leave her alone!" as he ran to the door and flung it open.

He found two of the servants holding a struggling Maurynna. His heart thudded at the sight of her; the heaviness smothering him lifted. "Let her go," he snapped.

The men jumped back from her as if she were on fire. At his curt "Leave us!" they bowed and retreated rapidly down the hall.

Maurynna rubbed her wrists. He could see marks where her bracelets had dug into her skin. Her lips were pressed into a tight line and her odd-colored eyes were sullen. She looked him up and down and then looked away.

He rubbed his chin nervously. His fingers rasped against beard. The amount surprised him; surely he had shaved recently? He couldn't remember. His exploring fingers met lank strands of hair. They felt greasy. He must look like hell.

All at once the familiar weariness overtook Linden, the flare of energy smothered under the weight of Maurynna's obvious contempt. He sagged against the doorframe. Forcing himself to speak, he asked, "What are you doing here?"

She drew herself up. Her nostrils flared proudly as she said, "I brought you a surprise. I think you'll like it very much."

Puzzled, he stared at her empty hands. The effort to think was too much. "What do you mean?"

"Let me in and I'll tell you."

Before he could move, she pushed her way past him into the room. He followed, shutting the door.

For the first time he noticed how stale the air in the room was. He'd not allowed the windows to be opened since his illness. Not even the window hangings had been opened; that the sun shone as always seemed a mockery.

The room stank of sickness. The sour smell of whatever he'd sweated out still lingered. Nor had he allowed the servants to clean. The room looked like a pigsty. Clothes lay strewn about. He had hazy memories of getting up a few times, meaning to dress, then tossing his clothing aside when it seemed too much effort. Half-eaten plates of food sat wherever he'd left them on the floor, chairs, and tables.

It was a wonder the room didn't smell worse than it did.

Linden slumped down onto the bed as Maurynna surveyed the room. The excitement of her presence faded. He retreated into his misery and stared at the floor.

Her voice came sharp as a dagger and cut as deeply. "Haven't you had enough wallowing in self-pity?" she said. "Aren't you bored yet with feeling sorry for yourself? Look at you! You couldn't get a berth on a fifth-rate cattle scow."

His head came up at that. He stared at her in disbelief; he hadn't thought her the sort to kick a man when he was down.

She stood, arms folded, glowering at him. Then she spun on one heel and strode to the nearest window. She pushed aside the hangings. The sudden brightness made Linden's eyes water. After a brief struggle with the catch she opened the window.

Maurynna came back. "For the sake of the gods, isn't it time you stopped playing the coward?"

White-hot anger burned in him for a moment, then died. "You don't understand," he said, despairing.

"Understand what?" she yelled. "I understand that you're behaving like a child!"

He said sullenly, "I can't tell you—"

"Bah! Can't tell me what? I think you're in the doldrums because a truehuman got the best of you—you, a Dragonlord!" she said. "Whoever they were caught you by the balls good and proper, didn't they? And you feel like a fool, don't you? Isn't that what this is all about?"

Linden leaped up. The anger was back and burning beyond white-hot this time. A tiny voice inside him dared to say she might be right. He ignored it.

He clenched his fists and yelled, "How dare you? You don't understand at all! I'm a Dragonlord! I can't make a mistake like—"

"Oh, really? Dragonlords can't make mistakes, is it?"

Maurynna planted both hands against his chest and shoved.

He fell back to sprawl across the bed and lay blinking up at her in surprise.

Maurynna slashed a hand through the air. "And since when is Dragonlord spelled g-o-d? Tell me that, Linden! Face it—even a Dragonlord can be tricked. Even a Dragonlord can make mistakes. It could have happened to Kief Shaeldar or Tarlna Aurianne—or any other Dragonlord. Maybe not the same way, but tricked they could have been. And yes, you were made a fool of—but it can't be helped now. Accept that and get on with your life, damn it, or *are* you too much of a coward to live with your mistakes? All the rest of us have to."

To his horror, Linden felt hot tears slide down his cheeks. "You despise me, don't you?"

She sat beside him and caught his hand in hers. "Never," she said. "Nor pity, you either; you would hate that even more, I think. I just hate to see you like this." Her lips trembled.

The shell of his numbing misery cracked. Linden pulled Maurynna to him. She wrapped her arms around him and buried her face in his neck. Her fingers clutched at his back.

Her voice muffled, Maurynna said, "Please, Linden. Otter denied it, but . . . You almost died, didn't you?"

Linden nodded, his cheek pressed against her head. He felt her breath catch in a sob as he stroked her hair. And in comforting her he found the strength to banish the last of the greyness. He longed for the day he could claim her as his soultwin.

Maurynna continued, "I know you've been ill, but you've got to try to go on, Linden. Please, it hurts so."

The pain in her words wrenched him. "I will, love," he whispered, shaken that she could already be so entwined with him. "For you, I will."

He tilted her chin back and kissed her.

It was a mistake. He knew it the instant he surrendered himself to the kiss. Maurynna pressed herself to him, answering him with a rising passion. Her hands stroked his bare back. Their touch woke a fire in him. Too late he remembered Kief's warning: *She will need you as much as you need her.*

And gods, how he needed her. A moment more, he told himself, only a moment, and then—

Rathan seized that instant of weakness with the lightning strike of a hawk sinking talons into its prey. The fire became an inferno as his dragonsoul sought the other half of itself.

No! Linden cried out in his mind. *No! You'll destroy us all!*

But Rathan would no longer be denied. Against his human will, Linden slid his hands beneath Maurynna's tunic. Her skin was soft and warm. She moaned with pleasure.

It was his undoing. Had she protested, he might have found the will to resist Rathan. But Maurynna knew nothing of the danger and, weakened from his illness, Linden hadn't the strength for both of them.

Caught in Rathan's desires, Linden eased Maurynna's tunic off. She helped him; then her hands slid down his chest to tug at the ties of his breeches.

He tried to say "No," but her lips covered his. Instead he wriggled out of his breeches and pulled off Maurynna's.

He rolled her onto her back. She welcomed him with a soft, glad cry. At first it was pure joy, this joining with the other half of himself. Within him Rathan silently roared in triumph.

Then the pain and terror began. He fell into a maelstrom of strange images, feelings, sensations. They sucked him down and tore him apart. Vertigo seized him as he was tossed about like a leaf in a storm-ridden sea of lurid colors. As alien visions overwhelmed him his mind screamed that he would be lost forever.

Pain racked him. His flesh was melting from his bones. He heard Maurynna cry out. The terror in her voice was worse than any agony of his body.

He tried to pull free. But Rathan drove him to consummate the union with his soultwin, heedless of the consequences.

A ghostly memory of his words to Otter returned to haunt him: "It sometimes happens that two Dragonlords—two *full*

Dragonlords—will destroy each other when they join.''

And Maurynna had not yet Changed. They would die— *were* dying. It was the only way this torment could end. The forces they'd released would devour them—

Something inside him snapped, shifted, wrenched itself free with a final burst of agony. Then his release took him in a rush of pleasure so sharp it was pain.

He had only enough strength to fall to one side of Maurynna. He lay gasping, fighting the darkness that threatened him.

A thought slid through the whirlwind in his mind: he was alive. He nearly wept with relief.

But what about Maurynna? Linden struggled to raise himself onto one elbow and leaned over her.

She lay still—too still. Her face was grey under the tan. A trickle of blood ran from the corner of her mouth.

''Maurynna?'' he whispered. ''Maurynna-love, can you hear me?'' Frightened, he touched her cheek.

Her head fell slackly to one side.

Fifty-seven

"Maurynna?" Linden whispered again. He gathered her up, cradling her against his chest. She lay limply in his arms. He panicked. Then he saw her breast move.

Relief flooded him—Maurynna was alive. But what if she guessed now what she was? And how to wake her from her faint? A thought came to him.

He carried her into the bathing room. The bathing pool was still filled with water. He stepped into it.

Kneeling, he gasped as the water slid over his stomach. He hadn't thought it would get so cold. Setting his teeth, he dunked Maurynna into the water.

Her eyes flew open; she squealed in outrage and swung at him.

Her fist caught him squarely on the ear. Startled, he fell backward and dropped her. She disappeared under the water. Faster than he would have believed possible, Maurynna surfaced again and surged to her feet, dripping and shivering, arms clutched across her breasts. Linden tore his gaze from her long, slender thighs and looked up.

"Are you trying to drown me?" she yelled. "Or freeze me? That water is *cold,* blast you! And stop looking at me like that."

He grinned. "Why?" he asked. "You're beautiful."

She blushed and looked away for a moment. Then she snapped, "And how do Dragonlords ever get anyone to bed them a second time if that's what it's like?"

Linden leaned back, nearly hysterical with relief. He stopped worrying she'd try forcing an early First Change. She had no idea of what had just happened.

"Stop laughing!" She kicked water at him.

He dodged and stood up. "Oh, love—it won't be like that the next time," he said, catching her in his arms. After a heartbeat or two, she relaxed. He held her, exulting in the feel of her body against his, running his fingers through the long black hair clinging wet and heavy to her back.

"Linden," she said. "The water really is cold, you know."

"Mmmm." He bent and dipped a hand into the water, muttering a short spell under his breath. Moments later the water steamed gently as if it had just come from the heating cauldrons.

Maurynna gasped.

"Is this too hot?" he asked.

"No," she said, then, with only the faintest tremor in her voice, "You heat-spelled it, didn't you?"

"Yes; any Dragonlord can do it. When y—" he began, then stopped in horror. Gods, if he couldn't watch his tongue any better than that! . . . He looked for a way to distract her before she could ask the question he saw in her eyes.

His gaze fell on the soap. He grabbed it.

"Shall I wash your back?" he asked.

Maurynna smiled and took the soap. "Why don't I do yours?" she said. She slipped behind him. Her hand on his shoulder bade him kneel.

Linden sighed happily as a short time later Maurynna's strong fingers kneaded his soapy back.

At long last he was one with his soultwin. For the first time in his life he felt truly complete.

As Linden ran a hand along his freshly shaven jaw, he remembered Maurynna's earlier words. "What's this 'surprise' you mentioned before?" he asked. He sat down on the bed and pulled on clean linen stockings.

Maurynna clapped a hand to her mouth, her eyes wide. Then she jumped for the rest of her clothes. "Oh, gods—I forgot all about him!" She struggled into her tunic and pulled on her own stockings. "Linden—hurry! Get dressed; he must be furious at waiting so long."

Linden tossed her her breeches and slipped into his own. "Who?"

Maurynna swore briefly as the legs tangled. She straightened them out and said, "Shan!"

Linden stared at her, not sure he'd heard correctly. "What? He can't be! How?" He shook his head. "I don't believe I said that; this is Shan. Chailen will kill me." He shoved his feet into his boots. "Come on; we'd best get to the stables."

"Who's Chailen?" Maurynna asked.

"Tell you later," Linden said. He scooped up a tunic, pulling it on as he ran from the room.

As he raced down the hall, he knew he was grinning like an idiot. He didn't care. Maurynna was right; he'd been tricked—the thought that he might have betrayed his fellow Dragonlords still burned—but it was time to go on.

And now they were Sealed to each other. He wanted to Change and trumpet his joy to the world. But the most he could do was pretend his happiness was caused solely by Shan.

Not that he wasn't happy to see his idiot horse. Linden whooped and jumped the last few stairs, Maurynna laughing behind him. He threw the door open before the steward could get to it. Once outside, he waited for Maurynna to catch up, then caught her hand in his. They raced toward the stable side by side.

"You sorry excuse for crowbait," Linden yelled. "Where are you?"

A stallion's ringing neigh, then the thunder of hooves, and Shan burst through the open doors of the stable.

Linden stopped and waited. Maurynna ducked behind him as Shan charged headlong. The stallion stopped just short of trampling them.

For a moment Linden simply looked at Shan, realizing how much he'd missed the Llysanyin. Then he threw his arms around Shan's neck. The stallion's big head dropped over Linden's shoulder as Shan returned the hug.

After a moment Linden noticed the odd sounds Shan was

making, tiny snorts and whickers. They had a worried, almost frantic tone to them as Shan snuffled him.

He pulled back enough to look the stallion in the eye. "You knew, then, that I've been ill?"

Shan nodded. He made another queer, very unhorselike sound.

"Otter told him," Maurynna said from behind him, "when we ran across him in the city. He took Shan off to one side and talked to him. Then I rode him here."

There was a catch in her voice. When Linden looked around at her, she was studying the woods in the distance.

"Ah," Linden said quietly. He scratched Shan's cheeks. No doubt Shan knew who Maurynna was, then; the stallion did not allow just anyone to ride him.

Linden rubbed Shan's nose, thinking.

Maurynna swallowed against the tears pricking her eyes. The big stallion's devotion to his rider moved her. Whatever happened between her and Linden after this, she was glad that she had been the one to reunite them. She sneaked a look from the corner of her eye.

Linden was rubbing Shan's face, leaning now against the stallion's shoulder; from the slight trembling of his legs, Maurynna guessed that the exertion of their lovemaking and the mad dash down the stairs had taken its toll. The stallion braced his legs to take the weight and stood with eyes half-closed, lipping at the front of Linden's tunic, no longer worried.

And Linden himself seemed different. Though still weak from his sickbed, he was more relaxed than Maurynna had ever seen him, as if a tenseness she'd not recognized before was now gone.

She drew a deep breath and realized she felt at peace as she hadn't since meeting Linden on the dock.

As if, as if—

Before she could catch the thought, Linden said, "Would you like to ride with me? Shan can carry both of us easily."

She nodded. "But are you well enough for it?"

"A gentle ride, yes."

She saw him look up at the windows of the house. Then he took a deep breath and vaulted to Shan's back. As he held his hand down to her, she noticed it trembled. She looked up at him in concern; he smiled ruefully at her and she understood—no doubt every servant in the place had watched that extravagant gesture. The word would soon go round of the remarkable recuperative powers of Dragonlords.

She took his hand, raised her foot to the instep of his braced foot and stepped up. It was a little awkward, but she managed to get onto Shan's back without sliding off the other side.

"Settled? Then hold on."

She wrapped her arms around Linden's waist as they started off. The unbound hair of his still-damp clan braid was cool on her skin as she rested her cheek against his broad back.

For a long time neither spoke as they rode through the sun-dappled woods and across small, grassy clearings. She could feel the strength flowing back into his body with the sunshine and the clean, sweet air of the forest.

Maurynna had never felt so deeply content in her life. This was worth all the earlier pain and terror. She wondered at it, then wondered if he'd spoken the truth when he said the next time would be different.

The next time. It sounded as if he wasn't planning to cast her off—at least not yet. True, this idyll would have to end when she—or he—left Cassori, but there should be time for a "next time." Her cheeks burned at the thought. She wished they could stop in one of the glades; the grass looked soft enough . . .

Stop that, or you'll be dragging him off this horse in another minute—and can you imagine the look on Shan's face? She snickered at the image.

He looked over his shoulder at her, one eyebrow raised. "And what was that for?"

"Nothing," she said, and hoped she wasn't blushing. "Linden, why are you called the Last Dragonlord? Hasn't there ever been such a long time between Dragonlords before?''

To her surprise, Linden said, "Longer—sometimes much longer—between Dragonlords coming to maturity with First Change. But always before the truedragons and some of the oldest Dragonlords have sensed the birth of potential Dragonlords between those times. Sometimes as many as five or six in a year, though nothing comes of it. Yet I was the last they sensed." Now he sounded distracted, as though some thought nagged at him.

"Potential?" Maurynna asked in surprise. "I thought the joining of the dragon and human souls happened before birth."

"It does. But not every Dragonlord lives until First Change," he said. His voice was quiet and sad. "Childhood accidents, war, plague—even the illnesses any child goes through can kill us; we tend to be a sickly lot as younglings. That ends for male Dragonlords about the time we can grow beards. For the women, when their first courses start."

Maurynna closed her eyes. So many Dragonlords whose lives had ended before they'd truly begun. And nothing since Linden was born. He would never have a soultwin. The thought saddened her.

He went on, "I daresay you were a . . . healthy little youngling, weren't you?"

"How did you know? I was hardly ever ill," Maurynna said.

"Wha—really?" A pause, then a puzzled-sounding "Oh" that she could make neither heads nor tails of. Perhaps someday she'd understand.

Then a tiny hope flared in her heart. She knew it was foolish; she shouldn't say anything.

But it was best to know now. "Could . . ." She faltered, then tried again, her voice the barest whisper. "Could you ever fall in love with a truehuman?"

He was silent for so long she feared she'd offended him. She let out a breath she hadn't known she'd been holding. As she inhaled again she noticed for the first time the faint scent of his skin, like sandalwood and myrrh mixed.

At last he spoke. "No," he said. "I will never fall in love with a truehuman." He said it gently enough, but with great finality.

Yet she thought she detected something else—a faint note of . . . triumph? No, he wouldn't be so cruel.

And she would love him forever. She said, "I should go back."

He nodded. Once again they rode through the woods in silence, angling toward the river now.

Far too quickly the trees ended. Before them was a small meadow, the road to the ferry cutting across it like a pale wound in the green. To the left lay the water glittering in the sun. The ferry boat wallowed in the middle of the river. It drew closer stroke by slow oar stroke.

Linden halted Shan at the edge of the meadow. He said, without turning, "You realize we must go on as before, Maurynna—don't you? You'd be in danger. . . ."

"I don't understand." She swallowed. "I—"

"It would be best if you left Cassori immediately—go on with your trading run."

She hated him for that, for his cool manner as he bade her go, his refusal to look her in the eye as he cast her off.

She hated him with all her soul until, voice shaking, he said, "If anything happened to you, I—I . . . Oh, gods. If you do go—and it would be safest—leave word with Otter which ports you'll be sailing to. I'll find you when this is over."

Confused now, she asked, "What are you afraid of? Surely those robbers have fled—"

"They weren't robbers," he said, his voice hard and flat. "Not with magery of that caliber."

"Then who?" she asked.

"The Fraternity of Blood. That attack was not a chance one on an unlucky traveler; it was prepared for a Dragonlord. And now that a direct attack has failed, what better way to strike at a Dragonlord than to hurt someone he cares about? Otter is safe, I think; his rank should protect him. As for Sherrine, I suppose her rank protected her as well during our dalliance. But you—you're vulnerable; you're neither noble nor Cassorin.''

She slid down from Shan, wondering at the frustrated anger in his voice, her head spinning from what he'd just said. She wasn't quite certain she believed her ears.

The Fraternity of Blood? But they were just a legend. . . .

He looked down at her, his face white and set. ''Will you leave?''

''I can't,'' she said. ''My hold is half empty. I can't ask my family to take a loss like that; I must have cargo to sell and trade at my next port.'' She reached up to him; he caught her hand tightly in his. ''But I promise you I'll be careful— I'll keep one of my crew with me as much as I can; most of them are good with a sword—and set sail as soon as possible. Until this is over?''

''Until this is over,'' Linden said as if he spoke a vow. He wheeled Shan around. They melted into the shadows under the trees.

The ferry was just making shore. Maurynna strode across the little sunlit meadow, her head held high. She never once looked back.

Linden rode through the tamed woods surrounding the river estates, trying to sort through his feelings. The terror he'd felt at their joining still echoed through his bones, but the joy of being Sealed at long last to his soultwin was more elusive, a quiet euphoria filling him like a slow and steady flood. It welled up at odd moments, ready to spill over, only to settle into a deep contentment a heartbeat later.

''I can't believe it's finally happened,'' he said in wonder.

Shan danced under him. Linden laughed and shifted his weight. The big stallion broke into a slow, collected canter, then pirouetted first one way and then the other, snorting exuberantly through the maneuver.

So this is what it is to be complete. In some ways I feel just the same as ever; in others . . . Gods, how did I ever think I was truly alive?

He and Shan explored the woods, riding slowly, until

Linden could no longer ignore his growing weariness. The sudden flush of strength that Maurynna's coming had brought was fading fast now. His illness had taken more out of him than he'd first thought.

"Good as it is to ride you again, crowbait, I've got to get some rest. It's back home for us, my lad."

As they made their way back to the estate, Linden plaited the now-dry hair of his long clan braid into its proper pattern lest he chance upon anyone else. That Maurynna had seen it unbound didn't bother him; he was only sorry that he hadn't thought to ask her to plait it for him as was a lover's right. That someone else might see him with it undone still struck him as somewhat indecent, though he'd heard that of late the old customs were not honored as they had once been.

"Ah, Shan," Linden said, "you've no idea how good it is to be able to do this and not have worry about you stopping at every blade of grass or spooking at some silly thing. And since I don't have any cords with me, you won't mind if I snatch a few hairs to tie this off with, will you?" Without waiting for a response, he tugged a few long black hairs from Shan's mane and bound the end of his clan braid with them.

Shan turned his head and snapped at Linden's boot toe.

"Missed you too, crowbait," said Linden.

Linden! Where in blazes are you? Kief's mindvoice thundered in his head.

Wincing, Linden replied, *No need to shout, Kief. Judging by the way you've rattled my brain, you're not that far from me.*

Bloody hell, you ass—we return home only to have the servants tell us you leaped from your sickbed and ran out the door with some young woman.

Tarlna interjected, *The servants described her as wearing wide gold bracelets. Maurynna?*

Then the grooms are trying to tell me some idiocy that Shan's here from Dragonskeep, Kief fumed.

Uh—he is. And it was—Maurynna, I mean, Linden said. *Could we wait to discuss this? I'm nearly back at the estate.*

A long, frustration-filled silence. Then, from Kief, *Very*

well. From Tarlna, *We'll look forward to . . . discussing . . . this with you*. The contact abruptly ended.

"Oh, joy," Linden said to Shan. "Kief and Tarlna are both madder than wet cats." Which puzzled him; why so angry? And if they were this upset now, wait until he told them what had happened.

A short time later he rode out of the woods onto the grassy lawns of the estate. Across the vast expanse of green he saw Kief and Tarlna, still mounted, waiting in the courtyard of the stables, their guards still surrounding them. Shan broke into a gallop. Linden waved, knowing that the motion would catch the sharp eyes of his fellow Dragonlords.

It did. Kief and Tarlna spurred their horses into a dead run and met him halfway. For a moment the three simply stared at each other, Linden uncomfortable, the others plainly furious.

Kief broke the silence. "Damn it all, Linden—do you *like* thumbing your nose at the gods? Are you out of your mind, riding around alone your first day up from a sickbed? Do you want to be waylaid again—perhaps killed, since whoever tried it didn't succeed the first time!" he yelled.

Tarlna, in her turn was quiet, but her voice shook with fury. "Don't you ever frighten us like that again. Ever."

Linden blinked in surprise. They were truly worried about him. The thought warmed him even as it astonished him. "I'm sorry," he said. "I didn't think about it. I won't do it again."

Kief, who'd had his mouth open to argue, shut it with a snap, the wind gone from beneath his wings by Linden's honest repentance. He muttered something under his breath, but Linden saw the tension leave the slender Dragonlord's shoulders.

Tarlna snapped, "See that you don't," sounding sorry that he wasn't arguing with them. She tried another gambit. "How did Shan get here? Did Chailen or one of the grooms bring him?"

"Ah—no. As near as I can tell, he got loose and made his

own way here.'' Linden smiled sheepishly. *Maybe they'll forget to ask about—*

''You,'' said Tarlna, ''and that horse deserve each other. And since he had no idea that you were here, someone had to bring him. Maurynna, I take it?''

Damn, he was in for it now. ''Yes.'' He took a deep breath. ''We're Sealed to each other. It . . . just happened; Rathan was too strong.''

''You fool!'' Kief exploded. Linden braced himself, expecting worse, but Kief suddenly checked his anger. A brief look of guilt flashed over his face. ''But you weren't the only careless one,'' Kief finished cryptically.

Tarlna said, ''What's done is done, Kief. And it may be for the best.'' Then, to Linden, ''Since you're riding blithely about, I assume she's well?''

He nodded, trying to unravel the meaning of their words.

She accepted his reassurance and said, ''It's time. Tell him, Kief—about Tsan Rhilin.''

Linden's hand went to his chest, seeking the wide leather strap of the baldric that supported the greatsword. Of course it wasn't there. It was back in his chamber. His conscience twinged for not having thought of the sword earlier. Then an uneasy feeling struck; he searched his memory, trying to remember if he'd seen the greatsword in his chamber.

No. It hadn't been there. Of that he was certain. A great hollow opened in the pit of his stomach. He licked dry lips. ''Where—,'' he began.

''Stolen.'' Kief wouldn't look at him. ''And it was a few days before I remembered that you had had it with you when you left here that night. You weren't wearing it when I carried you away from that field.''

It was hard to swallow now. ''So the men who attacked me—''

''Have Tsan Rhilin,'' Kief finished. ''That seems the only logical explanation. If we find the sword, we find the culprit.''

''Oh gods,'' was all Linden could say. The summer evening turned cold around him. To have lost the sword that was so interwoven with his life, that Bram had given him, shook him to his heart's core. What would he say to Bram—and, even worse, to Rani—when he finally passed on to the other side? It was almost all he had of the two people he'd loved the most for the better part of his life.

He burned to take Casna apart stone by stone. Instead he asked, "What has been done to find it?"

Kief made a hopeless gesture. "We deemed it best not to make a general announcement. Duchess Alinya has had agents from the palace hunting it. They've turned up nothing yet."

Linden found it hard to breathe. The loss of this mainstay of his life threatened to drag him back down into the grey misery he'd so recently escaped. He steeled himself against it and found a last reserve of strength deep inside.

"Kief, I think it best if I return to my own house. Let the people see that I'm well once more." To himself he added, *Perhaps that will somehow flush out the thieves.* Shan edged past their horses.

Kief nodded. "I think you're right. There have been rumors of your death. But, Linden—"

Linden halted the stallion. "Yes?"

Kief jerked a thumb over his shoulder at the courtyard. "This time take the blasted guards with you."

Fifty-eight

Althume waited on the battlements of the palace. It was cooler up here, a welcome respite from the humid heat. The ghost of a breeze drifted in from the south, bringing the scent of the ocean with it; if he squinted he could see the water glittering on the horizon.

He was tired. The power of the ceremonies he'd been working lately was draining him. True, he could tap the energies stored within the soultrap jewel to revive himself, but he preferred to save those. He yawned. Annoying as it was, he'd have to cease his magical workings for a few days. The whores of Casna would be safe once more.

The scrape of boots on stone came to his ears. A quick look told him no one else was about. Good; he'd not have to play the submissive servant. The act was becoming more tiresome with every passing day.

"Much better up here," Peridaen said as he joined the mage.

"Indeed. Cooler and more private than many places," Althume answered. "And a fine view of your kingdom-to-be."

Peridaen made the sign to ward off ill fortune. "Don't tempt the gods, Kas. It's not over yet and they don't like presumption."

Althume shrugged. Such superstitions had no fear for him. "I assume you've heard the news?"

"That Linden Rathan returned to his city house late yesterday afternoon? Yes. Now what?"

"Now we set the stage. First, the meetings must begin again—as soon as possible."

Peridaen stroked his beard. "You want the meetings to resume after all that effort to get them to cease? Kas, remember—I'm certain they're leaning toward Beren for the regency. We've got to think of something else or—''

"The regency is no longer the important thing, Peridaen. We have a chance—''

"No. I told you that already. I will have this regency," said Peridaen. "We will proceed with the original plan only."

"Forget the original plan! I already know it would work—I touched her once already using the soultrap jewel. That can be done at any time." Althume hissed in frustration. "Peridaen, think about it. This would be the greatest coup the Fraternity has yet scored. A regent loyal to the Fraternity would be useful, yes—but a tame Dragonlord? *Think*, curse it!"

"I have thought about it. You might kill Sherrine—and you will certainly kill Rann," Peridaen said.

"May I remind you, Prince, that it was your orders that doomed your sister and her husband? You already have the blood of your family—"

Peridaen shouted, "Dax knew too much and my sister had turned against me! They were adults. I do not kill children."

Althume pressed him harder. "Then what of the potion?"

"It merely keeps the boy quiet and biddable. You said yourself it won't kill him." Peridaen pushed off from the battlement he leaned upon. "I forbid you to consider this plan anymore. Do you understand?"

Mage studied prince; considered; decided there was wisdom in defeat—for now. "Yes, my lord."

"Good. I want that regency. See to it." Peridaen stalked away.

Althume watched him go, shaking with rage. The hell with Peridaen. He had betrayed the Fraternity—and for what? For personal gain and because he was soft, the mage thought with contempt.

The fool. There was no place for softness in this war. With Peridaen or without him, Althume would have Sherrine as a slave to the Fraternity.

He would have to move fast. Peridaen was not overly cunning or bloodthirsty, but even he would eventually realize that he would be safer without a certain wayward mage about.

And if he didn't, Anstella certainly would if Peridaen told her what he, Althume, had planned for her daughter. Althume had no intention of dying just yet.

It was time to gather forces magical and mundane. He had arrangements to make and a baroness to trick.

Linden sat in the library, turning over the pages of the book before him. He was sorry that he'd never taken the time before this to look more closely at Lady Gallianna's bookshelves; she was obviously well read, interested in a wide range of subjects. He settled himself more comfortably and began reading the book he'd selected, a history of Kelneth.

"Your Grace? I'm sorry to disturb you, but the Baroness of Colrane asks if you would see her," the house steward said from the doorway.

Anstella? Linden thought. *What does she want?*

Only one way to find out. "Very well, Aran. Show her here, please."

Aran nodded and withdrew. A few minutes later Linden heard him returning, followed by the hiss of satin slippers on tile and the rustling of a gown. Aran bowed Baroness Colrane in and withdrew once more.

Linden rose. "How may I help you, my lady?" he asked, polite but wary.

Anstella made him a courtesy. "I've come to beg a favor of you, Dragonlord. The Solstice is approaching and Sherrine—Your Grace, it is a hard thing to ask a young woman to miss the celebrations at the palace. My daughter has been looking forward to them for months. Of your kindness, Dragonlord, would you consider rescinding her exile?"

It would have to be this. But at least the mother had not sought to trap him publicly as the daughter had. And it wasn't fair to deprive the baroness of her only child's company; Anstella was blameless in all this. "It was not I who exiled your daughter, Baroness, but she herself. If she wishes to return I will not oppose it. It would be a shame if she missed the celebrations. So send to her, bid her return—but she is to remember that there is a condition to it. I think she'll know what it is.''

Anstella dropped another courtesy. ''I understand. Thank you for your kindness, Dragonlord. I will send for her this very day,'' she said, and left.

Fifty-nine

Linden lay on his back on the lawn, nibbling on a sprig of mint, watching the clouds float across an achingly blue sky. His thoughts drifted on the silken threads of melody from Otter's harp as Shan cropped the grass near his shoulder. Occasionally the stallion would stop and sniff Linden as though to make certain his person was really there. Linden stretched up a hand and scratched Shan's nose as the big black head once again loomed over him. A goblet of wine waited, forgotten, by his elbow.

He cast aside the last of the mint. Otter played softly; the tune now was a lullaby, old when Linden had heard it as a child. He closed his eyes, just this side of sleep, mulling over the news Otter had brought him.

That Maurynna was having such trouble worried him. Linden vividly remembered the terror he'd known before his First Change, the horrible certainty he was going mad, hearing voices in his head, his senses overwhelmed by the world around him. Judging by Otter's account, Maurynna was going through the same hell.

And there was nothing he could do to help her, save hope that her First Change would come soon. There was only one bright spot in Otter's tidings. "You say that this began before we were Sealed to each other?"

"Um, yes. I hadn't meant to tell you, but . . . The night you were attacked, Kief was so upset that he didn't think things through and Changed very close to Maurynna. He's been afraid that's what triggered all of this. He didn't tell you, did he?"

"No," Linden said dryly, "he didn't. But it does explain

something he said. When this is over, I believe I shall have a word or two with him.''

Otter smothered a laugh and returned to his playing.

"I'd like you to stay with Maurynna as much as possible, Otter. I'd rather she wasn't alone when these spells take her.'' The next words were hard. Linden forced them out anyway. "Sometimes . . . No, too damn many times fledgling Dragonlords have become so terrified they're going mad that they commit suicide. I nearly did. Lleld and my sister stopped me. Now I'm afraid for Maurynna. Please stay with her.''

The song faltered. "Gods help us; I never knew. Of course I'll do that, boyo. And I'll think of some excuse for it so she won't get suspicious.'' The bard's fingers trilled through an intricate run on the strings as if to make up for their earlier clumsiness and continued the song. "We'll have a problem with that, though. Maurynna and I were to part ways here in Casna. If I leave with her instead of staying, she'll know something's up.''

"Damn,'' Linden said. "You're right. Damn again. What to do, then?''

Otter chewed his mustache in thought. "Hm—perhaps I could tell her that this, while unusual, is something that some-times happens to truehumans close to Dragonlords. I already said something like it once.''

While Linden knew it was nonsense, it sounded as likely as anything he could think of. And if anyone could lie convincingly enough to get that bit of foolery believed, it was Otter. "Well enough. Make certain she understands that it's only temporary, that she's not going mad.''

"I will. Any word yet about Tsan Rhilin?'' Otter asked as the lullaby ended.

"None. It's as if it disappeared from the face of the earth,'' Linden replied, feeling heartsick. "I still can't believe it.''

"I can well imagine,'' Otter said. "I'm sorry; I know what it means to you.''

Linden nodded, saying, "At least there's some good news. Kief, Tarlna, and I are close to a decision on the regency. We want to hear a few more people out, look over the documents again, that sort of thing, but I think this will be over by the Solstice or shortly thereafter.''

"Thank the gods," said Otter. "When do the meetings resume?"

"Tomorrow."

"You're feeling well enough for that?"

"Yes, though I still tire more easily than I like and I sometimes get dizzy. We'll keep the meetings short to keep Healer Tasha happy and me from falling asleep at the table. Kief's worried that if we wait too long the factions will take matters into their own hands. I think he's right." Linden sat up, yawning and rubbing the back of his neck. Shan snuffled his ear; he tweaked the stallion's lip.

Strong white teeth clamped onto his clan braid. "Pull it, crowbait, and you'll never get another apple," Linden said.

Shan considered and dropped the braid.

"Wise horse. It has," Linden said as he rose in one easy movement, "been entirely too quiet. Something's brewing. I can feel it in my bones."

Sixty

Tomorrow the Solstice celebrations; now was the time for preparations. Tasha meandered around her office, collecting whatever empty dosing bottles she could find. Two kettles steamed on the hearth. One held the decoction she brewed every holiday. The other held hot water. She eased this batch of small pottery bottles into the water to join their fellows and ran a practiced eye over the number in the kettle.

Not hardly enough. I've a feeling there will be many more aching heads than usual after the celebrating. Bother, I want plenty of these to give out.

She called to Jeralin scavenging in the storeroom across the hall, "Any luck?"

"A bit. I found two baskets that had slipped behind that round-topped chest. One, hurrah, hurrah, has six empty bottles in it. The other one . . . A moment while I get the lid off of the basket. Ah, good! Here's another bottle—but it's full. Now what's in h—" Jeralin broke off, gagging.

Tasha ran across the hall. She found Jeralin sitting on a chest, coughing, a dosing bottle held as far as she could from her averted face.

"That is *vile*," the apprentice complained. She passed the offending bottle to Tasha's waiting hand. "What was it once upon a time?"

Tasha sniffed cautiously. Even that was almost enough to unsettle her stomach. "I don't know. Whatever it was, it's been fermenting nicely, hasn't it? But what could it have been?" She stoppered the bottle again. There was a scent she couldn't quite catch beneath the stink of fermentation, a scent that teased her. "There's something odd about this. I'll want a closer look at it later, I think."

Said Jeralin cheerfully, "Next mystery potion I find, I'm leaving it for Quirel to investigate when he gets back from the herb gardens."

Tasha nodded, hardly listening, examining the bottle in her hand. Then the girl's words sank in and stirred up something in her mind, but to save her life Tasha couldn't think of it. Ah, well, she'd busy herself with something else. She'd often found that when she stopped chasing an answer, the perverse thing would jump out at her. So she slung bottle, basket, and potion over her arm and went back to her office and the decoction bubbling on the hearth.

So close to the Solstice, even at deep dusk the streets of Casna were crowded. Early revelers and late errand-runners thronged the main ways. Maurynna caught snatches from the babble of conversation as she and Otter rode through the crowds.

"Gods, will this heat never break?" "It's the mugginess, I minds, I tells ya. Like takin' a bath with yer clothes on." "Don't care what they say out of the castle. A Dragonlord taken sick like that? It's magic; it must be. Who knows if he's really better?" "Gods, it's hot!"

They turned onto a less-traveled thoroughfare. Maurynna breathed a sigh of relief. "Too many people."

Otter smiled. "Easier on board ship, isn't it?"

"Gods, yes! And cooler, too." Maurynna wiped her forehead and struggled for something—anything—else to say lest she fall back into the dark mood that had gripped her for the past tenday, ever since she'd last seen Linden. "Black dog on my shoulder," she muttered.

"Hmm?" Otter said. Then, without waiting for a reply, "He said he'd be waiting in the garden."

She nodded; the black dog dug his claws in deeper.

"Have you ever been to the house? No? Likely just as well. I'm still not certain this is such a good idea, Rynna. While you're leaving tomorrow, there are still all those candlemarks between now and then for the Fraternity to strike at you. Hopefully no one will recognize you in the dark; Linden was wise to insist upon that.''

The black dog growled in her ear. She said, ''I hate this—this sneaking about as if Linden's ashamed of me.'' Though her mind said the noblewoman's taunt had no substance behind it, the poison of Lady Sherrine's words still lingered in her heart.

''Don't be an ass. You know full well it's not that at all. Now stop moping; we're nearly there.''

The bard urged his horse into a quick trot. Maurynna sighed again and followed. She wasn't moping—not really—but ever since she'd made the decision to leave, a deep melancholy had settled upon her; despite his promise, she feared she would never see Linden again.

So she had insisted on seeing him tonight. Perhaps if she threw the black dog this bone it would leave her alone.

Not bloody likely.

Tears stung her eyes, but she refused to let them fall. Blinking rapidly, she followed Otter into the large courtyard before Linden's house. Servants appeared, held their horses as they dismounted and led the animals away, all without a word spoken. She noticed they never looked directly at her.

For her protection, or for Linden's shame?

Otter led her to the side of the house where an arched passageway waited. Maurynna stared around her as she walked down the long passage. A lattice of thin stakes rose on either side to meet over her head. Roses fountained over it; their sweet scent wrapped her in a cloak of perfume that nearly overwhelmed her.

''Good gods!'' she said, stifling an urge to sneeze. ''I know Cassorins are mad about roses, but this is—''

''A bit much?'' Otter finished with a chuckle. ''Ask Linden to show you the maze when we find him.''

''The maze?''

''You'll see. Ah! I see a glow ahead—looks like coldfire. Thank the gods; we're nearly out of here, then. I like roses as much as another, but this is ridiculous—especially on such a muggy night as this. Damn near enough to knock you off your feet.''

They emerged into the garden. Maurynna caught her breath in wonder.

The garden was filled with animals. For one bemused moment she thought they were real. Then she realized that they were formed of living trees and bushes. She turned slowly as she walked, determined see as many as she could. A bold mouse, almost an ell high, watched her. Two ferrets played together while a brushy hare sat nearby. A stag touched noses with a wolf. There was even a goose chasing a fox across the lawn; one more step and it would have the fox's tail.

''That one's my favorite,'' a deep voice said behind her. ''Pity the poor fox!''

She turned into Linden's arms. He held her tightly, nearly crushing her, before letting go a heartbeat later.

He gestured and the coldfire at his shoulder fled to hover above a small table set between benches of white marble. A silver pitcher and three goblets waited for them. ''Shall we sit?'' Linden said. They followed him to the table.

''I've a better idea,'' said Otter as he poured wine for the three of them.

Maurynna took hers in silence, waiting for Otter to finish. The bard unslung the harp from his back.

''Why,'' Otter said as he deftly unpacked his harp, ''don't you show Rynna the rose maze while I sit here and play?''

She nearly kissed him. Her black mood lightened; more than anything she had wanted time alone with Linden—and now Otter was gifting her with it. But what if Linden didn't feel the same way? Perhaps—

The feeling in the Dragonlord's quiet ''Thank you'' set the black dog yipping into the night. She smiled up at Linden, lighthearted for the first time in days.

They left Otter sitting on one of the benches, the coldfire dancing above him as he tuned the harp. Linden led her past more topiary animals, going deeper and deeper into the garden. He suddenly stopped, a faraway expression on his face, as the first notes of a song rose into the night.

"Is something wrong?" she asked.

"No." He hesitated, then said, "I taught Otter that song nearly forty years ago; the tune is an old one—old even when I was young. Rani learned it in a dream from . . . from Satha—"

His voice faltered and Maurynna remembered Otter's warning to never ask about the undead Kelnethi harper. But Linden continued as if nothing had happened. "Bram wrote the words for her when they realized that they had to part for good."

He fell silent. Maurynna went cold inside; was the song meant for a warning? Before she could speak, he slipped an arm around her shoulders, pulling her close as they walked on.

"Thank the gods," he said, "for us it's just a sad but pretty song." He ducked his head. "I helped Bram with it a bit," he confessed shyly. "Not very much—just a little."

"But you helped," Maurynna said. Her arm crept around his waist; she rested her head against his shoulder, at peace now. The thought of leaving still made her sad, but she no longer feared she would never see him again. "What is this maze?"

"This." He pointed to a wall of roses before them that curved away to either side. "It's not truly a maze, since there's only one path; it just twists and turns upon itself as it goes to the center of the circle. The opening's this way."

He guided her to the right. "At least these roses aren't as heavily scented as the others in the passageway—or perhaps it's just easier to bear because there's no 'roof' to this; it's open to the sky. But come inside."

She followed him, curious. He sent a ball of coldfire ahead of them. The curving path was wide; three men walking abreast could fit between the hedges that rose above Linden's head. It turned abruptly and doubled back on itself as he had predicted. Maurynna soon lost track of how many turns they had taken and which direction they walked in at any moment.

He didn't speak as they moved deeper into the maze. Time

ceased to exist for Maurynna; it stretched on and on as it might in a dream.

Then all at once it was over; they reached the center. It was larger than Maurynna had expected, but empty. She didn't know what she had thought to find—but it wasn't a lawn of apple-scented chamomile.

She broke the silence. "Odd; I would have thought a bench at the least."

He moved away from her to the center of the lawn. The full moon shone down on him; he looked like a statue made of silver. Then he held out his hand and broke the illusion. "Sit with me."

She joined him. For a time they listened to Otter's harping. She rested her head on Linden's shoulder once more as he stroked her hair. Then he pulled her close and kissed her long and gently before releasing her.

She pulled back slightly, studying him. "Linden, I—I don't want to leave."

"I don't want you to, either, Maurynna, but it's safest. Otter said that your hold was filled three days ago. It would have been best if you'd left then. Why did you wait?" he asked.

She smiled. "My aunt asked me to stay. You see, the Solstice is my birthday, and I've never celebrated it with my family here. So we'll have a small feast in the afternoon and then I'll sail with the tide at dusk."

"Your birth—that wretch! He never told me!" Linden growled something in a language she didn't recognize and flopped back onto the grass. "Blast it; I wish I'd known."

She laughed and stretched out alongside him. "At least Otter didn't do what he'd threatened me with on board the *Sea Mist*."

"And what was that?"

"Make me wait until my birthday to meet you."

Linden rolled onto his side so that he loomed over her. "I would have had his head for that."

She touched his face. He smiled, a little sadly. "So little time, Maurynna-love."

"We'd best not waste it, then," she said and pulled him down for a kiss.

The night was quiet and still, the air heavy with unshed rain as Althume walked through the halls of Prince Peridaen's estate. He had no fear of anyone thinking it odd; wasn't Peridaen's faithful steward often up late at night tending to his master's business?

As he certainly was—in a manner of speaking. Althume held up his hand, letting the amethyst pendant dangle from the gold chain wrapped around his fingers. Time to return this pretty to its place on Peridaen's dressing table now that he was done with it. Then on to other business this night.

In a less savory part of Casna, Eel watched from the shadows. The little thief had marked his target—a burly man with a hard, square face, dressed well, and an air of prosperity if not riches—but now the man was talking to Nobbie, one of the many whores out this night plying the Solstice crowds.

Eel considered. He could nip in, cut the man's belt pouch free while the fellow was distracted by Nobbie, but that would mean the little prostitute would be out a fee. Worse, the man might think Nobs part of a scheme to rob him, and beat the living daylights out of the boy.

No, let Nobbie have this one. The boy was a friend and Eel didn't want him hurt. The thief watched whore and customer conclude their negotiations and go off together instead of slipping deeper into the alley to conduct their business.

Likes it private, I guess. Wonder which tavern the gent's got a room at? Eel wondered idly as he set off to find another mark.

Invisibility was an art, but a simple matter if one were subtle. There was no need for the stuff of ignorant tales, enchanted cloaks and helms or the like. And certainly no need of mystical chants and waving of wands, the overwrought display of fire and noise that was the mark of the poorly trained—and weak—mage.

A very simple thing indeed was invisibility. One did not, of course, actually become invisible. That was a waste of magical energy. Invisibility was merely the art of turning aside people's minds.

Which was exactly what Althume did as he walked through the palace that night. At this hour there were few people about; most of the nobles were still in the great hall. Those few who were in this wing of the palace were sleepy-eyed servants. It was child's play to Althume to turn their minds away from him. They might look straight at him, but he made no more of a ripple in their consciousness as they stepped aside for him than would a shark gliding through a midnight sea.

That he had kept himself inconspicuous all his time in Casna helped; "Peridaen's shadow" some called him. Ever the faithful steward waiting silently for his master's order.

Bah. But soon he would have his due as the greatest of mages, though the full truth would be known to only a few. He shifted the burden he carried from the crook of one elbow to the other.

A few minutes more brought him to the junction of this hall and a second. Beyond lay the chambers he sought. Two guards stood before the door. Althume stopped in the shadows.

Turning aside the minds of the serving cattle was one thing; trained soldiers were quite another. To make them ignore him *and* the opening of the door they guarded was a chancy thing at best. He could do it, but it would take more mage energy than he cared to expend.

He had more important uses for it. Time to see if the servant the scrying bowl showed him was still there.

Althume sent out a tendril of magic. He touched the mind of the servant: an old man, somewhat infirm of wit and body, but kept on for reasons of sentiment. Althume curled his lip at such weakness. To seize control of the man was simpler than a child's game of ring-toss. The mage left the shadows, carefully timing his arrival at the door.

The guards ignored him, but turned as the door opened

from the inside. The old servant shuffled out, leaving the heavy iron-bound door open behind him. Althume slipped inside.

One of the soldiers said "Where are you bound, Urlic?" and closed the door on Urlic's mumbled reply.

I care not where you go, old man; do not return until I call you, the mage ordered. He heard one guard remark, "Poor old Urlic; his wits have gone soft. Hope he don't fall down the stairs," and the other's grunted agreement.

Althume stood alone and unguarded. He sensed Urlic moving away. Good; he'd have the time he needed.

"I hadn't meant for this to happen," Linden said. His contented tone took any sting from the words.

His scar was rough under her cheek, shifting a little with the rise and fall of his chest. Maurynna raised herself up on one elbow so that she could look at him. "I'm glad it did. And you were right."

He lay with one arm cushioning his head; his free hand pushed her long hair behind her shoulder, then cupped her cheek. "I'm glad, too, though it was not the wisest thing."

She wondered what he meant. Was he afraid he'd gotten her with child? She longed to ask, but his lazy smile said that she'd wait a long time for an answer—and she'd not beg for an explanation. Instead she wrapped herself around the warmth of his body and said tartly, "Indeed? I thought it a fine idea myself."

He laughed. "So it was, with no harm done."

And what did *that* mean? How could he know already if he had gotten her with child? Aloud she said, "I would not consider it 'harm' to bear a—Oh! I forgot."

She rolled away from him. The grass was cool on her bare stomach. So, she would not have even the hope of a child from Linden. Nothing but memories when he finally left her. Not that she could raise a child herself; a ship was no place for a baby. Perhaps it was just as well.

He caught her chin, turned her face to look at him. "Even between ourselves children are very, very rare—even if the female Dragonlord doesn't drink *daishya* tea. Which most do; there is no guarantee that such a child would be a Dragonlord. And to watch your child grow old and die—no.''

''Oh gods, what a horrible thought,'' she said, and hunched her shoulders against it.

Linden sat up and reached for the untidy heap of his clothes. He said softly, ''I always wanted children. It's the one thing I regret about being a Dragonlord,'' and pulled his tunic over his head. ''We'd best go back.''

Maurynna bit her lip and nodded. She got to her knees. ''I wish . . .'' She let the words hang in the air. If she tried to finish, she'd cry.

''I, too, love. But I think this will be over soon and I shall find you wherever you've sailed to.''

''Truly?''

He met her eyes. ''Yes,'' he said, his deep voice quiet and sure. ''Yes. But for my peace of mind, Maurynna, promise me that you will leave tomorrow.''

She hated to, but what choice had she? ''I will.''

Althume examined the rooms, looking for a hiding place. It could not be too obvious; he didn't want his treasure found too soon. But it had to be somewhere large enough to hide the thing. Once again he shifted the heavy greatsword in his arms as he passed into the sleeping chamber.

Not the clothes cupboard, or someone would realize it should have been found long before now. And no one would believe under the mattress.

He frowned; there must be somewhere . . .

The windowseat caught his eye. Spanning the width of two windows, it was easily long enough for the greatsword. He hurried to it. Someone might find the wandering Urlic, bring him back; it would not do to be caught here.

His long clever fingers felt under the lip of the seat and quickly found a catch. ''Ah, good then; there *is* a chest beneath,'' he said under his breath. Releasing the catch, he swung the lid up, scattering the cushions.

The heavy scent of the herb bags within greeted him:

wormwood and tansy, lavender and lemon balm. He looked down at heavy woolen blankets and the thick curtains that would hang from the canopied bed in winter. Althume lifted the top blanket and laid the greatsword down. He replaced the blanket, tucking the bags of herbs into the folds. "Until the proper time, sleep well, Tsan Rhilin."

He set the scattered pillows to rights and left the sleeping chamber. Once more he stretched out his mind to Urlic, bidding the confused old man to return so that he might repeat the ruse and exit.

Althume was well pleased with this night's work. Peridaen would have his piddling regency—for however long events decreed. And the Fraternity would have a Dragonlord slave. But now it was time to meet Pol in the clearing.

A final cup of wine, and then Maurynna would have to leave. Barely suppressing a sigh, Linden pulled her close to him once more. She leaned against him, fitting along his body as if they had been molded for each other, as they watched Otter filling the goblets.

When they each had goblet in hand, Linden raised his and said, "To being together once more."

They drank.

Otter, a mischievous twinkle in his eye, raised his goblet for another toast. "Happiness to each of you: Linden, Maurynna, Rathan . . ." He smiled as he let his voice trail off and drank.

Nearly choking on a laugh, Linden followed suit, as did a puzzled-looking Maurynna. He wondered what name the fourth, unnamed one carried; he wouldn't know until Maurynna Changed for the first time.

Maurynna looked up at him and said, "Why name you and Rathan separately? Aren't you two the same?"

Linden shook his head. "No. We're two different beings who share the same body, and that body can shift between our forms. I have my own theory as to why—" Linden paused, remembering Rathan's amusement "—the dragon half slumbers with only occasional intrusions, but that's what

happens until the human half grows weary of living. Some
Dragonlords pass on while still very young as Dragonlords
go; it's not easy when everyone you loved and knew as a
truehuman is gone. Others of us, well, perhaps we're made
of sterner stuff or we're just more stubborn. When that weariness happens to me, I will cease to exist and Rathan will
come into his own as a truedragon.''

Maurynna said, ''You mean you'll . . .'' She reached up to
the hand he rested on her shoulder. Her face was pale in the
coldfire's glow.

He caught her hand. ''Die and my soul pass on like any
truehuman's. I'll simply have had hundreds of years more.
But it won't happen for many, many centuries, love. Not
now.'' *How could I become weary? There won't be enough
time to spend with you.*

Her fingers gripped his. ''Promise?''

''I promise,'' he said.

A tired but contented Eel sauntered through the byways of
Casna, eager to get to the little dockside hut he called home.
He'd done so well tonight that he considered taking a holiday
the next day. It would be, after all, the Solstice. Ah, he'd
think about it later. The night was fading fast; to the east the
sky was streaked with the coming dawn. Time to sleep.

As he turned a corner he came upon the panderer known
as Mother Sossie herding her little flock of prostitutes back
to the abandoned building that sheltered them. The youngsters—most in their early teens, a few younger, none older
than twenty-two, Eel knew—followed like sleepy chicks after
a hen.

''Heyyadah, Eel,'' Mother Sossie called. ''Stoppin' a moment, hey?''

Eel pressed his lips together. Mother Sossie catered to a
particular clientele that he didn't care much for. Even her
eldest whores looked to be little more than children; she
kicked them out when they looked too ''old.''

Still, no sense in making an enemy. Sossie could be a flaming bitch. He stopped. ''Heyyadah, Mother. What do for?''

"You seen Nobbie? Lazy sod not tartin' where he s'posed. Little bastard run, I beat his ass but good when I grab him. Third one this month." Mother Sossie spat in indignation at such ingratitude.

Eel scratched his head under the grimy cap. "Did see, but long ago—deep darktime. Shoulda been long time done. You say there been others, hey?"

"Oh, aye. Fillies and colts—mostly colts—been bolting the stables past month or so; mine, others too. Bah, Nobbie pure trouble. Always been. Little bastard." She stumped off, shooing her flock before her.

Eel continued thoughtfully on his way. He pondered Mother Sossie's news; now that he thought about it, he had heard about one or two other whores running away, but hadn't paid the gossip any mind.

But it was usually a few in the span of a year. This was as many in a month, and from only one panderer. It had happened to others as well, Sossie had said. Curious.

And disquieting. There were always a few whores who thought they could do better on their own. Sometimes they were right. Most often they were very, very wrong. He hoped Nobbie wasn't one of the last; little Nobs had helped him out once or twice when the pickings were lean.

Eel sighed. He'd nap a bit, then go look for the little idiot and try to talk some sense into him; even Mother Sossie was better than being out on the streets alone.

What in the world had possessed Nobbie to run, anyway? And all the others—what had happened to them, as well?

Sixty-one

Maurynna finished licking her fingers as Aunt Elenna brought out yet another tray. She groaned in mock misery, complaining, "Not another bite or the *Sea Mist* will founder under me! This is already the largest and best breakfast I've ever eaten. Um—what are those?"

Maylin laughed. "Sweetmeats; try one and tell me what you think. They're for those who'll come to visit after the Perfumers' Guild feast tonight."

Maurynna studied the dainty confections on the tray and selected one crowned with a crystallized violet blossom. She popped it into her mouth. "Mmmm—lovely. Now I'm sorrier than ever that I can't stay. Where is your feast this year?"

"At our new guild hall," Aunt Elenna answered. "Are you certain you can't delay one more day? You're welcome to go with us, you know."

"I know. But I promised Linden that I would leave today—and my crew is ready."

Her aunt held up her hands in resignation. "If a Dragonlord wills it . . . Ah, sweetheart, I wish *I* could stay longer as well, but I have to go help old Shaina oversee the final preparations for the feast. Happy birthday, dear heart, and good-bye."

Maurynna stood up from her chair, then bent to hug her tiny aunt and searched for words of thanks. Good-byes always made her feel awkward. "Thank you for everything. I know I haven't always been the best company this time around, but . . ."

"You have had," Aunt Elenna said wryly, "some small reason for that."

"Indeed yes," Maylin said. "More than enough to bear for any . . . truehuman."

*   *   *

A holiday it was; even a thief needed time off. Eel wandered through the streets looking at the vendors' wares. He even went so far as to buy, rather than steal, a meat pasty from an old couple doing a brisk business on a corner. Munching happily, he continued walking and enjoying the Solstice.

He was standing outside the door to the Juggling Cow and debating whether he wanted to start drinking now or wait a bit when the hard-faced man he'd seen talking to Nobbie the other night walked quickly out. From the way one hand rested on his belt pouch Eel guessed that the man had something important in there. Gold? At once the sharp, tiny knife was in Eel's hand; then he reconsidered. Could Nobbie have gone off with this fellow?

Eel plunged into the crowd after the man.

The late afternoon was even more oppressive than the morning had been. The heat did nothing to improve the usual harbor stinks: river mud, tar, dead fish, and other pungent odors that Maurynna preferred remain unidentified. Yet even through the miasma she caught the clean salt smell of the ocean. She yearned toward it, even as the greater part of her wanted to stay in Casna. That would have been the best birthday gift of all.

"Almost ready, Captain," Master Remon called from the *Sea Mist*.

She waved an acknowledgment and said to Otter standing by her side, "I'll miss having you on board, you know, even if you are a dreadful tease."

"And I'll miss you—even if you are more stubborn than a certain Dragonlord I know," he replied.

She smiled wanly at the joke. Gods, how she wanted to turn back and find Linden. But she had given him her word to leave this night. "I wish he could have come to say goodbye."

Once again Otter's hand closed over his belt pouch as it had done now and again all day. She wondered what was concealed in there.

"So does he," the bard said. "But Kief decided upon a surprise meeting of the council before the festivities begin in earnest. I think you might be seeing Linden a little sooner than you'd thought you might." He grinned. "Ah. Thought that would make you smile.

"And there's this: he gave me something for you for your birthday. His instructions were to give it to you in private and just before you left. I'll wager this is the right time and—blast it all, girl, I've no idea what it is and it's driving me mad! Where—"

"My cabin," Maurynna broke in, half laughing and consumed by curiosity. "Quickly, we must cast off soon if we're to make this tide, but there's a little time yet to spare."

She ran up the gangplank, Otter hot on her heels. "Master Remon! Hold off for a bit, if you please. Bard Otter will be leaving shortly."

Ducking into her cabin under the stern deck, Maurynna pushed the hangings over the window aside to let in the slanting light. As an afterthought she opened the window as well; the cabin was hot and stuffy. By the time she'd finished, Otter had placed a small wooden box on the table bolted to the floor. She picked it up—the weight surprised her—and studied it.

It was made of rosewood and inlaid with gold wire in a pattern of interlacing lines in the Yerrin style. The crafting was exquisite, from the tiny gold hinges and clasp to the enamelwork of the central design: a dragon in full flight. She tilted it gently; something inside shifted with a tiny *thunk!*

All she could do was stare at the beautiful thing in her hands, overwhelmed by the knowledge that this had to be a treasured possession of Linden's. One did not find work like this sitting about a marketplace to be purchased on a whim.

And he had given it to her.

Otter broke her reverie. "Rynna, if you don't open that thing before I die of curiosity, I shall haunt you!"

She laughed a little, nervously, and undid the latch. Holding her breath, she eased the lid back to reveal black silk folded over something. As if she opened the petals of a rose,

Maurynna turned back the layers of silk one by one.

A silver fox looked up at her, its amethyst eyes winking in the late sunlight, brushy tail wrapped around its feet. Caught by the laughter in the vixen's face—*How do I know it's a vixen?*—it was a few moments before Maurynna slid trembling fingers beneath the fox and removed it from its box.

She heard Otter gasp, "Gods have mercy!" at the sight of it, but paid no attention as she lost herself in her gift's beauty. It was a domed circular cloak brooch the width of her palm, the fox in raised relief against a granulated background, all within a frame of smooth, heavy silver wire. As she rubbed her thumb against the hundreds of tiny silver balls of the granulation, her other fingers noticed the thickness of the pin in the back. This brooch was meant for a cloak made of a loosely woven wool; she'd never before seen one like it.

"This is very old, isn't it?" she whispered, awestruck.

"Yes," Otter said. His voice was strained.

When she tore her gaze away from the treasure in her hands, she saw that he stared like one dumbfounded, shaking his head slowly as if he didn't believe what his eyes told him. It made her uneasy. "Otter?"

"It was Rani's," the bard said, sounding as stunned as she now felt. "Bram gave it to her; Linden said he always called her *Shaijha*—'little fox.' She gave it to Linden not long before she died. Save for his memories, that . . . that and Tsan Rhilin are all he has left of them. I—I told him once how much you loved the stories about them. He must have remembered."

She made it to a chair before her knees turned to water. "Dear gods, Otter; can he truly mean for me to have this?" she asked. The amethyst eyes winked at her.

"Ho! Captain!" Remon's bellow cut through her confusion. "We must cast off now or miss the tide. Time for shore, Bard, unless you're sailing with us again."

All at once Maurynna was aware of the tug of the tide against the *Sea Mist*'s hull. "Otter, Remon's right. I can't miss this tide; I promised Linden." *Though the gods know I want to stay more than ever. Why? Why give me such a precious part of his life?* "You'll have to leave now."

Somehow she scrambled out of the chair, legs shaking like the veriest landlubber in his first storm at sea. She laid the brooch in its box once more and hustled Otter out to the deck. He stopped, one foot on the gangplank.

"Rynna—remember what I told you about what's happening to you. It's only because you and Linden are so close. He said that in a short time it should end," Otter said. "*Please* remember that."

"I will. I promise," she told him, hardly knowing what she said. She was still stunned by her gift; she felt like a storm-tossed ship with its anchor ropes cut, not knowing which quarter the gale would come from next. "Go."

The bard looked no better off than she, trotting obediently down the gangplank like a sleepwalker. His face, when he turned to wave farewell from the dock, was pale. She suspected her own matched his very well indeed.

She never remembered what orders she gave to set the *Sea Mist* on her way again. But she must have done it right, for they neither ran aground nor rammed another vessel. Still, as the tide carried the little cog down the river to the waiting sea, Remon approached her.

"With your permission, Captain, you should go lie down. You look as bad as the bard did after that storm. It wasn't bad news about your family, was it?" the first mate said anxiously.

Maurynna said, "No. No, it wasn't bad news at all, Remon; not at all. But I—I think I will go to my cabin for a while. Take the helm, please."

She felt his eyes and the rest of the crew's on her back as she went to her cabin. Inside, she held the cloak brooch up in the sunlight sparkling through the stern window. The fox still laughed at her.

I don't understand. Why give me this? What does it mean? He said he could never love a truehuman, so it can't be that.

Never taking her eyes from the fox's, she sat once more in the chair and studied the brooch as if she'd find the answer there. But the little vixen kept her secrets safe behind her silver fangs.

Eel followed his rushing quarry as best he could. Sometimes he lost sight of the man, but he always managed to spot him again. When the man went into one of the public stables, he almost despaired. But when the man rode out—*that's no stable nag, not with those lines and tack like that*—Eel found that his job was, in fact, easier. The crowds kept the horse to a slow walk, and now that the man rose above everyone else Eel had no trouble keeping him in sight. The thief took advantage and dropped even farther back. No sense in taking chances.

Still, Eel ducked into a doorway when his man met another horseman near the edge of the merchants' quarter. He studied the second man: thin, with an ascetic, almost gaunt face—not someone to cross in Eel's opinion. This man wore a badge of some sort. Its gaudy scarlet and purple clashed with the man's sober grey and green clothing.

He watched the two men ride toward the nobles' section of the city. The trail ended here, then. Eel knew he'd stand out like a goose in a henhouse if he went amongst the gentry's homes. He chewed his lower lip, thinking. It was time to return to the beginning. He turned and retraced his steps.

To his frustration, Otter was unable to reach Linden's mind. He often could as a result of their long friendship, providing the Dragonlord was neither too far away nor too distracted. Now, however, he couldn't give Linden the "nudge" that would alert him to sustain the contact with his own strength. Since Linden was not that far, something must be engaging his attention.

Damnation, boyo, the bard fumed in solitary annoyance as he rode back to the Vanadin's comfortable house, *while I know it's her birthday, couldn't you have waited until after Maurynna's Changed to give her that? What if she guesses?* Another part of his mind pointed out, *Does anyone ever suspect they're a Dragonlord?*

Now there was a pretty puzzle. He wrestled with it for the remainder of the ride.

One of the apprentices let him in and then disappeared into the office. He could hear Elenna talking in there; by the sound of it someone was getting his ears pinned back. There was an edge to her voice that made him glad he wasn't the culprit. He made his way down the hall to the back of the house and into the kitchen.

Maylin sat at the table, a steaming pottery mug cupped in her hands. "Tea, Otter?" she asked. "You look as though you need it. Is something wrong? Maurynna set sail all right, didn't she?"

Otter shook his head. "No—nothing's wrong. I think. Maurynna is indeed on her way to Pelnar and all's well. It's just . . . I believe I'll have a mug of your mother's fine ale, if I may."

Maylin raised her eyebrows, but put her tea down and went to the buttery. She returned with a wooden tankard filled to the brim with rich brown ale that she set in front of him without a word.

He managed to make it to the bottom of the tankard before she began questioning him. Otter tried to fob her off with a few unimportant details, but he knew ahead of time that it was a wasted effort. "Don't you have a feast to go to or something?"

Maylin merely smiled—as she was doing now—and said, "I was planning to go a bit late. You might as well tell me, Otter. You'll have no peace until you do. Believe me."

"I do. You're very much like your cousin, did you know that?" Otter complained.

"Yes." The smile was wider.

"Oh, Gifnu's hells; I might as well. You'd find out with the first letter Maurynna sends you after she reaches port. When I saw him this morning, Linden handed me something to give her just before she sailed. It was in a box that he made me promise not to open, so I had no idea what it was."

He paused, hoping she'd be satisfied with that. It was the hope of a fool. Maylin took another sip and looked prepared to wait for the stone giants of Nethris Plain to come alive again.

"Every bit as bad as your cousin, girl. As I said, until Rynna opened it, I was as ignorant of what was in it as she. And if I'd known, I would have tried to talk Linden out of it. It was a cloak brooch—a silver fox cloak brooch."

"So? That doesn't seem an extravagance beyond a Dragonlord's means."

Otter said impatiently, "You don't understand. Rani eo'Tsan gave Linden that brooch. And he's given it to Maurynna."

Maylin rocked back in her chair as though she'd been slapped. But all she said was, "Did he now?" in an odd tone.

And not another word did she say while she took his tankard and her mug and washed and rinsed them in the water she drew from the kitchen cistern. But she paused on her way out of the kitchen to repeat, "Did he now?" still in that same odd tone, leaving Otter to stare after her.

Well and well and well. Dragonlords may not suspect what they are—but I think others might. It's a good thing Maurynna's safely away from Casna.

Sixty-two

Althume sat at his desk in the steward's quarters of the prince's city dwelling, his hands cupped before him. The soultrap jewel flared between them, icy blue light spilling over the stone.

The Solstice at last. Now was the time to gather the threads he'd spun. Now was the time of his triumph.

He would have preferred working this magic from the altar. But the distance would have been too great for the first part; he'd had to make do. Pol sat, back against the door, to guard against interruptions. Althume had done all he could to prepare for this. Time to begin.

The mage's mind stretched outward, seeking. He sifted through the minds he felt buffeting against his own, weak untrained things, mere thistledown against the steel blade of his resolve.

There. There was the one he sought. Althume reached out and caught the other's mind and will in his magic. Time for the first step in his plan.

"My lords and ladies of the council, I thank you for agreeing to take this time from your Solstice celebrating to meet with us this evening," Kief began.

Linden looked around the council room for what he fervently hoped was the last time. He was grateful that he could plead Tasha's orders to get out of the celebration tonight; he was tired and felt a touch dizzy now and again. *Please the gods,* he mindspoke Tarlna, *this will be the end of it.*

Let us hope so, Tarlna replied. *I miss—*

A sudden, far-off hubbub in the hall made her break off. She and Linden looked at each other, concerned and puzzled.

The noise was not yet loud enough to catch the attention of the truehumans but it drew closer with every heartbeat.

Kief faltered. Surprised, the councilors muttered between themselves. Then even they could hear the tumult in the hall. Many forgot themselves so far as to rise from the table, Prince Peridaen among them. The pendant he always wore flashed amethyst fire in the candlelight.

Then Linden heard a name that brought him out of his chair with a rush. He made for the door.

It swept open almost in his face. Captain Tev, commander of the palace guards, entered. Behind him tottered an old man with a heavy burden clutched to his chest. The moment the old man saw Linden, he held it out.

Tsan Rhilin.

"Old Urlic found it, Dragonlord," the old man quavered. "Hidden in the windowseat, it was, but I found it."

The council room erupted into bewildered uproar as Linden accepted the greatsword from the old servant's trembling hands.

Althume could feel Peridaen's surprise and consternation surge though the amethyst amulet. Things were progressing as they should, then. He began the incantations over the soul-trap jewel. Feeling the magical energies build within him, he formed it as a spear, holding it ready within his mind. He had already touched his intended victim once; this time he would strike in earnest.

Linden gripped Tsan Rhilin's hilt with both hands, exerting every ounce of self-control not to draw it. His voice tight with wrath, he said, "Urlic—tell me where you found this sword."

But the noise and confusion had upset the old man; he hunched his shoulders against the furor and fell to whimpering. "I don't understand. I just wanted to be certain the moths hadn't gotten into the curtains. It suddenly came into my mind, you see. I couldn't remember if I'd put the herb bags in. I forget so much these days." He trailed off, nearly weeping now. Turning to Beren, the old man pleaded, "My lord Duke, *you* understand, don't you? I didn't mean no harm. Why are they fussing so?"

Beren made his way to the man's side. He patted his old servant's shoulder as the man snuffled and muttered to himself. "I don't understand what's going on here, Urlic, but of course you didn't mean any harm. You just did your duty, old fellow."

"Oh, gods; Kief, get that poor old man out of here and somewhere quiet. I can't stand to see him like that," Tarlna said. "Please."

Kief motioned to one of the guards that had entered with Urlic. The guard slipped a gentle hand beneath the old servant's elbow and eased him from the press. As he left the room, the old man moaned over and over, "I had to. Didn't mean no harm. But I had to. I had to look in there."

Linden shuddered as the door closed behind the weeping servant. "Since Urlic is incapable, Captain Tev, I'll ask you to tell us as much as you know."

"As you wish, Dragonlord." Tev licked his lips nervously and began. "I was making the rounds of the guard stations and had just entered the hall that a number of the royal apartments open onto when I saw old Urlic come out of a door. He was carrying your greatsword, Dragonlord."

Lord Duriac asked, "Which door, Captain?"

Tev looked down, at the walls, the ceiling, anywhere that he didn't have to meet someone's eyes. But he drew himself up and said quietly but clearly, "The door to His Grace Duke Beren's rooms, my lord."

Linden whipped around to face Beren. The duke's jaw hung open. That look of astonishment was all that kept Linden from grabbing Beren and hurling the man against a wall, it so surprised him in his turn. The other Cassorins backed away from Beren as though the captain had named him plague ridden.

Beren finally recovered his wits enough to gasp, "It's a damned lie!"

The stocky guard captain said, "I'm sorry, sir. Truly I'm

sorry. But that's how it was. Poor Urlic was all upset; kept babbling about the windowseat. Then he said he had to bring the Dragonlord's sword back to him, that it broke his heart that his master had, had . . ."

Had damn near killed me, Linden thought grimly.

Beren stood, shocked into muteness now, shaking his head.

"Beren," Duchess Alinya said. "Have you an explanation for this?"

"It's obvious, isn't it?" Lord Duriac asked. "He was afraid that the decision would go the other way and tried to delay things. Or perhaps you're one of the Fraternity of Blood, Beren. Were you seeking Linden Rathan's death?"

The furor doubled at Duriac's words.

"Be quiet! All of you—this instant!" Duchess Alinya cried. She looked up at the Duke of Silvermarch. "Beren, you have heard the accusations and what proof has been brought against you. It grieves me, but until we have the truth of this matter I must hold you accountable. Guards!"

They came reluctantly, but they came. One on each side, they took Beren's arms and led him to the door. As if the movement shattered the hold on his tongue, Beren yelled, "I had nothing to do with it! Nothing—do you hear? I've no idea how that damned sword got into my chambers or what possessed Urlic to look there! Ask Peridaen!"

Peridaen's panic blazed through the amulet. It was time to strike. Althume concentrated a moment longer, honing the sleek and lethal power of the spear within his mind, then hurled it at his target. The soultrap jewel glowed more brilliantly than ever, crystalline fire under his fingers, glowing like the morning star. Althume smiled, admiring it. So beautiful—and so deadly. A lovely thing indeed. And soon he would accomplish what even Ankarlyn had not been able to do.

He would destroy the link that bound a Dragonlord's two souls.

Sixty-three

Sweeping a finger along the line of the coast on one of the charts spread out on the table in her cabin, Maurynna was reviewing their coastal route to Pelnar when all hell broke loose in her mind.

First, surprise; then an anger so powerful that it almost knocked her to her knees. She clenched the edge of the table for support. The anger was fury now, white-hot and blinding, burning throughout her body. She dropped to the floor and curled into a ball, paralyzed by the onslaught.

She clenched every muscle, armoring herself against the rage. Otter's last words to her came into her mind; she strove to fight the anger down.

Maurynna's breath came in short, hard gasps. An image flowered unbidden in her mind: a small, white-haired woman, seen from behind. The woman turned to face her. To Maurynna's surprise (yet somehow she wasn't surprised; she knew what to expect. How?), the woman was young despite the white hair, with a thin, sharp face and piercing violet eyes—a warrior's eyes.

A greatsword lay cradled in her arms. The woman's gaze met Maurynna's for an instant. Then the white-haired woman looked past Maurynna to someone standing just behind her. Torchlight (*But it's still light outside!* Maurynna's mind wailed) glinted on a round silver cloak pin at her shoulder as she offered up the sword she carried.

The image vanished like a moth in a flame, leaving only the rage behind. With all her will Maurynna forced the fury back. It receded, bit by reluctant bit, until she was once more in control. She sat up, shaking, wondering.

Her mind was too bruised and battered to make sense of

what she'd seen—if indeed there was any sense to be made of it. She bethought herself of the bottle of herbed wine in her chest, kept there for emergencies; Remon always joked one sip would rouse a dead man. It might not do that, but it might shock her brain back on an even keel. But before she could reach the chest, horror and fear stabbed her heart. She cried out, "No! *No!*"

Then, unable to bear any more, Maurynna fainted.

Beren raged as the guards dragged him away. Many of his supporters surged to and fro like sheep terrified by a wolf's attack, babbling and bleating among themselves.

Clutching Tsan Rhilin as though he'd never let it out of his sight again, Linden followed Kief and Tarlna as they moved to the far end of the room, there to watch faces, see what they revealed, listen to what was said—and what wasn't.

One moment the three of them stood together. The next, Tarlna gasped and collapsed, striking the floor before Kief could catch her. Kief fell to his knees, fingers at his soultwin's throat, desperately seeking a pulse.

Shocked, Linden stood staring. Then fear devoured him. "Tarlna? Oh, gods—no! No! She can't be dead!" he cried, and dropped to his knees at the stricken Dragonlord's other side.

If the reappearance of Tsan Rhilin had caused pandemonium, this was pure chaos. "Get back!" Linden yelled as the members of the Cassorin council crowded around them. He brought the sheathed greatsword up crosswise and pushed none too gently against the nearest councilors. By the grace of the gods, for once they didn't argue but fell back, taking the others with them.

Linden said quietly but forcefully, "Do not crowd us again, or it will go ill with you. Someone send for Healer Tasha."

He mindspoke Kief. *What's wrong with her?*

I don't know! I can feel her fading as though something's sucking the life from her, Kief said. He frantically patted Tarlna's face in an attempt to rouse her. She didn't respond.

Linden said, *I've never heard of any illness like—*

I don't think she's ill. This has the same feel about it as when I examined you in that field. Kief gathered Tarlna in his arms and cradled her against his chest. Her blond curls shone against the black of his formal tunic. He pressed his cheek against her forehead.

Linden guessed Kief was using the bond between them to seek along the "trail" formed by the magical attack. Judging by the growing pallor of the elder Dragonlord's face, he was also lending the strength of his life force to his soultwin in an effort to keep her alive.

Knowing there was nothing he could do to aid Kief, Linden stood up. He placed himself between his fellow Dragonlords and the Cassorins and drew Tsan Rhilin. At least he could guard them—not that anyone was likely to try an attack with this many witnesses. But his mercenary's training demanded he do something.

I . . . can't . . . follow, Kief's agonized mindvoice said. *Not strong enough.*

Before Linden could reply, a voice like thunder in the mountains rolled through his mind.

I will aid thee, humansoul Kief.

Linden started in surprise. Only deeply ingrained training kept him from forgetting his self-appointed duty. That mindvoice could only belong to Shaeldar, Kief's draconic half. For a dragonsoul to rouse on its own was almost unheard of; that he, Linden, could hear it was even more so. He wondered if Shaeldar would retreat as Rathan had done.

Linden forced his attention back to the truehumans. They stared at the motionless struggle going on behind him. The room was so quiet Linden heard only Kief's harsh breathing.

The silence stretched on for what seemed an eternity but was in truth only moments. Then a came a tiny, mewling gasp: Tarlna. He chanced a quick look over his shoulder.

Her eyes were still closed and she looked terrible, but now her chest rose and fell in a steady if shallow rhythm.

Damn!

The mindvoice was pure Kief. Linden heaved a sigh of relief. *What happened?* he asked.

We—Shaeldar and I—were following along the thread of magic when it just ended. I think the mage felt us and ceased his or her attack. Shaeldar said that this magic is tainted with much blood and death.

Blood and death. The words touched an echo in his mind. But the errant notion fled as Healer Tasha ran into the council room.

Damn, damn, damn! Althume slammed a fist against the desk, ignoring the pain. He'd been so close! Damn the Dragonlord. He hadn't thought the man would risk rousing the dragonsoul. But the bastard had indeed, may he rot in the deepest hells.

Althume reined in his anger and examined the events of the past few minutes. The soultrap jewel glowed more brightly than ever, but it was still not charged enough for what he intended. He would have to take the risk of using the boy after all. At least he had sensed the hunters coursing the trail left by the magical attack before they could find him. That was to the good. He needn't worry about anyone coming after him. And Peridaen no doubt had his paltry regency after the faroe just played out in the council room—as if that mattered a single copper.

He replaced the soultrap jewel in its silk-lined box and shut it away. Althume rose to his feet.

"My lord—did it work?" Pol asked.

"No. Kief Shaeldar—*both* parts of Kief Shaeldar—interfered. We'll have to move fast. You know what to do. Then meet me in the woods. Oh—and Pol? The girl knows too much."

Sixty-four

Sherrine watched with approval as Tandavi brought out
the new dress and arrayed it upon the bed for her inspection.
It was a beautiful thing, a lovely shade of green, and of a
most unusual silk brocade patterned with fern leaves, so rich
that the dress needed no further ornamentation of embroidery.
She stroked the fabric and nodded. "This, with the gold-
colored silk undergown and my necklace and earrings of em-
eralds and gold. And we shall see what we shall see."

She was pleased with herself. Surely Linden had come to
his senses by now—else why had he allowed her to return?—
and maybe the dress would remind him of their first tryst.
Who knew what such memories might lead to. Sherrine
spared a moment to think of the sailor and wondered if the
bitch had sailed away yet.

What matter? *She* would be the one to be with Linden at
the castle tonight, not that trull. Sherrine smiled as she made
her plans.

A knock at her chamber door barely interrupted her
thoughts. She left Tandavi to deal with it. But scant moments
later the servant broke in on those same pleasant thoughts.

"My lady? There's a note come for you—and the messenger says he must have your reply right away."

Sherrine sighed with vexation and snatched the folded
parchment sheet from Tandavi's hand. Then her mood bright-
ened; perhaps it was from Linden! She broke the plain wax
seal eagerly.

It was not, she saw as she quickly read the contents, from
Linden. It was, however, from another she dared not ignore.
"May you rot in the deepest hells!" she whispered. Then,
louder, "Tell the messenger 'yes,' Tandavi, then set out one

of my riding habits for me. I won't be going to the palace until later.''

She read the note again. *Damn you, you bastard.*

Tarlna lay on a bed in the queen's chambers, blankets tucked around her and Kief hovering anxiously over Healer Tasha's shoulder. She looked frail, even pathetic—most unlike the Tarlna Linden knew—and her skin in the candlelight had a transparent look that he didn't like.

He stood well back from the bed, having placed himself without thinking between his fellow Dragonlords and the door. Tsan Rhilin rode in its accustomed place on his back. The feel of the well-worn baldric across his chest comforted him.

Duchess Alinya stood at his elbow. ''This is the work of the Fraternity,'' she said quietly.

''I agree. Kief said that this had the same feel about it as the attack on me,'' Linden replied.

''And no idea what their goal was,'' said Alinya. ''Dragonlord, forgive the curiosity of an old woman, but what of your soultwin?''

''Well out of this, thank the gods. She set sail today. And no matter how strong a mage the Fraternity has, there's no possibility that he can work a magic to harm her over that much running water—even if he knew about her.'' Linden sent up a private prayer of thanks.

''And she still is ignorant of her true self?''

''Yes—though I think she may be within weeks of First Change now. There were . . . occurrences that may hasten the advent of that. But with her far away from any other triggers, there should still be time before it happens,'' Linden said, and crossed his fingers where Alinya couldn't see. He hoped he'd have that time to find Maurynna before her First Change.

Maurynna staggered to the open window to be met with darkness. Night had fallen while she lay unconscious. She was so frenzied now she didn't care that what she planned was dangerous; she only knew what must come next.

Find Linden.

It was the only thought her mind could hold. Find Linden—it was imperative. It never occurred to her to wonder what help she, a truehuman, could offer a Dragonlord who had been a trained warrior even before he'd Changed. It didn't matter.

She had to find him, to get away from the ship, to get *outside*. She seized the carved molding above the window and swung herself up so that she sat on the sill, her legs dangling out of the window. A deep breath, a strong kick, and she was falling into darkness. It took forever.

Then she was in the water. It rushed up her nose; she sank down and down. At first the water was warm, but as she plunged into the depths it chilled her to the bone. She kicked, swimming desperately for the surface as her lungs cried out for air.

What if there are sharks? The thought came unbidden as she broke the surface at last. She banished it from her mind, gasping and treading water, refusing to think what might glide through the dark fathoms below her. Her lungs still burning, she struck out for shore.

Only the need to find Linden gave her the strength for the longest swim she'd ever attempted. It drove her on mercilessly when she would have slipped, exhausted, under the water. More than once a wave caught her and she breathed water instead of air. Hacking and coughing, the salt water burning her nose, mouth, and lungs, Maurynna would tread water for a moment before forcing her weary arms and legs to move again.

The moon came out from behind the clouds. All at once the water around her turned to silver; she swam along a path of light to the beach. In some recess of her mind she remembered once again the Yerrin legend she'd invoked the night she'd cast the coin into the well and Linden had appeared. Something about when Sister Moon let down her hair to wash it, it stretched from horizon to shore.

Yes, that was it. And Sister Moon had helped her once already. *Please help me now. A fine thing it would be to drown on my birthday!* a small voice at the back of her head complained.

The waves were stronger. Maurynna raised her head, hoping to see the shore, and missed a stroke. A wave caught her, tumbling her like a bit of seaweed. She panicked and thrashed in the water. One arm scraped against a myriad of tiny knives.

Barnacles, her mind said.

Maurynna twisted in the water and seized a rock before the wave could drag her out again. She clung to it like another barnacle, ignoring the cuts the thousands of tiny shellfish inflicted. Her long hair floated on the water around her.

She let the next wave lift her a little higher on the rock so that her head and shoulders were well above the water. Resting, gathering her courage, Maurynna studied her surroundings.

She could see the shore now: a narrow stretch of pebbled beach at the foot of a cliff. Before she could despair of finding a way up the cliff, her vision changed once more. For a moment the moonlit world was painfully sharp, as if she saw with the eyes of an eagle.

There was a path leading up the cliff. She refused to consider that it might be no more than a mad vision. Before her unnaturally sharp vision faded and she lost sight of the way, Maurynna flung herself from the rock. She swam arrowstraight for the foot of the trail.

A final wave tossed her onto the beach, grinding her against the stones until she pulled free of the water. Her chest heaving, Maurynna fell on her side. Every muscle she had—and quite a few she was certain weren't hers—ached.

Gods help me—a beating couldn't be worse than this.

Slowly—too slowly—her strength returned. But so did the unnatural sharpening of her senses. The sound of the surf pounded in her ears, threatening to shake her head apart. And the salty scent of the air was so strong she thought she would drown in it. She felt every pebble beneath her as an exquisite pain. It felt as if she had been half-flayed and then flung onto thorns. She squeezed her eyes shut; one more assault on her overwhelmed mind and she would cast herself back into the waves to end the torture.

One moment she was in torment; the next, it was as though nothing had been amiss. *I am* not *going mad! I am* not! she told herself fiercely. She opened her eyes again.

Somehow she got to her hands and knees. Once more the stones dug into her, but this time it was no more painful than it should have been. She welcomed it as a reassurance of her sanity. Gingerly she crawled to the bottom of the path and looked up.

The moonlight showed her the trail. It was cruelly steep for one so tired. Tears flowed down her face; she doubted she had the strength to make the climb, yet she had to try.

She had to find Linden. Something inside drove her on, beating at her mind with wings of flame. It tormented her with the need for haste. Groaning, Maurynna inched her way upright, leaning heavily against the wall of the cliff. At last she stood; her legs shook like a jellyfish flung too high on a beach—but she stood. Holding herself erect by will alone, Maurynna began the climb.

The path was narrow and rose at a steep angle, turning back and forth upon itself as it climbed. To climb it seemed harder than flying to the moon.

I'd have trouble with this when rested, she thought. She forced her legs to move. The rough path hurt her bare feet as she inched her way along.

One more step; just one more step. The chant formed in her mind as she climbed. *One more step.*

She lied to her trembling legs, tricking them into climbing higher and higher. Almost to the top . . .

Just. One. More.

She staggered and tripped. Instinctively she put out her hands to break her fall. The left slammed into rock; Maurynna welcomed the pain. The right met—air.

Her body tried to follow it into the well of darkness below. Maurynna screamed. Yet a strange paralysis kept her from trying to save herself. A moment before she would have fallen to her death, her sliding fingers found a knob in the stone.

The paralysis lifted; Maurynna seized the protrusion and threw all her remaining strength into anchoring herself. A moment later she scrabbled a way back onto the path.

She lay on her stomach, gasping. Ahead of her was one more switchback, then the last stretch—only a furlong or so—to the top.

And if she slipped again?

She was more frightened than she had ever been in her life. Even nearly falling from the rigging hadn't frightened her so badly. For at those times she'd never felt the urge to jump as she had just now. Behind her desperate struggle to stay on the path had been a fierce voice urging her to fling herself from the cliff.

Ah, gods have mercy upon me—I am going mad.

She wanted to weep. But she still had to get to the top—and to Linden. Since she feared that if she tripped again, this time she would give in to the wild voice in her head, Maurynna crawled the rest of the way. It was slower, but at least she'd get there alive. At last she pulled herself over the edge and stumbled away from the cliff as fast as she could.

Something huge loomed out of the darkness over her. She cried out and fell to her knees before it, throwing her hands out to protect herself.

Quirel ladled yet another dosing bottle full of what he and the other apprentices irreverently called "Tasha's aching head anodyne." He popped a cork in and shoved it home with practiced ease, then passed the bottle on to Jeralin, who packed it into a basket with its fellows.

"We're short of the half gross that Tasha wanted," Jeralin reported. "Three more will do it."

"Bother. I don't have any more bottles," Quirel said. He groomed the hairs of his straggly mustache. "Do you really think we're going to need so many this time? What with Tarlna Aurianne taken sick like that, I don't think there's going to be much celebrating tonight."

"Maybe not much celebrating, but I'll wager there will be a lot of people who'll get drunk just to forget. And even if

I'm wrong, do *you* want to be the one to tell Tasha we decided not to follow her orders?''

"Ah—no. Point well taken. Shall we see if we can find any other bottles?" Quirel said.

Jeralin pushed the basket aside and got up. "I wonder if she cleaned out that mystery potion yet." She began browsing the shelves behind Tasha's desk.

Quirel followed her. "What mystery potion? Don't try to tell me that Tasha can't identify one of her own brews."

"Where did she? . . . Here we are—under her desk." Jeralin straightened and set a basket triumphantly down on the desk. "This one. I found it behind a chest." She pulled the lid off to reveal a dosing bottle snuggled down inside one of the partitions in the basket. "Have a care for your dinner if you sniff it."

Her fellow apprentice examined the basket and snorted. "Very funny, Jer."

"What do you mean?"

Quirel fingered the shoulder strap. "See that knot where the lacing broke? I did that myself. This is the basket I used to carry Prince Rann's medicine every morning. I'd been wondering where it was. Behind a chest, you say? How did it get there? But let's see this mystery bottle." He plucked it from its pocket. "Oh, for pity's sake. This is Rann's tonic, the same that I make for him every day; I recognize the bottle—there are two of them with this streaky glaze. Stop trying to scare me, you wretched cow."

Jeralin said, "Quirel—whatever that is, it is most certainly not Rann's tonic. I think that Tasha had best know of this right away."

Sixty-five

Stone. Her outthrust hands touched stone. Maurynna ran her fingers down the cool granite, then sat back on her heels and pushed the hair back from her face, brushed tears from her eyes. The mad compulsion to find Linden was gone as suddenly as it had seized her.

Shaking with exhaustion, she found herself kneeling before a tall, pillarlike stone. For a moment she stared, uncomprehending, then memories from previous voyages along the coast of Cassori came to mind: a headland, jutting boldly into the sea, crowned with standing stones.

Could it be the same place?

Using the menhir to steady herself, Maurynna rose to her feet and began to explore. There were stones to either side of hers, more than the three that she was familiar with, which could be seen from a ship. The stones formed a circle with a trilithon in the center. It was the trilithon that drew her. Step by unsteady step she approached it, wary at first, then more quickly as she came closer.

At last she stood inside the trilithon. She tried to span the distance between the uprights, but she guessed her arms would need to be half again as long as they were. Overwhelmed with fatigue, Maurynna leaned against one upright; the next moment she slid down and curled up against it, her cheek pressed against the stone. Somehow she felt welcomed, cared for. She could even imagine that the stone sang to her.

She was safe here. Beyond wondering at the strangeness of it all, Maurynna closed her eyes and let whatever sang in the stone take her, hardly noticing when the golden voice in her head joined it.

*   *   *

It was some three candlemarks before Tasha's eyes flickered open. She looked dully around her.

"There's nothing more that I can do, Dragonlord," Healer Tasha said. She stood up to let Kief take her place at Tarlna's bedside.

Kief rubbed his forehead. His face was grey with exhaustion. "I understand, Healer. Thank you for your help."

Linden mindspoke him. *I've been thinking—what if there's another attack on Tarlna? Will Shaeldar be able to respond quickly enough?*

You knew about that? Kief asked, surprised.

I heard him quite clearly, thank you, Linden said dryly. *It was like standing with my head next to a war drum.* He was rewarded with a flash of weary amusement. *I was thinking that if there is—may the gods forbid—a second attack, you might be better able to fight it—*

—As a dragon. You may well be right; if nothing else, it will be easier to call upon Shaeldar if I need to do so. Aloud, Kief said, "Healer—would it hurt my soultwin to be outside this night? I wish to keep watch over her in my other form."

Tasha looked thoughtful. "No, Your Grace. The night is dry enough. It might even be cooler in the gardens and more comfortable for her. I'll have the soldiers make up a litter to carry her."

Kief nodded. "Well enough, then. I'll leave the arrangements to you. Just pick out an area large enough for me to Change."

Panic flared in the Healer's eyes. "Ah, Dragonlord—"

Linden took pity on her. "Healer Tasha—I'll go with you. I know how much room he'll need."

They went out together. Linden waited as the Healer gave the soldiers outside the door directions for the litter. Part of him felt that he neglected his duty; the other, more logical part, said anything that could get past this many soldiers and an enraged Dragonlord defending his soultwin would hardly notice one Linden Rathan in its path.

Still, uneasiness rode heavy upon his shoulders as he followed Tasha down the hall.

* * *

Balls of coldfire bobbed around the garden like giant fireflies. Linden watched as the soldiers carefully set the litter down. Kief and Tasha transferred Tarlna from it to the featherbed that had been brought outside.

Kief fussed over her a moment more. Then he walked away from the bed. Linden waved the soldiers and the few nobles to accompany them back and moved aside himself. He found himself next to Prince Peridaen who gave him a distracted nod.

Kief stood alone in the moonlight, perfectly still, his thin face stern and remote. Then his body dissolved into red mist. Someone behind Linden stifled a scream and more than one of the soldiers gave breath to something between a curse and a prayer.

A flicker of an eyelid later a brown dragon filled the lawn. Kief stretched his wings a moment before settling himself by Tarlna's side. He curled his long tail around her still form so that the tip touched her cheek. She wrapped her fingers around it.

"Comfortable?" Linden asked them.

Well enough, Kief replied. His head jerked up as someone approached the circle of soldiers; Linden heard the rumble of flames building in his chest. Tasha, on her way to her patient's side, evidently also heard it; she hesitated midway between the onlookers and Tarlna.

The rumbling subsided when the newcomers proved to be Tasha's two senior apprentices. They made straight for their master like arrows to the gold and began a hurried conference. Linden guessed the subject to be a basket that the worried-looking Quirel clutched in both hands.

Linden's eyebrows went up in surprise when Tasha let loose with a curse fit to scorch a salamander and grabbed the basket. She wrestled the lid off and flung it to the ground. Intrigued, he joined the others drawn to the curious spectacle.

"You're certain?" Tasha demanded of Quirel as he joined the semicircle. "You're completely certain?"

Kief stretched out his neck so that his head hung over the

group. *What is all this about?* Everyone was so intent on the bottle Tasha now held that they ignored the long fangs only a foot or so above their heads.

"Quirel says that this is one of the bottles he regularly uses for Prince Rann's tonic after he makes it each morning," Tasha said. "But what's—"

One of the nobles demanded, "You entrust an apprentice with Prince Rann's medicines? He's not even a Healer!"

Tasha treated the speaker to a withering glare before replying, "My lord, not everyone trained at the College of Healers' Gift heals by magic. There are, in fact, very, very few of us. Quirel is one of the finest Simplers—herbalist, you would say—to come out of Healers' Gift. Yes, I trust him to make Rann's medicines. He makes most of the healing potions used in the palace—including the one that cured your dropsy, Lord Nelenar."

She held up the bottle so that they could all see it. "But what's in here is not Rann's tonic. Neither of us made this, nor can we identify what's in it. And that scares me. Who *did* make it? Why did they? And what is it meant to do?"

Quirel said quietly, as if musing to himself, "Each morning I give Gevianna the bottle of medicine. She gives it to Rann when she gets him up, and later in the day I retrieve the bottle from her." He paused, licking his lips. "It's—it's always washed before I get it back. The only time that I can think of that it wasn't was the day of the picnic, Healer."

"No wonder Gevianna looked sick with fright," Tasha said grimly, "if she's the one switching potions. And I thought it was just because she's afraid of deep water."

A murmur went around the crowd.

"Whoever it is," Linden snarled, "damn him or her to Gifnu's deepest hells. They're poisoning the boy." He fought down the rage burning inside. To attack a child—any child, but especially one who looked to him . . . "I'm placing the boy under Dragonlord protection—*my* protection. Tev—get Rann and bring him here."

And bring this Gevianna here as well—under arrest, Kief said so that all heard.

The captain saluted smartly. "Dragonlords!" He hurried off, taking a few of the soldiers with him. Prince Peridaen went with them.

Those left behind waited. And waited. After a time the nobles exchanged surprised glances, then worried looks and whispers. Even Tarlna roused enough to notice something was wrong.

"This is taking far too long," she said, her voice weak and shaking.

"You're right," Linden said. "Rann's chambers aren't that far from here." He would give them a little more time.

That time, and more, passed. Just when Linden had decided to go look for Rann himself, Captain Tev and the soldiers returned.

Without Rann.

Otter fiddled aimlessly with the strings on his harp as he sat on his bed in the little sleeping chamber. He had a vague idea for a melody, but the tune would not make itself known beyond a few tantalizing notes. A knock at the door was a welcome diversion.

"Come in," he called.

Gavren the apprentice's head peered around the edge of the door. "Bard, there's someone to see you. He's, um, he's . . ."

Curious at Gavren's confusion, Otter asked, "What's his name, lad?"

"Eel, sir. He came looking for the captain, but when I told him she'd sailed, he asked for you."

Now Otter was intrigued. What did the little Cassorin thief want with him? "Send him up."

A few minutes later Otter heard the patter of quick, light feet on the stairs followed by the heavier tread of the apprentice. Gavren said, "In there," and the thief slipped into the room.

Eel pulled the cap from his head and stood twisting it, then burst into speech. "I don't like it, Bard! I tell you I don't like it at all! There's summat up and if it bodes well for your friend the Dragonlord, then I'm captain of the bleeding City Watch.''

Startled, Otter said, "The nine hells you say. Sit down, Eel, and tell me more.''

Maylin quietly closed the door to her sleeping chamber. She stood in her shift, back against the door, and considered what she'd overheard. Then she crossed the room and knelt by the bed. A moment's blind fumbling found her father's old sword in its hiding place. She pulled it out and tossed it onto her bed beside the gown she'd planned to wear for the guild's festivities. Maylin ran her fingers down the silk, biting her lip in regret, but her mind was made up. She pulled off her shift.

When she was ready, she went down the hall.

"Where's the boy?" Linden demanded.

The sturdy captain look half sick. "My lords—Prince Rann is not in his chambers, any of the chambers nearby, or the great hall. Nor can we find his nurse. It's as if they've . . . they've disappeared.''

Kief bellowed in everyone's mind, *Find the boy! Rouse everyone, search everywhere—I want Rann found. Go!*

Linden ordered most of the soldiers to go with Tev; only a handful stayed behind to guard Tarlna. Even the nobles joined the search; Tasha sent her two apprentices with them, electing to stay with her patient. Linden debated accompanying the searchers, but knew he'd be of little use. They knew the castle; he did not. But doing nothing was hard. He paced the garden, muscles knotting with tension, Tsan Rhilin a slightly comforting weight on his back, as the search took far too long.

One thing at least he could do. Beckoning two of the remaining guards, he said, "Bring Duke Beren here."

It didn't take long. Indeed, Beren arrived at a run, ahead of his escort. He halted before Linden, his face pale.

"What's this about Rann missing?" he said.

"The soldiers and others are searching for him," Linden

said. "Duke Beren, tell me what you know of his nurse, Gevianna."

Beren slammed a fist into the palm of his other hand. "I *knew* it. I knew she was up to no good. That's why I had Beryl—Your Grace, all I know about her is that she came from Lord Duriac's lands."

"And Duriac is Peridaen's supporter," Linden said heavily.

He neither needed nor appreciated the tickling at the back of his mind. Angry, he lashed out, *Damn it, Otter! What is it? I don't have time—*

You'll have time for this, boyo. I've a friend of Rynna's here who's been telling me some very interesting things, Otter shot back.

They had better be, Linden said grimly. *Someone damn near killed Tarlna and Rann's missing.*

Surprise, horror. *What? What happened?*

Linden quickly told the bard of everything that had come to pass since the council meeting. *So now I've got to wait here while other people look for the boy,* he said. *Otter—I have to know: Maurynna is out of this, isn't she?*

I stood on the dock and watched the ship until it was out of sight. She, at least, is safe.

Linden sighed in relief. *Thank the gods for that much. Things happen in threes, and to find out she's still in Cassori would have been the crowning touch. Now—who's this friend of Maurynna's and what has he to say? Wait; I want Kief and Tarlna to hear this.*

He touched his forehead with the two middle fingers of his right hand and looked at his fellow Dragonlords. Kief nodded; after a moment, so did Tarlna. Linden brought them into the link with Otter. *Go on,* he said.

Otter began. *Rynna's friend is named Eel. He's a Cassorin thief, knows the streets well. He tells me that for some time now prostitutes have been disappearing, never to be seen again. The other night Eel saw someone with a prostitute he knew—a boy named Nobbie—and the next morning Nobbie's panderer told Eel that the boy was missing. Eel saw that same man come out of an inn today and followed him. I think he suspected the fellow. Eel saw the man meet with another who looked to him like a noble's servant; Eel thought he saw a steward's chain of office. He didn't dare follow after that. Instead he went back to the inn. To make a long story short, there's a storeroom there that Eel contrived to investigate. Among other interesting things it contains a mage-spelled chest. Next to that he found a bit of dried herb. He's certain that it came from inside the chest.*

Otter paused; Linden felt him withdraw slightly. When the bard continued, his mindvoice was colored with embarrassment. *I did something very stupid; I crumbled a bit and tasted it. Knocked me flat on my ass for a good long while. Good thing both Eel and Maylin were here. I might have cracked my skull when I went down. But I'm fine now.*

Linden silently thanked the gods that Otter was well and refrained from snapping the bard's fool head off. He let Kief and, to a lesser degree, Tarlna do that as he withdrew slightly from the mindlink.

Why the hell were prostitutes disappearing—and why prostitutes, but not anyone else? A moment later he had the answer: because no one would miss them but their pimps. And no pimp would approach the City Watch with a tale of a missing bawd. If any group was safe to prey upon, it was the whores of Casna.

But why? A moment later he thought he had the answer. It made him sick. He reentered the mindlink. *Kief—Shaeldar said that he felt blood and death in this magic, yes?*

Yes.

Why? both Tarlna and Otter asked.

A memory rose up in Linden's mind. He felt unclean. *The altar. Remember I said it had been used for sacrifice? I think that—* What he'd felt that night almost overwhelmed him. *I think that's what happened to those missing whores.*

He said aloud, "Healer Tasha, what kind of herbs would Healers keep in a mage-spelled chest?"

The Healer looked surprised at the question but answered immediately. "We don't, my lord; we use locks on chests of medicines. Our form of magic doesn't work well with others, even simple locking spells. To my knowledge the only kinds of herbs kept like that would be those used in magery, especially dark magery."

"Such as?" Linden asked.

"Hm, the most notorious is—Oh, dear gods—that's what the smell is in that potion! It was so faint I couldn't recognize it at first, but it's the same as you sweated out, Dragonlord."

At first Linden didn't understand what she meant. Then he said, "What is used in a Cassorin farewell cup?"

"Honey for the sweet, my lord, wormwood or rue for the bitter, and ginger for the warmth of memory."

He closed his eyes, sickened. He knew the taste of those herbs; none had the metallic aftertaste he remembered. "What was in the cup that I drank that night?"

"*Keftih,*" Healer Tasha whispered. "I'm certain of it. It takes some time to work when it's mixed with something. If you know it's there and purge yourself of it quickly enough . . . I'm sorry, my lord."

"So, my good Healer," Linden said quietly, "am I." He turned his mind back to the others waiting for him. *Otter, ask Eel what the noble's servant looked like.* He waited while Otter spoke with the thief; he had a fair idea of what the answer would be.

He remembered Sherrine's tear-streaked face that night at the feast. To himself he thought, *And was it all, even from the beginning, a sham?* Anger at the betrayal would come later. Now there was only pain.

The description, when it came, confirmed his suspicions. Linden turned to the soldier nearest him. "You will seek Prince Peridaen and arrest him. Dragonlord's orders." He took a deep breath. "You will also arrest Lady Sherrine of Colrane."

He started across the garden. Kief asked, *Where are you going?*

Linden replied, *To find Kas Althume, Peridaen's so-called steward. He'll be at the altar—and so, I'm afraid, will Rann. I can't wait for the soldiers; it will take too long to gather them. Send them after me.* He broke into a run.

Sixty-six

"Dear gods!" Otter exclaimed. He tried to get to his feet, then his head started spinning again and he fell back onto the bed.

"Stay down or I'll sit on you!" Maylin said, fierce as a snow cat. "What happened?"

"Linden suspects Rann was kidnapped for sacrifice," Otter said; the thought made his stomach turn. "Something about an altar in the woods, and—"

Maylin was on her feet in a flash. "I knew it! I knew something would happen tonight!" She ran for the door, pausing only long enough to say, "Eel—don't you dare let him leave this room, do you understand? He's too ill. And Otter—Rynna is Linden Rathan's soultwin, isn't she?"

Otter considered lying. "Yes," he said, ignoring Eel's yelp of astonishment.

"I thought so," Maylin said, and disappeared from view.

Otter yelled after her, "Where are you going?"

"Where do you think?" he thought he heard her say, and then the front door slammed.

Shan's hooves skidded as they rounded a sharp corner, his shoes striking sparks from the cobblestones; a moment later the big stallion had regained his balance and was racing down the street. Late revelers scattered out of the way as Linden guided the stallion through the streets of Casna. He thanked the gods that he rode Shan now and not the pied gelding. The gelding hadn't a hope of getting to the altar in time to save Rann; Shan's Llysanyin strength and speed might be enough.

He swore. If only he could fly there, but the clearing wasn't large enough for him to maneuver on the ground as a dragon.

Nor could he remain airborne and use his flames—too much chance of catching Rann as well. He thought about Changing once there, but abandoned that thought when he realized the dark magic there would catch him at his most vulnerable and might well unmake him.

A pity Lleld wasn't here; the madcap little Dragonlord was small enough to fight within the clearing as a dragon. But she was far to the north; that left him as Rann's best hope. He prayed he'd get there in time.

They were nearly to the city gate. "Make way!" he bellowed at the stragglers blocking the passage. "Make way!"

Soldiers and celebrants alike fled or threw themselves aside before the thundering stallion. Linden ignored the cries behind him, hoping no one had been hurt.

At last they were outside of the city walls. No time for the road and the leisurely way he'd taken before; Linden hastily recalled what he knew of the area and set Shan to run cross-country. A wave of dizziness made his head spin, reminding Linden that he was still not completely recovered. It passed and he settled into the saddle to ride as he'd never ridden before.

"Is he awake yet?" Althume asked.

"Still groggy, my lord," said Pol. "He seems to have been hard hit by the sleeping draught. Is it necessary that he be fully alert?"

Althume paused a moment in his preparations. "Yes. The greater his terror, the more it will feed the jewel as he dies. And for this working we will need as much magical energy as possible. But we've time; our guest of honor has yet to arrive. And she's certainly taking her time." Once more he ran the honing stone along the blade he used for sacrifices. "Still, just a little more patience and the prize will be ours."

Captain Tev has just reported finding the nurse, Kief said. *She was hidden behind a bush in the garden. Her neck was broken. Prince Peridaen cannot be found.*

Linden considered that. *He left with the guards on their*

first search for Rann. If he rode hard he could reach the altar soon.

And you?

Another wave of dizziness. *Not too far behind him, I hope.* He shook his head; the dizzy spells were coming more frequently. But worse yet was the fatigue spreading through his muscles. Whatever Sherrine had given him still visited her revenge upon him.

Linden—are you well?

Worry about Tarlna, Kief, he said, clenching his jaw. *Not me.*

The boy was finally waking up. Althume leaned over him, smiling coldly. "Well met, young prince," he said to the frightened brown eyes that focused on him. "I'm glad to see you've decided to join us. Oh, no you don't—stay where you are, boy." He trilled a note on the bone whistle.

The *dragauth* approached the altar. Althume stepped aside so that nothing was between it and the terrified child cowering on the stone. The mage held up a hand; the *dragauth* halted. Its foul reek hung in the warm night.

Althume laughed quietly. "No, it isn't very pretty, is it, little prince? And you know what it is, don't you?"

Rann nodded. "A *dragauth*," he whispered.

"Clever boy. And it looks to me for orders." Althume grabbed the boy's face in one hand, forcing Rann to meet his eyes. "You will stay right where you are and obey my every order. Run and my pet will hunt you down and eat you. Disobey me and I will give you to him. Do you understand?"

Rann's white lips formed "Yes."

Pol said, "Someone's coming, my lord," and set off down the slope.

Althume took a moment to listen the snap and rustle of a horse breaking through the underbrush. "Back to the woods," he ordered the *dragauth*. "As for you," he said, shoving Rann flat onto the altar, "stay there and not a word out of you. Remember the *dragauth*." He flung a cloak over the boy's trembling form and went to meet his guest.

The horse broke through the last of the trees. Auburn hair glinted in the torchlight as the rider dismounted. Pol led the horse away.

"My dear Lady Sherrine," Althume said as she came up the hill. "You've no idea how happy I am to see you."

Maylin clung to the horse's back like a burr as it galloped across the grasslands. She wondered if this were a fool's errand; after all, she didn't know just where the altar was. Indeed, until this night, she'd been half inclined to consider it a legend.

Ah, well—if she was meant to find it, she would. The gods knew their business. Hers was to get to the woods opposite the standing stones as soon as possible.

"What is that?" Sherrine asked as they reached the flat crown of the hill, pointing to the cloak-covered form on the altar.

Althume said, "Nothing that concerns you."

To his annoyance the girl stopped. "Why did you tell me to come here? What do you plan to do?"

He cursed under his breath. His voice tight with suppressed fury, he said, "Just do as you're told."

"No. Linden nearly died of that potion—the potion *you* had me give him. You didn't tell me that might happen," said Sherrine.

"That was a mistake; he would have had an antidote if I hadn't been interrupted. Now go stand at the foot of the altar; after tonight you will have power as you've never dreamed of—and Linden Rathan will be yours for all time."

That caught her as he knew it would. Still, there was a rebellious light in her eyes and her gaze kept returning to the form on the altar.

"You want Linden, don't you? Some things must be bought with blood, Sherrine. This is one of them. Decide now." He waited. He was certain he knew what the outcome would be; if he was wrong Pol was between her and her horse. Willing or not, Lady Sherrine would play her part this night.

Her lips trembled. Then she held her head up a fraction higher and walked past him to take her place at the altar.

At last, the final wards were set. Only one last thing to make ready and the ceremony could begin. Althume nodded to Pol. At once the servant brought out the small chest that contained the soultrap jewel from the saddlebags by the base of the altar. He started to open it.

"No, Pol!" the mage said sharply. "It's too powerful now for you to handle; you're not magically shielded. Touch it and you'll destroy it and yourself. Give the chest to me."

Pol gingerly passed the chest to him. Althume opened it, reverently pulled back the silk covering inside. Light welled out of the chest to drip like falling water to the ground. Sherrine gasped as he raised the soultrap jewel in his hand and offered it the stars. Then he set it at the head of the trembling boy still hidden under the cloak. "Such a good boy to listen so well," he murmured, amused. Then, louder, "It is time."

He began the chant of invocation. He called upon the dark powers to witness, aid him, protect him. He promised them blood, blood with the taste of magic in it. The ancient words, in a tongue so old it was half forgotten even in Ankarlyn's time, rolled off his tongue with a rumble like an earthquake.

The power grew. Althume rejoiced deep inside; at long last he would see his dreams made real. The time of the Dragonlords was at an end.

Then a crashing in the woods made him pause; an exhausted horse collapsed into the clearing. Althume recognized Prince Peridaen as he leaped from the saddle.

"Rann! Rann!" Peridaen screamed as he ran up the slope.

Rann sat up. Althume tried to shove him down again, but the boy squirmed and the cloak fell aside, revealing him.

Sherrine turned and ran like a deer. Althume snapped out, "Pol!" as he held Rann against him. He cursed. The wards were meant to keep out malevolent spirits and turn aside casual intruders. They would likely fall before a determined invader. Still, they might slow Peridaen down just long enough. Althume raised the knife.

The wards didn't slow Peridaen down in the least. He charged through them with the fury of an enraged bull. And he was upon Althume before the mage could do anything. As they struggled for the knife, Peridaen yelled, "Get away, Rann!"

The younger prince jumped down and fled into the woods. Enraged, Althume slammed a fist into Peridaen's stomach. The man fell back across the altar, gasping.

Althume sprang upon him. "You'll do just as well, Peridaen!" He slashed the razor-sharp blade across Peridaen's throat.

Blood fountained up. Peridaen made a last gurgling sound, then the light faded from eyes filled with terror. Althume seized the soultrap jewel, bathing it in the blood of the sacrifice as he began chanting once more.

Pol dragged Sherrine before him and threw her down. The jewel glowed now like a tiny sun; Althume held it up and directed its light upon the girl sprawled on the ground, blinking groggily up at him. She screamed in agony as the light touched her.

Sixty-seven

Linden heard a scream as he guided Shan through the woods. He urged the tired stallion onward. "This way!"

They plunged headlong through the woods, balls of coldfire lighting their way through the thick underbrush. As he rode Linden drew together his last reserves of strength and prayed he'd be in time.

They burst into the clearing. Shan took the hill at a heavy gallop. But even the Llysanyin would not approach the altar. Shan came to a bucking stop as his front hooves touched the barren soil at the crown of the hill. Linden jumped down. Shan whirled and retreated.

The Dragonlord stopped in horror at the scene before him. Peridaen lay dead upon the altar; Sherrine crouched in pain on the ground nearby, bathed in the cold light from something that a chanting Althume held in his upraised hand. There was no sign of Rann. *Let that,* Linden thought, *be a good omen.*

Then Linden understood what Althume held and what had happened to Tarlna, and why the whores of Casna had died. But for what end?

"You're too late, Dragonlord," Althume said, laughing. "She's mine." The jewel pulsed; Sherrine cried out. "You can do nothing to save your soultwin."

For a moment Linden gaped in astonishment. In that instant a heavy weight fell on him from behind.

Danger!

Maurynna snapped out of her dream of singing stones with a scream. She scrambled upright, clinging to the pillar for support, and looked wildly around.

Nothing. There was no danger here. Just the night, the stars, the standing stones glowing in the light of the full moon.

Glowing? She rubbed her eyes. Even in this bright moon-light, the stones shouldn't be glowing. Yet glow they did, soft silver and gold, pulsing like a heartbeat. Then she realized that she saw past the granite exterior to *inside* the stones, to the magic that was their heart. The feeling of peace was gone; the song the stone circle sang to her now throbbed in her bones, a war chant to raise an army from the depths of the earth itself. The golden voice in her head trumpeted a paean of wild victory.

I don't care what Otter said—I am *going mad!*

Maurynna ran. She didn't know where she ran to, nor did she care. She had to get away—from the stone circle that suddenly closed in on her, from its mysteries, from herself.

It was only after her panic-given strength had faded that Maurynna realized that she was being called. She stopped, panting, feet planted wide to keep from collapsing, and looked back over her shoulder. She could still see the standing stones; their glow was fainter now but still visible. In the distance before her she could make out a darker line on the horizon: trees. It was the forest—or something within it—that called her. The summons was honey-sweet, seductive—and set her skin crawling. It wanted nothing less than her soul. She fought it.

And realized that she was losing when, unbidden, her feet stumbled of their own accord toward the dark woods. "No! Help me!" she begged the standing stones.

Their light flared brighter, but with it came another surge of power from the forest. The two powers fought over her, tugging her to and fro like a bit of sea wrack upon the waves. The forest was winning; Maurynna felt its dark fingers claw-ing into her soul. In desperation she turned to the voice within her, the voice that terrified her more than anything else. *Come,* she said to it. *Come to me.*

And instantly regretted it. She might have been able to fight whatever was in the woods. But now she was dissolving in pain, unable to scream, to fight back, to do *anything*, while the voice inside her roared in triumph.

* * *

Rann fled through the woods, running as fast as he could. Behind him the *dragauth* crashed through the underbrush. Rann found he had an advantage; he could slip between or under bushes and branches that the *dragauth* had to fight a way past. Frightened as he was, Rann remembered his mother telling him, *Never give up.*

He found a thicket of brambles and dropped to his stomach, squirming along the ground. He had no idea where he was going; he'd think about that later when he'd gotten away.

If he got away.

A little later he was out the other side. He risked stopping to listen. From the sound it appeared the *dragauth* was having trouble wading through the thorny tangle. Good; every moment helped. He dove into another patch of bushes.

He was clambering down a bank when something grabbed his belt. Rann yelped and bit the hand that instantly clamped over his mouth.

"Stop that!" a voice ordered as he was drawn into a hollow in the bank.

He struggled, then recognition filtered through his terror-fogged brain. "Maylin?" He clutched her. "There's a *dragauth* hunting me," he whispered. "We have to run!" He struggled to rise.

Maylin stopped him. "The woods end not far from here. We'd have no chance in the open." She drew the sword at her waist.

They held hands as the slow trampling of bushes drew closer. Rann prayed as he'd never prayed before.

A shrill whistle pierced the night. Silence; then to Rann's almost hysterical relief the crashing footsteps receded. When they had faded away, he tugged Maylin's sleeve. "We've got to get out of here," he said, "and tell Linden what's happening. He'll make it better."

"He already knows. But let's get you back to Casna, Your Highness. My horse is tied at the edge of the woods."

When they found it a few minutes later, Rann protested at

being lifted into the saddle. "But what about you? You can't walk all that way."

"I'll do what I must, my lord." She patted the horse's neck.

They had barely left the shelter of the trees when something winged past overhead, blotting out the moon and the stars for an instant.

Rann stared after it. "That was a dragon, wasn't it?"

"Yes," Maylin said. "But which one?"

Linden rolled, striking out, but his illness had taken a heavy toll; he was too slow. His attacker jumped out of the way. Then a boot crashed into his head and Linden went sprawling.

Althume blew upon a whistle.

But Linden was ready the second time. When his attacker tried the same trick, he caught the man's foot and heaved, sending the man flying. Linden staggered to his feet, blood running down his face. He drew Tsan Rhilin.

The man was up and charging. *Harn? No, but kin.* Linden brought the greatsword up, then hesitated. His attacker was unarmed. Cursing, Linden waited until the man was almost upon him, then sprang aside, reversing the greatsword. He brought the pommel down on the back of the man's head. The man dropped like a downed ox.

Then Linden was free to deal with Althume. He approached the mage cautiously, Tsan Rhilin held out before him.

"Put your cold iron away, Dragonlord," said the mage. "You know that its presence can send a working awry—and that would be a very dangerous thing. Do you truly want to destroy all of us?"

Linden clenched his jaw. Damn the mage; he was right. Linden stabbed Tsan Rhilin into the earth and stepped away from it.

"A pity you had to be here for this, Dragonlord. For I'll have to kill you so that I can keep control of your soultwin once I've forced her into First Change."

So that was the game. Linden said, "You're wrong. Sherrine's not my soultwin."

The mage's thin nostrils flared. "I don't believe you." He resumed his attack upon Sherrine.

Gods help him; he didn't dare attack the mage outright. There was only one thing Linden could do to save Sherrine—and it might mean his death. He reached out with the magic within himself and drew away the magical energy that Althume poured into Sherrine from the soultrap jewel.

It burned through him. What he'd gone through before was nothing compared to this. Still he kept on. It was Sherrine's only hope.

But the dark magic within the jewel frayed the joining of his souls. "Althume—stop! Sherrine is not the fledgling!"

"It won't work, you know. You'll just save me the trouble of killing you later."

Linden believed him. The pain was incredible; it forced him to his knees. But he continued deflecting the searing energy away from Sherrine, taking it into himself.

"The sailor," Sherrine rasped. "It's the sailor, isn't it?"

"Yes," Linden whispered. "Sherrine—run; I won't last much longer."

She got slowly to her feet. Her eyes met his. "Good-bye, Linden," she said—and flung herself upon Althume.

Her clawing fingers closed upon the soultrap jewel. It flared; the mage threw himself away from it. For a moment Sherrine held the jewel before her. Then it exploded and Sherrine burned in a magical fire, screaming as it consumed her, melting flesh from bone. Moments later there was only a soft scattering of ash that fell gently to the earth.

"Oh gods, no," Linden said, unable to believe what he had seen. Tears slid down his face. He tried to stand, but his legs wouldn't support him.

The mage had no such difficulty. "Damn you," he said as he stood up, his eyes and voice filled with hate. He beckoned to something behind Linden. "Now you die."

Linden smelled the stench of rotting meat. At once the centuries fell away as the old terror swallowed him. "Satha?" He slewed around as best he could on his knees.

It was not the undead Harper. He wished it was. Instead,

nightmare incarnate stalked him. And he was too far away from Tsan Rhilin to reach it before the thing was upon him—even if he had had the strength to wield the greatsword.

He hoped Maurynna would survive his death.

Sixty-eight

The dragauth *snarled. It stretched* itself to its full height, towering high over him. Somehow Linden got to his feet and backed away. Step by step the *dragauth* closed the distance between them.

"Kill him," the mage said.

The *dragauth* roared and charged. Linden turned and tried to run; his legs gave out. He fell just short of the beginning of the slope.

A shriek of rage tore the sky above him. Linden rolled onto his side and looked up.

A dragon, almost as large as the one he himself Changed into, hovered over the clearing, its wings beating furiously to hold it in place. It screamed again, its fury-filled gaze locked on the *dragauth*. The mouth opened; long fangs gleamed in the moonlight. Linden heard the telltale rumbling and threw himself to tumble down the slope away from the one form of fire that could harm him.

Scarlet flames poured forth, spread across the earth. The *dragauth* burned with a sickening stench of cooked meat. The dragon landed on the scorched crown of the hill. One foot touched the altar; the dragon screamed again, this time in pain. It whirled and struck the altar a tremendous blow, sending the top stone flying. The stone shattered when it slammed into the earth dozens of feet away.

But the touch of the altar sent the unknown dragon into a frenzy. Linden crawled up the slope once more as the dragon spun again. He saw Althume, badly burned, attempt to flee. The dragon's front foot slashed through the air and pinned the mage to the ground.

Scales glittered blue and green in the moonlight, iridescent as a dragonfly, something Linden had never heard of before. It was no dragon he'd ever seen.

Blue and—"Dear gods—it can't be! Maurynna!" he cried. "No—don't!"

The dragon's head whipped around. *I am Kyrissaean,* she proclaimed. *This one is evil; he has killed many times. I feel it in him.*

"You are also Maurynna and my soultwin," Linden said.

The dragon—*I must think of her as Maurynna,* Linden told himself—hesitated at his words. Her head tilted in a way that made him think of Maurynna. He thought she would let the mage go. But then Althume sealed his own fate.

Linden saw the mage's hand go up; something glittered in his clenched fist. Before he could shout a warning, the hand came down and the sacrificial blade bit deep into the tender skin between Maurynna's toes.

Maurynna disappeared beneath Kyrissaean's wrath. The forefoot clenched; claws pierced the mage's chest like a handful of swords. Kyrissaean flung the torn and bloodied corpse away and leaped into the sky, bellowing her rage and pain.

"Maurynna, come back—you don't understand the danger!" Linden yelled after her but in vain. The dragon was winging out of sight. He tried to reach her mind, but she had shut it against him. He had only one hope if he couldn't reach Maurynna in time. *Kief!*

The frantic mindcall rocked Kief back onto his haunches. The fear in it sent his head snapping up in an instinctive search for danger. He looked down at his soultwin.

She nodded. *You know what to do.*

Tsan Rhilin in hand, Linden slipped and slid down the slope. He had to get to a larger open space. "Shan! Shan!"

The big stallion slunk out of the trees, looking everywhere at once. Linden shoved the greatsword into its sheath and somehow forced his exhausted body into the saddle. "She's gone, you coward. Did you think that she was going to eat you?" he said as they headed into the woods.

Shan nodded and broke into a run, dodging around the trees. Linden cast his pride to the winds and grabbed the high pommel of the saddle, content with staying on Shan's back any way he could.

After far too long for Linden's peace of mind they reached the grassland. In the distance he could see two people and a horse. One person led the horse; the other perched on the saddle. He didn't care who they were as long as they didn't interfere.

He brought Shan to a sliding halt and tumbled from the saddle. "Get back," he ordered. When the stallion had moved to a safe distance, Linden initiated Change—and prayed.

Thank the gods, it was beginning. Linden felt his body begin to flow, then—nothing. He was as solid as ever. *This can't be happening; I* must *reach Maurynna before it's too late.* As if the gods teased him, Maurynna winged back into sight, circling as though she was drawn to his vicinity. But she didn't land.

To Change when he was so exhausted was dangerous; this was his magic's way of telling him to stop. He'd just have to take his chances. He tried again.

This time when it ended he found himself flat on his back, shaking. A face appeared in his circle of vision.

"It *is* you," Maylin said.

Rann also appeared. "Linden—what's wrong?"

Linden blinked, unable to believe his eyes at first. How on earth did—? It didn't matter. He had to get up, get to Maurynna. She wasn't strong enough to fly for so long. She had to land soon—or die. He struggled to sit up.

As if in response to his agitation, Kyrissaean trumpeted in alarm. To Linden's astonishment it was answered from even higher in the sky. Another, smaller, dragon arrowed out of the sky, diving for Kyrissaean. She screamed in anger and lashed out at the intruder. But the second dragon would not be turned away; from Linden's viewpoint it looked as if the smaller dragon landed on her back and was forcing her to spiral lower and lower.

Kief's mindvoice thundered in his head. *You will retreat, Kyrissaean, and await your proper time.*

Kyrissaean snarled, but there was an edge of exhaustion in it now. She was too tired to fight back.

"Dear gods," Linden whispered. "Let her land before it's too late." He could see where Kief was herding her. Maylin and Rann helped him to stand. Shan came forward; he hung on the stallion's saddle and as quickly as Linden could move, the four of them hurried to the site.

He nearly panicked when he lost sight of Kyrissaean and Kief, then realized they were in a hollow. When at last he stood upon the lip of the shallow depression, he forgot how tired he was.

Maurynna—Maurynna, not Kyrissaean—knelt in the bottom of the bowl-shaped hollow. Kief, still in dragon-form, lay curled in a half-circle around her. Linden ran down the gentle slope.

Maurynna looked up at him, one hand pushing the long black hair back from her face in a gesture he knew well. He caught her to him, holding her tightly, afraid to let her go. "Welcome, little one. It is so good to have you here at last."

Maurynna said, "Is it true, Linden?"

He touched her face, smiling. "It is indeed, little one. It is indeed."

She buried her face against his shoulder, laughing and crying at the same time.

Sixty-nine

Linden and Maurynna stood together before the fireplace in his sleeping chamber in the city house, a single ball of coldfire dancing in the air above them. All the other players in this night's drama were still at the palace; he'd pleaded fatigue—his own and Maurynna's—and left the others to untangle the last threads in the plot; a plea met with too many too innocent looks, and a barely concealed smirk from Otter, blast him. He'd get the bard back one day. But not tonight . . . He rubbed his cheek against Maurynna's hair.

Together at last.

The words sang through him again and again as he held her close. She, in turn, held him as tightly as if she intended to never let him go again.

Gods, but he'd never known such happiness. He smiled, wishing the moment could go on forever.

She said, "I'm dreaming, aren't I?" Wonder filled her voice.

He chuckled. "No, thank the gods. This is very real."

She ran a hand down his back. "Don't believe you."

"Shall we see if this convinces you?" he teased, and tilted her face up to meet his.

He kissed her, a long and lingering kiss that left them both breathless when it finally ended.

"Well?" he asked, smiling down at her.

She looked thoughtful a moment. Then, grinning mischievously, she said, "Perhaps just a little more . . . convincing?"

He laughed aloud and set about the pleasant task with a will.

Seventy

It was quite the gathering in one of the palace gardens. Rann and Kella romped with Bramble the wolfhound. Otter played his harp. Eel sat near him, resplendent in a new jerkin and cap, nodding his head in time to the music. The older Dragonlords and Duchess Alinya talked in the shade of the pavilion; Tarlna looked healthier already. Maylin, Quirel, and Jeralin sampled the various delicacies on the laden tables. Elenna and Tasha were discussing, of all things, methods of distillation. Linden supposed it was something common to perfumery and herbalism, but he was too lazy to really care. Instead he pulled Maurynna a little closer, so that her head rested on his shoulder for a moment. She smiled up at him.

He half-closed his eyes, wondering, if he tried hard enough, if he would see an auburn-haired shadow by the edge of the garden. Despite her part in the plot that had brought them all to the edge of disaster, they owed this happy ending to Sherrine. *I hope you find your own happiness in the afterlife,* he thought sadly. *You deserve it. Fare thee well, Sherrine.*

Maurynna turned her head and smiled up at him. "I still don't believe this," she said.

"I'm very happy to," he replied.

"Wait until I drive you mad. I'm very stubborn, you know," she warned.

"So am I. I foresee some interesting centuries ahead of us." He kissed her; her head went back down on his shoulder as she laughed quietly.

After a time she asked, "When do we go to Dragons-keep?"

"As soon as we have word that your crew knows you're safe. They can tell your Thalnian family the tidings. Beren sent a fast ship out this morning to overtake them, so stop fretting, love; your crew won't have long to worry.''

"Remon must be worried sick," Maurynna said. "I feel awful about that.''

"We'll make it up to him and the others somehow. Ah— there's Beren. I'd been wondering where he was.'' Linden waved to the new regent of Cassori as the man entered the garden, his newly betrothed lady on his arm. Now that the stress of the council meetings were over, both Beryl and Beren had changed tremendously; Linden found that he liked them both. Beren made for them as if the wave had been a summons, pulling Beryl along with him.

He greeted them with a slight bow as Beryl made a courtesy. "Dragonlords.''

Linden felt Maurynna shift under his arm; she was not yet at ease with her new rank. It *was* a hard thing to get used to. "Duke Beren, my lady Beryl," he said, nodding in return. "Will you sit with us?" he asked, secretly hoping they would decline.

"Thank you, but—may I speak with you a moment, Linden Rathan? Alone? My apologies, Maurynna Kyrissaean.''

Linden frowned. There was something in Beren's tone. . . . "Wait here, love. I won't be long.''

Beryl took his place on the bench; she and Maurynna began talking.

Beren led him to an empty section of the garden, well away from the gathering. "Your Grace," the duke began, "I've a double confession to make.''

Oh, gods—what was the man about to stir up? "Indeed, my lord?''

"Beryl admitted to me that it was she who hid the warrant, Dragonlord. She only thought to spare me shame when you found out; we feared you would be able to tell . . .''

"Tell what?" Linden asked.

Beren's face turned as red as his hair. "The warrant of regency, my lord. It is a forgery.''

Whatever Linden had expected, it wasn't this. "But you swore—''

"That I didn't forge it. I am not forsworn, my lord. I didn't; my brother Dax did."

"The prince consort," Linden said, bewildered at the turn of events. "Why?"

"Dax never trusted Peridaen and his influence over Desia. She was a good queen, but too softhearted about her younger brother. Dax had some kind of evidence proving that Peridaen had dabbled in dark magery; I don't know what it was. But I believe he spoke the truth about it. So when Dax told me what he'd done, I kept my mouth shut. I didn't believe Peridaen would really do anything, but I didn't want to get my twin into trouble." Beren shrugged. "I still don't know whether everything that happened was due to Peridaen and his mage, or if some was just coincidence. I don't think we'll ever know the whole truth.

"We're tracking down as many members of the Fraternity as we can, Dragonlord. I don't know if Alinya told you: Anstella has been exiled for life after confessing as much as she knew—or said that she knew. Neither Alinya nor I have the heart to put her to torture, Your Grace; we felt she'd been punished enough, losing lover and daughter like that. You'd understand if you saw the emptiness in her eyes."

The duke faced him squarely. "Now that you know the truth, my lord, what do you intend to do?"

Linden said, "Nothing. One of Rann's parents considered you the best choice for regent and I happen to agree. Besides, who else is there but Alinya? And I am not," he added with some heat, "sticking my hand into *that* hornets' nest again."

Beren laughed. "Dragonlord, I can't fault you for that. And may I say, I'm glad you've found your soultwin at last."

Linden looked back to where Maurynna now laughed with Beryl. As if she felt his gaze upon her, she smiled at him, a smile full of happiness.

He smiled in return. "Thank you, Beren," he said, his eyes still on his soultwin. Smile turned into wide grin. *I wonder if she really is as stubborn as I am?*

Here's a special sneak preview
of Joanne Bertin's next novel,
the sequel to *The Last Dragonlord*...

Dragon and Phoenix

Prologue

The old dragon stirred as something blazed like a shooting star through his dreams.

Something new. Something . . . unbelievable.

He drifted toward waking. In all his long life he had never known such a thing and he trembled with joy. The waters of the deep lake above him rippled, echoing his movement.

Then, like a morning mist, it was gone, hidden once more from him.

He sank back into sleep, to dream the centuries away.

Chapter One

Year of the Phoenix 1008
The Harem of the Imperial Palace
Jehanglan

Lura-Sharal was dead.

Shei-Luin bowed her head as her sister's body was carried away for burning, borne away upon a litter of ebony by four burly eunuchs. A cloth of the imperial gold silk covered the girl's slight form. What did it matter?

Lura-Sharal was dead.

Shei-Luin knew she should be proud of that mark of the Emperor's favor. But all she wanted was her elder sister back. What would she do without the wise and gentle words of Lura-Sharal guiding her?

She watched as the litter disappeared through the door. Tears streamed down her cheeks; she wanted to run screaming after it, to hurl herself upon her sister and beg Lura-Sharal to tell her it was but a jest, to hold her, to sing and dance with her once more. To run away and ride the wide open plains again as Zharmatians with Yesuin, their childhood friend.

Ah, Phoenix, if they could all be free once more . . .

But now Yesuin was a hostage to the uneasy peace between his father's tribe and the Jehangli.

And Lura-Sharal was dead.

A hand came down with jarring force upon Shei-Luin's shoulder. She jumped, and looked up to find Lady Gei's masklike face hovering over her.

"Come," the lady said. Her voice held no sympathy. "Come; the Phoenix Lord has seen you and grants you the favor of his company. For you are also of the seed of Lord Kirano; it is time to do your duty, girl. At thirteen you are old enough.''

''But I am n—'' Shei-Luin broke off. To speak the truth would be to close the path she suddenly saw open before her. Shei-Luin turned her head to hide her slip of the tongue.

The fingers on her shoulder tightened like bands of steel. Empty inside, Shei-Luin went where they led. Eyes filled with jealous hate followed her as she went deeper into the perfumed sanctum of the harem to be made ready.

And afterward . . .

She bowed her head. But only for an instant; she would not shrink from her fate or from Xiane ma Jhi, Phoenix Lord of the Skies. For she knew a thing that no one else alive now remembered.

She stared straight ahead, her eyes dry now.

Chapter Two

Dragonlords—those who are both human *and dragon. They come to Jehanglan. They will bring war to the Phoenix.*

So said the rogue Oracle. And the words of an Oracle were truth.

But now his Oracle was dead. She would never See for him again.

Lord Jhanun pondered the prophecy once again. Had he known the girl had a weak heart, he would not have ordered her given such a large dose of the forbidden drugs. But her words had been so tantalizing . . .

His fingers smoothed the piece of red paper on the desk, discovering its texture, gauging its precise weight. Each piece of *sh'jin* paper was subtly different. A true disciple revered such individuality.

He made the first fold. "This is a true thing, these—" he hesitated over the uncouth foreign word—"Dragonlords?" He glanced at the man who knelt a few paces before the desk.

"It is, lord. There are a certain few, far to the north, who are born with the joined souls of dragon and human," Baisha said.

Fold, crease, fold. "And these weredragons—they are able to change forms as do the weretigers that haunt the mountains?" Jhanun asked.

"Yes, lord. But they may change form whenever they wish, not just at the full moon."

Jhanun ran one end of his long mustache through his fingers and shuddered. Abomination! He must calm himself, else the paper would sense his disturbance. Fold, fold, a quarter turn of the sheet . . . "The creature now beneath the mountain—it is not one of these . . . ?"

"No, lord; it is a northern dragon, else it would have Changed and escaped as a human."

"I see," Jhanun said, thinking.

One alone—the Hidden One—means the end of the Phoenix. But four will give you the throne—

A pity the girl died with those words; more would have been useful. How was one more dangerous than four? he wondered. He would get no more; he must gamble with what he had. The crisp red paper hummed as he slid a thumbnail along a crease.

Jhanun said, "The Phoenix must live. You will lure these unnatural creatures to the sacred realm. You know the prophecy; you know what must be done and the best way to do it."

After all, according to the prophecy, the vile creatures were coming no matter what. He would merely make certain that it would happen in the most advantageous manner—for him.

Turn, fold, crease, fold.

Baisha smiled to the precise degree allowed a favored servant to master. The hands resting on his thighs suddenly turned palm-up. They were empty. Then he pressed them together and brought them up to touch fingertips to forehead. Then he laid them palm-up in his lap once more.

This time a silver coin lay in one hand.

The Jehangli lord nodded in understanding; the creatures would be tricked. "You're certain they will come?" asked Jhanun.

"Yes," Baisha replied. "They will come, the noble fools."

"So be it." He studied this, one of his three most faithful and trusted servants.

Pale skin, yellowed now, wrinkled and lined; a bald head fringed with thin white hair bleached by the powerful phoenix of the sun. A *baisha,* a foreigner indeed.

The Jehangli lord went on, "I raised you from slavery. I covered you with the hem of my robe though you were not one of the children of the Phoenix. I gave you what your own people denied you.

"Now I give you this task. The journey will be long and hard, the task difficult. Do not fail me." A final fold, a last crease, and a paper lotus of a certain style lay before Jhanun.

"It will be done, lord. I will bring you the required number of Dragonlords." Baisha rose and bowed. His eyes burned with fervor. "I know what will bring them. I won't fail you."

Stirred by such devotion, Jhanun rose from his desk and came around it. Bending slightly, he rested his fingertips on his servant's shoulders, a mark of great favor. "I know you will not fail. Now go; there's much to be done." He let his hands drop once more to his sides.

Baisha bowed once more, backed the three required steps, then turned and strode to the door.

With a satisfied smile, Jhanun folded his hands into his wide sleeves.

It was beginning.

Shei-Luin fanned herself as she watched the tumblers with their trained dogs and monkeys performing in the open space between the two gazebos. She sat by the railing of the Lotus Gazebo in the choicest spot as befitted her current status as favorite concubine. Her eunuch Murohshei stood at her left shoulder, keeping the lesser women from crowding her.

The Lotus Gazebo and its companion, the Gazebo of the Three Golden Irises, stood in the heart of the Garden of Eternal Spring. Winter never came here; the leaves of the plum and peach trees never withered with the cold, the bright green of the grass never turned sere and brown. The might of the Phoenix ruled here, a gift to its royal favorite, the Phoenix Lord of the Skies. Or so said the priests who chanted here at the solstices.

To one side sat the Songbirds of the Garden. A group of boys and young eunuchs chosen for the incredible purity and beauty of their voices, their sole purpose was to sing for the emperor whenever he chose to visit the Garden. They were silent now, except for giggles as they watched the performers. They were, after all, just boys.

Shei-Luin hid a smile behind her fan as she glanced at the youngsters. Many rocked back and forth, holding their laughter in lest it disturb his august majesty in the Gazebo of the Three Golden Irises. One boy eunuch, Zyuzin, the jewel of the Garden, had both hands clapped over his mouth as he doubled over in mirth; his three-stringed *zhansjen* lay forgotten on the grass before him as he watched.

For one of the tumblers ran in circles, waving his arms and crying exaggerated pleas for mercy as a lop-eared, ugly, spotted dog chased him. Each time the dog jumped up and nipped at the man's bottom, the man would grab his buttocks and leap into the air, squealing like a pig with a pinched tail.

The Songbirds giggled and pinched each other in delight.

A loud, braying laugh shattered the air. Shei-Luin winced delicately, careful that no one should see it, and looked into the opposite gazebo.

Xiane ma Jhi hung over the railing, laughing as the ugly dog persecuted its master. He called encouragement to it, slapping the shoulder of the man standing by his side and pointing at the tumblers. The man grinned and said something in return.

Shei-Luin's heart jumped at the sight of the second man. Yesuin, second son of the *temur* of the Zharmatians, the People of the Horse, the Tribe. Yesuin, once her childhood love and now hostage to his father's good behavior. How she'd cried when he first came to the palace, knowing what it meant to him to lose the freedom of the plains. She'd remembered all too well what she'd felt when the walls of the imperial palace closed around her. But his misfortune had become her salvation.

Between the Phoenix Emperor and Yesuin was a certain resemblance; the concubine who had borne Xiane had been a woman of the Tribe.

Yet such a difference! Yesuin was all fire and grace; Xiane . . . *Bah; Xiane does not bear thinking about,* Shei-Luin told herself. *He looks like a horse and brays like an ass.*

As if he sensed her thoughts on him, Xiane looked across the lawn into the gilded structure where Shei-Luin sat with the other concubines and their eunuchs, the only males allowed there beside the emperor himself. Their eyes met. He made a great show of licking his lips and leering at her. Shei-Luin's stomach turned; she knew that look. Unless he drank himself into oblivion, he would come to her chamber tonight.

She pretended modest confusion and hid behind her fan, gaze lowered. Later she would send Murohshei to bribe Xiane's cupbearer into seeing that the Phoenix Lord's wine bowl was kept full.

The other concubines tittered. Shei-Luin considered ordering them all flogged. But no; she had not the power for that yet. She must become *noh,* a servitor of the first rank; she must give Xiane an heir.

An heir that he could not give himself. But she had found a way; for she alone knew the ancient secret of the palace. And then . . .

The scene before her changed. The tumblers and their animals gave way before the female wrestlers that were Xiane's current mania. Shei-Luin sat up straighter.

Not because she enjoyed the wrestling. Far from it. She thought these women hideous beyond belief. They were as ugly as the women soldiers who guarded the harem; big women, solid as oxen, and muscled like them, too.

But this was the fourth troop of wrestlers in the past span and a half of days, and if Xiane remained true to form . . . She watched the women, naked save for loin cloths and breast bands, grapple and struggle with one another, and waited as patiently as she could.

At last! Xiane stood up. A servant ran to take the robe he shrugged from his shoulders. The loose breeches beneath came off next and the Emperor of Jehanglan stood only in his loincloth. He vaulted over the railing, calling over his shoulder, "Let's have some fun!"

Laughing, the other young men in the gazebo followed suit. For once they were freed of the restrictions of the imperial court where every move was ancient ritual, every word and glance noted, debated, dissected for insult or weakness.

Only in this garden and among the troupes of entertainers that he delighted in, could the Emperor of Jehanglan, Phoenix Lord of the Skies and Ruler of the Four Quarters of the Earth, relax. Shei-Luin felt a momentary pang of sympathy. The Phoenix was cruel, setting this man upon the Phoenix throne instead of making him a performer.

But that moment was lost as she watched Yesuin run lightly across the lawn to stand beside the emperor. Her heart hammered in her chest; it was a wonder that all could not hear it.

They might almost be brothers, they look so much alike standing together!

But similar as the men were in build, it was the thought of Yesuin that thrilled her. The memory of Xiane's body on her's made her feel ill. It amazed her, how differently she could react to two men so much alike.

Neither was tall but both were well made and athletic. Xiane's skin was the paler legacy of his imperial father, and smooth; Yesuin's scarred here and there from the battles he'd fought before coming to the Imperial Court as hostage. Some of the courtiers cast glances of mixed admiration and disdain at the sight of the scars; when those gazes fell upon the Zharmatian's thigh and the brown birthmark there, they were pure contempt.

So the People of the Horse don't kill their children for every little blemish, Shei-Luin thought fiercely, dismissing those contemptuous glances with an unconscious flick of her fan. *They're not the cowards you are. They don't fear your demons.*

She watched him, and him alone, as he wrestled first with the women, then with any of the courtiers brave—or foolish— enough to challenge him. She knew what was to come.

It happened all in a heartbeat. Yesuin and Ulon, one of the courtiers, rolled across the lawn as they grappled; Yesuin caught his opponent in a choke hold. As if by chance he looked over Ulon's head and into the Lotus Gazebo where no man's gaze but the emperor's might fall. Shei-Luin was ready.

She dropped the fan. *Tonight,* she mouthed, quick as a thought. He blinked. Then Ulon twisted, and he and Yesuin rolled away once more.

It was enough. She would be ready.

Chapter Three

As he warmed himself by the brazier at his feet, Haoro, priest of the second rank, received the messenger in the outer room of his private quarters in the Iron Temple.

The man bowed to the small image of the Phoenix that adorned one wall of the plainly furnished room before kneeling to Haoro. Reaching into his wide sleeve, the messenger carefully withdrew something.

It was a single sheet of rice paper, folded in the form known as Eternal Lotus. A *red* lotus. It was exquisite. Every graceful line spoke of a master *sh'jer*'s touch.

So, Haoro thought as the man held the message out with both hands, careful to never let it sink below the level of his eyes, *it is time.*

He took the paper lotus and held it up, admiring it. His uncle had exceeded himself this time. He would have to congratulate Jhanun. With eyes only for the flower resting on his palm, Haoro tossed the man a token and intoned a brief blessing. "You may refresh yourself at the inn of the pilgrims," he said negligently. "You also have my leave to attend the dawn ceremony tomorrow in the inner temple if you wish. Tell the lesser priests I said so."

Joy spread over the messenger's face. To be allowed to hear the Song without having made the full pilgrimage beforehand was a rare privilege. The man knocked his forehead against the floor three times. "Thank you, gracious lord!"

He crawled backward, touching his forehead to the floor now and again, until he was at the door. Then the man stood up and left.

The moment the messenger was gone, Haoro cupped the paper lotus in both hands.

By this one's color, he knew its message as if it had been set before him in the finest calligraphy.

Be ready.

So—the time had come for the realization of the ambitions he and his uncle shared. *And what,* Haoro pondered, *has my revered uncle devised for his part?*

No matter; he would find out when his uncle made his pilgrimage to the Iron Temple. Jhanun would never set his schemes to paper; this would be for Haoro's ears alone. Again he wondered what his uncle had planned. Whatever it was, it would be bold.

The priest looked once more at the lotus. Had the messenger guessed the import of what he'd borne? The Eternal Lotus was by custom worked only in paper of the purest white. Therefore, this one could not exist.

With a thousand regrets, Haoro let the masterpiece drift into the brazier and watched it burn.

Many spans of days after he started his journey, Baisha stood beside a crude dugout canoe on a desolate beach on the northern shore of Jehanglan. He rubbed his forehead as if he could rub away the lingering effects of the illness that had delayed him. Damn that he'd ever caught the shaking sickness! It had made him late to leave Jehanglan.

"You are certain the Assantikkan ship will be leaving shortly?" he said to the trembling man the temple soldiers had forced to kneel before him. "Answer me or they die." He jerked his head.

"They" were the man's terrified family—a wife and a babe in arms—standing behind him within a ring of more soldiers. Swords pricked the hostages' throats.

"Yes, lord," the man stammered. "They never stay very long—a few hands of the sun. You must hurry." He tried to look back at his family. A soldier seized his long black hair and yanked his head around again. Tears of pain filled the man's frightened eyes.

It mattered not to Baisha. He looked over to the priest from the Iron Temple. "Did your master give you what I need?"

The priest nodded and reached within his robes. When he brought out his hand again, a crystal globe filled it. Inside floated a golden image of the Phoenix. The captive whimpered at the sight of it.

Baisha took it and hid it away inside the ragged and salt-stained robes he had donned a little while ago. "The rest?"

Once more the priest reached into his robes. This time he brought forth a jar of ointment. "Smear this upon your face and hands, and all other exposed flesh. It will redden and irritate the skin so that you'll look as if you've spent days drifting in the boat. Remember to smear some upon your lips, as well; they must be swollen and cracked as if from lack of water."

Grimacing, Baisha took the jar and removed the oiled paper lid. So he must look as wretched as he felt. With a sigh, he scooped some ointment out and smeared it on his bare arm. The priest signaled the acolytes who flanked him to aid.

Soon Baisha was ready. He stepped into the dugout; two soldiers ran to catch the sides and push it out to sea. Baisha picked up the single paddle and set to work, cursing under his breath. The damned ointment was doing its work quickly and too well.

The priest called out, "What about these cattle?"

Baisha barely glanced over his shoulder. "Kill them, of course. We want no witnesses."

He ignored the anguished screams behind him and bent to his work.

Chapter Four

To rule the heart of the Phoenix Lord—that is power. Yet what is power if one lives confined? Though the bars of the cage are of carved jade, banded with gold and hung with silk, they are still bars.

Shei-Luin *noh* Jhi turned from the screened window. Her silk-shod feet padded softly against the floor as she went once more to read the message on the desk.

Such an insignificant bit of paper; the merest strip that would fit around the leg of a fast messenger pigeon. But all the world hung in its words.

The emperor is dying. Come at once—Jhanun.

Shei-Luin studied it, tracing the words with a long, polished fingernail. Her finger paused over the signature: *Jhanun.* Just that. No title, no seal, not even an informal thumb print.

Were I as stupid as you hoped, Jhanun, it would have worked. And you would have wrung your hands over my death, vowed vengeance against whoever used your name, and grinned like the dog you are in private.

She could well believe Xiane claimed he was dying; that did not surprise her. A stomachache from green mangos and Xiane ma Jhi, august Emperor of the Four Quarters of the Earth and Phoenix Lord of the Skies, squalled that he was poisoned.

She'd seen it too often to be frightened anymore.

But whether Xiane were dying or not, it would mean her

death to approach him before her time of purification was over. Which was exactly what Jhanun wanted. He had lost much of his former influence over the Phoenix Emperor since Xiane had become enthralled with her.

Was Jhanun mad that he thought she would obey—or did he think her a fool? No matter. He would learn. She was not to be taken by such ploys. Fool he was, to place such a weapon in her hands; if Xiane saw this, Jhanun would not escape banishment a second time. She would keep this safe to use one day if necessary.

But that the emperor's former chancellor thought to order her as though she were still a simple concubine—that was arrogance.

And arrogance was not something she need tolerate. Not even from one as powerful as Jhanun *nohsa* Jhi—Jhanun, second rank servitor of the Jhi. Not when she herself was *noh*, first rank. Not when she was the mother of the Phoenix Lord's only "heir," born just three weeks ago.

A cloud of black hair spilled over her shoulder as she bowed her head at a sudden thought. Her hand clenched on the fan beside the note.

Was all well with her son? Xahnu was with his retinue in the foothills of the Khorushin Mountains, sent there to avoid the lowland fevers that carried off so many children every hot season. He should be safe. Even those as ambitious as Jhanun or the faction he headed would never dare harm the emperor's heir—the Phoenix would destroy them.

Even so, she wanted her baby by her side. Tears pricked at her eyes.

No! She must not be weak. Her breath hissed through clenched teeth. She must be the coldest steel—especially if the emperor were truly dying. There would be a throne to seize if that came to pass. A throne that Shei-Luin already had ambitions for.

And Jhanun must be taught a lesson. That he thought to fool her by so transparent a trick angered her. He must be removed from the game that was the Imperial Court. Without him the Four Tigers would be masterless, scuttling in every direction and none like a centipede with its head chopped off. They would cease their endless attempts to manipulate the weak-willed emperor. More importantly it would end their attempts to depose *her*.

"Murohshei!" she called. Her voice rang in the airy pavilion like a bell. At once she was answered by the slap of bare feet against the polished wood floors of the hall as her eunuch obeyed the summons.

Murohshei—slave of Shei. Idly she wondered if even he remembered what name he had carried long ago, before being given to the then child Shei-Luin for her own.

The eunuch entered the room. He fell to his knees before her, forehead pressed to the floor. She stood silent a moment, pale hands clasped before her, holding the fan of intricately carved sandalwood and painted silk like a dagger.

"Murohshei." Her voice was clear and sweet.

The eunuch looked up at her.

"Murohshei, I desire the head of Jhanun."

"Favored of the Phoenix Lord, Flower of the West," Murohshei said. "It shall be done. However long it takes, it shall be done." He touched his forehead to the teak floor once more.

Shei-Luin smiled. She imagined Jhanun's head on a pike outside her window. It would look very well indeed.

Then, as it had done all too often of late, the earth trembled violently. Shei-Luin staggered, would have fallen had not Murohshei sprung to her aid.

The Phoenix was angry once again.

Chapter Five

The dragon flew rapidly to the north, urgency in the rapid beating of its wings. Soon it dwindled to little more than a speck in the brightening sky.

Maurynna paused in the doorway to the balcony, wondering which Dragonlord was abroad so early and with such pressing need. She knew it for one of her kind and no truedragon; whoever it was, he—or she—was much smaller than her soultwin Linden's dragon form. And even he, she'd been told, was no match for a truedragon.

She finished wrapping the light robe around herself and continued into the new day, considering what it might mean.

She'd caught only a glimpse, just enough to tell her that the dragon was dark, either black or brown. Jekkanadar or Sulae, perhaps? She knew they were both black in dragon form; but then so were a few others. If brown, well, there were too many to hazard a guess. Maurynna pursed her lips in frustration. She was too new at Dragonskeep to know her fellow Dragonlords by sight in both of their forms.

Ah, well; no doubt she would find out eventually. She would put it from her mind and enjoy the early morning. It had always been her favorite part of the day.

The thought brought back a memory of the sea and the feel of her ship beneath her feet; she pushed it away and concentrated on what was before her. This was her life now.

The mountain air was still cold with the passing night; she

shivered but made no move to go back inside. Instead she marveled at the colors of the mountains as the light spread across them, reaching bright fingers across the great plateau to the Keep.

First came the grey of the mountains' granite bones peering through their skin of earth. Then, as the growing light flowed down the mountainsides, it revealed the pine forests standing guard between frozen peaks and living valley below, hidden now in the morning mist. Below their windswept green ring blazed the autumn leaves of maples, oaks, aspens, and many other trees Maurynna couldn't name, turning the valley walls into a tapestry of frozen fire that inched downward day by day.

Autumn in Thalnia, her home country, never announced itself with such a fanfare of color, nor did it begin so early. Maurynna refused to think of what was to follow: snow that would bury the passes, trapping those who could not fly within Dragonskeep until the spring. She would *not* think of that; she would think only of the beauty before her.

Remember how you dreamed of this when you were a child listening to Otter's tales before the fire.

How she'd dreamed, indeed—and now it was real. Joy blazed in her heart. She, Maurynna Erdon, was one of the great weredragons.

Maurynna Kyrissaean, a sleepy voice corrected in her mind. *Your dragon half would not like to be neglected,* the voice added with a chuckle. *She's a most opinionated lady— for all that she won't speak to me, Rathan, or anyone else.*

Maurynna made a wry face at the reminder, then concentrated; mindspeech was another thing new to her. *I'm sorry. Was I shouting again?* As always when she used mindspeech, she felt what she could only describe as an "echo" buzzing in her skull. It made her want to open her head and scratch.

Only a little; no further than me, anyway. You're doing much better. What are you doing up so early, love?

On the heels of his words, her soultwin Linden Rathan padded out onto the balcony in his bare feet. Linden's long blond hair was tousled, his dark grey eyes still heavy with sleep. He rubbed at them, yawning. Maurynna caught a glimpse of the wine-colored birthmark that covered his right temple and eyelid—his Marking. He wore only a pair of breeches against the chill.

Maurynna shivered at the sight and shrank into her robe.

One eyebrow went up as he smiled. "Are you cold? Silly goose, did you forget you could call up a heat spell now? Come here."

She went happily into his arms, turning in them so that she could look out over the mountains once more. Sometimes there were advantages to forgetting one was a Dragonlord, she told herself smugly as she pressed her back against her soultwin's broad chest. Linden must have called up a heat spell even before getting out of bed. Someday such things would become second nature, but for now she was content to stand with Linden's chin resting on the top of her head, his arms warm around her, and gaze out at the mountains that were her home now.

Yet try as she might, she could not think of them as home. They were beautiful, yes. But they were not the refuge of her heart. She admitted it to herself: she wanted the *Sea Mist* back.

I'd only just become a captain, she thought sadly. *It was still all bright and shiny and new.*

And the thought of being trapped in the Keep for the long northern winter nearly made her scream in panic.

Though she knew it would do her as much good as beating her head against the proverbial stone wall, she had to try once more. "Must we stay here? I'd like to see my family and friends in Thalnia one last time. I never had a chance to say good-bye to them."

Linden sighed and rubbed his cheek against her hair. "I'm sorry, dearheart, but you know what the Lady has decreed. She's concerned because you can't Change; she feels it's safer for you here. Besides, there is the matter of Kyrissaean."

Ah, yes; the matter of Kyrissaean. The recalcitrant, irritating, inexplicable dragon half of her soul. Who refused to speak to any Dragonlord or even another dragonsoul, yet always lurked in the back of Maurynna's mind. Who would not let Maurynna Change, who kept her earthbound and chained to the Keep.

Damn Kyrissaean. It would be long and long indeed before she forgave her draconic half.

Maurynna fumed. "I hate being coddled. And you're coddling me—all of you."

"Yes," Linden agreed equably. Maurynna wondered if he guessed how tempted she was to kick him for it. "We are; I am," he went on. "It's been far too long since there was a new Dragonlord. And I waited far too long for you, love. Bear with us."

And if you all drive me into screaming fits because you're smothering me? Then what? But she held her tongue; the last thing she wanted to do was fight with Linden first thing in the morning. Especially not when he nibbled her neck so gently.

Eyes closed, she let her head fall back against his shoulder to make it easier for him. His hands slid up to her breasts. Oh, yes; a fight could wait at least until after breakfast.

But when, much later, they reached the great hall where the meals were served, something drove all thoughts of argument from Maurynna's mind.

A young man stood with his back to her. As tall as Linden, though not as broad of shoulder and chest, he conferred with Tamiz, one of the *kir* servants. His hair glinted red-gold in the late morning sunlight pouring through the tall, narrow windows. He wore it in the Yerrin fashion, as Linden did his: shoulder length save for a long, narrow clan braid hanging from the nape of his neck and down his back. But where Linden's braid bore the four-strand pattern of a noble and was bound with the blue, white, and green of Snow Cat clan, this man sported Marten clan's black and green tying off the three-strand braid of a commoner.

Curly, reddish hair was common among Yerrins, and Marten a large clan. It might be anyone. Still. . . .

Tamiz nodded, a sudden grin appearing on her short-muzzled face. She beckoned the man to follow. The set of shoulders and head was distinctive, but it was the horseman's walk that gave him away beyond a doubt.

"Raven!" Maurynna gasped. Then, louder, "Raven—what are you doing here?" She ran across the wide floor.

Raven stopped, looked back over his shoulder; his face lit up at the sight of her. "Beanpole!" he cried as he caught her in a hug.

Maurynna hugged him back, forgetting that she was now much stronger than she had been as a truehuman.

"Ooof!" Raven wheezed in surprise.

"Oh, gods, Raven—I'm sorry. I forgot," Maurynna said, laughing in delight. What was her best friend in all the world doing here?

Raven avoided her eyes. "So did I," he said at last. "I'm sorry, Your Gr—"

Maurynna went cold. Not from Raven. Please—not from the boy she'd traded black eyes and heartfelt secrets with all her life. She couldn't stand it.

"Finish saying it, lad, and you'll be lucky if all she does is knock you down," Linden said as he came up. He clapped Raven on the shoulder. "Remember me? We met when you were a child. When did you arrive?"

"Late last night, Dragonlord." Raven bowed, then stared a moment before blurting out, "But you're not as tall as I remember, my lord."

Linden laughed. "And you're not as little as I remember. You'll certainly not be sitting in my lap any more. Otter warned me a while ago that you'd grown. Speaking of him, isn't your disreputable great-uncle awake yet?"

"I kept him up last night," Raven said with a smile.

"No excuse for him—not today," Linden said. "Lazy wretch. Tamiz, if Otter's playing slug-a-bed this fine day, tell him I said you could pour a bucket of cold water over him to rouse him. Dragonlord's orders, in fact."

Tamiz laughed and went off. There was a wicked glint in her eye.

Oh, my—she wouldn't, would she? Maurynna turned back to find Raven staring at her.

"So it's true," he said.

"Yes." She swallowed. Why was her mouth suddenly so dry?

Linden said nothing, only shifted so that their shoulders lightly touched.

"I used to tease you about your eyes, that they were a Marking because they were two different colors," Raven said. His voice was flat and tight. "I never thought I was right." A long silence, then, "You won't ever come home again, will you?"

There was pain in the words, and resentment. But what hurt most were the unshed tears she heard. He shifted his gaze to Linden. A long look passed between them.

"Ah," said Linden at last. In her mind he said, *I think there was more on Raven's side than just friendship, love. You two had best talk. Take him to an out of the way corner; I'll see that you're not disturbed.*

Confused, Maurynna said, *What do you mean, 'more than—'*

Talk to him, Maurynna.

And Linden left them alone. Maurynna studied Raven; it was like facing a stranger. "This way; we can talk over here." She hoped she didn't sound as lost and lonely as she felt.

He followed her without speaking. She led him past the Dragonlords and visitors dining at the tables to one of the little alcoves that opened off the great hall. Cushioned benches lined the walls, a cozy place for friendly confidences. It seemed a mockery. She took a seat; Raven hesitated as if unsure whether he should sit in the presence of a Dragonlord.

Maurynna glared at him. He sat. Not as close as he once would have, but not as far away as she had feared.

A stiff silence hung over them for too many long, awkward moments. Then Raven asked again, "Will you ever come back?"

Maurynna bit her lip. "They'll have to let me go sometime—I hope."

Raven started in surprise. "They're keeping you here against your will?"

She shrugged. How to explain this? And should she? She knew that Dragonlords kept secrets from truehumans lest those few against the weredragons find a weakness to exploit.

But this was Raven. She made her decision and damn anyone who disagreed. "Not quite. The Lady says it's for my own safety. The Lady would likely also say I shouldn't tell you, but . . . I—I can't Change at will. Something . . . happened the first time. It was agony and it's not supposed to be. Now Kyrissaean, my dragon half, won't let me become a dragon. She stops me whenever I try. Did you hear what happened in Cassori a few months ago, the regency debate?"

Raven nodded. "Yes, we got the news when the *Sea Mist* came home to Stormhaven. How the Dragonlords had been called in as judges, how you'd gone to trade there and that you'd become—" His voice nearly broke. A moment later he went on, "I heard it from Master Remon himself."

The breath caught in Maurynna's chest at the mention of Remon, her former first mate. She wondered what he'd thought when the Cassorin ship caught up to him with its astonishing news. Never mind that; what had the poor man thought when he'd found her missing from the *Sea Mist*? She imagined how Remon had felt when he'd walked into her cabin only to find it empty, the open window bearing silent witness to his captain's disappearance.

Raven continued, "Great-uncle Otter told me more last night; that's why we were up late. But he didn't tell me everything; he said some was your tale to tell me if you wished."

It was a moment before she could say, "We didn't discover the problem, you see, while we stayed in Casna. Then, because Linden's Llysanyin stallion Shan had escaped from Dragonskeep and made his way to the city looking for Linden, we decided to ride back. It seemed the best thing. Shan made it plain he wouldn't tolerate another rider and Linden was afraid I'd overreached myself on my first flight. The other two Dragonlords who had served as judges with Linden, Kief

Shaeldar, and Tarlna Aurianne, agreed. They flew home the day we set out.

"All seemed well, but one day on the journey Linden wanted to show me something from the air. It was to be a short flight, nothing difficult—and that's when it happened. I couldn't Change again."

Maurynna swallowed against the memory; even remembering that pain made her queasy. "Not that time, not the other few times I've had the courage to try. It's never happened before in anyone's memory, and there's no mention of such a thing in any of the records. Both the Lady of Dragonskeep and her soultwin Kelder as well as the two archivists Jenna and Lukai, all of the *kir* recorders, Linden and I have spent candlemarks searching them. I keep hoping there's an answer. . . ."

"I'm sorry for that," Raven said. "Truly sorry." Then, "You and . . . Linden Rathan. . . ."

The pain was back in his voice. Maurynna suddenly understood. "Raven—did you . . . did you think that we would . . . ?"

He turned bright red. "Um, ah—yes. I did. We got along so well, you see. And we always made up after a fight. We wouldn't have to get used to another person's ways, either of us."

"Raven, you don't really consider *that* a good reason to get married, do you?" The thought boggled her. She had certainly never felt that way.

Raven said, "It's better than some."

She had to admit that he was right; indeed, it was a better reason than many she'd heard.

But it still wasn't enough.

"It seemed so simple. We've always been comfortable together," he finished plaintively.

If she'd had something to hand, she would have thrown it. Marry her because she was comfortable, like a pair of old boots? Because it was the easy way out? She considered hitting him but remembered her new strength in time. "What!"

From the corner of her eye she could see heads turning to

look. She didn't care. "Oh, for—! Raven, yes, I love yo...
you idiot, but as a friend." She relented at the hurt in his
eyes. More gently she said, "Don't you see? We would never
have had a chance. Even if we had married, I would've had
to leave you once I'd Changed the first time. Try to understand; I don't just love Linden. He's part of me—literally.
That's what being a soultwin means. I would have had to go
to him no matter what."

He nodded. His voice shook when he spoke. "I'm trying
. . . to, to understand. I do here," he touched his forehead. He
continued, "But I'm having trouble here," and laid a hand
over his heart. "I'd always thought we'd marry, then go to
my aunt in Yerrih. You know she wants me to help her raise
and train her horses."

The words shocked Maurynna. Not *his* plans; she'd known
about *his* plans for years. But she'd never known of his plans
for *her*.

Feeling the walls of the Keep closing in, she got slowly to
her feet. Suddenly there wasn't enough air to breathe. "You
thought I would give up the sea so easily? That I could?"

She couldn't believe it. Raven of all people should know
what having her own ship meant to her. He had dreams as
well. "Hang it all! Don't any of you understand?"

Maurynna bolted from the alcove and out of the great hall.
Through the halls of the great Keep she ran, ignoring those
who called to her, running like a deer from the hounds, running from those who wanted to bury her alive.

It was silly and childish—she knew that. But neither could
she sit still any longer. She'd suffocate.

One of the postern doors was open to the fresh morning
air. Maurynna went through it like a bolt of lightning looking
for a target.

She didn't stop until she reached the paddocks behind the
Llysanyins' stable. A leap that she wouldn't have even considered trying a few short months ago carried her over the
fence to her Llysanyin stallion's yard. She landed, nearly lost
her balance, but caught herself before she sprawled facedown
in the dirt.

Boreal trotted to her, snorting concern over his person's agitation. Maurynna buried her face in his mane and wrapped her arms around the dappled grey neck, fighting back tears of frustration and anger.

I can't be a proper Dragonlord, I can't be a ship's captain at all, and everyone wants to either wrap me in wool like some glass bauble or drag me off to fulfill their *dreams. Damn it, it's not fair!*

Boreal draped his head over her shoulder and pulled her closer. Encouraged by the intelligent animal's sympathy, she drew breath to recite her list of grievances.

With my luck, the horse will be the only one who understands. The sudden thought made her break into a wry, hiccuping laugh.

''Thank the gods,'' a lilting—if ironic—voice said behind her, ''you're not crying after all. I had wondered about that from the way you fell on Boreal's neck. For alas and alack, little one, you're a wee bit large for me to cuddle on my lap for comforting.''